Dear Reader:

We at Berkley invite you to enjoy Kristie Knight's exciting trilogy of glorious romances set in Charleston, South Carolina, during the Revolutionary War in 1780–1781. The Charleston Women are three beautiful, brave, and thoroughly memorable cousins who face the war in vastly different ways and who fall in love with heroic men who will delight you as soon as you meet them.

Each heroine is featured in her own book, but her cousins appear in her story so you never lose sight of these very special women. Noelle Arledge confronts Indians and Redcoats *(Crimson Sunrise)*; Erin Banning embarks on dangerous supply runs to aid Patriot soldiers *(Midnight Star)*; and Lilly Arledge must follow her heart and her own beliefs despite pressure from her Loyalist father *(Carolina Moon)*.

Their adventures, bravery, and romantic spirit will give you hours of reading pleasure you won't want to end. Each romance stands on its own, but together they form an unforgettable trilogy about love and courage in the midst of America's fight for independence on the coast of South Carolina.

Happy reading!

Judith Stern

Judith Stern
Senior Editor
The Berkley Publishing Group

THE CHARLESTON WOMEN by Kristie Knight

CRIMSON SUNRISE
MIDNIGHT STAR
CAROLINA MOON

CAROLINA MOON

KRISTIE KNIGHT

DIAMOND BOOKS, NEW YORK

CAROLINA MOON

A Diamond Book / published by arrangement with
the author

PRINTING HISTORY
Diamond edition / September 1991

For information address:
The Berkley Publishing Group,
200 Madison Avenue, New York, New York 10016.

ISBN: 1-55773-579-4

Diamond Books are published by The Berkley Publishing Group,
200 Madison Avenue, New York, New York 10016.

PRINTED IN THE UNITED STATES OF AMERICA

10 9 8 7 6 5 4 3 2 1

For Sandra Chastain
who loves me enough to critique every word I write
without hesitation. Her invaluable words of wisdom and
insight challenge me to explore the complexity of
writing and to discover new worlds in my own mind.
Her friendship is one of the most precious gifts
I've ever received.

To
Donna Ball, Marion Collins, and Shannon Harper
who, along with Sandra,
comprise a special critique group
devoted to discovering the talents
that lie within each of us.
Without their encouragement, my books would still rest
within the cobwebs of my mind.

CAROLINA MOON

CHAPTER 1

October 1781
Charleston, South Carolina

LILLY ARLEDGE STRODE TO HER WINDOW AND stared out into the night. Lifting the sash, she stepped through the opening onto her piazza and inhaled the cool salt air. The crisp breeze ruffled the hem of her silk gown, and she hugged herself to keep warm as she watched the mist rolling across the juncture of the Ashley and Cooper rivers into Charleston Harbor to envelope King George's ships in a veil of gray.

Tonight felt almost springlike. She could almost catch the delicate fragrance of Carolina jasmine and oleander if she closed her eyes and imagined hard enough. She looked at the large vines that grew to the height of her piazza and smiled with pride. Her plants were among the largest in all of Charleston. She bent down, reached between the wrought-iron rails, and broke a stem with lush green leaves. Sniffing gently, she closed her eyes and recalled the scent of jasmine for a moment, shutting out her problems—the gathering crowd downstairs, the War for Independence that had gone on for so many years, and, most of all, her father. But she couldn't remain in her fantasy world for long.

She glanced down at the street. Below her, carriages lined up outside her gate, and guests clad in gaily colored silks and satins poured from them into the twilight. Some of them called greetings to one another, but no one seemed to notice Lilly as she kept her silent vigil above them. From the look of my guests, she thought, you'd never know a war was going on. The War for Independence seemed far away as she prepared for her father's party.

A man emerged from a carriage and waited for the second occupant. As both men walked toward the lower piazza, the first man, a stranger, glanced up to where Lilly stood. In the dim light filtering through the palmetto fronds and live oaks, he gazed at her for a long moment. Lilly knew she should step back into her room, but she didn't want to appear rude. He was with one of her good friends, Gregory Weston.

The stranger smiled and touched his hand to his forehead in greeting before catching up with Gregory. Lilly felt a blush sting her cheeks and shrank back into the cool anonymity of the shadows. As she stepped back through the window, she thought tonight might not be such a trial after all.

She knew her father would be angry with her if she delayed her entrance any longer, but Lilly didn't hurry to embrace the duties thrust on her for the past few years. She wanted to be a typical seventeen-year-old, and as such she sometimes risked his anger to do so. She wasn't too happy with him, either. Twirling the jasmine stem between her fingers, she looked for a hairpin. In the springtime she would have worn the fragrant yellow blossoms so that when the evening became tedious, she could inhale their scent and hide in her private world of dreams. Tonight she sprinkled a bit of perfume over the leaves and pinned them in place. Tartuffe, Lilly's cat, leapt into her lap and purred, rubbing against the bodice of her gown. Lilly felt the prick of a claw on her thigh and jerked the cat's paw free.

"Ouch! Tartuffe, you naughty boy. You'll ruin my gown." But she couldn't be angry with her friend for too long. Lilly stroked the white cat's fur and scratched between its ears. "Now, run along and chase mice."

She watched the cat prance independently across the floor, grinned in spite of the pick in her skirt, and pinned the stem in place. She stood and tilted her chin jauntily to one side. "You'll do," she whispered to herself.

By now her father would be enraged over her lateness. The bells of St. Michael's were tolling the hour of eight, and she should have been downstairs thirty minutes ago. Her father controlled most of her life, but these few stolen moments were her form of revenge. These people were not her guests but his. The gown she wore was his choice and not hers. This evening, like so many others orchestrated by her father, promised to be a long, tiring event—except for the presence of the gallant stranger who might provide some entertainment. He certainly didn't look like most of her father's associates.

She shook the fine yellow silk of her skirt to make sure it hung gracefully over her petticoats and swished out of her dressing room. Hesitating a moment to gain her composure, Lilly placed her hand on the banister and inhaled deeply. From now until the early hours of the morning she would have to smile sweetly and dance with many British soldiers she hardly knew. Since her mother was dead, Lilly served as her father's hostess. He seemed to notice her only on evenings like this.

Jonathan Arledge, her father, worked very closely with the British authorities. The British occupying force required great amounts of food, and her father was getting rich procuring supplies for them from the outlying parishes. Lilly was forced to assist, but she couldn't stop her feelings of shame.

She could delay her entrance no longer without incurring Jonathan Arledge's wrath. Forcing a smile to her lips, she tugged at her low-cut bodice, trying to make the almost indecent gown presentable, and started down the stairs. Jedediah was opening the door to admit more guests as Lilly reached the foyer.

"Lilly, how lovely you look." Marigold O'Grady linked her arm with Lilly's and peeked into the parlor. "A room full of men—looks like a girl's idea of heaven!"

"Ugh," Lilly groaned and wrinkled her nose. Mari had pointedly refused to acknowledge the presence of several Charleston matrons scattered among the male guests. "Not one interesting person in the lot. Except you, of course." Knowing that her friend would make too much of the incident, Lilly failed to mention having seen the handsome stranger earlier.

"Love the saints, my prayers have been answered." Marigold gripped Lilly's arm and pointed across the parlor to a tall man standing near the harpsichord. "Who is that Greek god?"

Lilly looked at the man and shook her head. He was the man she'd seen from her piazza. "He's certainly very handsome, but I don't know who he is. And he's wearing far too many clothes to be a Greek god."

"You're the hostess. Go introduce yourself and then introduce me." Marigold nudged Lilly forward. "It looks like he's with Gregory Weston."

Marigold was right, although Lilly didn't confirm her friend's conclusion. Gregory and the stranger were engrossed in their conversation and didn't appear to notice the girls' approach. Lilly could hardly keep from staring. The man wore no uniform, and she was glad. British soldiers kept trying to impress her by regaling her with accounts of their heroism in battle. Though the Arledge household—including Lilly—remained loyal to King George, Lilly hated to be reminded of war every time a man spoke to her. They seemed to have completely forgotten all other topics.

As she made her way across the parlor with Marigold, Lilly paused here and there to welcome her father's guests. With their arms linked, Lilly did all she could to restrain her best friend, who seemed to want to rush past everyone else to reach the handsome stranger.

Gregory Weston spotted Lilly crossing the room and gestured to the man standing with him. "Ah, here's our hostess. Miss Arledge, may I present Ethan Kendall. Ethan, Lilly Arledge, the loveliest of Charleston's young ladies."

Before Lilly could reply, Marigold elbowed her way between Lilly and Gregory. "Shame on you, Gregory, for not introducing me. I'm Marigold O'Grady. Call me Mari. Everyone does."

Ethan barely glanced at Mari but gazed at Lilly with a warm smile. "So nice to meet you . . . both."

Lilly felt herself grow warm under Ethan's gaze. Her eyes met his, and she smiled genuinely for the first time this evening. His eyes seemed to devour her, to lock out everybody else. His grin deepened, and he cocked his head to one side. Lilly felt as if he'd come just to see *her.* Something about him made her feel important for the first time in her life. But then, she admonished herself, he probably made every girl he met feel important.

Suddenly Lilly felt proud of herself. Her decision to remain loyal to King George sprang from deep within her, though almost no one credited her with the sense to reach such a conclusion on her own. Most people felt it was because of her father's loyalty.

Rather than inspire Lilly, Jonathan Arledge's self-serving stand was an embarrassment. He'd clearly chosen sides based on greed—not personal convictions. Now she'd met a handsome man who seemed to make her decision easier to live with. There were a few nice young men left in Charleston these days, and she met only the ones her father picked because of his greed or political aspirations. For a fleeting moment she wondered if Ethan was one of those, but dismissed the idea. Her thoughts returned to the conversation around her, and Lilly knew she'd spent too much time with this little group.

The foursome talked a few minutes before Lilly excused herself to make sure all her guests were comfortable. Her gaze kept drifting back to Ethan Kendall, and she found that he, too, was watching her. Color suffused her cheeks as she strode back to the kitchen to check on the preparations for supper.

Zipporah, Lilly's mammy, stepped from the dining room and nodded. "Supper 'bout ready. Go on back to you comp'ny."

"Thank you, Zip. We're ready to eat." Lilly smiled at the older woman. She leaned close and whispered, "I'd like to be in bed by midnight. Do you think there's a possibility?"

A roar of laughter burst from the parlor, and Zipporah shook her head. "Sound like a rowdy bunch of geese. Them folks ain't gonna leave afore mornin', don't you know? I bet they be powerful hungry, too."

Lilly laughed and hugged the servant. "Oh, well, I can hope, can't I? Have Jedediah announce supper."

Returning to her guests, Lilly hesitated at the double

doors to the parlor and studied Ethan Kendall. She wondered what he was doing here, why his gaze followed her as she walked from one cluster of people to another.

"Lilly!" her father called over the din of the crowd. "Come here."

She could no longer waste time wondering about Ethan Kendall. Her father sounded angry, and she knew better than to keep him waiting when he was upset.

Ethan Kendall watched his lovely hostess as she crossed the room to her father. The yellow gown drifted around her like the froth that rode the waves along the beach, making her appear to float as she strolled gracefully to the hearth, where a small knot of men stood talking. Her hair, braided and pinned securely to the nape of her neck, shone like chestnuts in the soft glow of candlelight. He wondered how it would look hanging free down her back, blowing gently with the breeze that blew off the rivers.

Her eyes were the rich, glittering color of brandy. Ethan felt drawn to her and walked across the room, nearer to the hearth so he could see her lovely face better. A wisp of hair slipped free of its confinement and caressed her cheek. Without seeming to think about it, she brushed it back with her small hand. He wanted to reach out and touch her; she looked so soft and gentle.

As Ethan watched, Jonathan Arledge snatched his daughter's hand and jerked her to one side. Ethan couldn't hear the conversation, but he was surprised by the violence of the act that took place in full view of the people assembled in the parlor. He noted the color that rose in Lilly's cheeks, and suddenly he felt protective. He'd heard of Jonathan's temper but hadn't really believed the tales until now—and, beyond that, couldn't believe that the man would inflict his foul temper on his daughter.

He studied Lilly's reaction. Rather than cower before her father's anger, she lifted her chin and listened as he berated her for some grievance of which he alone was aware. Ethan sensed a detachment in her, as if she were oblivious to the verbal abuse her father inflicted. In that instant Ethan understood that Lilly would do her father's will with dignity—as it seemed she always had—but something didn't quite fit. Her eyes were alert and challenging—not the cowed gaze of a dutiful daughter who never risked disobedience. She possessed spunk.

With her chin tilted high, she turned and strode away from her father. To leave the room, she had to walk past Ethan. For a moment he looked down at her as she glanced up to see who stood in her way, but he moved quickly to one side. He didn't want to add to her troubles, but he decided to ask Greg if he knew anything about the relationship.

For a few seconds she gazed at him and then murmured, "Excuse me, please, Mr. Kendall."

"Certainly, Miss Arledge." He smiled, hoping to bring the light back into her eyes. "We didn't have much of a chance to talk earlier, but I know your cousin, Mrs. Gallagher."

Lilly had started to move past him, but when he mentioned her cousin, she stopped. "Erin? Is she well? I haven't seen her since . . . since her marriage."

"She's well, I understand. They're expecting a baby soon." Ethan smiled. He'd seen Erin a week ago. She and Bowie were still hiding from the British.

Lilly smiled and nodded, wondering whom Ethan had spoken with who seemed to know so much about her cousin. "She'll be a good mother. I wish I could see her. Do you . . . do you know where she is?"

He'd hoped to avoid lying to Lilly, but now she'd asked a question he'd pledged not to answer. "No. They haven't been seen in some time around Charleston."

He admired Erin and Bowie a great deal. Both of them had fought for the Patriot cause, risking their lives to assure that the Continental Army received supplies that were vital to the winning of this war. Ethan wanted to play as important a role as Bowie, to contribute to the victory. But Ethan hadn't yet found his place. He knew he could have a significant impact on the outcome of this war if only he could discover his fated role.

Ethan wasn't afraid to fight. He'd fought since he turned eighteen. He'd been in Charleston when the first British ships arrived in June of 1776. He'd seen action at Port Royal Island in 1779. He'd fought at Flat Rock, Thicketty Fort, and at the Battle of the Blackstocks before joining Light-Horse Harry Lee in December 1780 soon after General Greene took over the Southern Department of the Continental Army. Ethan was proud of his record, even prouder of his new assignment. He'd been sent to Charleston to infiltrate the British Army, the occupying force.

He looked at Lilly and smiled. What part would she play, if any? Many women were finding ways to serve during this seemingly never-ending war. Jonathan Arledge was a Loyalist. Ethan guessed that Jonathan's loyalty to the British was solely a financial one. He believed that the British would win and he wanted to reap the benefits of remaining loyal to the winning side. Ethan prayed that Jonathan was wrong.

But he wondered where Lilly stood. Did she believe as her father did? If she'd remained loyal, he instinctively believed her reasons would be heartfelt. Almost all young women he knew had taken the same side as their parents, and Ethan felt that Lilly was probably no exception. He would have to be careful.

Ethan smiled down at her. He understood the pain of the experience he'd witnessed between her and her father. His own father had been abusive to a degree. With a desire to divert her attention from her father, Ethan asked, "Have you known Greg for very long?"

Glad for a moment's distraction before she would have to move on to other, more probing guests, she tried to smile back at him. "Since my early childhood. Greg, Mari, and I grew up together. We played together as children. And you—how long have you known him?"

"Not nearly so long," Ethan answered truthfully. "I met him in school. We've been friends since we were about fourteen years old."

"He's a fine man and a fine soldier." Lilly glanced at her friend, who was deep in conversation with Mari.

Ethan never doubted her words for a moment. Greg was the kind of man who attacked a task wholeheartedly or not at all. He, too, held strong beliefs about this war. Wondering how close Lilly and Greg were, if there was any feeling beyond friendship, Ethan looked down at her speculatively.

Lilly gazed at Ethan. He was staring at her in the same way other men did—a way that made her feel uncomfortable. The corners of her mouth tilted into a smile. She had smiled the same way at other parties or suppers when she wasn't particularly interested in the guests. Her smile faded. He had seemed so intriguing to her, so exciting, but maybe her assessment was wrong.

She lifted her chin and eyed him casually. "I'm sorry,

Mr. Kendall, but I have other guests who need attention. Perhaps we can speak again some time."

Without waiting for his acknowledgment, she moved away from him. Glancing quickly about, she spotted Mari and strode toward her. Mari and Gregory were still deep in conversation and didn't notice Lilly's approach. "Hello, you two. Are you having a nice evening?"

Before either of them could reply, Jedediah announced dinner. As usual, Lilly sat at the opposite end of the table from her father. Silently she thanked whoever wrote the rules of good manners for dictating that host and hostess should be separated by such a distance. She didn't want to sit near her father if possible. Then, to her dismay, she found the place cards rearranged. Ethan Kendall was seated to her right and Gregory Weston to her left. Mari sat beside Gregory while a woman Lilly didn't know took the chair on the other side of Ethan.

At first Lilly thought that Ethan might have rearranged the place cards but decided that he wouldn't have done such a thing. So far he'd shown no particular interest in Lilly, except for that moment when their eyes met, that moment when the real Lilly flickered to life for the briefest span of time.

Studying her carefully, Ethan held the chair for Lilly before sitting beside her. He smiled at the woman on his left, but then turned to face Lilly. She seemed to observe him briefly before turning to Gregory to ask about his mother. Ethan watched the interplay between them without participating. The two had been friends for a long time, Gregory had said, and Lilly had confirmed it.

He allowed his thoughts to drift. Earlier in the evening Ethan had seen her standing on her piazza, a vision in soft yellow as she stood looking across the rivers. He'd been enchanted. He'd watched her from the window of the carriage for a few seconds before he climbed out. She hadn't noticed him, not until she finally glanced down at the street as he stepped from the carriage, and a smile had lifted her lips. She'd been lovely, almost as if a promise had been spoken between them. But her reception had been cool. Ethan had seen nothing of that promise when they met in person. Could he have been mistaken? Could her smile have been for Gregory?

The muscles in Ethan's jaw twitched as he observed the easy flow of conversation and laughter between the two of them. Glancing at Mari, he ate an oyster. She'd pursued him relentlessly, practically throwing herself at him. He already knew that she could never mean anything to him, however. Her head was stuffed with silly fripperies and flirtatious banter. The most serious thought Mari would ever consider for any length of time would concern her attire or hair.

Ethan never wasted time on such women. He studied Lilly. More beautiful than Mari, he doubted that Lilly would spend the hours most women did on their appearance, yet she didn't seem to be interested in news of the war, either. He felt that she was a devout Loyalist, was almost certain because of the way she talked, but she seemed to freeze up around the soldiers except for Gregory. Getting to know her would be entertaining, he thought and raised an eyebrow as he considered how to approach her without causing a stir.

"Well, it gave me quite a turn, I assure you," Lilly said and sipped her wine. "I never expected to find a cow in my garden."

Gregory and Mari laughed. Ethan grinned to cover his embarrassment at not paying attention to the conversation. He hoped nobody asked his opinion on the subject, but he didn't escape quite so easily.

"And, you, Ethan, what do you think of Lilly's discovering a cow in her garden?" Mari asked, batting her eyes playfully.

Ethan cursed his lack of attention but grinned again and tried to bluff. "I suppose that finding a cow in your garden is better than finding a cow in your bedchamber."

Poor Gregory nearly choked with laughter as he apparently tried to keep from spitting wine on his hostess. Resolving to pay closer attention to the conversation, Ethan sipped his wine and continued to eat. His comment must have been adequate since nobody asked him what he meant.

"You're quite right, Mr. Kendall." Lilly patted the corner of her mouth with a damask napkin and placed it back in her lap. "I'm sure I don't know what I would have done with a cow in my bedchamber, and beyond that, I don't know how a cow could get there. But I don't know how she got in the garden, either."

"What did you do with her?" Mari asked.

"I led her to the stable." Lilly placed her fork across her plate and gazed at her friend. With a slight lift of her eyebrows to include the listeners in her confidence, she whispered, "I decided that if someone missed her, he could come looking for her."

"And has anyone come?" Gregory inquired, leaning forward slightly.

"No, she's still there." Lilly laughed and shook her head. "Applejack milks her twice a day. For the first time since the occupation, we have plenty of fresh milk."

Conversation lapsed into a discussion of shortages caused by the war, and, with a sniff of jasmine fragrance, Lilly allowed her thoughts to drift. Her gaze moved to

Ethan. Why was he here? He must be a Loyalist or he wouldn't be bold enough to walk into this party, let alone be so friendly with Gregory and the other British officers.

But he spoke of her cousin Erin as if he knew her well. Lilly puzzled over this enigma. She'd never discover the truth by thinking about it, but she liked challenges, and in that moment she made the mystery of Ethan Kendall her new project. She'd unshroud the story of his presence. Besides, he intrigued her.

She picked up the thread of conversation as Ethan said, "It's a lovely old place on Goose Creek." His voice lowered to a softer, more loving tone as he apparently recalled a favorite place. He darted a glance at Lilly, hoping she would forgive him for not telling the complete truth. He was proud of Carolina Moon but didn't want to risk having this group connect him with the Patriots. "My family's been there since before my birth."

"It sounds wonderful." Lilly smiled, not knowing exactly how to respond to a man who so obviously wasn't ashamed to show his emotions. Her eyes met his, and she noticed them for the first time. They were as green as the Atlantic and glinted with gold like the sun's summer rays off the water. With a slight catch in her voice she whispered, "I'd love to see it some day."

Ethan gazed at her. Her voice had changed. In that short time span, was it possible that her opinion of him had changed? Something in her tone, the soft throaty whisper, said much more than her words. "And so you shall. After all this strife is over, I'll take you there."

A wisp of mahogany-colored hair again fluttered across her cheek, and she absently brushed it away. Her fingers were long and tapered, and the graceful movement added to the aura of natural beauty that he kept seeing even when he turned away. But her eyes were spectacular. Wide open and the color of roasted chestnuts, they studied him with vitality and honesty. Nothing of the coquette abided within her, or if it did, she kept it well hidden from him.

Color suffused her cheeks as she realized that she'd allowed herself to reveal far too much to this stranger. She knew nothing about him except that a hank of his tawny hair refused to be bound by the tie in back. He'd mentioned Erin and attended this party with Gregory, but many people knew both Erin and Gregory—people on both sides of this horrible war. She watched him for a moment; he seemed more complex than most of the men she knew—and definitely more interesting.

Ethan turned to answer a question asked by the woman at his right. Greg and Mari were debating the merits of some soldier's feats. Smiling vacantly, Lilly withdrew into herself as she did so frequently these days.

The flames on the candles danced as the breeze wafted through the sheer draperies from the fully open windows. Lilly looked toward the harbor, which she could barely see because of the houses that stood between the Arledge house and the water. Dark clouds gathered on the horizon, and a storm seemed to be approaching. Lilly loved storms. They made her feel alive, vibrant. The hint of the coming disturbance lifted her spirits, and she grinned wickedly to Ethan, Greg, and Mari. "Jedediah, lower the windows a little. I'm afraid the wind will blow the biscuits off the platter."

The butler stared at her for a moment as if to determine whether or not she was serious, but the next puff of wind blew out several candles, and he scurried to lower the windows. The room grew quiet. As he pulled them down, a soft whisper came from the inner recesses of the walls where the weights slid up to allow the sash to be moved downward.

"Well, these are light biscuits, but not quite that light," Mari observed as she broke the crust on one. With her mouth full she added, "Good, though."

Lilly allowed herself to sink back into her personal world as the chatter resumed around the table. She found the normal sounds of routine relaxing. The windows, like most in Charleston, could be raised completely into the upper story to allow people to walk from the interior of the house to the piazza and gardens. On warm summer nights all of the windows were opened to allow the breeze off the ocean to blow through the house, chasing away the heat of the day. Now the window allowed a fresh breeze to cool the night. Lilly longed to walk outside, where she could feel the approaching storm. Instead, she was forced to signal for the next course.

After a custard for dessert, everyone moved into the ballroom. A string quartet played softly as several couples meandered to the dance floor. Lilly watched as they lined up. She didn't enjoy dancing with the soldiers because they were quite often too ardent for her. Several of them had already proposed to her, and she'd turned them down. She refused to be a pawn in her father's devious tricks and, as a result, rarely accepted any invitations from the soldiers he invited to parties or suppers.

"Miss Arledge, may I have this dance?" Ethan bowed from the waist.

"How kind of you to ask, Mr. Kendall."

They joined the other couples on the polished hardwood floor. Lilly curtsied, and Ethan bowed. She laid her hand on his arm, and for a few moments they executed the steps without speaking. Lilly didn't know what to say to him. His touch seemed to chase all rational thought from her mind. "Mr. Kendall, have you been in Charleston for long?"

Ethan accomplished the next few steps before responding. He didn't know how to answer her truthfully without breaking a confidence that might jeopardize the Patriot efforts. "Miss Arledge, I've lived northwest of here all my life."

"I understand that, but—"

Lilly had no time to ask how he knew Erin. The dance ended, and Ethan walked her back to Mari and Gregory. Immediately Gregory asked her to dance, and she allowed him to lead her to the floor. Over his shoulder she watched as Ethan and Mari began to dance. Though she wanted to remain with Ethan—to find out how he knew Erin, what he was doing at this party—she managed to enjoy herself. She'd much rather dance with Greg than those other soldiers her father insisted on pairing her with.

Living with Jonathan Arledge was a constant fight. He insisted on her being friendly with the British soldiers he brought home. Lilly, basically a shy person, hated being pushed by her father into friendships that would always be one-sided. Though she heartily believed in the British cause, she refused to consort with the soldiers—particularly on the level her father was aiming for. She sometimes sensed that he wanted her to be . . . well . . . loose. As a result, she shied away from men almost completely—or had until tonight.

The ballroom was lit with fat white candles nested in jasmine bowers, and the scent of jasmine and candle wax filled the room. Lilly smiled. She loved the fragrance. Every year she dried the flowers and crushed the petals to save the scent for winter. At times when the weather became intolerable, she'd toss them onto a burning log, and the room would smell like summer again.

The music stopped while the musicians prepared for the next dance, and she walked with Gregory to the edge of the dance floor. She sat beside Mari and watched as couples began to whirl about the room to the next melody. Ethan and Gregory left to find the punch bowl.

"Lilly, I want to tell you that Ethan Kendall is the most exciting thing to happen in Charleston since the day we sat on the roof and watched the bombs flying through the air from the British ships." Mari leaned close and tugged on Lilly's arm. "More exciting."

Lilly smiled at her friend's obvious joy with the newcomer, who now headed back toward them carrying two punch cups with Greg trailing behind. But Lilly's thoughts ran deeper. She studied him. As he skirted the dance floor, he paused to speak here and there, occasionally a smile breaking across his face. Yet he seemed a bit reserved, aloof, as if he were above all that was happening. Intrigued, she kept a secret eye on him while she pretended to watch the dancers as they passed and called greetings to her.

Ethan listened to the chatter of a matron who appeared to be intent on keeping him from returning to Lilly and Mari. He listened as she pointed out the merits of her daughter, who more closely resembled the horse he rode than the human race. He smiled and nodded, hoping the old baggage would tire of prattling on. When it seemed she would never stop, he became almost desperate in his attempt to escape.

Desperate situations called for desperate measures, he thought, and wondered what could end this tirade. By now his arms were tiring from holding the two cups of punch he was carrying to Lilly and Mari. Punch. That was the answer to his dilemma. Nodding in agreement with the matron's faulty assessment of her daughter's virtues, he admitted, "I've seen none who compares to her in Charleston."

The matron beamed and turned to nod reassuringly to her coltish offspring. When the woman moved, Ethan seized the opportunity and adjusted his position so that her action caused him to spill a few drops of punch onto the sleeve of her gown. "Oh, I am sorry. How clumsy of me," he groveled. "I can't seem to do anything right. Here take my handkerchief."

He handed the embroidered linen to the woman and stepped back. She dabbed at the garnet-colored liquid and muttered something. Ethan repressed his smile. His assessment had been right. Her dress was more valuable to her than marrying off her daughter.

"I do apologize." Ethan attempted to help and jiggled the cups again. This time the punch fell harmlessly to the floor, but the matron stepped back out of his way. He felt horrible about using such a ruse to escape her grasp, but he didn't want to stay long enough to have to turn down the inevitable offer to drop by for supper. "Goodness!" he cried, an anguished look wrinkling his face into a mixture of a scowl and a grin. "Do let me carry this punch to the ladies for whom it was intended before I inundate you with it. Simply too careless of me," he muttered as he stepped around the woman and her still speechless daughter.

By the time he reached Lilly, he was grinning broadly. His good manners, ground into him by a mammy who threatened to restrict his riding, abandoned him as he handed Lilly and Mari their drinks. With a twinkle in his eye he shook his head briefly and inhaled deeply.

"Your good friends"—He glanced back at the woman—"the old woman with the—"

Lilly interrupted. "Are you referring to Mrs. Montaigne? One of our most outstanding matrons? A pillar of society? One of the most vigorous workers for the Loyalist cause?"

Ethan sóbered somewhat and peered down at Lilly. At the corners of her eyes, those wonderful warm brown eyes whose sparkle beckoned like a campfire on a cold night, he noticed tiny wrinkles. She was teasing him. Her laughter welled up and spilled forth like a hundred tinkling bells, ebullient and carefree on a spring morning. The sound surrounded him and wrapped him in a cloak of pure happiness.

Ethan gazed down into her eyes once again and felt a catch around his heart. He hadn't felt like this since the war began.

CHAPTER 2

LILLY WATCHED SEVERAL PEOPLE LEAVE AS THE SUN began to rise over the harbor. Zip might be a servant, but she was a good judge of Lilly's guests. This crowd was one hungry for gaiety and companionship, one that didn't want to go home.

Going home meant facing reality. Reality these days could be ugly and painful. It could also be dangerous. People who were living on the edge of hysteria over the continuing occupation were quick to fling nasty remarks at those on the opposite side—and almost as quick to throw more substantial objects like bricks or rocks.

So far Lilly had managed to avoid these confrontations by drifting into her own fantasy world. When she felt threatened, a wall came up and protected her from all the pain—both physical and mental. She kept to herself, said little to those outside her small circle of friends, and seldom ventured from her home. Her father encouraged her to accept the offers of carriage rides and other entertainments with some of the British officers, but Lilly tried to remain as secluded as possible.

She gazed at her father, thinking back to when the change in their relationship had occurred. The way he used her made her feel uncomfortable with men. He insisted that her gowns be cut lower than any of the other girls'. He suggested that she might consider using rouge to heighten the color in her cheeks. Jonathan Arledge, it seemed to Lilly, regarded her as an enticement, much like oleander to a hummingbird—a lure made more attractive by her lush coloring and lavish unsuitable gowns.

At first Lilly hadn't understood. Her father had never paid any attention to her until she began to develop as a woman. Then a metamorphosis occurred, and he began to regard her differently. She had been a pale and listless child, shrinking from his anger, but as she grew up she became more attractive and, according to Mari, Lilly's dark hair and eyes combined with her pallor presented an exotic appearance.

Lilly had thought that Mari had been tippling in Jonathan Arledge's brandy that afternoon a few months ago, but now her suggestion seemed almost believable. When Lilly caught her reflection in the mirror over the little table in the foyer, she saw the same dark eyes and hair she'd always seen. Her face seemed no more and no less pale than it had always been. But there was a difference now. The planes of her face were sharper, and the baby fat had disappeared from her cheeks. Above her eyes long thick lashes had replaced shorter ones.

Forcing her thoughts to return to her present predicament, Lilly smiled at the young soldier standing by patiently. Judging from his apprehensive appearance, he must have asked a question she hadn't heard. "My, but this is a noisy crowd," she observed, knowing that the noise level would hardly interfere with her hearing. "Could you repeat your question?"

"Your father said . . ." Color stained the young man's plump cheeks, and he smiled tentatively. "Uh, I would like to take you for a walk some afternoon, Miss Arledge."

"A walk? Me?" Lilly groaned inwardly. If another lonely soldier asked her to marry him, she'd scream. When she married, it would be for love, nothing less. "What a lovely offer, but I'm afraid I can't. But if I have the need of an escort when I go on errands, I'll call on you."

The soldier mumbled something and left. Feeling a little guilty, she turned and smiled at Mrs. Montaigne and her daughter Mignon as they followed the soldier out the door.

Lilly grinned as she heard Mrs. Montaigne call, "Sir, oh, sir. I couldn't help overhearing your offer to walk with Miss Arledge as she . . ."

Knowing that the young soldier didn't stand a chance against the well-practiced and overwhelming coercion of Mrs. Montaigne, Lilly felt even more guilty. If she'd talked with him a few moments longer, he might have escaped without meeting the bumptious woman, but the old woman had snared him now, and Lilly could do nothing. Within a few days Mrs. Montaigne would probably announce the betrothal of her daughter to the young soldier.

She glanced around the parlor, where her remaining guests had gathered. Mari slumped into a chair near the harpsichord, while Ethan and Gregory peered through the windows and across the garden. From her vantage point she could study Ethan's profile without his knowledge. His face was strong, with high cheekbones, proud brow, and square jaw—a face that invited trust. But with the onslaught of war Lilly had learned that many people appeared trustworthy and proved themselves otherwise.

Mari said something that caused the two men to smile.

Lilly didn't really want to join them, not right now. The intensity of feelings that seemed to spring from conversation with Ethan was something she wanted to avoid.

She looked further and spotted her father. He frowned at her, and she realized that he must have heard her refuse to go out walking with the soldier. Why Jonathan Arledge demanded that she be overly friendly toward the British soldiers, she couldn't understand. Her geniality should have no influence on his business dealings with the British Provost. The group clustered around her father argued amiably as they always did about the war. Lilly wanted nothing to do with that conversation.

Mari and her parents were heading toward the door, and Lilly accompanied them. "Do come again soon," she called as they left. Lilly returned to the parlor.

Several ladies were sipping strong tea as they tried to stay awake while their escorts discussed the latest developments in the war. The ladies weren't really talking. Most of them were fighting sleep and boredom. She heard one of them mention Mrs. Montaigne, and Lilly smiled. Then one of them said something about the cut of Lilly's gown, and the wall went up around her heart. She glanced toward Ethan to see if he'd heard. His eyes met hers, and she knew he had.

The women of Charleston often said unkind things about Lilly, and usually she didn't mind so much. If they were talking about her, then some other woman was getting a rest. But tonight she cared. Ethan had heard. He now knew what Charleston society thought of her. Embarrassed, she fled the room.

Without caring where she was going, Lilly headed into the garden. She ran along the little brick path that led to her favorite spot. Disregarding the possibility of getting her gown dirty, she scurried across the soft grass until she reached a bower of live oaks. The leaves and small branches fluttered in the breeze that ruffled the hem of her gown.

The chill of the morning seeped through the fine silk dress, and she shivered, but continued on until she found the little marble bench she always sought when she was disturbed. Dusting it off with her palm, she wished she'd stopped long enough to bring a shawl. The air was cool around her.

She sat down and, with a practiced hand, arranged her skirts in a flattering manner about her. Why? she wondered. Why couldn't the old crows wait until later to make unkind remarks about her clothes? Lilly rose. She paced back and forth, hardly noticing her surroundings until she bumped her head on a low-hanging limb. She wrapped her arms around the thick branch and rested her cheek on it. The rough bark and smell of foliage comforted her a little as she fought to maintain control of her emotions.

Lilly hoped that Ethan had dismissed the remark as being catty. She thought he had sense enough for that, but it hurt for him to hear. If only for an evening she wanted him to like her.

The crackle of a twig startled her. Had someone followed her? She listened intently, straining to hear the slightest sound, but could hear nothing. She was alone in her world.

This was her place, her limb. Many times as a little girl she'd climbed into the comfort of this old live oak and hidden from the world. The world had always seemed hostile to her, even before the war began. It would be improper to climb the tree now—at her age and dressed as she was—but she wanted to. It beckoned her.

Lilly glanced around to be sure she hadn't been followed, but she hadn't heard anything since the first noise. Who would know? The urge to climb was very strong.

The thick branch swung a little under her weight but cradled her away from the realities of life. Nobody would think to look for her here. She shifted slightly to make herself more comfortable and leaned back against a crook in the gnarled limb. While she adjusted her position, she snagged the hem of her gown on a rough piece of bark. She hesitated, feeling foolish for giving in to a whim that would no doubt ruin her gown.

"Balderdash," she muttered aloud and pulled herself more securely onto the limb. "You don't like the dress anyway."

"I thought it a lovely gown," she heard a man say from the shadows at the edge of the little grotto.

Lilly froze. She peered through the branches but couldn't see who had spoken. She felt like a little girl who'd been caught doing something naughty. Then she hesitated. She wasn't a little girl. She was an adult who could do whatever she pleased. *As long as it's all right with Father,* a little voice inside reminded her, but she ignored it.

Maybe if she remained still and said nothing, the man would think he was mistaken. Knowing the possibility of that happening was almost nonexistent, she tried to prepare herself for the inevitable question. How could she tell one of her guests that she'd climbed a tree in an expensive gown? Silk was quite expensive these days. She hesitated to think what Father would have to say to her when the opportunity arose. She could almost hear the conversation now and the laughs that would follow.

None of this would happen if she could stand up to her father and refuse to wear these revealing dresses. The man standing at the edge of the glade probably assumed that since she wore such inappropriate attire, she would act accordingly. Sometimes she felt that her father really wanted her to relax her stiff demeanor toward the British soldiers he invited into the house, but she couldn't be sure.

"I say, you look rather like a yellow bird perched on that limb," came the voice again. "Could I interest you in sitting on the bench instead?"

He wasn't going away. Wishing she could fly like a yellow bird into one of the trees that lined Oyster Point, she peered once again through the branches. She could see the outline of a figure where the brick walkway joined the little glade. There seemed to be nothing left for her to do except respond. Anything less and she would appear more foolish than she already did.

Gathering her courage, she answered, "Had I preferred the bench, I would be sitting there now."

"Aha! The bird speaks."

The man walked into a shaft of light, and Lilly recognized the profile of Ethan Kendall. Her eyes closed in dismay. He, of all the people at the party, was the last one she wanted to find her perched in a tree like a bird. With the sunrise the shadows were lightening, and she could see his face more clearly with every step he took toward her. He looked amused.

Ethan smiled, hoping to put her at her ease. He didn't want to startle her into toppling from the limb. Lilly Arledge was far different from any woman he'd ever met, and he'd hate to be the cause of a broken bone or worse. He didn't know why she'd sought the sanctuary of the live oak, but he could almost guess. He'd heard the remark one of the women made about Lilly's attire.

"Miss Arledge, do you mind if I join you?" he asked

as he approached. "I do find a brief perch in a tree to be most relaxing, don't you agree?"

Gaping at him as if he were mad, Lilly wondered if she'd heard him correctly. His smile assured her that she had, and what's more, he lifted himself easily onto the limb beside her. After a moment's uncertainty her bravado returned. "Quite relaxing. I come here every evening to watch the moon rise over the harbor."

Every evening? Ethan couldn't believe she meant it. "Then I hope you won't mind if I join you from time to time when I'm in Charleston."

Lilly grimaced. Why had she told that lie? Now, for a few days at least, she'd have to be in the garden at moonrise. If he came looking for her, she'd be there waiting—not for her own amusement, but because Lilly didn't lie. She prided herself in telling the truth. She'd known this man but a few hours and already had lied to him. She'd simply have to make sure it wasn't a lie.

"Er, how did you come to such a practice?" he asked and shifted his weight to make himself more secure. He had to admit that trees were much more comfortable to a boy of nine or ten than to a man of twenty-five.

Lilly thought back to the first time she'd climbed this old oak. Tartuffe had been a kitten then. Lilly's father had kicked the poor cat, scaring it so badly that Tartuffe had leapt out of the window and raced across the garden with Lilly running after. She'd found the trembling creature in this very tree. When he wouldn't come down, she'd climbed up after him and liked the spot. From that day on, whenever her father did something she didn't like or when she was insecure or frightened, she had come here for solace, often finding Tartuffe already there, licking his paws.

She couldn't tell a stranger that her father abused animals, so she simply left out some details. "I came here to rescue my cat, Tartuffe."

"Tartuffe?" Ethan asked. "Rather a pretentious name for a cat, isn't it?"

"He's a pretentious cat." Lilly remembered the first day she'd seen him, lying atop a fence and preening. She'd stopped to stroke him, and he'd followed her home. He always pretended that it was she who needed him, rather than the other way around.

"I see." Ethan wanted to laugh. He'd never met a woman with so much imagination. "And does Tartuffe still live here?"

"Yes, he does, although he frequently is gone on trips of an unknown nature." Lilly giggled. "And, just as frequently, he returns with his fur tattered and torn, as if he'd been in a horrendous battle."

"Cats will do that," Ethan agreed, liking the girl all the more. "I once had a cat. She kept the barns free of mice. That cat could spot a mouse a mile away and catch him before he could hide."

"Sounds like a handy cat to have around. Tartuffe's getting older now." Lilly caught sight of a movement above Ethan's head. Tartuffe was creeping down a limb toward Ethan. Before she could warn him, Tartuffe leapt the remaining distance and landed on Ethan's head.

"Damn cat!" Ethan swore as he wobbled back and forth precariously on the limb and fought to retain his grip. His efforts were futile, and he fell from the branch to the ground with a thud.

"Ethan!" Lilly exclaimed and scrambled down to help him. "Are you hurt?"

Ethan shook his head groggily and then tried each of his extremities. "I seem to be unbroken."

"Oh, dear, let me help you up." Lilly grasped his arm

and helped him to his feet. "I'm so sorry. I should have warned you. Tartuffe is a little stuffy about the company I keep."

"Your cat attacks like a dog?" Ethan asked as he brushed the dirt and debris from his clothing.

Lilly laughed and gazed up at him. "Well, not exactly. I never knew of a dog climbing a tree."

Ethan stared at her for a moment and then joined in her laughter. "I suppose you're right. Still, this has been an adventure beyond my greatest expectations."

Though she didn't know for sure, Lilly thought that his comment included the party as well. Did he find someone interesting? He seemed to be in a happy bent of mind, regardless of his tumble from the live oak. Lilly felt a pang of jealousy. Nobody ever seemed to be that happy to see her.

Well, she couldn't be angry with Mari. Ethan Kendall was a handsome man. Any woman would be foolish not to be flattered by his attentions. Lilly almost wished that she were the object of his interest, but she knew that she could never be alluring to a man like Ethan. He seemed so worldly, so . . . She couldn't even describe him in adequate terms, and she was considered well read.

Lilly decided to end the meeting as quickly as she could. Their absence would be noticed by the same women who'd remarked about the cut of her gown. "I'm delighted that our little party amused you, Mr. Kendall. You'll have to visit with us again. Now I really should return to the remainder of my guests."

Ethan took her arm, and they strolled along the narrow brick walkway toward the house. He couldn't recall ever being so captivated by a woman. This guileless woman intrigued him, and he wanted to come here again when there were fewer guests to distract her. He wondered if Gregory could wrangle an invitation for supper one evening. He would definitely have to pursue the issue, he decided.

Lilly lifted her chin before returning to the parlor. When she and Ethan entered the room, only a few guests remained, but the women noticed her. Ignoring the color rising in her cheeks, Lilly resumed her role as hostess while Ethan drifted over to Gregory's side.

"You seem awfully cheerful," Gregory commented as Ethan turned to glance at Lilly. "What happened?"

"Happened?" Ethan asked, wondering what he could tell Gregory. If Ethan said anything about his little adventure, then he instinctively felt he would be betraying a confidence even though Lilly hadn't told him to remain quiet about the event. But he didn't really know her. For all Ethan knew, she could be well known for sitting in trees, but he thought not. He'd simply have to skirt the truth. "Nothing really. Just taking in a little fresh air. Gives one a decided lift, wouldn't you say?"

"A lift? Fresh air?" Gregory stared at his friend blankly. "I've known you for years and never heard you say anything so ridiculous in my life. I know that look. It has to do with women."

"You've consumed too much brandy." Ethan cocked his left eyebrow and gazed at Gregory. "Far too much, from the looks of it."

"I have indeed drunk too much brandy and loved every swig, but that has never been an issue. I've seen you swill down enough brandy to sink a sailing vessel, and you know it. The amount of brandy I've consumed has nothing to do . . . You're changing the subject."

Ethan couldn't contain his mirth. He suddenly felt as if the war had been won . . . but why? He glanced at Lilly. She was standing by the door and bidding goodbye to some of her guests. Ethan realized that if he didn't leave soon, he'd make a spectacle of himself by ogling her. "Gregory, old chum, let's end the night with breakfast at the inn."

"Sounds wonderful. I'm famished." Gregory elbowed his friend. "Drinking does that to a man, wouldn't you say? Makes him hungry, I mean."

"Exactly," Ethan agreed too quickly.

The two men sent Jedediah for their cloaks and said their goodbyes to Jonathan. He seemed eager for both of them to return.

"You're always welcome here, son!" Jonathan exclaimed. "Always. Drop in. Glad to count a true Loyalist among our friends, I must say."

"Thank you for your kindness, sir. I hope to see you again soon." Ethan stepped away and took his cloak from Jedediah while Gregory spoke further with Jonathan.

Ethan took the moment to approach Lilly. "You certainly have shown a stranger the benefit of your charming hospitality, Miss Arledge. I hope to call on you again."

Lilly gazed into his sea-green eyes. She could almost feel the tide pulling her into them, but she resisted. He stared at her with an intensity that made her shift uncomfortably. "Please do come again, Mr. Kendall. You're always welcome in the Arledge home. I . . . we'll be happy to see you whenever you can call."

Ethan opened his mouth to respond, but before he had a chance to speak, Gregory interrupted. "Ah, Ethan, here you are, basking in the beauty of Miss Arledge."

Lilly felt herself blush. Gregory was always a flatterer, but she didn't like his timing above half. "Gregory, you are as charming as Tartuffe."

"You mean that old cat's still around? I should have thought that someone would have gaily strangled the old soldier by now," Gregory declared and shook his head. "Ethan, did I ever tell you of the time Miss Arledge and I were sitting in the garden and that fat old feline leapt upon me from a limb hanging over the bench?"

Ethan could hardly suppress his mirth but managed to gaze at Gregory without feeling too foolish. "Why, no. What could you have been doing that caused the animal to do such a thing?"

Lilly bit her lower lip to keep from laughing out loud. Gregory would be fascinated to hear of the attack on Ethan, but he didn't seem to be willing to discuss the event. She glanced at Ethan. He, too, was experiencing difficulty keeping from laughing. She lifted her chin and composed herself as best she could. "I'm afraid, Mr. Kendall, that Tartuffe and Mr. Weston don't get along very amiably. Mr. Weston has been known to provoke my little darling's anger."

Ethan couldn't look at Lilly. He knew instinctively that she was baiting Gregory, and Ethan could ill afford to cause hard feelings with Gregory. Their friendship meant more than mere companionship to Ethan. Gregory was a lifeline, a source of information. Ethan decided that Gregory could take the good-natured jest. Gregory always had a sense of humor, and though he was a little embarrassed now, he'd soon join their laughter. Ethan watched the color rise in Gregory's cheeks and couldn't resist the chance to tease his friend a little. "My, but you're a brave sort, Gregory. How cunning is Tartuffe in battle?"

Gregory glared at his friends, first one and then the other. "Actually, he's quite a competitor. I must say he has no sense of honor. A true son of England would never attack from behind, nor would he use such devious battle plans."

"Devious? You're accusing a kitten, a darling little ball of fur, of being devious?" Lilly asked, feigning astonishment. "Why, that's like accusing a tiny babe of malice."

"She's right, Greg. I'm afraid you've overstated the kitten's abilities." Ethan patted his friend on the shoulder and winked at Lilly.

"Overstated? Just you wait until that little demon leaps upon you at a moment when . . . well, when you're seriously discussing your future." Gregory looked at Lilly and smiled. "A most untimely moment."

Ethan stared at Gregory and then at Lilly. Could this be the woman Gregory had spoken of earlier this evening? Ethan paid little attention to Greg when he prattled on about his conquests, but had he mentioned Lilly? Surely not. Lilly's face, radiant with innocence, turned to Ethan as if she were waiting for him to make some reply.

If Lilly was as innocent as Ethan believed, then Greg must be referring to an honorable relationship. Could Greg be in love with her? Unconsciously Ethan stepped back. The conclusion irritated him.

Lilly gazed at Ethan, silently imploring him to disregard Greg's exaggeration. She never doubted for a second that Greg would one day ask for her hand, but she felt nothing for him beyond friendship. They'd grown up together. Now no one seemed to be able to speak. How could Lilly deny what Greg had implied without making herself appear foolish?

Ethan finally broke the silence. "Well, it seems I must be careful when I call on Miss Arledge. She's well guarded by a proficient soldier."

"I fear that Mr. Weston exaggerates the skill of Tartuffe in battle. He's merely a cranky old cat, nothing more." Lilly peered through her dark lashes at Ethan, hoping he'd believe her, perhaps understand what she was really saying.

"And I, Miss Arledge, fear that Mr. Weston embellishes the truth to enhance the tale, wouldn't you say?" Ethan asked and noticed that Lilly seemed to relax a little.

"You must judge our friend for yourself, Mr. Kendall. He's a delightful fellow, but a bit brash on occasion." Lilly smiled and patted Gregory on the arm.

"You're both talking as though I weren't here. And," Greg continued, scowling at each of them in turn, "I sense that I'm being mocked."

"Mocked?" Ethan stepped backward and clamped his hand over his heart. "Mocked? My dear Greg, you've wounded me. To think that I . . . that Miss Arledge and I would stoop so low as to mock you . . . I'm mortally wounded."

Lilly giggled. She could no longer maintain a serious expression. "I fear that both of you are in your cups. Your humor is diverting, but the hour grows late. Heavens, the sun's risen. Take yourselves to breakfast and then sleep off this evening's entertainment."

"Miss Arledge is correct," Ethan agreed. "What's called for is a strong cup of tea and a good night's rest, though we'll have to sleep during the day."

"Sleep? I must be at my duty station in two hours' time!" Greg cried, shaking his head sadly. He stepped through the doorway and donned his cloak. "I'll be a worthless chap for the day."

"You're always a worthless chap," Ethan retorted genially. He was reluctant to leave such amiable company.

Lilly certainly possessed a delightful sense of humor. Greg could be fun, too, but Lilly retained his interest. "I'm afraid, Miss Arledge, that we worthless chaps must bid you good morning."

"I believe I've grown fond of worthless chaps. 'Tis a weakness developed most recently." Lilly watched Greg walk down the steps and turned to Ethan. She wanted to say something else, something significant, something that would tell him she wasn't as featherheaded as many of the girls she knew. Then again, maybe he liked girls with fish eggs for brains. "Good morning," she said simply and closed the door.

She danced to the door of the parlor and glanced inside. Nobody seemed to notice her. There were but a few people left, mostly soldiers and their escorts. Knowing she should act the proper hostess, Lilly grimaced and stepped into the room, then paused. No one paid any attention to her. She stepped back. Still nobody looked her way.

Feeling better suddenly, she flew up the staircase as fast as she could run. Her father would be furious later, but she didn't care. She'd been congenial to his boring—and sometimes rude—guests for too long this night.

Inside her room she ran to the window and threw open the sash. She stepped onto the piazza and looked down on Charleston, now bathed in the soft rays of early morning sunlight. Loving her beautiful city, she peered up and down Meeting Street as far as she could see. In the distance she could see two men dressed in formal attire, walking along. Ethan and Gregory were wending their way toward the inn.

She sat on a low chair and rested her chin on the wrought-iron railing. Closing her eyes, she could easily recall the smile that broke across Ethan's face as he teased Greg. The memory of Ethan's expression when Tartuffe had leapt upon him, knocking him from the tree, brought a smile to her face. How he'd tormented Gregory without ever revealing that a similar incident had occurred no less than twenty minutes earlier. Ethan seemed to be able to keep a secret.

That knowledge made Lilly feel happy. Her secret—being caught in a silk gown in a tree—would go no further.

Lilly grinned. This night had changed her life. Ethan's presence had subtly altered her outlook. Without knowing exactly why, Lilly jumped to her feet and whispered, "Good morning, Charleston. I love you."

CHAPTER 3

LILLY SLEPT FOR MOST OF THE DAY. WHEN SHE FINALLY arose shortly before two o'clock, her father had already gone out on business. She stretched luxuriously and pulled on her dressing gown before ringing for Zipporah to bring tea.

While she waited, she washed the sleep from her eyes and slipped into a day gown of soft peach-colored muslin. Tying a kerchief across her bosom, she sat down at her dressing table and then began to brush her hair.

Before Lilly could arrange her hair into its customary chignon, Mari burst into the room. "Tell me everything. If you hold back the teensiest detail, I'll tell all of Charleston that you're a Whig."

"Mari!" Lilly exclaimed and leapt to her feet so quickly that the stool toppled over behind her. Using the confusion to cover her embarrassment, she righted the stool and then faced her friend. "You wouldn't dare."

"Wouldn't I? Well, maybe nothing that drastic." Mari flounced over to the settee and made herself comfortable. "I told Zip to include a cup for me. I hope you don't mind."

Relieved a little, Lilly joined her friend in front of the cold fireplace and sat on her favorite rocking chair as the bells of St. Michael's tolled two o'clock. She didn't really want company, but Mari would carry most of the conversation—relating the latest gossip and news—allowing Lilly to think about last evening. "Of course, I don't mind. It'll save her the trip for another cup."

"So tell me all about Mr. Charming," Mari persisted, hugging herself. "He's the man of my dreams."

Lilly frowned. Why would her friend call Ethan "Mr. Charming"? Had Mari spent enough time with him to make such a determination? Maybe she meant someone else. Lilly sometimes couldn't tell what Mari was thinking. Though she thought Mari was talking about Ethan, Lilly didn't want to give the impression that she understood the question. "To whom do you refer, Mari? I know many charming men."

"You know who I'm talking about. Stop playing the innocent and tell me what happened." Mari settled back and crossed her arms primly.

"That's a lovely dress you're wearing." Lilly tried to change the subject. Mari was always happy to talk about fashion—hers and everyone else's.

"Thank you, and don't you dare try to change the subject, Lilly Arledge," Mari insisted. "I won't allow you to veer away from my question so easily."

Lilly rose and walked to the window. She peered down onto the street without really seeing anything. How much should she tell Mari? How much was there to tell? "Well, Mari, I can't see why you place such importance on an event, but I assume you're referring to my walk in the garden with Mr. Kendall."

"You don't fool me, Lilly Charlotte Arledge. You were blushing when you returned to the parlor." Weaving her fingers together, Mari edged forward on the settee. "And your gown was soiled."

"Don't be ridiculous." Lilly returned to her chair, sat

down, and began to rock. "You are a foolish child. The color in my cheeks was . . . was due to the cool air outside. And my gown was soiled from sitting on the marble bench in the garden."

"You are the foolish one, Lilly, if you think to fob me off with such stories." Mari grinned conspiratorially and wriggled excitedly. "Tell me, did he kiss you?"

"Kiss me? You've taken leave of your senses. I hardly know the man. In fact, I've seen him but the one time." Lilly did her best to summon a semblance of outrage but fell short of her goal. The best she could do was seem shocked. "Had he tried to kiss me, he would have received a resounding slap for his efforts."

Mari looked a little disappointed. "Well, then, what happened? You were both gone for so long, I naturally assumed—"

"You assumed incorrectly." Lilly hoped to end the discussion before Zip returned. Zip despised the way Jonathan made his daughter dress and act—having said so on many occasions—and wouldn't hesitate to chastise her charge for inappropriate behavior if she knew Lilly had walked alone in the garden during the wee hours of the morning with a stranger.

Mari stared at her and grimaced. "Lilly Arledge, stop with all this flowery talk and tell me the straight of the matter. Did you or did you not kiss Ethan Kendall?"

"With or without flowery talk, the answer is still no." Wondering how to change the subject, Lilly stopped rocking and glared at her friend for a few moments. Then she decided to shift the weight of the conversation to Mari's conduct. "Did you?"

"Did I what?" Mari asked.

Feeling a little relieved, Lilly grinned, settled back, and started rocking again. "Did you kiss Mr. Kendall?"

"Why, you know I didn't. He was mooning over you the entire evening," Mari replied and crossed her arms. "Nobody else had a chance with him."

"Mooning? Over me? What a ridiculous thing to say. Why, I'd venture to say that this afternoon he won't even remember my name. I'd even wager—"

"Miss Lilly," Zip called and tapped on the door. She opened it and peeked inside. "Miss Lilly, does you want me to serve tea in the parlor? Mr. Ethan Kendall is come a-callin' on you."

"Ethan Kendall? Here? Now?" Lilly felt the shock of hearing his name through her entire body. Hoping that neither of the ladies noticed the slight quiver, she glanced from Zip to Mari and back again. "Well, of course, we'll serve tea downstairs. I hope you made Mr. Kendall comfortable."

"Yas'm, I did." Zip closed the door as she left.

"Aha! You planned this last night, didn't you?" Mari pounced on Lilly much like Tartuffe would when he was hungry.

"You are a silly twit, Marigold O'Grady. I can't think for the life of me why we're best friends." Lilly hoped to still Mari's already bouncing enthusiasm. "Would you have me keep Mr. Kendall waiting, or will you join me downstairs in the parlor?"

Mari rushed to the door. "Lilly, there's no place in Hades you could hide if you didn't let me go down with you. I promise I'll—"

"Spare me the promises you won't keep, Mari." Lilly glanced in the mirror to make sure she looked presentable. "Except for one. Please promise me you won't embarrass me by asking Mr. Kendall the silly questions you've been plaguing me with this afternoon."

"What kind of woman do you think I am? Would I

embarrass my dearest friend?" she asked with wide-eyed innocence.

"Yes, you certainly would." Lilly checked to make sure her skirts hung gracefully, patted her chignon, and opened the door. "Miss O'Grady, will you join me in the parlor?"

Mari almost leapt out the door. When she reached the stairs, Lilly placed a restricting hand on her friend's arm. If she hadn't, Mari would have raced down the stairs like a schoolboy. "Remember, we're ladies and not hoydens."

Ladies and not hoydens. As the two girls walked down the stairs, Lilly thought back to the previous evening when she'd sat in the tree with Ethan. If a hoyden lived in Charleston, she was certainly the one. Did he think badly of her for acting so strangely? Feeling a little foolish, she opened the door to the parlor and allowed Mari to walk through first.

"Mr. Kendall, how kind of you to come by." Lilly strode across the room and smiled graciously at her guest. "I'm sure you remember my dear friend, Miss O'Grady."

"Certainly," he replied, glancing briefly at Mari and then back at Lilly. He wasn't happy to see Marigold O'Grady here. He had wanted to see Lilly privately, to see if she was as wonderful as he remembered. "May I say how lovely you ladies look this afternoon?"

Mari held out her hand in greeting and gushed, "Of course you may. How kind of you to notice."

"Won't you be seated, Mr. Kendall?" Lilly gestured to a chair for him and seated herself in the blue brocade wing chair while Mari selected the sofa near Ethan. Lilly smiled sweetly at Mari, hoping she'd behave properly. "I do hope you can stay for tea, Mr. Kendall. Mari and I were just about to have ours. Zip should be serving—"

A tap on the door interrupted her, and Zip swept into the room with Jedediah in her wake. "Missy, here the tea."

"Thank you." Lilly watched as Jedediah placed the silver tray on a small Queen Anne table. As the two servants left the room, Lilly glanced at Ethan. "As I said, I hope you can join us for tea."

"You're very kind." Ethan gazed at the tray. He'd eaten almost nothing today, and the little tray of delicacies looked tempting. "I would be happy to have tea with two of the loveliest ladies in Charleston."

Ethan listened idly to Mari's chatter. Though she was charming in a shallow sort of way, she lacked the spirit that made Lilly so attractive to him. Still, spending the afternoon chattering about nothing with Mari would bring him closer to Lilly than if he'd gone back to his lodgings. Ethan had slept little. Thinking about the party last night had kept him awake.

Looking from Mari to Lilly, he tried to determine why he found Lilly more attractive. If he'd met Mari on the street, he would have flirted with her. She was pretty enough in an esthetic sense—honey-blond hair, cornflower-blue eyes, slender figure—but not a woman he could spend the rest of his life with.

Lilly, on the other hand, was not only beautiful, but also she seemed to be more serious, more thoughtful. She certainly wasn't a shallow flibbertigibbet who thought of nothing but clothes. Sitting in a tree in a silk dress suggested that her thoughts were more precious than her attire.

He wondered again why she'd climbed into the tree. He'd never seen a woman do that, not even in her everyday clothes. By the gods, he liked a woman who would do a thing like that. Grinning, he looked at Lilly apprais-ingly. He wished that she'd take the pins out of her hair and let it fall around her shoulders. He suddenly wanted to bury his hands in its rich fullness.

He noticed that when she laughed, little lines appeared at the corners of her eyes, and her whole face took on a cherubic appearance. Her day gown was much more modest than the stunning yellow one she'd worn last eve-ning. Its simplicity adorned every curve and highlighted her tiny waist.

"Ahem, won't you, Mr. Kendall?" Mari repeated and reached over to touch his arm.

"What?" he asked, feeling a bit foolish for not paying attention. With Lilly there, he should keep his mind on her. There would be plenty of evenings when he would have only a mental picture of her rather than the pleasure of her company, and he wanted to remember every facet of her appearance. The way Mari had phrased her ques-tion seemed to require a positive response. "Oh, yes," he said.

"I knew it." Mari clapped her hands together. "Seven-thirty this evening? Lilly you'll come, too, won't you? I'll ask Gregory. We'll make it a small party. Papa will be out, and Mama is visiting with Mrs. Montaigne this eve-ning."

Lilly glared at her friend. Mari knew her parents would refuse to allow her to entertain a stranger without a chaperon, so she'd included Lilly and Gregory as a buffer. Lilly averted her eyes and caught the smile on Ethan's face. How could she refuse to go when he seemed so pleased that she would be along as well? "Well, I don't know, Mari. I mean, after all—"

"You'll come. Don't try to get out of it, either." Mari

jumped up. "I must go and tell Cook to prepare. Don't forget."

"But, Mari—" Lilly's objection came too late. Her friend disappeared out the front door. With a stunned look on her face, Lilly glanced back at Ethan. "Well, I guess we're going to Mari's for supper."

Ethan could hardly control his pleasure. He couldn't have asked for a better entrée into Charleston society. Bowie had suggested that Ethan could wriggle into Lilly's good graces if he mentioned Erin. With a few more contacts like the ones he'd made in the past three days, his ability to infiltrate the ranks of British officers seemed more assured. He'd received his uniform and commission with Gregory's help. Tomorrow Ethan would sport the red uniform of a British major, having recently been promoted. He gazed at Lilly. How would she feel about him if she knew he was really a Patriot spy?

He couldn't worry about that now. She was staring at him as if he'd turned green or something, and he decided that it was because he looked so serious when the conversation had been light and fun. Smiling, he shook his head and chuckled as he forced his gaze to the door. "What a whirlwind she is. Is she always so impulsive?"

"Oh, yes. She's quite impetuous." Lilly laughed as she remembered some of Mari's more foolhardy plots. "Once she wanted to stow away on a ship bound for France. We were hardly out of the schoolroom. She wanted to get a firsthand look at French fashions."

"Stow away?" Ethan asked and cocked his eyebrow.

"Yes. Her father refused to let her go to Paris. After all, the war had started, and he considered it unsafe for her to sail from here," Lilly explained and shook her head in consternation. "I don't know what we would have done if I'd allowed her to convince me to accompany her!"

Ethan didn't want to even consider the possibilities. He was glad Lilly had a good head on her shoulders. "I don't think it would have been a very good idea."

"That's the least of her silly schemes." Lilly liked Ethan's smile. She liked to see him laugh, too. Not enough laughter could be heard around Charleston these days—not since the occupation began. People on both sides found too little to laugh about. But when she was with Ethan, she could almost forget that a war was going on. "Tell me all about your plantation."

Ethan grinned and sat back. "I love it. It's the most beautiful place on earth. Spanish moss hangs from the cypress trees in the swampy areas. The yard is dotted with fine palms, palmettos, and live oaks. The loblolly pine dominates the forest, but there are some good hardwoods interspersed among them."

Lilly leaned back and curled one foot beneath her. She knew the posture was impolite, but she didn't care. She simply rested her head on the back of the chair and let his deep, rumbling voice flow over her like a warm tide. The rhythmic pattern of his speech, coupled with the timbre of his voice, lulled her into a peaceful comfort that, had she not been so interested in what he had to say, would have put her to sleep as effectively as the best lullabye.

"The soil is fertile enough that the flowers are abundant and as lovely as any you'll ever find. The hunting and fishing are the best in the area." Ethan paused, noticing that her eyes were closed. Had he bored her to sleep?

After a moment Lilly realized that he was silent. Was he waiting for some reply from her? She opened her eyes and gazed at him. He was studying her thoughtfully.

Feeling the color creep into her cheeks, she cleared her throat and wrung her hands. What could she say to make him realize she'd been listening intently? "Mr. Kendall, your plantation sounds like a special place."

"It is," Ethan answered simply. He regretted omitting the name of his family's plantation, Carolina Moon, but he couldn't provide too many details without endangering his holdings. If the Tories should discover that he was spying, his home and all his family's possessions would be lost to him forever. He recalled the devastation of Sumter's home, burned to the ground by Tories, and vowed that would never happen to Carolina Moon.

Lilly gazed at him. He appeared to be reminiscing about the good times he'd had as a boy growing up on such a wonderful plantation. She experienced a twinge of envy. Her father never owned a plantation, but she'd been out to her cousin Erin's on occasion and loved it. "I hope it has been untouched by the war."

He looked at her. He hoped it would remain untouched, but he doubted whether it could escape unscathed. "I hope so, too, Miss Arledge."

Looking into the depths of his lovely green eyes, Lilly felt as if she could drown. She'd never met anyone who could maintain such disciplined eye contact before, and she felt as though nobody else in the world mattered to him but her. When Lilly could no longer stand the intensity of his gaze, she averted her eyes.

"Another cup of tea?" she asked, reaching for the teapot.

"Another? Eh, no, thank you." Ethan placed his cup on the tray and stood. "I'm afraid I must take my leave. If I'm to join you for supper this evening at Miss O'Grady's, I must attend to my errands."

"I see." Lilly put her cup beside his and rose. "I can't

tell you what a pleasant time I've had. Please come again."

Ethan walked to the front door with her and stopped. He lifted her hand and kissed it gently, even though he wanted to linger there. The soft fragrance of violets filled the air around her, and Ethan knew that if he remained much longer, he'd go beyond the bounds of propriety. He stood erectly and smiled. "May I stop by and escort you to Miss O'Grady's home this evening?"

"I'm sure that won't be necessary. You don't have to worry about walking me here and there." Lilly felt warm with happiness. He must like her or he wouldn't have asked.

"I'd consider it a privilege, not a worry." Ethan felt his body moving closer and stiffened. "May I call for you about a quarter after seven?"

Lilly smiled broadly. "That will be fine. I'll be ready."

Lilly made sure all her chores were done so she'd have plenty of time to dress for supper. She wanted to look nice this evening. As she sat in her small parlor, or her sun room, as she liked to call it, she stitched carefully on a napkin she was making for her trousseau.

She felt much happier about placing the tiny stitches as she sat in the late afternoon sunlight streaming through the window. She put down her work and thought of Ethan. The memory of his smile brought a smile to her own face. There was something about him that touched her, that reached deep inside her and heightened her senses. Humming, she forced herself to return to her embroidery.

"Lilly!" came her father's thunderous voice from down the hall.

She jerked so hard that she pricked her finger. She

dropped her embroidery hoop and sucked her finger for a few seconds before responding. She wanted to hide. Her father sounded in a terrible mood. "In my sun room, Father."

Jonathan Arledge flung the door open so hard it banged against the wall and bounced back in his face. Lilly couldn't help giggling, even though she knew he'd be even angrier.

He almost leapt across the room and jerked her from her chair. His strong hands bit into her arm, and she was afraid he'd break it, but she didn't cry out. She lifted her chin and stared blankly at him, as if pretending not to see him and wishing he couldn't see her.

"The fires of hell would roast that look off your face! You'd better learn proper respect for your father." He grabbed her other arm and shook her. "Tell me why you refused the offer to walk with young Madison."

Young Madison? The words echoed in Lilly's mind. Of course, he was the young man she'd turned away last evening. She should have known her father had put the boy up to it. Madison must be from a prominent family, or perhaps his father was a high-ranking officer. "I didn't want to go walking with him."

"I've told you to be kind to these soldiers. They're fighting for our country, for God's sake. Have you no compassion?" Jonathan tightened his grip. "The next time he asks, you'd better go, or there'll be hell to pay."

"Father, I can't go walking with every man who asks. If I do, my reputation will be no more valuable than the oyster shells that cover Oyster Point." Lilly knew she should simply have agreed with her father, but she had to make him realize that she had some pride, that she wanted to be liked for herself—not for whatever these soldiers thought they could get away with because of her father's attitude.

"You'll go when someone asks, or else. I'm tired of your silly false morality." He thrust her back into her chair and leaned over to glare at her. "I don't want to hear that you rejected a friend's invitation again."

Lilly looked into his eyes and saw the fury that raged there. Something else had caused his foul mood. He was taking it out on her because there was no one else who was so easily intimidated. She said nothing; anything she answered would merely add fuel to his already frenzied mind.

"I see you've adopted your childish attitude. Speak or not, I don't care. You'll do as I say if I have to beat you every step of the way." He moved toward the door but stopped short of leaving. "Soon I must leave for a few days. I expect to find a change in you when I return."

She heard the front door slam and then rose and went to the window to watch him leave. Her arms were red where he'd held her so tightly, and she knew the marks would turn to bruises soon. She rubbed her arms gently, knowing she'd have to wear something with long sleeves for a few days to hide the marks that would look like black fingerprints on her arms.

"Honor thy father and thy mother," she quoted from the Ten Commandments. "Lord, did you know about Jonathan Arledge when you issued that commandment?"

Lilly scowled. She couldn't defy her father openly without risking a beating, but she could do little things, get her own small revenge. This evening would be one of those times. She watched the sunset and then smiled. Jonathan Arledge had little use for Greg and Mari. Lilly wondered what he thought of Ethan?

Ethan! She hurried from her sitting room to her dressing room. So little time remained before he would be here. Where had the time gone? She'd promised to be ready at seven fifteen.

"I'll be ready," she repeated to herself at seven fifteen, knowing she'd be late. She hated to be late for anything, and this evening she especially wanted to be on time. "What shall I wear?"

Lilly rifled through her dresses, tossing them here and there before finally selecting an apple-green satin brocade with layers of lace at the sleeves. The neckline, cut square, fit snugly and barely covered her breasts. "I know I shan't be ready on time."

"It don't hurt a man to wait," Zip said from across the room. She looked at the pile of dresses accumulating by the wardrobe and shook her head. "This'n must be a powerful attractive man fo you to go to such trouble. I ain't never seen you in such a fix."

"I'm not in a fix," Lilly said. "I merely want to look nice."

"Harrumph," Zip groaned. "If'n you jus' want to look nice, any of them dresses'd do. Don't you be tellin' me any tales. I'se done raised you up from a sucklin' babe. I knows you and that's that."

Lilly rolled her eyes. Zip's opinions, once formed, couldn't be changed. Besides, Lilly admitted privately, she's right. I do care how I look for Ethan Kendall. She noticed that Zip had stopped what she was doing and turned to listen for an answer. "Oh, hush up. You'll have to smooth my hair again. It got caught in the lace."

"Well, if'n you'd a-dressed first and fixed yo hair last, I wouldn't be a-havin' to do it again." Zip took the brush and teased it lightly over the smooth curls that hugged the nape of Lilly's neck. "I tole you and I tole you. Put on the dress first."

"How do I look?" Lilly asked, peering nervously into her mirror.

"You looks like a princess." Zip stared at her critically. "But if'n your pa don't stop buyin' them dresses that low-cut, I'm gonna stick a pitchfork in his bee-hind. It ain't decent. It just ain't. And I see'd them marks on yo arm. Don't you think I didn't. That man don't know what's right fo his girl."

Lilly didn't have much time left to dress. She pinched her cheeks, hoping to bring fresh color. "Where is he tonight?"

"Lordy, I can't say as I know. Keepin' up with that man is worser than tryin' to catch a bullfrog with a bonnet." Zip surveyed her work. "You looks like you could be a fashion doll. Jus' you don't go gettin' low morals 'cause you be wearin' clothes like a wharf woman."

Lilly rolled her eyes. She couldn't listen to this speech again without screaming. This dress was no worse than the others. In fact, it probably was the most modest of her gowns. "Zip, go and see if Mr. Kendall has arrived yet. If he has, tell him I'll be down soon."

"Since when you go traipsin' round Charleston with a stranger?" Zip crossed her arms and narrowed her eyes as she studied her charge. "If'n I'd a know'd you was goin' with a stranger, I'd a tied you to the bedpost."

"Go on, Zip. I can't keep him waiting."

Ethan stood in the parlor. He spotted a portrait over the fireplace and strode over to look at it. The woman's hair was quite red, coppery almost, but her eyes were the warm brown of Lilly's. He guessed that the woman must be Lilly's mother. He considered the portrait and compared it with the memory of Lilly's face.

The parlor door slid open, and a black woman peered inside. "Mistah Kendall? Miss Lilly be with you in a minute."

"Thank you," he replied and glanced back at the portrait. "Is this Miss Arledge's mother?"

"Yessuh. That's Miss Thera. She been dead since my po' Lilly was born." Zip seemed to relax a little and stepped inside the room.

"She's lovely, but not nearly as lovely as her daughter." Ethan looked at the servant and saw by her nod that she agreed.

"Miss Lilly's a finer woman. Not that Miss Thera weren't fine, but Miss Lilly cares 'bout everybody." Zip glared at Ethan for a moment. "Sometimes she cares too much 'bout the wrong peoples."

Ethan tried not to grin. He realized that the servant adored her mistress and would be offended if he made some flippant remark. He also recognized the warning contained in her words and never doubted that the same warning had been issued to Miss Arledge many times. "I'll guard her with my life."

"Harrumph," the old black woman said as she stepped back into the foyer and hesitated briefly. "Who gonna guard her against you?"

CHAPTER 4

"I APOLOGIZE FOR BEING SO LATE, MR. KENDALL." Lilly swept into the room and stepped to his side. "I encountered a problem that required a change of my attire at the last moment."

Ethan glanced at her appraisingly. Whatever the problem, he was grateful for it. If anything, she looked even lovelier than he remembered. "You look stunning. Well worth the moment's wait."

"Thank you for your kindness." Lilly pulled her lace shawl about her shoulders. When Ethan reached to help, their hands touched, and she gazed up at him as the intensity of the contact surged through her. Knowing she should move away from him, find a way to escape the magnetism of his green eyes, she cleared her throat and asked, "Shall we be going?"

Ethan longed to prolong the contact with her, but he quickly remembered Zip's parting comment. He also didn't want to risk extinguishing the fire that lit up Lilly's eyes when he looked at her. Extending his arm, he waited for her to place her hand in the crook of his elbow, and then they walked out of the parlor.

The butler, Jedediah, opened the door for them. Ethan found the servants in this household extremely protective of Miss Arledge, and he wondered if their concern was due to Jonathan Arledge's treatment of his daughter. From what Ethan gathered, all the servants adored Lilly.

He stepped carefully down the steps, exerting extreme caution to prevent Lilly from stumbling over her long skirts. The touch of her hand on his arm sent little tingles through his body as they strolled along Meeting Street on their way to Queen. Ethan didn't know when he'd been so excited about escorting a woman down the street. He inhaled the warm salty air and glanced around to see who might be watching.

They soon arrived at Mari's house and found Gregory already waiting. He jumped to his feet as they walked through the doorway into the parlor. "I say, but it's tops to see you again so soon, Lilly. You, too, Ethan, old man."

"It's lovely to see you, Gregory," Lilly replied and allowed him to kiss her hand. "Where's Mari?"

"You know her. Late as usual. Her maid came down a while ago and said Mari would be here shortly." Gregory motioned for Lilly to have a seat. "We may as well make ourselves comfortable while we wait."

Ethan and Gregory talked of the war, but there wasn't much happening—at least, not around Charleston. For now the British and the Patriots seemed to be avoiding conflict.

Studying Gregory, Ethan finally asked, "What do you think will happen next?"

Greg shook his head. "I don't know. We seem to be doing nothing. I personally think morale is low as a result of the lack of engagements."

"You may be correct," Ethan agreed and shot a glance at Lilly. She listened intently but remained quiet. Was she listening with interest or simply pretending? Ethan wondered. He knew he shouldn't waste valuable time trying to figure out what was in a woman's mind, especially in view of his mission. He returned his attention to Greg and said, "We're having a hell of a time finding food for all the troops and horses."

"I know that's true. I wonder what we'll do if there's another big battle? Hungry men are not likely to be effective fighters." Greg stood up and walked to the window. "I can't understand the thinking of the British commanders. Why aren't we doing something?"

Ethan wondered the same thing but for other reasons. One of his tasks was to determine what, if anything, the British planned to do in the near future. "Perhaps they're lulling the Patriots into a sense of security. Maybe they plan an all-out attack soon."

"God, but I pray so." Gregory returned to his seat. "I want some action. Everybody does."

"Right," Ethan agreed. "Everybody does."

Gregory couldn't know how close he was to the truth, Ethan thought. The Patriots were ready to end this war. With the British Army now virtually held prisoner in the city of Charleston, there seemed to be no reason to maintain a militia. Many of the soldiers who'd fought so gallantly were now home with their families, preparing to plant crops, repairing damage incurred through battles and neglect. Ethan wanted to be home, too, but he refused to return as others had until his job was done, when all the king's men were out of Charleston and America.

Ethan thought of his mother. He'd stopped in to see her on his way to Charleston a few weeks ago. She'd been fine, but he could see the strain of the war on her face. He wanted to be home, to start preparing the soil for the spring planting, to begin living a normal life again.

"Oh, I'm so sorry. You can't imagine how much trouble I had picking out a dress." Mari barged into the room with a flourish. She held her hand for both of the men to kiss and then hugged Lilly. "Oh, my dear, you look lovely. I simply can't wear that color without looking like a green fig. On you it looks wonderful."

"Of course you wouldn't look like a fig. I never heard anything so silly." Lilly smiled and comforted her friend.

Mari, although quite brash where men were concerned, frequently exhibited an insecurity that Lilly couldn't understand. The young woman had everything. She was beautiful, a blond goddess with eyes as blue as the summer sky. Her figure was petite and well shaped. Her parents were quite well to do and treated her with nothing less than love and affection.

Lilly, on the other hand, had every reason to be insecure, but she chose to go on with her life as if her problems didn't really exist. She treated people well and expected the same from them, though she rarely received it. Those women who'd made the remarks about her gown were beyond the bounds of decency, she knew, but she could do nothing about it.

Gazing at Ethan, Lilly realized that for the first time in her life she wanted to leave Charleston. She hated the whispers, the innuendo about her life and the way she dressed. Didn't her detractors realize that she had no choice? Couldn't they understand that she hated what her father forced her to be? Couldn't they see her bruises?

Lilly glanced at her friends, both old and new. She didn't know what she'd do without them. Greg and Mari had stuck by her when many of her old friends seemed to forget who she was. Ethan, though he'd most assuredly heard the cutting remarks about her dress last night, appeared not to care. Still grateful that he'd chosen not to mention it, Lilly smiled at him when he turned to face her. She could almost hug him for being so kind.

Ethan gazed at Lilly. When he'd glanced her way, she'd smiled broadly, and a glimmer of gold sparkled in her eyes. What had made her so happy all of a sudden? Nothing in the conversation had been amusing, nor had it centered on her. He had no idea what gave her the glow that warmed him from across the low table. He smiled in return, hoping that she wouldn't think him rude for not doing so immediately.

Basking in the warmth of her lovely smile, Ethan felt as if they were alone in the world. He longed to take her hand and lead her away from the aggravations of day-to-day living. In short, he wanted to take her to Carolina Moon. She belonged there in the tranquility of the countryside, in the silken glow of moonlight as it trailed across the neat gardens and pooled in the fountains like clusters of diamonds.

He could easily imagine her strolling among the loblolly pines or dangling her feet off the end of the dock on a warm summer afternoon—or maybe perched on the limb of a live oak. The image renewed his smile.

"Yoohoo," Mari called.

Ethan jerked his mind from its reverie. Lilly, Mari, and Greg were staring at him as if they were waiting for an answer to a question. He'd have to learn to keep his mind on the conversation instead of allowing his mind to wander. "I . . . I, well, I guess I was thinking about . . . What was the question?"

Mari frowned slightly but repeated her question. "I asked how long you are going to be in Charleston."

Her question was another that Ethan couldn't truthfully answer without endangering his position. "I don't really know. I suppose as long as there's a need for my services."

There. He'd found a way to be truthful. Let her

think—let them all think he would be here as long as the British needed him. He glanced at Lilly. Her smile made him feel guilty for being dishonest. His answer wasn't completely dishonest, but he *was* withholding the truth.

"Where will you go after the war is over?" Lilly asked and leaned forward a little. She couldn't look directly at Ethan for a moment because she didn't want him to know how important his answer was to her. What a silly thought, she mused. I've hardly known the man two days, and already I'm concerned about . . . about his future.

His future. Lilly knew that she wanted to know for herself, not out of concern for his future. Her inquiry sprang from a selfish desire to see him as frequently after the war as she had during the past two days, silly as that seemed. She glanced at him and found him gazing at her in that deep penetrating way that made her feel as though the two of them alone populated the earth. She wondered why his gaze made her feel that way; many men had stared at her, even gaped and gawked like schoolboys, but Ethan was different, and she felt warm all over.

Ethan noticed the blush tinge Lilly's cheeks pink and decided it made her look even lovelier than he could have ever imagined. He supposed she was embarrassed for asking a question, which on the surface seemed innocent enough, but down deep may have meant more to her. He hoped it did. In the past few hours he'd thought of nothing but her—and if that didn't change, he'd be in great danger.

Ethan addressed his answer to all three friends. "I plan to return to my plantation. I hope that we can gather there soon, that this war will be over soon. We can have the grandest lawn party ever, and the four of us will be joined in victory."

"We'll count on that," Gregory answered. "Especially the soon part. I'm ready for this war to be over. Enough good men have died."

"You and I certainly agree on that." Ethan glanced at his companions and wondered how they would feel after the war was over.

Would they hate him for his part in the war? He couldn't dislike them, even though they were on opposite sides. After the last shot was fired and the treaties were signed, there would be a period of adjustment—regardless of who won. Neighbor had fought neighbor, friend had fought friend, brother had fought brother. How long would the healing take? Or were the injuries so severe that past friendships would die without a chance of survival?

"Well, then, let's plan the biggest party ever to be held in South Carolina." Mari, always one to concentrate on the fun aspects of anything, latched on to the party idea. "We can call it a victory party."

Ethan winced. Victory for whom? "Why not call it a . . . a closing-the-gap party or a forgetting-the-war party. Something like that? I mean, somebody has to win and somebody has to lose, but we all have to learn to live together again."

"I'm for that," Lilly chimed in for the first time in a few moments. She'd been listening to the conversation, wondering why she felt so close to Ethan in such a short time. He seemed to be honest and trustworthy, level-headed. His suggestions were well thought out and appropriate.

Mari's cook announced supper, and Lilly allowed Gregory to take her arm. She would rather have walked into the dining room with Ethan, but Mari claimed him too quickly, and Gregory took Lilly's arm.

"It's only fair. Ethan accompanied you over here, so I'll escort you to supper." Gregory smiled at Lilly, and they followed Mari and Ethan into the dining room.

Mari's dining table was small, and they could sit close enough together so that conversation wouldn't be a chore. The meal was pleasant, and the little group chatted and laughed so much that Lilly hardly noticed the food, even though Mari's cook was excellent.

While appearing to listen to the discussion about the lull in battles, Lilly studied Ethan. His blond hair refused to be tamed into a queue, and several curls had freed themselves of their bondage, curling across his forehead. Lilly decided the curls made him appear happy. His green eyes were splendid. Set deeply, they were the dark green of a forest glade, cool and remote even though earlier they were speckled with gold. Must be the candlelight, she mused.

Suddenly her eyes met his, and she realized she'd been caught staring. He seemed amused by her discomfort.

"Well, of course, they occasionally search for forage for the horses, but as far as I know, we haven't seen any real action in some time," Gregory was saying. He shook his head and sighed. "I tell you, the men are getting anxious. They feel that the damned Whigs are up to something devious."

Ethan smiled and nodded. "I know what you mean. I feel it as well. What are the officers going to do to combat the monotony?"

"Who knows? The repercussions of Cornwallis's leaving South Carolina are still being felt." Gregory scraped the last piece of pie from his plate, ate it thoughtfully, and then gazed at Ethan. "Why would he leave here with Charleston's future still uncertain? I simply don't understand his thinking. After all, Clinton's orders were for him to remain here."

"I don't know," Ethan answered truthfully. "I, among many soldiers, believed Cornwallis would be here until the end of the war."

Lilly looked from one man to the other, feeling a little anxious herself. Did Cornwallis's abandonment of Charleston signify something she couldn't understand? Worry beset her. What would happen to the people who'd remained loyal to their king, the people he was supposed to be here protecting? Until this moment she'd never really fretted about the war's outcome. She'd assumed the British would win easily; now she couldn't be sure.

"Mr. Kendall—" she began.

"Ethan," he corrected. "Both of you should call me Ethan. I know you call Gregory by his given name."

"Well, I . . . Ethan, surely you don't think the Patriots have a chance of winning, do you?" she asked and placed her napkin beside her plate. "I mean, we still hold Charleston and Savannah."

"True, but . . . well, who can be certain?" Ethan chose to answer as tactfully as possible. He wanted to boast that the Patriots outnumbered the British and Tories. That wasn't exactly true, but the Patriot force seemed more motivated at the moment.

"We can only hope and pray that King George sends Cornwallis back soon. Without him our troops are likely to lose their zeal." Gregory leaned back in his chair and patted his stomach. "Fine meal, Mari. Fine."

After dinner they took turns playing draughts in the parlor. First Mari lost to Ethan; then Lilly beat Greg.

"Now you two must play," Mari announced and motioned for Ethan to seat himself opposite Lilly.

"First-rate idea. A championship of sorts." Greg stood. "Come now, Ethan old boy. Can't let the women-folk best us, can we?"

Ethan held back his stinging reply. Lilly had beaten Greg with such ease that the game had been over far too soon to boast of a fair fight. Lilly's skill far surpassed most of the players with whom Ethan had played. "Where did you learn to play so well, Lilly?"

Lilly toyed with one of the draught pieces and then gazed up at Ethan. How could she tell him that out of loneliness she'd learned the game and then taught her groom to play? Applejack had grasped the game almost immediately. The two of them had spent long hours studying the board, searching for ways to triumph over the other in their spare time. "My groom, Applejack, has little to do on cold winter nights. I taught the game to him, and we play as often as possible."

"You're jesting!" Greg exclaimed. "You actually taught a slave to play draughts?"

Forcing a smile, Lilly recalled Applejack's skill. He was a far more wily opponent than Greg. "Yes. He's very good at it, too."

"Well, Ethan, are you up to beating Lilly at this game?" Greg asked, glancing at Ethan, who stood with his elbow resting on the mantel. "You will have to defend our honor."

Lilly shot a glance at Ethan, and before he could speak she said, "I'm afraid I must leave. The hour is growing late, and Zip will take a yard broom to me if I don't hurry."

"I'll escort you, Lilly." Ethan turned to Greg. "We'll play again. Perhaps you and Mari can play another game tonight and polish your skills for a rematch."

Greg opened his mouth to say something, but closed

it without uttering a sound. Lilly hid her grin behind her shawl as she drew it around her. She would never embarrass Greg by laughing at him and most certainly not in public. It was enough that she'd beaten him resoundingly at a game that was considered to be a man's pastime.

She could tell that Greg wasn't particularly happy with the arrangement, but she could do nothing to change it. She and Greg had been friends for a long time, even longer than she and Mari. While Lilly looked at Greg almost as a brother, he had less fraternal feelings for her. He wanted to marry her. Lilly smiled at Greg, as if her kindness could compensate for not loving him.

Watching as Lilly smiled up at Greg, Ethan felt a twinge of jealousy. Though he'd hardly admit it to anyone, he envied the happy and loving relationship among these three people. Growing up with an indulgent, adoring mother and an abusive father had hardened him, impairing his ability to form close ties. The confusion resulting from living with such vastly different parents kept him aloof and estranged even from those who would become friends.

Ethan had reached a crossroads. Lilly seemed to be a sweet and unaffected woman with high ideals, and he wanted to know her better, to learn of the complexities that made her so attractive to him. Could he risk such a relationship?

The outcome of such a venture seemed indisputable. When she learned of his ties with the Patriots, would she come to hate him? Ethan watched her thoughtfully and wondered how he truly felt.

Feeling slightly let down because the evening was ending, Lilly tugged on her shawl and turned to hug Mari. "Good night, dear Mari and Greg. I'll see you both soon."

Hurrying out into the cool fresh air, she almost fell down the brick steps that led to the street. Ethan caught her before she tumbled down to an inevitable injury.

"Lilly! Are you hurt?" Ethan pulled her close and held her briefly before looking down into her eyes. "By the gods, what happened?"

Lilly said nothing for a moment, waiting until she could speak calmly. "I . . . I'm fine. Thanks to you. I'm sure if you hadn't been so alert, I would have tumbled down the steps like a clumsy pup."

Ethan held her a moment longer and then took her arm, directing her carefully onto the silent street. He realized that she must be embarrassed and wanted to call no further attention to the incident. As they strolled along Meeting Street, he glanced up at the moon. "Lovely moon tonight, don't you agree?"

Lilly looked up. Ethan's face was silhouetted against the silvery disk, and she studied him for a moment. "The Carolina moon is the loveliest in all the world."

Ethan chuckled. He felt the same way. She didn't know that Carolina Moon was the name of his plantation, but he was amused by her comment. Uncharacteristic giddiness overcame him as he thought of home and then turned to face her. "The Carolina moon, eh? I never thought of it as being our moon. Somehow I assumed that it belonged to everyone."

"Oh, I suppose it does," Lilly agreed.

They continued walking until they reached her house. Ethan hesitated as he swung the wrought-iron gate back so they could enter. "Would you like to sit in our tree for a while?"

Our tree? she repeated to herself. A smile of pleasure caught the corners of her lips and tugged them upward. "Why not?"

Why not, indeed? she wondered. Ethan probably thought she was mad for doing such a silly thing in the first place. Goodness knows, what he must be thinking now that she'd agreed to repeat the folly.

They strolled silently down the brick path until they reached the little glade with the marble bench. "If you'd prefer, we can sit on the bench since your gown is so delicate."

Lilly nodded. She could ill afford to damage another gown. Two ruined dresses in two days would undoubtedly bring her father's wrath down upon her.

Ethan removed his cloak and laid it across the cold marble for Lilly to sit upon. When she had arranged her skirts, he sat beside her. For a moment neither of them said anything. The silence wasn't a strained silence, but a thoughtful one.

Moonlight filtered through the fluttering leaves of the live oak, and Lilly watched the changing patterns of the shadows on her gown. A fresh breeze ruffled the lace at her sleeves, bringing along the clean scent of wind off the rivers, and she caught the lace between her fingers, toying with it as the silence lengthened. "Mr. Kendall, do—"

"Ethan," he reminded gently.

"Of course. Ethan, do you think the war is almost over?" She'd heard every other man in the city make predictions, but she sensed that Ethan wouldn't try to gloss over the facts. She looked into his eyes, knowing that the deep green-colored orbs were fixed on her. "When is this horror going to end?"

"I wish I knew the answer to that, Lilly. Nobody wants the war to end more than I do," he said.

Lilly rose and walked over to the limb of the live oak that she and Ethan had sat on last night. "Where will it end? Will Charleston be a smoldering ruin before the war is over? We'll have to pick up the pieces and go on with our lives, but will the pieces be worth picking up?"

For a moment Ethan stared at her as she bowed her head and cradled her chin in her hands, using the branch for a resting place. He stood and strode to the other side of the limb, facing her as she looked up. He placed his hands on her shoulders and squeezed gently, as if his gesture could offer her some hope that the fighting would soon end. "Lilly, we'll just have to deal with events as they happen. Nobody wanted this war. Nobody. But when both sides faced unacceptable choices, war was inevitable. Now maybe we're facing the end. How we handle the division our country has suffered could determine how people live for centuries to come. I hope and pray our leaders make the correct choices."

He was staring down at her, his face half hidden in shadow as the light played across his features. Ethan was closer to her than he'd ever been, except for that embarrassing moment when she'd almost fallen. His face was so close she could feel the soft warmth of his breath caressing her cheeks as time slid by unnoticed. His hands relaxed on her shoulders and, after a few seconds, slipped further down her back until he embraced her with the thick tree limb between them.

Both delighted and disheartened that the branch separated them, she felt a shiver of excitement race along her spine and wondered what would happen next.

Ethan slowly closed the distance between them. His lips touched Lilly's, and a surge of desire swept through him. He hadn't meant to kiss her, even though he'd thought of little else all day. One tiny kiss, he'd told himself as he moved closer to her. Now he realized that one kiss would never be enough. He wanted to draw her fully into his arms, mold her body to his, and surrender to her charms, as he hoped she'd succumb to his.

Damnable tree! he cursed silently as his lips sought hers again. Her mouth tasted faintly of spices, and he held her more tightly, feeling the urge to devour her sweetness. At first Ethan expected her to resist, to rouse the neighbors with her outraged cries, but her response was more tentative. Though she didn't react as an experienced lover would, she didn't withdraw from him. Encouraged, Ethan held her closer and opened her lips gently with his tongue. For a few seconds he probed hungrily, seeking some sustenance that would carry him through the next few weeks.

Lilly drew back and stared at Ethan. She didn't know what to say or what to do. She'd allowed, no, she'd *encouraged* a strange man to kiss her and had been a willing accomplice to the act. Shame and indecision fought within her. Part of her knew that to act as she had would invite further liberties; and another part of her wanted him to take those liberties. Ethan's kiss awakened a desire she didn't know she possessed. Even though she had pulled away, she knew she could easily succumb to his advances if he continued them.

Suddenly confused and embarrassed, Lilly stepped farther away from him. Cold air enveloped her, and she stammered, "I . . . I, er, good night, Mr. Kendall. I must . . . I must go inside. Zip will be waiting for me."

CHAPTER 5

LILLY PEERED DOWN AT THE GARDEN FROM HER WINdow. Ethan stood among the oleander and shrubs as still as a statue. Did he intend to stay there all night? she wondered. Finally he moved and slowly walked out of the garden.

When he disappeared from her view, Lilly ran to her other window. He opened the gate and paused. After a moment he looked up at her window. Then he closed the gate and strode down the street. Lilly watched until he was gone and then sat at her dressing table. Why had she allowed him to kiss her? Why hadn't she raised such a screech as to awaken her neighbors? Any self-respecting woman would have, and yet not every woman had been kissed by Ethan Kendall.

Lilly had been kissed before, though not often. Once Greg had become amorous after a party, but he hadn't kissed her the way Ethan did. Her fingers went involuntarily to her lips. She peered into her mirror. Her mouth felt branded. Would Mari notice the difference? Would Father? Would Zip? Of the three Zip would be the most likely person to notice a difference in her, if indeed there was one.

Removing the pins from her hair, she let it fall around her shoulders. She picked up her silver brush and began to brush gently as she continued to think of her appearance. She leaned forward and gazed at her reflection. She couldn't see any difference at all, but other people might be more perceptive than she.

Her father never really looked at her except as an object with which he obtained the cooperation of British soldiers. Lilly wondered at times if her father would eventually barter her off for some favorable position in the government or a sum of money. The day might come when he'd announce her engagement to a man she barely knew.

If that man happened to be Ethan Kendall, she didn't think she'd mind so much. But Ethan probably had too little to offer her father. Someone high in the British government or army would be the man Father selected. She shook her head to clear her thoughts. Father wouldn't sell his only daughter, she told herself sternly. Even as the words formed in her mind, she knew they weren't true. Jonathan Arledge would stop at nothing to obtain prestige, power, and position with the British government.

Lilly grew tired of trying to second-guess her father. Besides, no matter how hard she tried, she could never come close to predicting the depths to which he would sink next. Only time would reveal his plans for her.

She thought again of Ethan. He had changed her life in the span of a few seconds, although his kisses seemed to have lasted much longer. She began to wonder how she could face him again without blushing profusely. Lilly had a lot to learn about relationships between men and women.

"Lilly!" came a roar from downstairs.

"Oh, no," she murmured, wondering if she should hop in bed and pretend to be asleep. Her father sounded even angrier than usual. She'd learned early in life to face his anger rather than cower and cringe like a frightened kitten. She missed Tartuffe and glanced around to see if he might be hiding somewhere in her room. She hadn't seen him all day.

Heavy footsteps bounded up the stairs, and Lilly steeled herself against her father's fury. Without warning, the door banged open and knocked a painting off the wall.

"Where in the name of hell have you been?" Jonathan Arledge stormed into the room, his face scarlet with anger. "I've been looking all over for you. Can't make any sense of the servants. They babble on so."

Lilly lifted her chin and stared at him a moment before picking up the painting to see if it had been damaged. The paint had chipped off in one spot, but she could repair it if she could match the color. She faced her father again. "I've been to Mari's for supper."

"That girl's no good for you. Why do you persist in going around with her when there are so many suitable young men—soldiers—fighting for our king?" Jonathan's gaze followed Lilly as she moved to her divan and sat. "Answer me, girl."

Lilly sighed. This was an old argument that flourished in the Arledge household. "She's my best friend, Father. We've been friends for years and—"

"Her father can do me no good," he interrupted.

Jonathan moved closer to her, obviously working himself into a rage. Lilly stared at him, refusing to be intimidated by his blustering. She'd seen him like this many evenings. His face was flushed, his eyes were red, and the smell of whiskey was strong on his breath.

"How many times must I tell you that if you want to live well after this war is over, to have pretty gowns and all the geegaws that girls like, you must cultivate the friendships of the soldiers or one of the men—"

"And how many times must I say that I'm not going to purposefully cultivate the friendship of a man so you can—"

Jonathan slapped her and then held her tightly so he could glare into her face. "You will do as I say. Tomorrow evening we'll have guests for supper. You wear something pretty and act like you're interested even if you're not. I won't suffer this insubordination! If you don't behave as I expect, then I'll take a strap to you."

Lilly squeezed her eyes closed to prevent the tears from spilling over her eyelids. His grip was like steel bands on her forearms, but she finally opened her eyes defiantly and stared blankly at him.

"Don't you get that faraway look. I'll beat the defiance out of you yet." He flung her hands away from him and moved to the door. "You'll do as I say."

Lilly said nothing as he strode out the door. Answering back would cause her further injury. Slumping back against the divan, she allowed her eyes to fall shut. In a deliberate attempt to close out the ugliness of her life with her father, she pictured Ethan. She didn't have to try very hard. His image came to her mind almost unbidden, an oasis in a world of strife.

Without stopping to think, she moved to her piazza and stared at the tree where she'd perched herself with Ethan last night. If she willed it, would he appear there suddenly and make her laugh? Deep inside she knew he wouldn't, but she didn't really care. She wanted to be close to him and walked to the end of the piazza where the trellis of jasmine grew.

Lilly pulled her skirt through her legs and tucked it in front to keep from becoming entangled in it. Carefully she edged over the railing and climbed down. Once on the ground, she ran for the glade, her special place, the place she'd always gone when she was angry or scared.

She'd long since gotten over being scared of her father. He could hurt her physically, but she now blocked out his mental cruelties. Until tonight she hadn't known that he was aware of the wall she erected around herself when he railed against her. Well, it didn't matter if he knew. He couldn't do anything about what went on in her mind.

Past the oleander and roses she hurried until she reached her tree and pulled herself onto the low-hanging limb. This time, instead of remaining in the curl of the limb that had cradled her and Ethan, she sought refuge higher up in the thicker foliage. She soon found a safe place to sit on one of the fat twisted branches. The loop in the limb curled enough for her to settle herself safely and provided a place to rest her back.

Above her wisps of thin clouds moved past the moon and sent shadows scurrying across the garden like apparitions. After a few minutes she began to breathe easier and leaned back against the support of the branch.

As a child, she'd considered running away. But Lilly had nowhere to run. Her mother's family lived far away, too far for a young girl to reach without help. Erin and her parents lived a few blocks away, but Jonathan Arledge would have looked there first. There had been no escape for Lilly.

She tried to concentrate on Ethan and conjured up his image once again. She envisioned him smiling, running his fingers through his thick blond hair. She could almost see the twinkle reach his green eyes when he smiled and cocked his left eyebrow. The sound of his voice brought a smile to her lips as her mind heard him say, "Lilly, what are you doing in the tree?"

The sound was so real that she opened her eyes and looked around. She heard nothing and closed her eyes again. Maybe if she wished hard enough, Ethan would appear and distract her mind from her father and his silly supper tomorrow with the soldiers. She would, no doubt, have a new dress to wear that would embarrass a wharf woman.

"Lilly, what are you doing out here at this time of night?" she heard from the shadows.

"Ethan?" she asked, hoping the reply would be affirmative. "Is that you?"

"Yes." Ethan crossed a patch of moonlight and rested his arms on the tree limb below her. "Fancy meeting you here."

Lilly giggled. "I could say the same about you."

"Well, I suppose you could. What if I said I returned to find my hat?" Ethan climbed into the tree until he reached her, straddled the limb, and scooted down into the loop closer to her until his legs were touching hers.

"I'd say that's a fine excuse except for one thing," Lilly retorted, feeling the warmth of his legs on her own.

"Oh? And what might that be?" he asked. Ethan felt an immediate surge of desire as she shifted slightly.

"You didn't wear a hat tonight." Lilly covered her mouth and giggled again.

"Ah, I've been caught." Ethan leaned back and looked at Lilly. He'd seen Jonathan Arledge returning home and followed. Arledge seemed angry about something. When Ethan reached the gate, he'd heard Jonathan shouting at Lilly and knew she would be upset. Ethan had decided to wait until Jonathan would be asleep and then try to talk to Lilly.

He had had no idea how he would attract her attention, but he'd wanted her to come to the garden, and she'd come. This tree seemed to be her refuge from all her problems. For some reason Ethan felt protective of her. She seemed so fragile, but had thus far demonstrated a strength he couldn't have guessed she had. Saving a woman from a vicious lecher like Jonathan Arledge wouldn't be easy to do. Arledge had the backing of several high-placed officials in Charleston. Ethan would have to exercise extreme caution.

He'd considered kidnapping Lilly and sending her to his mother at Carolina Moon but wasn't sure how Jonathan would react. If he found Lilly, he might do something worse to her than shout.

Ethan gazed at Lilly in the darkness. Had Jonathan done worse? Ethan's eyes were accustomed to the dim light, but he couldn't see her face well enough to tell how distressed she was. His stomach turned when he thought that Jonathan might have struck her. Was her father that cruel and insensitive?

From what Ethan knew, Jonathan could very well be. Gossip, if reliable, reported that Jonathan Arledge was well known for fits of temper and had, upon occasion, struck a subordinate. Ethan bit his lip to keep from asking Lilly if her father ever hit her, but he reached out instinctively to comfort her, for he knew how cutting Jonathan's words had been. Ethan couldn't tell Lilly he'd heard the argument; she'd be too embarrassed by the revelation. Instead, he stroked her hand gently and said nothing.

Lilly watched Ethan for a moment. He held her hand and patted or stroked it like he would a kitten. She decided he must be quite lonely. "Well, since we've eliminated your alibi for being in my tree, would you care to tell me the truth?"

Ethan felt cornered for a moment, but he distorted the truth a little and told his story without giving away the information that would embarrass her. "Miss Arledge, I found myself walking past your house when I saw someone shinny down the trellis outside your window. Feeling a sense of duty to protect your lovely person, I entered your garden with the intent of thrashing the culprit."

Finding his words both comforting and flattering, Lilly smiled. She wasn't frightened since she was the person he'd seen. "Then I must thank you for caring about my well being."

"Your thanks isn't necessary." Ethan rubbed against the rough bark of the limb to scratch an itchy spot in the center of his back. He patted her hands again, relishing the softness that was so different from his own. "Ah, but this is a lovely night to be sitting in a tree."

"I daresay that most people would disagree with you, sir." Lilly chuckled and shook her head. "At least, those above the age of ten."

Ethan gazed at her and squinted. "You look lovely with your hair soft around your face."

The quick change of subject surprised Lilly, and she blushed. "You're very kind to say so. Thank you."

"It's the truth." He continued to study her, fighting the urge to reach out and touch the curls that lay so softly on her shoulders. "I will never understand why women want to wind their hair up in those knotty things and tie it around their heads."

"To be honest," she began and touched her hair self-consciously, "I don't know, either. A woman's whim, I suppose. I guess it's much easier to do chores without a mass of hair in your way."

Ethan considered her point for a moment. "That may be true for the times when chores are being done, but what about evenings? Parties? Since women wear such delicate gowns, much like that one you've probably ruined this evening, why not leave their hair down?"

"I'm afraid I can't answer that. And you're probably right," she admitted, fingering the delicate fabric. Lilly had forgotten that she'd pulled the hem of her skirts up between her legs to climb down the trellis. She tugged the fabric out of her sash and shook her head. "My gown is ruined. Zip will never be able to iron the wrinkles out."

"She's going to wonder how you're ruining so many dresses in such a short time," Ethan agreed. "But I admit climbing down a trellis in a full skirt would have to be difficult."

"I should have come out the front door. I would have except that my father . . ." Her voice trailed off. Lilly wasn't prepared to explain her father to anyone, even though Ethan seemed understanding.

Ethan perked up. He felt the pain of her words and knew that when she said no more, it was because she couldn't. She didn't know him well enough to discuss family business. Ethan already knew about her situation, or thought he did. He became furious all over again and tried to think of a way to spirit Lilly away from Charleston.

Of course, he knew her cousin, Erin Banning Gallagher. She would gladly take Lilly in, but getting her to Erin might prove difficult. She and Bowie were the topic of angry conversation among officers who'd been outsmarted by the couple. Bowie worked occasionally with Francis Marion, the man called the Swamp Fox, but generally kept out of sight.

For now Ethan could do nothing without jeopardizing his own cover. If Jonathan and his friends delved too deeply into Ethan's past, they would discover that he was a Patriot. Within days he would leave to rejoin Marion, but for now Ethan wanted to spend as much time as possible getting to know Lilly.

The sun began to rise as they talked, and Lilly suddenly noticed the warm pink glow spreading over the rivers. "I must go. Father will . . . He can't find out that I've spent so much time sitting in a tree with you."

Ethan jumped down and reached up to help Lilly. "How will you get in?"

"The same way I escaped." Lilly stood close to him, peering up into his eyes. She wanted to stay with him, but knew she couldn't. With guests coming for supper this evening, she needed to rest. "Father has guests coming this evening. As I am his hostess, I must try to sleep or I'll seem like a dullard to them."

"I doubt that you could seem like a dullard even to a bunch of soldiers." Ethan felt her shiver and drew her into his embrace. "I can't remember when I've enjoyed an evening as much as this one. I hope we can do it again."

"Me, too." Lilly could hardly breath. Every time she inhaled, her breasts pressed against Ethan's chest. The contact sent tingles throughout her body. His firm embrace kindled a warmth in her that defied the chill of morning, and Lilly realized that Ethan was going to kiss her again.

Longing to feel his lips on hers, she stood on tiptoe and met him halfway. She slid her arms around his neck and clung to him as their lips joined. Ethan pulled Lilly closer until their bodies seemed to be molded together as they shared a kiss that she reciprocated easily. He tasted slightly of brandy, which she found pleasantly enticing.

When his tongue slid between her lips, she was surprised but didn't pull away. She found the gentle exploration exciting and opened her mouth farther, wishing she knew more about kissing. Lilly's body felt warm despite the cool morning mist that rolled in from the juncture of the two rivers.

After a moment Ethan pulled away and gazed at her. "I think . . . maybe you'd better go inside. It won't do for us to be found in the garden together at this hour."

She nodded and reluctantly started to walk away, but Ethan drew her to him once again. This time their kiss was neither gentle nor exploratory. A rush of passion brought them together for one last intimate moment before the sun rose over the harbor.

Then, without speaking, Lilly twisted out of Ethan's arms and ran away from him. When she reached the trellis, she glanced over her shoulder to see if he'd followed, but she could see nothing. Hesitating no further, she climbed the trellis, darted lightly across the piazza to her window, and dashed inside. Her chest heaving, she watched the garden to see when Ethan left, but never spotted his departure.

Good, she thought. If she didn't see him leave, then maybe no one else did, either.

Knowing that Zip would be poking her head in early this morning, Lilly slipped out of her gown and into her night dress. As she slid between the covers, the bells of St. Michael's tolled six times. Lilly knew that sleep would be difficult after such an exciting night, but fell asleep more quickly than she could have imagined.

Ethan's face haunted her sleep, and his lips taunted her dreams. Lilly dreamed in vivid detail of their kisses. She could almost feel his arms around her, cuddling her. "Ethan," she said aloud, the sound of her own voice jolting her awake.

Zip was scowling down at her. "Why you callin' out that man's name, missy?"

There was no way Lilly could hide the scarlet that blossomed in her cheeks. Zip spotted it immediately and continued, "How come you so embarrassed?"

Lilly desperately sought for a way to change the subject. If she allowed her servant to continue this line of questioning, Lilly would end up telling everything. "Don't be silly, Zip. You misunderstood what I said. Now, get me some tea."

Zip stood erect and eyed Lilly suspiciously. "I ain't misunderstood nothin' 'cept why you callin' out that name. Don't you be tryin' to fool ole Zip. I might be ole, but I ain't dead and I hear as good as a fox. I heared 'Ethan.' "

Lilly sighed in exasperation and took another tack. "All right. If it'll get my breakfast any faster, you heard 'Ethan.' Now, go and get my tea." Lilly slid out of bed and pulled on her dressing gown. She puttered over to the mirror and patted her hair while muttering loudly enough for Zip to hear, "Silly woman. I'll never understand what makes her so suspicious."

Zip stood watching her for a moment and then left the room. Lilly sank onto her chair and cradled her chin in her hands. Glancing in the mirror, she saw circles under her eyes and knew that Zip would spot them as well. There was no help for it. Lilly rose and walked to the pitcher. She poured the water into the bowl and proceeded to wash her face. Maybe the cool water would help her appearance.

When Zip returned with the tea, Lilly was wearing her quilted silk petticoat and bodice. She sipped tea while Zip took a simple gown of homespun from the wardrobe and held it up for Lilly to see.

"That's not necessary, Zip." Lilly placed her cup on the tray and stood. "I'm not feeling well this morning. I have a headache. I believe I'll lie down for a short while to see if it goes away."

"Harrumph. You's got more'n a headache if'n you think you foolin' me." Zip placed the dress back in its place and turned with arms crossed to face Lilly. "Yo papa say some new silks come in up at Miz Hawkins. You supposed to go look and pick out some. Miz Hawkins'll make you some new gowns. That woman and yo papa is tryin' to make a . . . a loose woman out'a you, and you jus' go right on a'lettin' 'em like you was happy 'bout it."

Lilly had heard this argument before. In fact, every time Lilly bought fabric for a new gown, Zip railed for days about the rumors that would be spread. Lilly had since discovered that she needn't reply. Zip had her opinions and she'd express them no matter what. Even though Lilly agreed with her, she was helpless to do anything about it.

She'd long since given up the idea of marrying well. If she didn't find someone soon, her reputation would be so damaged as to be nonexistent. Lilly doubted seriously whether she and her father would ever agree on a man. He wanted someone who could further his career; she wanted someone to love who would reciprocate her devotion.

Zip left the room, and Lilly fell across her bed in utter

exhaustion. She'd sleep for a couple of hours and then go to see the silks. Any other woman would be delighted with the generous allowance Jonathan Arledge gave Lilly for clothing, but not her. Every time she bought a new gown, it was more daring than the last. Pretty soon, Lilly mused, there will be nothing left to hide.

When Lilly awakened, she felt refreshed and eager to get out. She hurried into her clothes, ate a small bowl of oyster soup, and pulled on her shawl. She'd stop off at Mari's to see if she could go, too.

Mari seemed happy to see her friend. As usual, the vivacious blonde scampered off to find her shawl while chattering away like a bird. Lilly smiled. She loved Mari dearly but sometimes tired of her constant babbling.

They were soon on their way. Mrs. Hawkins's shop was several blocks away. When they reached the door, Lilly inhaled deeply as she opened it. She really hated to choose new clothes.

"Ah, Miss Arledge, how delightful to see you again. And Miss O'Grady," Mrs. Hawkins continued as she rounded the counter to stand beside them. "I'm happy to see you, too."

"Thank you, Mrs. Hawkins," Lilly replied dryly and glanced around. "Father sent me to see your new silks."

"Oh, yes. Come with me." Mrs. Hawkins led them across the room to the stairs.

Lilly spotted a fashion doll and stopped. "Oh, how lovely. May I see that doll, Mrs. Hawkins? The one in the pink and black striped taffeta."

Mrs. Hawkins retraced her steps and lifted the doll from its case. "Here you are. This is a lovely fabric. I'm sure it would look stunning on you."

"Oh, Lilly, it would. This is exquisite," Mari cooed as she stepped closer.

Fingering the fabric thoughtfully, Lilly agreed and nodded. She liked the style and cut of the gown. It hung gracefully over double panniers and an underskirt of pink taffeta. The pagoda sleeves were lined with lace ruffles and black velvet bows. While not modest, the dress had an elegant bodice that tapered to the narrow waist.

"Mrs. Hawkins, I'd like a gown made similar to this." Lilly handed the doll back and smiled. "I'll see the silks now."

She spent the afternoon looking at roll after roll of silks, satins, brocades, taffetas and velvets. When she thought she could see no more, she leaned back in her chair and scanned the fabrics again. "I'll take a dress of the cherry-colored silk. I want it made *à la française* with the deep pleats in back. I realize it's useless to say, but please make it as modest as possible. I know my father will countermand that order, but I wish to make it anyway. Trim it with white lace."

"That sounds lovely," Mari agreed and pointed to the robin's-egg-blue satin. "I think that color would be good for you."

"Yes, I had my eye on that as well." Lilly instructed Mrs. Hawkins to make three other gowns for evening wear. "And I'll take a new riding habit like the one on the other doll."

"Well chosen, my dear. Is there anything else?" Mrs. Hawkins asked, writing furiously.

Lilly thought a moment. "Yes, please. I'll take a new cap of fine lawn trimmed in lace. And a cloak of that lovely garnet-colored velvet."

When they left the shop, Mari asked, "Do you think she'll make the dresses as you required?"

"No. She never does. While I'm there, she agrees with everything I say. Lilly stopped to look at the display in the cobbler's shop. "But she'll do exactly as Father says."

"Such a pity. I mean . . . I can't stand for—"

"Don't waste your pity, Mari. I can fend for myself." Lilly pointed to a pair of ladies slippers. "Those embroidered kid slippers are lovely, don't you think?"

"I do."

Before she left the cobbler's shop, Lilly had ordered a pair of slippers like those she'd seen in the window and two others to be sent to Mrs. Hawkins to be covered with fabric matching the dresses she'd ordered. "Well, I suppose I'd better go home. We're expecting guests for supper."

"Who?" Mari asked, almost dancing with glee. "Did you invite that dashing Mr. Kendall?"

"I didn't invite anyone. Father did and he didn't provide me with a guest list." Lilly left Mari at her gate and walked the remaining distance alone.

She wondered if Ethan could be one of the men her father had invited to supper but doubted it. Ethan could offer no more prestige or power to Jonathan Arledge than she could herself. Lilly plodded along, reluctant to return to her home and the burden she perceived would be hers for the evening.

Since her father had invited but three officers, Lilly would have to wear a particularly revealing gown. Tonight wouldn't be the first time. Each of the guests would be someone particularly selected because of her. Jonathan loved to taunt the men with Lilly, almost telling them that if they gave him what he wanted, she would be theirs—for an evening or for a lifetime. Fortunately, so far, she hadn't been forced to stay for more than supper or an occasional late dessert.

Lately, however, Jonathan seemed to be growing more restless, more frantic. Lilly knew that soon an evening of conversation wouldn't satisfy the men Jonathan brought home. She didn't know what she would do when that evening arrived.

Lilly could delay no longer. Raucous laughter welled up from downstairs, and she knew that her father's guests would be well into their cups by the time Dulcie served supper. She'd been tugging at the bodice of her gown for more than a quarter of an hour, hoping to find some way to cover herself decently. With a sigh, she realized her attempts were futile.

Her dress was of scarlet silk that hung gracefully over her panniers and fell into several layers of ruffles along the hem. Her bodice was laced with black and decorated with black satin bows and a sprig of artificial violets. Her hair had been pulled severely away from her face and piled high on her head. Zip had woven a strand of black pearls through the braids.

If anything, Lilly thought she looked like a wealthy strumpet. The black velvet ribbon tied around her throat held a small cameo that had been her mother's. Knowing how much her father claimed to love his deceased wife, Lilly used the broach on occasion to make him feel guilty for treating their daughter so badly.

With a final glance in the mirror she rose and then headed downstairs. Zip had told her that the four men had all been there before, most more than once, so Lilly wondered what her father could be up to this time. He seldom invited guests more than once or twice unless they were well placed within the British government.

As she reached the last carpeted stair, she heard the roar of laughter break the silence once again. Steeling herself for an evening of boring conversation, she thrust open the doors to the parlor. One by one she glanced at the soldiers. Yes, they were high-ranking officers. One man she couldn't identify wore no uniform. To her surprise, the fourth man was Ethan Kendall! That he and her father were good friends was obvious from their jovial chatter. Somehow that surprised and saddened her. She'd hoped that Ethan would despise her father.

Smiling brightly, she crossed the room and kissed her father's cheek as any dutiful daughter would. "Sorry I'm late, Father, but I simply couldn't decide what to wear."

"You look lovely." Jonathan looked from one man to the next as if to verify that each man thought Lilly was lovely. "You know Colonel Wilkins, Major Hobbes, John Cruden, and Major Kendall, my dear."

"Of course. How good of you to come." Lilly tried to smile but felt herself faltering under Ethan's watchful eye. She lifted her chin and extended her hand to him. "Major Kendall, I'm delighted to see you again so soon."

Ethan bowed and kissed the back of her hand. "It is I who am delighted to see you again."

Forcing a smile, she withdrew her hand and seated herself on the brocade sofa. Her father smiled and nodded. His expression told Lilly he liked Ethan a great deal.

A little irritated because she didn't want her father to like Ethan, she hardly listened to the conversation. They were talking about the prospects of peace or the likelihood of another all-out assault. Lilly wasn't really opposed to discussions of the war, but lately nobody had anything different to say. Nobody knew anything, yet everyone continued to talk.

Without appearing to be forward, she gazed at Ethan. He was listening to the animated conversation and ignoring her, or so she thought. Her thoughts wandered back to Ethan and the exquisite sensations his kiss had caused. She wondered if she walked in the garden later tonight, would she find him there waiting for her? Should she dare to find out?

The idea intrigued her. But the evening droned on and on, and she wished there were some way she could feign illness and leave. She knew the consequences of such an action—her father would be furious for weeks.

"Well, I'm sure an astute man such as General Cornwallis has a plan. He's biding his time," Jonathan blustered, trying to make himself appear to know more than he actually did. "When the time is right, he'll chase those rebs right out of the colonies. Then we'll celebrate, men."

"Come, Arledge, what do you know of the subject? Are you hiding something from us?" Major Hobbes put down his glass. "We have a right to know what lies in our future."

Jonathan chuckled. "Afraid I can't say more. Break a trust, you know, that sort of thing."

Ethan studied the other men. Only Colonel Wilkins and John Cruden remained silent, leaving Hobbes and Arledge to their verbal jousting. Neither of them knew anything. Wilkins might, but Ethan didn't know anything about Cruden. Ethan decided to ingratiate himself to Wilkins. "I say, Wilkins, fine piece of work that last battle you commanded, I hear."

Wilkins gazed at Ethan a moment. "So they say. I lost a lot of good men to gain almost nothing."

"Well, a victory is a victory." Ethan decided that Wilkins might be evaluating the men in the room for some task to be assigned at a later date. Although Ethan felt that he wouldn't be selected, no matter how much he flattered Wilkins, the pretense must be maintained. "I think we have the rebs on the run. What sort of government do you think King George will set up once the war is ended?"

"I don't try to anticipate our good king's judgment." Colonel Wilkins glanced at Lilly. "My dear, I must apologize to you. We've excluded you from our conversation by discussing matters far too weighty for a lovely young lady like you to understand."

Lilly was offended, but she managed a smile. "Why, thank you, sir, but you needn't apologize. I'm used to having a parlor full of men talking about the war. It's all so complicated but fascinating."

"Still, we were thoughtless." Colonel Wilkins cleared his throat. "Gentlemen, I forbid any of you to discuss war while in the presence of this lovely young lady."

Lilly would have much preferred the men to go on talking about the war than to pay attention to her. Now she had to appear to be interested in the conversation around her when she would like to have continued studying Ethan.

Supper lasted forever, or seemed to. Lilly wanted to run shrieking through the house by the time the men rose and returned to the parlor for cigars and brandy. After seeing to their comfort, she excused herself and hurried up the stairs.

How long would she have to wait for them to leave?

Her wait wasn't long. Jonathan knocked on her door scarcely an hour later and entered without waiting for her reply. "My dear, you looked wonderful tonight. I stopped by at Mrs. Hawkins's shop and signed the vouchers for your new dresses."

"I suppose you canceled the orders for modest attire and requested something more scandalous." Lilly sat on her divan and glared at her father.

"Of course I gave her some ideas for style. You have

no head for fashion." Jonathan stepped outside the door and then hesitated. "By the way, I'm leaving in the morning on that trip I mentioned to you earlier. I'm off on important business with John Cruden. Very important business. Our future is almost secure."

Our future is almost secure echoed in Lilly's mind. What could he be doing that would affect their whole future? Had he selected a rich husband for her? Or was it something else?

Lilly began to brush her hair angrily. Why couldn't he be like other fathers? Every time he said something, she knew he was up to no good. She stood and paced back and forth across her room, wondering what she could do to prevent him from acting so foolishly.

Other men either worked for or fought for the king for the noblest of reasons. Even the rebels felt they were working for a justifiable cause. Jonathan Arledge was simply working to better himself.

She needed fresh air. Lilly stepped out onto the piazza and glanced across the garden, wondering if she would find Ethan out there. Whether she found him or not, she couldn't stay here any longer. She needed the freedom and innocence of her special place.

Waiting a few minutes until the candles were extinguished in her father's bedroom, she turned and stared between the houses at the river. From her piazza she could hear the whisper of waves lapping at the sand and shells. The moon poked its face above the trees and bestowed a golden glow across the houses and water. Peering down at the street, she saw a movement. Someone was coming toward her garden between the houses.

"Ethan!" she exclaimed and then clapped her hands over her mouth. The man crossing the neighbor's yard had to be Ethan.

She tiptoed past her father's window and paused a moment. If he discovered her sneaking into the garden at this hour, he'd become so enraged that she'd never hear the end of his lecture—or there might be worse punishment. Shrugging, she continued to the trellis and climbed down easily.

Feeling a surge of energy and happiness, she ran the short distance into the garden where she knew Ethan would be waiting by this time. As she approached the spot where they would meet, she stopped and inhaled deeply. She didn't want him to know she'd been so eager to meet secretly with him that she'd run all the way.

While feigning an air of nonchalance, she strolled leisurely into the glade. She reached the bench and sat down to await the moment when he'd make his presence known. Her wait was short.

"Ahhh! Damnable feline!" came an anguished cry from the live oak.

Lilly sprang to her feet as Ethan fell into the soft shrubs beneath the tree. "Ethan! Are you injured?"

She ran to his side and knelt beside him. "Let me help you up." She held his arm steady as he rose. Lilly glanced at her cat sitting conspicuously on the limb where she and Ethan always sat. "Tartuffe, you are a bad cat."

"I can't say as I disagree," Ethan snarled and glared at the pair of greenish eyes staring calmly back at him. "Devilish bad."

"Oh, I do apologize." Lilly tried to dust the leaves and dirt from Ethan's cloak. "But I did warn you."

Ethan stretched and tested to see that no bones were broken. He chuckled as he rubbed his derriere and nodded his head in agreement. "You certainly did. Little did I know that you weren't exaggerating. You would think the little devil would know me by now. Would you mind sitting on the bench instead of in the tree this evening?"

Lilly giggled as she watched Ethan hobble over to the bench and wait for her to sit. Not wanting to cause any further discomfort, she hurried to comply. "Are you sure you aren't injured?"

"I'm sure of nothing at this moment except that my . . . except that I'm in a certain degree of pain in a place that will cause riding to be difficult." Ethan lowered himself gently to the bench.

"Are you going riding?" Lilly asked, hoping to divert his attention from his pain. She arranged her skirts and sat erectly from habit more than from a desire to remain prim and proper.

"I'm afraid so." Ethan shifted his weight in an attempt to get more comfortable. "I have to leave Charleston on business for a few days."

"My father is going away for a few days, too. Are you going to be with him?" Lilly asked, wondering if this could be the reason that her father found Ethan interesting enough to invite back after the first visit.

"I don't think so. I'm going with a detachment to find forage for the horses and another shipment of food." Ethan found that by balancing on one hip, he could sit in reasonable comfort. "I won't be gone very long. May I call on you when I return?"

Lilly held her breath. She liked Ethan more than she'd ever liked any man before. His question confirmed that he liked her, too. "I should like that."

"Call it settled then." Ethan slipped his arm around her. "I enjoy being with you, Lilly."

His mouth closed over hers, and Lilly felt as though she were flying, wheeling and turning on currents of air as free as the gulls. When he pulled her closer in his embrace, she slid her arms around him and clung like he was trying to leave her forever.

The kiss ended too soon, and they stood. Lilly's heart pounded loudly enough to wake up all of Charleston, and she could hardly breathe. "I . . . I'll miss you. Goodbye."

Lilly ran along the brick passageway until she reached the trellis and climbed as quickly as she could. When she darted through the window into her room, she leaned back against the facing and tried to calm down. Her face was damp with perspiration, but the cool air made her shiver.

She spun around the room, dancing a jig and giggling. He wanted to call on her. That was different from coming to supper with a group of soldiers or government men. *He* wanted to call on *her.* Lilly hugged herself and fell across the bed. The world was wonderful.

CHAPTER 6

ETHAN RODE SLOWLY OUT OF TOWN WITH HIS SORE posterior a constant reminder of his folly. He'd allowed himself to become involved with a woman—a Loyalist woman. No matter how many times he berated himself for his foolishness, he still kept her image in his mind.

He'd never seen such rich, lustrous hair, and it framed a face men would kill for. That Lilly didn't seem to realize how lovely she was puzzled him. He could see that her father showcased her, hoping to gain some recognition with the British. "Damn him!" Ethan swore and then stopped his horse.

He carried letters in his pouch for Colonel David Fanning, the leader of the Loyalists in North Carolina. Before Fanning ever read the letters, General Marion of the Patriots would see them.

Because he didn't want to be away from Charleston and Lilly longer than necessary, Ethan had been riding hard. He would use an extra day looking for Marion and would have to make it up somehow, so he was riding as quickly as possible and resting little.

Ethan was intrigued by Lilly. Her regal carriage and seeming innocence confused and delighted him. Her sweet response to his kisses caused a tightening in his loins even now as he walked along, leading his horse.

Shaking his head to obliterate the image of Lilly, he remounted. He should encounter Bowie Gallagher any time now, and Ethan wanted to remain alert.

The moon sailed gracefully overhead, and he recalled Lilly's description. She'd called it a Carolina Moon. He'd said little. The connection between the name of his plantation and her name for the moon caught him off guard. In normal times he would have been proud to tell her the name of his plantation. It had been well run and productive before the war. Nowadays, he was rarely home, and the servants simply couldn't run it alone. They needed guidance.

His mother tried, but she wasn't capable of keeping the entire plantation running. She made sure they had food, but that was about the limit of her abilities when supplies were so hard to procure. Most of their valuables, seeds, and tools were hidden well, so well that no intruders could find them unless she told them where to look. Ethan knew with certainty that his mother would rather die first.

He hoped and prayed it wouldn't come to that, but many women had died because they refused to abandon their homes or reveal the whereabouts of their valuables. Ethan was constantly tempted to withdraw from the army and go home. He realized that if he did so, he could never live with himself. Every man in the Patriot force must be facing the same dilemma. With every passing day he hated the war more.

Now he really had something to fight for. More than ever he wanted the war to end, for times to return to normal. It would take a lot of patience, understanding, and forgiveness, but Ethan felt convinced that Americans could someday simply be Americans, all together, for the same goals.

Time. He hated the time he spent away from Carolina Moon. He didn't want to leave Lilly in Charleston with her degenerate father for too much time. He didn't want to spend time fighting and killing anymore. What would the future bring?

He envisioned a day when he could approach Lilly openly, when she would be fully aware of his role in the war. He visualized her acceptance of his decision to go with the Patriots rather than remain on the side of the Loyalists. He prayed that she wouldn't hold a grudge against him forever.

He'd heard rumors that if the British lost the war, many Tories were going home to England. Some spoke of settling in the Tropics or Canada. Would Jonathan Arledge leave? Would he take Lilly with him, or would she remain?

There were so many questions that could be answered only by the passage of time. Ethan chided himself for thinking of the future instead of concentrating on the present, but he couldn't get Lilly's image out of his mind.

He heard a sound and stopped. The crackling of twigs came from his left, and he placed his hand on the stock of his gun to be ready in case there was trouble. He suspected that Bowie was out there somewhere trying to decide who rode up the trail.

After a few seconds Ethan made a call like a nightingale and waited. His call was soon followed by another identical one, and he relaxed a little. That sound was his signal to Bowie.

Within a few seconds the shape of a man leading a horse materialized on his left. Ethan said nothing until the man spoke.

"Good evening to you, sir."

"And to you, Bowie Gallagher." Ethan swung down

from his horse and shook Bowie's hand. "I must say you startled me."

"I never meant to. I intended to be just far enough in the brush to see the road." Bowie gestured back into the woods. "I didn't realize how difficult it would be to pick my way through in the darkness."

"Where's Marion?" Ethan asked as he remounted. "I'm in a hurry. If I don't get these letters to Fanning quickly and rush back to Charleston, I'm afraid my absence will arouse suspicions."

"Aye, that it would." Bowie mounted and led the way. "We've been hiding out while we awaited these letters. General Marion knew that some sort of communication was expected this week."

"Does he think this is important?" Ethan inquired and patted his horse. "I'm afraid I need to rest a bit if we have too far to go. I've been pushing myself to find you."

Bowie looked back and then slowed his horse a little. "Not far. What's happening in Charleston?"

"Not much. The war is causing a lot of talk. Everybody wants to know what's going on. Nobody admits to knowing anything." Ethan smiled as he recalled the parties and suppers where he'd listened for any clues and heard only the same sort of conjecture he was spreading. "I've become friends with the Arledges. I mentioned to Lilly that I knew Erin. I think Lilly would like to hear from her."

"I know Erin would like to see Lilly. They were close until the war." Bowie stopped his horse and dismounted. "We need to walk from here."

"Lilly seems lonely. She has her father, but I think he's quite mad." Ethan recalled the look on Jonathan Arledge's face when they'd passed on the street. "I wouldn't put anything past that man."

"And what of Lilly?" Bowie glanced at Ethan speculatively. "You've called her by her first name. Does that mean you know her very well?"

Ethan stopped walking. He hadn't intended to give away any details about his relationship with Lilly, but in talking about her, he had. He resolved to speak of her to no one else. He could be endangering her. Of course, Bowie wouldn't harm her, but someone else might. "We're . . . friends."

Lilly peered into the night. Hoping to see Ethan, she'd gone for the last few nights to her garden as the crispness of fall air settled in. She'd been disappointed each time, but she still felt closer to him there. She didn't know whether to expend the time to try again or not, but she couldn't stay away.

She stepped through her window onto the piazza and started to walk toward the trellis when a sound coming from the street distracted her. Could it be Ethan? She didn't think so. He never made so much noise. Whoever was coming down the street was raising a ruckus and was more than likely in his cups. As the sounds came closer, she recognized her father's glorious bass voice booming out some unintelligible song.

Thankful that she'd been undecided about whether to go to the garden or not, she stepped into the cool darkness of her bedroom. If she had decided one minute earlier to go to the garden, her father would have caught her outside—or worse, climbing down the trellis.

She removed her clothes quickly and slid between the covers of her bed to feign sleep. The slamming of the front door almost brought her to her feet, but she tried to lie still. Perhaps her father wouldn't bother her.

The door to her room flew open, and Jonathan Arledge bustled inside. "Wake up, Lilly, girl. We've struck it rich."

Lilly's eyes opened reluctantly. She didn't want to know what he'd done. It could have been dishonorable, and she didn't want to be a part of it. "What is it, Father?"

"I've a plantation. One of the finest. Up on Goose Creek, a splendid place. Cruden came through at last." Jonathan Arledge danced around the room and stumbled against the mantel. "Damnation. Aren't you happy?"

Lilly sat straight up, all pretense of sleep abandoned. "What do you mean, you've a plantation? And what has Cruden to do with all this? We have no money to buy a plantation."

"A gift—or very nearly so, my dear, from King George." Jonathan whirled about, clapping. "I'm rich! I'm finally a planter!"

"Father, please talk sensibly." Lilly felt the hairs on her neck rise, and fear sent shivers to each cell until she felt like a mass of jelly. "Tell me what's happening. Why would King George give you a plantation, and where did he get it?"

"What? Are you questioning the king's authority?" Jonathan grimaced and glared at her. "I'm a servant of the king, loyal to the true ruler of this land. Why shouldn't I be given a plantation? Many men who've done less than I have received beautiful plantations."

"Father," Lilly began and wondered why she even bothered to try to find out what he was talking about. Obviously he'd been drinking for some time and would have no reasonable answers. "Where have you been?"

"I told you. I've been to Goose Creek with John Cruden to choose a new home for us." Jonathan moved toward the door.

"What has John Cruden to do with our getting a plantation?" Lilly asked again.

"John Cruden is the Commissioner of Sequestrated Estates for the province of South Carolina." Jonathan grinned foolishly. "He's finally allowed me to select our new home. I've always wanted both a town house and a plantation. Be ready to move in one week's time."

Dread filled her heart. As soon as the door closed behind him, Lilly threw back the covers and rose. She couldn't remain in bed when she felt this way. Her father had stolen a plantation. She knew it. She'd heard that many plantations belonging to Whigs had been confiscated and given to loyal Tories. Lilly didn't like the idea. Thinking it an abhorrent practice, she had given it no further thought. Now she and her father were going to move into someone else's home and claim it as their own!

Lilly slept little. She kept thinking of some poor woman and her children being put out of their home with no place to go. She hadn't cried in a long time, but this thought almost made her weep.

How could she face her friends when they found out? True, the king was rewarding loyalty, but at what cost? She felt that once the war was over, people would try to get along again, to resolve their differences. If the king's men continued to confiscate property, there would be little chance of reconciliation.

She wondered if Ethan had anything to do with this. After all, he'd been at her home several times lately. Could he have been instrumental in her father's good fortune, as he called it? Lilly could forgive a lot of things, but she doubted if she could overlook this. Still, she didn't want to judge Ethan without asking him for the truth.

* * *

Every night for a week, after spending each long day packing, she'd gone to her garden to see if Ethan would come. So far he hadn't. She took this as a good sign. Maybe he was involved in some other department and had nothing to do with the horrendous practice of confiscation.

Her father gloated about his good fortune. Everybody in Charleston knew he had been awarded the property. Lilly refused to leave her home all week. She saw only Mari and Greg. Both of them understood her humiliation. Both felt the same way she did.

At last there was nothing left to pack. Lilly fell exhausted into her bed. When the sun rose the next morning, she, her father, and their servants would sail up the Ashley River toward Dorchester where they would find Goose Creek. The house would be grand, she knew, or her father wouldn't be so gleeful. She couldn't imagine how it would feel to walk into someone else's home and claim it as her own. She was thankful she wouldn't have to face the previous owners.

For now Lilly couldn't sleep. She tossed and turned until she could lie abed no more. Without really thinking about what she was doing, she rose and went to the window to peer down into the garden. What if Ethan came tonight? Or even worse, tomorrow night when she was gone? What would he think?

Lilly pulled on her wrapper and made her way gingerly across the piazza. If she couldn't see Ethan before she left, she'd do the next best thing. She'd sit where they always sat.

When she reached the glade, she realized she'd made a mistake. Even though she desperately wanted to see

Ethan, she couldn't tell him about what her father had done. She was simply too embarrassed to talk about it.

She lifted herself to her favorite limb and balanced herself carefully before leaning back against the branch. Tartuffe scooted down the trunk and into her lap, overbalancing her and almost causing her to tumble to the ground. "You're dangerous, but I love you."

"Are you addressing me?" she heard from behind the shrubs.

"Ethan, is that you?" Lilly felt her face flame with color. "I was talking to Tartuffe. I didn't know you were there."

"Alas, always my luck." Ethan appeared beside the tree as if by magic and hefted himself up beside her. "There you are, you scruffy cat. Don't you try to sneak up on me this time."

He wagged his finger at Tartuffe, who summarily ignored the man lecturing him.

"Unimpressed, wouldn't you say?" Ethan asked and straddled the limb to keep from falling.

"Looks that way to me." Lilly stroked Tartuffe's fur as she tried to think of something sensible to say. She had to find a way to tell Ethan goodbye. "Did you have a good trip?"

"Business for the government. Lots of discomfort, no fun." Ethan looked at her closely. For a moment he was speechless. Lilly was sitting within inches of him and wearing nothing but her nightdress and a wrapper! Something must be terribly wrong for her to have come out after she dressed for bed. "Is something wrong?"

"Wrong?" Lilly repeated and then followed the direction of his eyes. She'd forgotten she was wearing her bedclothes. She clutched the opening of the wrapper and pulled it closer around her. "Oh, how embarrassing."

Ethan chuckled. "Don't be embarrassed. I'd say you're quite modestly covered."

Lilly knew he was right. Her father never questioned her bedtime attire, and, as a result, it was considerably more modest than her dresses. "You're correct, but I'm still embarrassed. I must go in."

As she started to climb down, Ethan stopped her. "I've missed you, Lilly."

"And I missed you," Lilly admitted, still clinging to her wrapper. "I hoped you'd be here tonight. I . . . we—my father and I—are leaving Charleston tomorow."

"Leaving?" Ethan was surprised. He'd thought Jonathan would remain in Charleston until the last British soldier was either killed or left town. He didn't like the idea of never seeing Lilly again. "Where are you going?"

She sighed and shook her head. "I don't know exactly where we're going. Somewhere around Dorchester . . . the Goose Creek area."

Goose Creek? At least he could find her and see her fairly frequently there. "Do you have a home there?"

"We . . . yes." Lilly couldn't tell him the truth. She was so ashamed of her father that she couldn't repeat the story again.

Ethan studied her. Something wasn't right. Lilly seemed to be disturbed by this move, more than he would have thought. Maybe she thought there was still too much fighting going on there for her to be safe. Or maybe she thought she wouldn't get to see him again. Ethan's spirits lifted, and he smiled. She'd said she missed him.

"It's getting late, Ethan." Lilly touched his arm, initiating the contact between them for the first time. "I must go in."

"Oh, yes, of course." Ethan jumped down and caught Lilly as she slid into his arms.

For a moment neither of them moved. Ethan held his breath, thinking that if he dared to move, she'd scamper off and leave him alone. He couldn't resist kissing her upturned mouth and soon closed the distance between them. Lilly responded with much more abandon than she had the last time he'd kissed her.

Ethan wondered again if she was scared she wouldn't see him again. When he drew away, he kissed her forehead and held her close to him. He whispered against her hair, "Don't worry, I'll find you as soon as I can get away again."

Lilly nodded and turned to receive a second kiss. She knew she couldn't linger here with him dressed as she was. When he held her tightly in his embrace, she clung to him for a moment longer. "Goodbye, Ethan."

This time Lilly walked rather than ran away. From the moment she left his arms, a strong urge to return to the haven they provided almost overcame her. She'd never felt such a connection with anyone in her life and was loath to leave it. A tenuous thread had begun to weave them together, and she was afraid it wasn't strong enough to stand the pressure of separation. Realistically she might not see Ethan again until the war was over—if then.

Now more than ever she prayed that there would be no more fighting. She couldn't stand to think of Ethan charging with his bayonet fixed toward people who were once her neighbors. It seemed that the longer this war continued, the more reasons she found to hate it.

Tartuffe wound himself between her legs as she reached the trellis, and she almost tripped. She couldn't carry the cat up with her, so she decided to leave him outside until she could come down and let him in through the front door. She didn't think she'd have time in the wee hours of the morning to be looking for an adventuresome cat.

She hurried up the trellis and into her room. She wished she'd thought to ask her father where they were going. If she'd had the fortitude to find out whom they were displacing, she could have told Ethan where to look for her.

The time for that was past. She could do nothing about it now. Lilly left her room, ran lightly down the stairs, and opened the front door. "Tartuffe, where are you? Come, kitty."

Tartuffe strolled leisurely in, brushed against her legs, and then ran up the stairs. Lilly latched the door and returned to her room to find Tartuffe stretched out on the bed, purring luxuriously and washing his paws. She blew out her candle and climbed into bed, relishing the soft feather mattress that cradled her so gently.

Lilly planned to take Tartuffe with her when she left. She decided that he'd like the country—lots of mice and lizards to catch. Maybe he could find a mate upcountry. She didn't dare consider the same idea for herself. After her father's latest escapade, she doubted whether she'd ever have friends again, much less suitors.

The only man she would even consider to be a suitor was Ethan, and he'd shown no inclination to become more than a secret lover in the bower beneath the trees—or *in* the trees. She didn't know what he intended to do, but he said he'd look for her. She had to cling to that hope.

"What are we going to do, Tartuffe?" she asked and stroked him gently. "We're going to be alone in a place where we have no friends."

Tartuffe gazed at her and then licked his paws. He didn't seem to care what happened.

Lilly felt sadness settle in as the time to depart came closer. "We're going to be alone—but worse, we're going to be without Ethan."

CHAPTER 7

LILLY AROSE BEFORE THE SUN CAME UP. SHE'D SLEPT little with so much on her mind. There seemed to be no way to resolve her problems. Her father refused to allow her to remain in Charleston, even though she believed it would be safer for her. He planned to install her in their new plantation and return to Charleston to continue his work. Occasionally he would bring friends or government officials to visit.

When Lilly considered the implications, she felt a little relieved. At least in Goose Creek she wouldn't be constantly paraded before wife-seeking men like a cow at a cattle auction. Maybe she could even dress normally.

They were finally aboard the schooner. Tartuffe traveled in a large box. Zip grumbled about being moved, but the rest of the servants kept quiet except for Applejack. He was delighted to be moving out of Charleston. He'd have a place to spread out, to tend the animals and farm as he'd always wanted, as he'd always told Lilly when they played draughts.

"Miss Lilly, you think we gonna have some horses at our new house?" Applejack asked, peering at her with wide eyes of anticipation.

Lilly couldn't fault Applejack for wanting to have some space around him, where he could really pursue his love of animals. "I don't know, Applejack. I . . . I sort of hope so."

"I'm gonna miss that cow. Mistah Arledge say they ain't room to take her, but she'd a fit fine. I could'a kept watch after her, and she wouldn't a been no trouble." Applejack glanced around the schooner and gestured with his hands to indicate the space. "See? It ain't nearly so filled up as Mistah Arledge said."

"I know. Maybe we'll have a cow at our new . . . on the plantation." Unlike Applejack, Lilly couldn't yet call the place they were going hers. She probably wouldn't be able to do so for a long time, if ever. The idea of evicting someone from their property was somehow degrading to her.

Applejack brightened up. "Yas'm. Maybe we will. I shore hope so. Applejack shore likes to fool with animals."

Lilly smiled indulgently. Applejack was an enigma. With no formal education, the huge black man had been passed over by her father as being stupid. Consequently, Applejack was assigned the tasks that were most menial and demeaning. Apparently only Lilly knew of his inquiring mind and sharp wit. Her father would never have allowed her to teach a sophisticated game like draughts to a slave, much less an outdoor dolt—which Jonathan considered Applejack to be.

Everybody knew Applejack doted on Lilly. From her early childhood she remembered happy days in the barn spent watching him shoe horses or curry them after her father returned. Quite often the animals were in a lather from rough treatment. Applejack always managed to keep them healthy—despite Jonathan's ill handling.

When Lilly needed a friend, she came to Applejack. Now his short bristly hair was graying—the only sign of his aging. No one really knew how old he was—probably not even Applejack himself, but Lilly didn't care. He was more a father to her than her own father ever could be.

"Applejack, do you suppose . . . I mean, is it right what we're doing?" Lilly asked, voicing her misgivings for the first time. "I know it's legal. We have a decree from the king's agent, but is it moral?"

Applejack peered straight ahead for a long moment until Lilly thought she would have to ask the question again. As always, he seemed to be thinking of all sides of the problem.

"Miss Lilly, I don't think God would like it. But he ain't a-likin' this war anyhow." Applejack shook his head and sucked air through the gap between his front teeth before looking at her. "It's right that you don't think it's right. You's a good girl, in spite 'a everything that devil make you do. You ain't got no choice a'tall. Some day that man gonna pay for the things he done to you—and to ever'body else."

Deep inside Lilly knew Applejack was right. Jonathan Arledge would someday have to face his Maker to answer for the wrongs he'd done during his life. " 'Judge not that ye be not judged,' " she quoted, more for her own benefit than anyone else's. She glanced at Applejack, who stood close enough to hear her, and she decided to change the subject. "So, how's your courtship coming?"

"Laws, I can't git nowhere near that woman. That Zipporah think she too good fer me." Applejack grinned and winked. "But I ain't givin' up."

Wishing it would rain, Ethan scuffled along in the dust. Though the fall nights were getting cooler, the days were hot and dry. Lilly hadn't been gone a day yet, and already he was lonely.

His uniform was clean and bright red. Soldiers stood at attention when he passed, giving him the deference due his rank, but in his mind he saw only Lilly. He recalled how lovely she looked that first evening in the sunny yellow dress, how the sprig of green leaves softened the effect of her tight chignon.

In his mind he could hear her lilting laughter ringing all around, sending shivers of joy through him. But most of all he recalled how fragile she felt in his arms, how delicate her fragrance, how tender her touch when she thought he had been injured, the soft caress of her lips on his.

Ethan felt a tightening in his groin and knew that if he didn't find a way to get her out of his mind, he'd be embarrassed beyond endurance. He heard Greg's voice coming from behind and stopped to await his friend.

"Say, Ethan, hold up." Greg loped along until he reached Ethan. "I just heard the most ridiculous piece of gossip."

Ethan perked up. He knew that Greg wouldn't have chased him down all the way out here at the fortifications if it weren't more serious than mere gossip for the ladies' circle. "Well, speak up. What's so pressing?"

"I can't confirm this, but I hear that one of our officers is going to be accused of treason." Greg grinned, apparently happy to be able to pass his gossip on to someone who hadn't heard.

"Any idea who the culprit might be?" Ethan asked with a heavy sense of foreboding. Could he have been found out? What should he do?

"All I can get is that the man is a major," Greg admitted ruefully. "I'll go back and see what else I can find out. You keep listening for details, too."

"Thanks. I shall." Ethan watched his friend return toward headquarters. Ethan faced a real dilemma. Should he remain here and wait to be arrested, or should he escape while he could? He knew that if he waited much longer, he'd be tried and hanged for treason. Intuition told him that he was the major to whom Greg referred. "Captain!"

A young officer snapped to attention. "Yes, sir?"

"I must be away for a few moments. I'm leaving you in charge. If this unit doesn't complete the reinforcements of this battery, I'll have you doing night duty for the next month." Ethan knew this punishment would be the worst he could offer the young captain, who happened to be in love.

"Yes, sir. You won't have to worry, sir. Take your time." The young captain turned and barked an order at one of the soldiers who seemed to be loitering.

Ethan forced himself to walk slowly, to appear normal. He couldn't do anything that would arouse suspicion. He cut through the side streets until he came to his lodging, where he gathered a change of clothing and his weapons. As he started to open the door, he glanced out his window and noticed a crowd of soldiers gathering outside his residence.

Fighting his rising panic, he hurried to the back of his house and peered out. From there he could see no one, but he knew it would be useless to try and escape by the full light of day. He would somehow have to find a place to hide and wait until dark.

Lilly slept briefly in the shade of the sail. She opened her eyes and looked around. Cypress trees towered above them. Cypress knees jutted out of the water in the swampy areas adjacent to the stream, and frogs sang noisily along the banks. She spotted a heron and watched as the boat startled it into flight.

Here and there she could see deer and other creatures hiding in the misty glades and watching her pass. A thick snake slithered into the water nearby, and Lilly shivered. She offered a silent prayer that the boat wouldn't sink. In addition to the poisonous snakes, these waters were inhabited by alligators.

The schooner turned off into one of the tributaries and slid silently through the water until the sails had to be lowered. Several black men rowed for a while until the boat reached a dock jutting out into a wide lagoon.

Jonathan helped Lilly onto the dock, and some of their trunks were unloaded. By that time a contingent of troops, smartly dressed in the distinctive red and white of the British Army, arrived on horseback.

"Good afternoon, Arledge," called Colonel Wilkins. "I see you made good time."

"Quite. We had a favorable wind for most of the distance. Isn't this a lovely spot?" Jonathan fairly bubbled with joy. He turned to Lilly. "I can't wait for you to see the house."

Colonel Wilkins signaled to a young soldier, who dismounted, strode to the large bell hanging on a stand by the dock, and rang it several times. From her vantage point Lilly couldn't see the house at all, but after a moment several black men appeared over a hill and edged toward the group on the dock.

"Oh, Lawsy, gimme strength!" one man shouted at the sight of the British and fell to his knees.

Another turned and ran as quickly as possible over the ridge and disappeared. Without waiting for an invitation,

Colonel Wilkins and his men rode toward the direction from which the slaves came. Lilly and her father were given horses, and they followed along behind.

When she reached the crest of the hill, Lilly gasped. The mansion sprawled out before her was huge—and beautiful. She'd never seen such a lovely home with such incredible dimensions. The stately home sat on the hill like a crown, magnificent in its splendor. White columns rose, strong and graceful, from a piazza that encircled the house and reached through the porches to the uppermost floors. The front steps, two curved staircases that formed a semi-circle leading to the lowest piazza, were of brick and cement, and sported pineapple carvings to welcome guests to the plantation.

Lilly imagined the gay parties that must have taken place here. She could almost see beautifully dressed young women strolling along those porches, pausing here and there for a secret kiss. Now, all that had ended. There were few gay parties and little laughter out here where everyone was involved in the war.

Lilly had often wished to become mistress of such a grand place, but not this way. Not because of someone else's political choices. She turned to her father. "Surely there must be a mistake. This can't be our—"

"Of course it's ours," Jonathan snapped. "Come along. Don't dawdle. We've plenty to do."

Lilly stared at the house a moment longer and then fell in behind her father. The group of men gathering in front of the mansion started to dismount as she arrived.

To her surprise, a petite woman appeared at the door. "And what might you want? You've already taken everything that could possibly be of value to you."

Open-mouthed, Lilly studied the woman. She presented such a picture of dignity. Wearing a simple dress of homespun over her petite figure and a cap of lawn over lovely graying hair, she glanced at the crowd without appearing to be frightened by the armed soldiers.

Colonel Wilkins removed a paper from his cloak and began to read. "Know all men by these presents: In the name of George the Third, by the grace of God . . ."

Lilly dismounted and walked toward the house. The woman standing at the top of a double staircase never moved a muscle, and Lilly was intrigued. Who was she? What was she doing here? Colonel Wilkins's words flowed over Lilly with chilling clarity. *This woman was being evicted from her home!*

"Lilly! Come back here," Jonathan called to his daughter.

She paid no attention and kept walking. Tears were beginning to form in her eyes as she sensed the anguish the woman must be feeling. Lilly bit her lip to keep from crying. How could her father be so uncaring?

When she reached the bottom step, Lilly hesitated a few seconds. She wanted to comfort the woman, to assure her that this wasn't really happening, that no harm would befall her.

"And according to John Cruden, Commissioner of Sequestrated Estates, you are to leave these premises, never to return. You must be out by sundown." Colonel Wilkins finished reading, folded the form, and handed it to Jonathan. "Mr. Arledge, I'd like permission to assist Mrs. Kendall in packing and moving." To Mrs. Kendall he said, "Mrs. Kendall, Commissioner Cruden will allow you to take one trunk and one personal servant. Everything else becomes the property of Mr. Arledge and his daughter."

Lilly winced and froze before she reached the top step. Kendall? She couldn't be Ethan's mother, could she? No, of course not. Ethan was a Loyalist. This plantation belonged to a man who fought for the Patriots.

For the first time the woman Wilkins called Mrs. Kendall glanced at Lilly. Color sprang to Lilly's cheeks, and she reached out to touch Mrs. Kendall's hand.

Mrs. Kendall jerked away, as if she'd been burned. "Colonel Wilkins, this plantation isn't subject to confiscation. It is owned without mortgage. The taxes are paid. You have no right—"

"Mrs. Kendall," he interrupted, "the matter is decided. Your son is fighting for the rebels with that swamp rat, Marion—a traitor and a spy. As the decree says, the property of people who harbor enemies of the king is subject to confiscation."

Lilly's tears fell now, and she closed her eyes. Why couldn't she control her emotions when this woman who was about to lose everything she owned remained so calm? "Mrs. Kendall," she whispered. "Please, you won't have to leave. . . . I'll think of something."

"You? What can you do?" Mrs. Kendall fixed her attention on the girl—a lovely young woman who apparently felt terrible about the turn of events. "Don't worry, young lady, I'll be out of here by sundown."

"No!" Lilly exclaimed. "No," she repeated more gently. "I won't allow it. You will remain here in your home. I refuse to take advantage of your misfortune."

Jonathan Arledge came up behind Lilly and heard her words. "Damnation, Lilly, stay out of this. I'll brook none of your nonsense this afternoon. This house is ours. This woman has no claim on it."

Octavia Kendall glanced from the girl to her father. The girl—young lady—was more decent and caring than the man would ever be. Feeling a surge of sympathy for a young woman who was related to such a brute, she took the girl's hand. "Never you mind, dear. I'll go and never cause you a moment's trouble, nor hold a grudge against *you.*"

Lilly met Mrs. Kendall's eyes. The older woman tried to smile, and Lilly squeezed Mrs. Kendall's hand. "No, Mrs. Kendall. We'll not take your home and property from you. If you'll give us lodging for the night, we'll return to—"

"Damn you, Lilly Arledge!" Jonathan jerked Lilly around to face him and slapped her resoundingly. "I said this is our home, and it is. Any more of this rebellious talk, and I'll take a strap to you."

Just as Applejack started toward Jonathan Arledge, Octavia Kendall stepped between the two of them and prevented the servant from defending Lilly. Octavia knew that the servant would be beaten severely if he interfered. She glared at Jonathan and poked her finger in his chest. "Sir, striking a woman is a cowardly crime I refuse to allow on my property. If I ever see you raise a hand to strike this child again, I'll come back here with an ax and lop off your worthless head!"

"You'll—"

"Lop off your worthless head and every protruding part of your body." Octavia took Lilly's hand and led her inside, leaving Jonathan sputtering epithets behind them.

Lilly's tears came in full now, and Octavia gathered the girl in her arms. "Don't you worry. That'll keep him straight for a while."

"Mrs. Kendall, please don't worry. I'll find a way to convince Father that we can't stay here. I refuse to become a parasite just to . . ." Lilly searched for the right words. "Just to make him feel more like a man."

Octavia smiled and patted Lilly on the back. "Dear girl, what's your name?"

"Lilly Arledge. Again, let me apologize for my father's behavior. He has no manners." Feeling foolish for crying, Lilly wiped her eyes. "Give me a chance to talk to him in private."

"Public or private will make no difference." Jonathan stepped into the house behind the ladies. "This house is mine."

"Temporarily, perhaps." Octavia glared at him. "When the Patriots have routed the Tories, you'll be where you belong. Back in the streets."

"Now, see here—"

"You see here. This child doesn't deserve such treatment from you. I meant every word I said to you." Octavia moved Lilly out of Jonathan's reach. "Mr. Arledge, I won't leave this girl for you to abuse."

"You've nothing to do with how I treat my daughter."

Several servants peered from behind half-closed doors, and Lilly got an idea. "Father, why not allow Mrs. Kendall to remain here in the capacity of . . . of companion to me?"

"That's the most ridiculous notion I ever heard. Why would I do that?" Jonathan asked and glowered at his daughter.

"Well, Father," she wheedled, hoping to convince him to see her point, "I'm sure the servants will more readily obey Mrs. Kendall. She can be . . . our liaison."

Jonathan studied the proud woman who too quickly took his daughter's side against him. Lilly had never had a mother. Feminine company might do her some good. He nodded slightly. "Perhaps, as long as she knows her place."

"Thank you, my dear, but no. I cannot remain." Octavia smiled at the girl's attempt to prevent the inevitable eviction. "I could never live in the house with this brute."

Lilly saw her dreams shatter. She knew that her father would never consent to leaving the plantation, so she had to convince Mrs. Kendall to remain. "Is there a guest house on the property? If there is, you could live there. That way . . . you wouldn't have to see my father."

"Truly, Miss Arledge, you are kindness itself, but I must refuse." Octavia hugged the younger woman, who must be at least five inches taller than she. "I've been expecting this for some time. I'll go."

"The idea intrigues me." Jonathan stepped back through the door and called to Colonel Wilkins. "Mrs. Kendall will remain on the plantation. I'll need several men to take her belongings to the guest house."

Suddenly Lilly realized what she'd done. In her desperate attempt to keep Mrs. Kendall from being put out of her own home, she'd done something far worse—exposed her to Jonathan's misguided sense of justice. He obviously felt that he was far better than Mrs. Kendall and that she should serve him in some way. Making a servant of a planter's wife would thrill Jonathan Arledge.

Trying to gauge the effect of her father's statement, Lilly glanced at Mrs. Kendall. Her shoulders were squared, her chin high—her dignity intact. Jonathan would have to go a long way to break the spirit of Mrs. Kendall.

Chuckling to herself, Lilly followed Mrs. Kendall up the stairs. When Mrs. Kendall stopped outside one of the doors, Lilly looked at her questioningly. "I'm sorry. I . . . I merely wanted to help."

Mrs. Kendall smiled and put her hands on Lilly's shoulders. "My dear, you've done more than you know. I'd about given up on humanity. Nobody seems to care about anyone anymore. You do. I'll always be grateful that you cared."

Mrs. Kendall stood on tiptoe to kiss Lilly's cheek. With a smile of apology, Lilly hugged the woman. "I hope we can be friends in spite of my father."

Lifting one eyebrow conspiratorially, Mrs. Kendall whispered, "I think we shall be friends *because* of your father."

For the remainder of the afternoon Lilly helped Mrs. Kendall move her personal belongings to the guest house. They worked well together, and Lilly really hoped they could become friends. She enjoyed listening to the stories the older woman told about the house and its history.

It had been built not long after the Yemassee Massacre and was quite sturdy. Brick instead of wood, it was designed to resist fire. Although the interior would most certainly burn, the fire would be contained in a single room because of the brick walls that served as room dividers. Over the interior bricks thick paneling shined bright with polish, and the hardwood floors gleamed. There were no rugs in most of the rooms and no curtains. There were shutters on the inside and outside of the upstairs rooms.

"We've tried to make the place as fireproof and impregnable as possible. I never had any idea that my own people would become my enemies." Octavia removed a portrait from the wall. "My husband. Do you mind so much if I take it?"

"Take everything you feel will make you more comfortable. I won't abide my father's riding roughshod over you any longer." Lilly helped her new friend take down the heavy portrait. She stared at it for a long moment. There was something familiar about the man.

* * *

Ethan lay under the load of fish as the little boat moved up the Ashley River. He'd almost been caught as he left his townhouse but had managed to escape through a neighbor's open door. When he reached the river, he found his contact waiting to help another rebel to escape. Instead of one passenger, the fisherman had two.

The small boat was equipped with a false bottom. It had barely enough room for one man to lie in for a short journey. Since Ethan was the extra passenger, he had to lie on the bottom of the boat and be subjected to the smell of fish as they were shoveled over him. There was no other way for him to leave Charleston.

If Greg hadn't been so eager to pass on the exciting gossip that one of their men would be accused of treason, Ethan would be in jail now. One of these days Ethan would have to thank his friend for saving his life.

Now that Ethan had time to stop and think, he wondered how the British had found out that he was a spy. He tried to recall every conversation, but he couldn't. Did that mean there was a spy in Marion's group? Probably not. Marion's men were hand-picked.

Somebody within the British ranks must have known Ethan from a previous battle. Regardless of how it happened, Ethan's usefulness as a spy was over. General Marion would be displeased but understanding. Ethan, on the other hand, was furious. He'd been given a job to do and he hadn't completed it.

The fishy odor was about to stifle Ethan when the boat coasted to a stop. He heard voices—obviously soldiers—asking questions about missing officers, traitors. The boatman answered each question calmly, and when the soldier inquired about the boatman's papers, Ethan heard the shuffling of paper.

"If you blokes feel like searchin' me boat, then have at it," the exasperated fisherman said. "But don't be bruisin' me fish. Else leave me be on me way afore these fish take to smellin' too bad and I have to dump 'em."

"They already smell bad if you ask me," came the reply. "You don't plan to eat these, do you?"

"I plan to sell 'em."

The soldier laughed. "Be sure you sell them to the rebs and not to the British army. I don't relish the idea of finding one of them on my plate."

The boat was underway again. Ethan breathed a sigh of relief. He'd been holding his breath for fear of moving the fish. The slippery ones on top would slide off, leaving him exposed.

They'd passed the last British outpost. Soon Ethan would be free of his stinking prison. He didn't know exactly where Marion was, but he would do his level best to find him. Marion deserved to know that Ethan had been discovered. Because of this event others might be in danger, too.

Finally the boat skidded to a scratchy stop on some smooth rocks. The boatman helped Ethan up, and the two of them rescued the other passenger. Ethan had been exposed to the awful smell, but the other man had been nearly suffocating in his little space beneath the pile of fish.

Ethan was heartily glad to be free. He removed his British major's uniform and buried it in the woods. He'd never wear it again. Wearing a hunter's jacket and breeches, he made his way along the bank and turned northward. He wouldn't stop until he reached Marion, but he had to see his mother first. She needed to know that she might be in danger because of her relationship to him.

* * *

Lilly watched while Mrs. Kendall and her maid, Prudence, disappeared down the walkway to the guest cottage. While Lilly would have much preferred to go with them, she had her own unpacking to do.

Her father had walked through every room, clucking with glee like a fat chicken over a worm. There was no way for Lilly to convince him that taking a person's home by force was wrong, so she saved her arguments for later. She found that if she argued less frequently, he was more likely to see her side of the story—as he had when she'd suggested that Mrs. Kendall be allowed to stay on. That suggestion had placed Mrs. Kendall at more of a disadvantage, but at least she had a comfortable place to sleep where she would be relatively safe.

Now that she was alone, Lilly wondered about the relationship between Mrs. Kendall and Ethan. Colonel Wilkins had said that Mrs. Kendall's son was a spy. Could he have been talking about Ethan? Lilly probably wouldn't be able to find out for some time. Mrs. Kendall probably wouldn't talk about him until she discovered she could trust Lilly.

Lilly chose a bedroom that overlooked the river on one side. She couldn't see the dock but spotted a crook in the river that was north of the dock. The view was splendid.

That evening the house servants were cold toward Lilly and almost belligerent toward her father. Lilly could understand their animosity. Their mistress had been turned out of her own home, and they didn't know what to expect from a man who would do such a thing.

She'd wait a few days and let them get to know her. Lilly felt sure that she could get along with them given a little time. In the meantime, she treated them courteously. Her father felt no such compulsion to do so and was therefore treated even worse. Lilly realized that the situation would soon erupt into an all-out refusal to obey his orders, and she regretted it. He wouldn't hesitate to beat one or all of them.

As darkness settled over the plantation, Lilly felt the urge to explore by moonlight. Tartuffe had fled the moment she released him from his prison, and she wanted to make sure he was still around. She crept quietly down the stairs and exited through the back door. Most of the soldiers were camped out front, so she avoided that area.

Strolling along, she noticed the candles burning in Mrs. Kendall's cabin. Instead of bothering her, Lilly decided to walk the perimeters of the property.

The moon rose silently over the river as Lilly passed the furthest point from the main house. Using the silver glow provided by the full moon, she walked easily along the bank until she came to the woods that bordered the south side of the property.

Lilly looked at the low-hanging limbs of the live oaks and smiled as she recalled the pleasant times she'd spent in such a tree with Ethan. She wondered what he was doing tonight. Did he miss her already? She doubted it.

Wishing she could see him now, she sighed and continued to walk. After a few moments she heard a sound and stopped instantly to listen. Who—or what—could be there in the woods? Knowing that it was probably an animal didn't make her feel any better. These woods were full of wild animals, and she knew better than to tempt them. Wolves, bears, and bobcats roamed the area, and Lilly suddenly felt foolish for having come so far from the house.

She turned her back to the woods and began to walk purposefully toward the house. Lilly knew better than to run. The sight of rapidly fleeing prey would cause an instant attack. Slow, Lilly, walk slowly, she chanted in her mind.

When she heard the sound of something rushing toward her, she knew it was too late. Before she could escape, her attacker launched himself at her and threw her to the ground.

CHAPTER 8

LILLY STRUGGLED AND FOUGHT WITH THE PERSON who had her face down on the soft grass. "Let me go!" she screamed and found a stinking hand clapped over her mouth and nose.

"Silence!" commanded the deep masculine voice. "I won't hurt you if you're quiet."

Lilly lay completely still, hoping her attacker would remove his hand before she suffocated. He'd twisted her arm behind her back until she thought it would break and planted his knee in the middle of her spine.

"I'm going to move my hand. If you scream, I'll kill you."

Listening carefully to the familiar voice, Lilly nodded that she understood. When the hand moved slightly away, she gasped for air. "Get off me. Who do you think you are, attacking me on my own . . . in my own . . . here?"

Once again Lilly couldn't claim the plantation as her own. She doubted if she'd ever be able to do so.

"Lilly?" the man asked quietly. "Is that you? What are you doing at Carolina Moon?"

He knew her name. It was him! "Ethan?"

"Good God, Lilly, I could have killed you!" Ethan slid off her and drew her into his arms. He kissed her forehead gently and held her close. "What in the name of all that's holy are you doing on my plantation?"

My plantation. My plantation. My . . . The words echoed through her mind. This was Ethan's plantation. Mrs. Kendall was his mother. Now she knew why her father had asked Ethan back several times. Her father knew that Ethan's property was about to be confiscated and wanted to know more about it. She felt sick. Disgusted.

"Ethan, oh, I'm so sorry. Oh, God, forgive me." Tears shimmered in Lilly's eyes. What had her father done?

"What are you doing here, Lilly?" Ethan asked again, this time a little more forcefully.

"Oh, Ethan, this is horrible. How can I explain to you that . . . well, my father . . . he's apparently been looking at several . . . Oh, please forgive me."

Ethan tried to see her face, but the moon was hidden behind a cloud. "Tell me, Lilly. I deserve an explanation. How did you know Carolina Moon was mine?" He recalled the night when she'd first mentioned the Carolina moon. Had she known then that Carolina Moon was the name of his plantation?

Lilly inhaled deeply. She didn't want to tell Ethan what had happened, but someone had to, and she'd heard Colonel Wilkins say the plantation owner's son was a spy. Ethan a spy?

She drew back to stare at him. That meant he was a rebel. "Oh, dear God in heaven. This is worse than I thought."

"Where is my mother? What the hell's going on around here?" Ethan felt his anger rising unchecked. He sensed that his mother was in danger and that Lilly had something to do with it. He shook her shoulders until her head bobbled back and forth. "Talk to me! Tell me the truth!"

"I . . . oh, please, Ethan. Please forgive me. I didn't know. Honestly I didn't."

"Didn't know what?"

"Ethan," she whispered and let her chin fall forward until it reached her chest. She simply couldn't look him in the face and tell him that her father now owned the plantation. "Your plantation has been confiscated."

"Like hell it has. I'll kill any Tory I find in my . . ." His voice trailed off, and he stared at her as she raised her gaze to meet his. She'd betrayed him. It had to be her.

His words were like a knife plunging into her chest. The pain was so intense that Lilly could almost feel the blood pouring forth from her heart. The next words tumbled out involuntarily. "You're a spy."

Ethan peered at her. He could almost feel the anguish of her words. The two of them had started a special relationship, and the war still stood between them. A war and his plantation. "Where's my mother?"

"In the guest cottage," Lilly replied simply, all feeling gone from her body.

Ethan jumped up and jerked her after him. "Come on. Keep up, or I'll drag you."

Together they ran toward the guest cottage. When they were in view of the main house, she dug her feet in and stopped. "No, Ethan. Don't go there."

"Why not? I'm going to toss you and your wretch of a father out of my house." Ethan started to move again, but Lilly held back. "Now what? I warn you, I won't tolerate this. Come along."

"No. There are soldiers camped in the front yard." Lilly bit her tongue. She'd warned the enemy, someone who in his rage might kill her on the spot. Unable to believe that he would intentionally harm her, she held her ground. "Please. Please, believe me."

"Why should I believe you?" Ethan demanded sarcastically.

"Because I . . . I mean, we . . . oh, for heaven's sake, why would I lie to you?" Lilly couldn't answer any other way. She'd almost said she loved him, but she didn't—she couldn't. Lilly Arledge couldn't love a rebel, a rebel spy at that. "Please believe me. Let me take you to your mother."

Ethan studied her for a moment. Why indeed should he believe her? He'd mentioned that he knew Bowie and Erin. He'd told her he was leaving the city. She must have informed one of her soldier friends who figured out the rest of the story. Maybe she'd been instructed to obtain information from him all along. Was that why he found her so willing? Was Jonathan Arledge smarter than Ethan thought? Could Lilly's innocence be an act?

There were too many unanswered questions, and they were making Ethan angrier. As they strode across the lawn, he tried to calm down. Ethan couldn't remember ever being this furious with anyone, and certainly not a woman he . . . what? How did he feel about Lilly? He didn't love her. Of course he didn't. But he did like her quite a bit—until tonight.

Nearing the guest cottage, he could see the warm glow of candlelight filtering through the windows and quickened his pace. His mother would be distraught, and Ethan wanted to be with her, to comfort her for a few moments before he went to the big house and killed Jonathan Arledge. He stopped without warning. Kill? Was he actually thinking of killing a man who would probably be unarmed?

No. No matter what had happened, Ethan couldn't

kill an unarmed man. Not even Jonathan Arledge. He took a deep breath and looked down into Lilly's puzzled face. The moonlight bathed her features in a golden glow that made her dark eyes seem darker and the softness of her lips more inviting.

Without hesitating further—which might cause him to lose his resolve—he jerked her along with him and finally reached the cottage. He tapped lightly on the door and waited. Prudence, his mother's personal maid, answered the door.

Dragging Lilly along, he brushed past the maid and found his mother seated near the fireplace. She was occupied with her needlework, much as she had been every night of his life. "Mother, are you all right?"

Octavia put down her needlework and smiled broadly, though she was stunned by his sudden appearance. She stood and put her arms around her son. "Ethan, you reckless dear, you must leave at once."

"Not before I exterminate a rat in the house." Ethan glared at Lilly over his mother's head. "You stay put until I'm ready to deal with you."

"Ethan!" Octavia exclaimed and drew back to look at her son. "Since when do you treat a lady in such a crude manner?"

"It's all right, Mrs. Kendall. I . . . I deserve it. He knows that my father . . . that we . . ." Lilly's words trailed off. She slumped down in the nearest chair and hung her head in her hands. What an awful mess this was.

"Nonsense. Ethan, apologize to Miss Arledge at once," Octavia demanded and stared at her son.

"Mother, don't you understand what she's done?" Ethan asked, protesting his mother's stand in the situation.

"I understand that you're acting like a total boor, and if it continues, you may leave." Octavia knelt beside Lilly and took her hands. "My dear, this is not your fault. And once Ethan understands that, he'll—"

"Mother, for the love of God, they've confiscated our property, and here you sit coddling her as if she were the one wronged." Ethan glanced at Prudence to see how she was taking this and was surprised to find her glaring at him, too. "Will someone please tell me what's going on?"

Octavia patted Lilly's hands and stood. "Sit down, son. We have a lot of talking to do. Prudence, close the shutters, please."

Waiting for Prudence to finish, Octavia sat back in her chair and picked up her needlework. "Sit down, Ethan. I'm not accustomed to being ignored."

He chose a chair opposite the two women. He felt like a boy again, being punished for the infraction of some rule. He said nothing, knowing that his mother would speak when she felt like it, and nothing he could do would speed her along. When he thought he would bound up from the chair in sheer frustration, she looked up, first at him and then at Lilly.

"Ethan, my son, you owe this young lady an apology." Octavia stopped sewing and leveled her gaze at her son. "I note that her gown is torn and stained. Do I assume correctly that you are the cause of that accident?"

"Yes, Mother, but—"

"Apologize to her at once. The very idea of you tackling her like a chum of yours—I can't believe that you've stooped so low." She glanced at Lilly and shook her head. "My dear, my son is a brute, nothing less. I had hoped that you two would get along, but I can see now that my son isn't worthy of the attention of a lady like yourself."

"Mother! Listen to me. They've confiscated our house, our property, everything you and Father worked for," Ethan began, wondering when all of this would sink in. "And now I'm branded as a spy because of her."

"Ethan!" Lilly jumped to her feet and stared at him in shock. "How can you say such a thing?"

"It's true—it has to be." Ethan saw the color rise in her cheeks and knew that he still cared for this woman even if she was a traitor to him and to his country.

Octavia rose, walked over to Ethan, and pinched his ear! "I say apologize at once or leave my home. In addition to acting like an ape, you're smelling up my house. You smell worse than a kettle of fish that's been sitting in the sun for a week."

As a child, this particular punishment was one of the worst, but as an adult, it was demeaning. "Mother, you're treating me like a boy."

"You're acting like a boy."

Ethan inhaled deeply and gazed at Lilly, who was standing just behind his mother. "I apologize for all my shortcomings, Miss Arledge, and most particularly if I have misjudged you in this matter. And I apologize for offending anyone with the smell. I was forced to leave Charleston under a boatload of fish."

"Ethan, I didn't turn you in. You must believe that." The sting of his accusation still hurt, but she knew she wasn't guiltless. She *was* living in his house—a home she knew he loved. "But I wish I could rectify the situation. If I'd known that my father was doing this, I would never have allowed it. Somehow I would have stopped him."

"Nonsense," Octavia stated flatly and resumed her seat. "You could no more stop that . . . weasel than I could stop him from striking you today."

"What!" Ethan roared and leapt from his chair. "He hit her? I'll kill that bastard."

Ethan strode toward the door. Lilly bolted from her chair and caught him before he could leave. "No, you can't. It's suicide."

He looked down at her in the light from the candelabra and saw for the first time a trace of a bruise across her cheek and lips. Rage mounted in him, controlled him, and he tried to shake her loose. "I won't allow him to treat you this way. I'll—"

"Ethan, she's right. You can do nothing. A British contingent is sleeping on the front lawn. It's a wonder they didn't catch you coming across the back a while ago." Octavia saw the anger in her son's eyes. She'd never seen him so enraged before and glanced at Lilly. She realized that they knew each other already. How deeply did their feelings run?

Octavia smiled. She already liked Lilly. The girl wasn't afraid to work, she was honest, and she was caring. More than that, she seemed to be in love with Ethan.

"Mother, I can't let this pass. I've heard the way he talks to her, but for him to strike her is beyond—"

"Ethan, the choice isn't yours." Octavia put her hand on Lilly's arm. "We can't change the world overnight. I'll find ways of protecting her as much as possible, but you can't risk your life over this."

"She's right, Ethan." Lilly loosened her grip on him now that it seemed he wouldn't storm out the door and blunder into the British Army. "I have ways of shutting him out. Don't worry about me. He can't hurt me."

Ethan had seen the way she shut Jonathan out, but did she shut out all men because of her relationship with her father? The pain in her eyes was evident. The physical pain would be nothing compared to the emotional torture that she must have endured.

Before he realized what he was doing, Ethan put his arms around her and tried to comfort her, to wipe out the pain she must be feeling. "Lilly, let me talk to him. I'll—"

"No. You can't. Not only will you be endangering your own life, but think of me. You'll make the situation worse. And think of your mother. She's living here, too." Lilly felt desperation rise in her. If Ethan tried to speak to her father, she'd never hear the end of it.

Octavia watched the two of them in astonishment. Her son was comforting the young woman he'd wanted to thrash moments ago. She'd have to look into the situation. Maybe Lilly would talk to her after Ethan left.

"Son, sit down and tell me why you came here." Octavia returned to her chair, and the others did, too.

"I was in Charleston," he said and glanced at Lilly. He didn't know how much she knew, and he didn't want to give her any information she could later use against him. He still didn't know whether she was the person who passed along information to the British or not. "I heard that a British major was about to be accused of treason. When I went to my lodgings, I found troops there and escaped."

"Oh, Ethan." Lilly clasped her hands together joyfully. "Then it's not true. You're not a spy."

Ethan gazed at her. What had she heard from her father and the other soldiers? How much could he say without damaging his cause further? Ethan found that he didn't want to be dishonest with her, even if it jeopardized him further. "Lilly, I know this is hard for you to understand. I . . . I am a rebel. I don't deny it."

Lilly's eyes closed for the briefest moment. She'd

wanted him to say no, he wasn't a spy, but he hadn't. She wondered if she would have preferred him to lie to her and decided that she'd rather know the truth, no matter how hard it seemed. "I see," she whispered.

"I know we're on opposite sides, but—"

"Posh. There's no time to talk about such weighty matters now," Octavia interrupted. "Ethan, you must leave before you're discovered. There'll be plenty of time later to discuss this."

Lilly tried to smile. "She's right, Ethan. Please go. Don't tell me any more. I'll leave you alone with your mother." Lilly rose and walked to the door.

Ethan followed. He turned to his mother for a moment and said, "I'll be right back. I'm going to walk her part of the way to the house."

"No, Ethan, you mustn't," Lilly protested. "It's too dangerous. I can walk alone."

"Nonsense. Let him go a short distance with you." Octavia put her needlework in her basket and rose. "Prudence, leave the door unlocked. Ethan, when you return, all the candles will be extinguished. I'm using the first sleeping chamber. Come directly there, and we'll talk briefly before you leave." She turned to Lilly. "Good night, my dear, and thank you for all you've done."

"Good night, Mrs. Kendall." Lilly let herself out, and Ethan followed.

Ethan guided her through the formal gardens. They strolled among the tall boxwoods and ornamentals, the roses and other florals. He knew the layout of the garden as well as he knew anything in the world. As a child, he'd played there almost every day.

"Lilly, let's talk a moment before we get too close to the house. Do you think your father will be looking for you?" Ethan asked and pulled her toward an alcove with a marble bench.

"I doubt it. He probably doesn't know I'm outside." Lilly sat on the bench and glanced up at the moon. "A Carolina moon. Your plantation is called Carolina Moon. It just occurred to me that you were talking about the plantation earlier."

"Yes. I don't want to mislead you. I . . . I like you a lot and want to remain friends, but if it's difficult for you, then I won't—"

"Ethan, I hope we can be friends. This is torture, knowing that you're fighting for the other side, but I understand. At least you're fighting for your convictions, not simply for whoever pays the most." Lilly was thinking of her mercenary father. "Just don't tell me anything. Don't tell me about battles or what your plans are."

"I won't." He sat down and put his arms around her. After a few seconds he lay his cheek against her hair, and for a long time neither of them spoke. "I hope we're strong enough to survive this."

Lilly looked up at him. "If we're not, then the nation is doomed, regardless of who wins."

Ethan hugged her close and tried to memorize every curve of her body. Later, when he was standing watch or hiding in a tree or sleeping on the cold hard ground, he'd have something pleasant to remember. The scent of jasmine clung to her and surrounded him in the most pleasant of atmospheres.

Their lips met. Lilly wanted him to kiss her until her memory was blocked out, until she remembered nothing of war and fighting. She was searching for good memories, too.

Lilly wanted the moment to last forever, to transcend the strife life and war created. Her arms were around him, clinging to him. Her eyes were closed, and she shut out everything except the sensations Ethan created with his lips. Her mouth opened to him, and he began a slow, gentle probing that sent shivers of fire down her spine. His kisses were intoxicating, and she felt herself waver in his arms.

He withdrew from her and held her tightly. Ethan didn't want to release her, to leave her. "Lilly." He whispered against her ear and nibbled on the lobe. "Lilly, don't hate me."

"I don't," she replied breathlessly. "Don't hate me."

Ethan held her away from him slightly and looked into her eyes. "Somehow we must surpass this idealistic difference of opinion. We may face difficult times, but we'll survive."

Lilly wanted to believe him. She didn't want him to leave but knew he must or face the consequences with the British soldiers out front. "Ethan, I . . . do be careful. I heard Colonel Wilkins order sentries posted along the river. I don't know how you missed them when you arrived, but please, oh, please be careful."

Ethan could hear her voice cracking as she spoke to him. The cost to her must be dear because she was giving away information that would ultimately help the Loyalist cause. "Thank you, Lilly. I'll see you soon. Maybe sooner than you think."

He kissed her again, this time reveling in her touch and fragrance as might a man who'd been condemned to death. Reluctant to leave, he clung to her for a moment longer and then whispered, "When I'm gone, remember me."

Before she could reply, he disappeared into the darkness. Lilly sat there for a long time, partly because she didn't want to go inside, but primarily because she wanted to watch for the sentries. If one of them heard something, she'd simply explain it as noises she had made while out walking.

She suspected that Ethan would remain with his mother for a short while and then sneak away while he could during the darkest hour prior to dawn. After about fifteen minutes she rose and walked slowly toward the house. Apparently he'd reached his mother's cottage undetected.

Lilly quietly slipped into the house so no one would see her torn, soiled gown. When she went into her new room, she looked around. She hadn't paid too much attention to the decor earlier because she hated being here. She still hated what had happened, but now that she knew this was Ethan's plantation, she liked the idea a little more. She would make sure that it was kept in prime condition and somehow find a way to return it to its rightful owner after the war ended.

The heavy furnishings told her that the room was a man's, possibly Ethan's. She didn't want to disturb anything, but by now all personal belongings of his had been removed and replaced by her own. She'd inquire in the morning about where they'd been put. She wanted to make sure everything of his was made available to him if he should want it.

Ethan slipped silently into the cottage. He waited long enough for his eyes to adjust to the darkness and then proceeded up the stairs to his mother's room. He found her with the shutters closed and a single candle burning.

She came to him and put her arms around him. "Ethan, dear boy, what has happened?"

He explained about the tip he received from his friend Greg and how the soldiers had come to his lodgings.

Ethan knew they were looking for him. He didn't know how they found out he was a traitor.

"I've gone over every conversation I had with Greg and with Lilly. I can't think of a single thing that would have tipped them off, except that I mentioned to Lilly that I knew her cousin, a known Patriot." Ethan sat on the hearth and watched his mother.

"That girl never reported you, I'm sure of it." Octavia smiled as she recalled the look that had passed between her son and her enemy's daughter. Neither of them realized it yet—or she thought they didn't—but Octavia could see the fresh seedling of love just reaching the sunlight. She hoped that nothing happened to trample the fragile growth.

"How can you be so sure?" Ethan asked with hope in his voice.

"I'm sure. Now tell me the rest of it." Octavia understood Ethan well enough to know that he'd deny any attraction to Miss Arledge and, perhaps because of hearing the words spoken aloud, might avoid her in the future. Octavia didn't want that at all, so she kept her feelings to herself. There would be plenty of time to broach the subject later, when she knew Lilly better and when Ethan wasn't in such a dither.

Ethan related the events simply. He didn't know any other way. After he finished, he expected his mother to agree with him that Lilly was probably the culprit.

"I think your accusation of Miss Arledge is nonsense," Octavia announced. "You need someone to blame, and you've chosen her. I'll hear no more about it."

"But, Mother, think about your own situation. She's mistress of your plantation now. You're in the guest cottage," Ethan argued.

"Yes, and if it weren't for her intervention, I'd be

homeless." Octavia stood and faced her son. While he was seated on the hearth, she was tall enough to look into his eyes. She wanted this matter of Miss Arledge's innocence to be over before it had a chance to blossom into hate.

"What do you mean?" Ethan's attention was rapt. He was clutching at straws in a whirlwind. He wanted to believe Lilly, he really did, but he couldn't, not without more evidence.

"I mean that when the officer read the proclamation, it stated that I could take one trunk and one personal servant and leave the premises before sundown. There was no mention of where I'd go nor of how I'd get there." Octavia closed her eyes briefly and then wrapped her arms around Ethan. "Miss Arledge refused to allow them to put me out. That's why her father slapped her."

"I don't understand." Ethan slid his arms around his mother's waist and laid his head on her breast. "Tell me all of this sordid story."

Octavia did. She left nothing out. "Needless to say, if it wasn't for Miss Arledge, you'd have walked into a trap here tonight. I don't believe she knew anything about this until she arrived."

"That's hard to believe."

"She may have known about the plantation being confiscated, but I feel sure she thought the occupants had already been relocated." Octavia held her son for a moment longer. "Ethan, you must go. The time is growing late."

With a knapsack full of food, Ethan left Carolina Moon. He resolved to return before long and talk about this whole affair with Lilly. For now he had a war to fight.

* * *

Lilly went to the side window and peered out. The guest cottage was visible from this window during the day, but now it was shrouded in darkness. Was Ethan still there with his mother? Was it coincidence that Lilly had ended up at his plantation or fate? As the hour was late, Lilly couldn't think about the situation any longer.

She blew out the candle, offered a silent prayer for his safety, and then crawled into bed.

CHAPTER 9

LILLY SLEPT WELL FOR THE FIRST TIME IN DAYS. When she awoke, the sun shone brightly through her window. She rose and walked over to it to peer out. She could see the cottage easily now and wondered if Ethan had gotten away without harm.

She stepped onto the piazza and walked as far as she could to see better but could see nothing amiss. She smiled and looked for a trellis, just in case she wanted to escape at night as she often had back in Charleston.

When she entered her room, Zip was waiting for her. "Yo breakfast ready. Set down and eat while it's hot."

Lilly obeyed without speaking. She was too deep in thought about Ethan. How could she have been so easily fooled? She tried to recall how he'd responded when she'd asked questions about the war, about who was winning and when it would be over. None of his answers had made her suspicious.

When she remembered his accusations last night, she felt like shriveling up and dying. He was right about many things, except that she didn't report him. Even if she suspected him, she would never have said anything to anyone.

She wondered if her father might have been the informant, but decided that Jonathan knew less about Ethan

than she did. He might have said something unwittingly, though, that tipped off the British provost. The more she considered her father's motives, the more she wondered about him. Her father was quite capable of making up the story about Ethan being a spy.

Jonathan had been on several trips lately, on the premise of procuring food for the soldiers and fodder for the animals. She wondered if he'd been here and liked this place well enough to lie. Lilly made up her mind to ask Mrs. Kendall if she'd ever seen her father before.

When she got downstairs, Lilly found Mrs. Kendall in the kitchen supervising the servants. "You don't have to do that, Mrs. Kendall. I already feel bad enough about taking your home without seeing you act as housekeeper."

"Nonsense. I've been doing this for years." Octavia finished instructing the maid about dusting the upstairs rooms and turned to Lilly. "Come with me. Let's talk."

Lilly followed Mrs. Kendall out the back door and down into the garden. When they reached the spot where Ethan had stopped last night, Mrs. Kendall sat down and patted the bench beside her. "Please join me."

They talked pleasantly for a while about the beauty of Carolina Moon and the area in general. Then Octavia decided to talk seriously to Lilly. "Lilly, my dear, I appreciate what you've done for me."

When Lilly started to protest, Octavia waved her off and continued. "I'm going to be very honest with you. I expect Ethan to come back here occasionally. Without your cooperation—and silence—I doubt if he could do so safely."

"Mrs. Kendall, if you're asking for my permission for Ethan to come here, you have it, but I don't see that it's necessary. He's your son. This is your home." Lilly clasped Mrs. Kendall's hands in her own. "I am the intruder. I shall do nothing to endanger him and shall endeavor to protect him while he visits you."

"Thank you. I knew I could count on you." Octavia smiled and nodded. She'd been right about Lilly. The moment Ethan's name was mentioned, Lilly's eyes began to sparkle. "Another thing. Please call me Octavia. You make me feel ancient. I was never one to stand on ceremony."

"That would be disrespectful," Lilly said and tried to smile.

"Not as disrespectful as ignoring my wishes. I insist." Octavia put her arm around Lilly and hugged her. "As badly as I hate this situation, I feel that you and I are going to be close friends. Friends don't address each other so formally."

"I'll try, but please don't be angry with me if I occasionally forget." Lilly gave in. She was delighted that Octavia wanted to be friends.

"And please indulge me if I try to mother you. I'm forever expanding my brood to include all those I love. I'm sure I'll love you, too." Octavia smiled and clapped her hands together. "Now, let's get to work. If we work hard, we can put in some onion sets and cabbages that might ripen before cold weather. Maybe a few greens."

Lilly was amazed. She and Octavia, along with Applejack and one of the plantation's field hands, soon had a full kitchen garden that would withstand the cool weather of fall. There were radishes, onions, cabbages, greens, and beets planted in the dark, rich dirt. In a month some of the vegetables would be ready to harvest.

They worked every day in the gardens. In addition to the vegetables, Octavia kept a full herb garden. Lilly crawled among the rows, pulling grass and weeds until she was exhausted. Time passed much more quickly here than it had back in Charleston.

Her father was gone frequently, and Lilly enjoyed the freedom of being in the country much more than she ever thought she would. One day her father returned with several soldiers in tow. He called for her, and she went to see what he wanted.

"We're going to be entertaining quite a bit over the next few weeks. Please be on your best behavior. I've brought your new clothes and will expect you to wear them." Jonathan lit a cigar and puffed absently for a few minutes. "We'll dress for supper this evening."

Lilly left him and felt terrible. All of the fun she'd had with Octavia seemed to be lost to her now that her father had returned. She went out to inform her friend that she'd be unable to help in the garden for the remainder of the afternoon.

Octavia smiled indulgently and took the young woman's hand. "I understand, my dear. I'll see you tomorrow."

Lilly agreed and went to the kitchen to instruct Dulcie about the menu and number of guests. Lilly had sent the Carolina Moon cook to the cottage to help Prudence care for Octavia. Dulcie seemed to be fitting in well with the remaining staff in the kitchen.

Her task complete, Lilly asked Applejack to bring water for her bath. She didn't want to entertain tonight, but she knew she couldn't get out of it. She spent the afternoon in her room, pacing back and forth. The gowns her father had brought were indecent. Lilly didn't know how she would find the courage to wear any of them. Her father would expect her to wear one of them this evening, and Lilly dreaded facing his guests.

The wharf women in Charleston who plied their trade

openly might not even have dared to wear such revealing gowns in public. Lilly decided that she had no choice. As time for supper neared, Zip came to dress Lilly's hair.

"Have mercy! Ain't you got nothin' to wear over that?" Zip clapped her hands across her heart. "Sweet Jesus, take me now. I cain't stand no more."

"Don't take on so, Zip. I already feel awful about having to wear these . . . these garments." Lilly looked at herself in the mirror. If Mrs. Hawkins had made these dresses as Lilly specified, she would have been proud to wear them. But the bodices were cut so low that when Lilly leaned over, she could see her nipples—and she didn't have to lean very far.

She wore a gown of crimson silk decorated with black lace and satin ribbons. Instead of an innocent maiden, she felt like a brothel owner. If she ordered any more new clothes, then she would have to paint her breasts to match because each new outfit was more revealing than the one before.

With all the dignity she could muster, Lilly went down to supper. When she reached the parlor, several soldiers leapt to their feet in unison and hurried over to kiss her hand. Lilly glanced over their heads at her father, who was beaming with pride.

Lilly knew she looked pretty. Zip always managed to tame Lilly's long curly chestnut hair into a presentably fashionable coiffeur. Tonight the braids were thick and wound around the crown of her head. Interspersed were the tiniest artificial red flowers—a gift from her father—that matched the sprig of roses at her waist.

She didn't know a single one of the men surrounding her, but they proceeded to introduce themselves without her father's assistance. Lilly had a difficult time keeping from laughing at their eagerness. She noted that her father's friend, Daniel Boyd, sat near the hearth warming his hands, and Colonel Wilkins was beside him. When she entered, both men had risen and were now watching her carefully.

After the young men had completed their introductions, Lilly excused herself and walked over to greet Mr. Boyd and Colonel Wilkins. After the greetings were said, Dulcie announced supper. Lilly found herself seated between Colonel Wilkins and Simon Owens. Simon was a major and proud of his rank. Colonel Wilkins obviously liked the young man and smiled at his youthful exuberance.

Lilly found the conversation trying, to say the least. Colonel Wilkins inquired about how she had settled in and whether or not Mrs. Kendall had caused any problems.

"Oh, no. Mrs. Kendall has been most helpful," Lilly replied, wondering why Colonel Wilkins seemed so interested.

"Has she many visitors?" he asked absently, not looking directly at her.

Smiling sweetly, Lilly fluttered her eyelids flirtatiously. "I don't think she has any visitors. With the dangers of war so prevalent, few people are to be found making social calls."

When Colonel Wilkins nodded, Lilly thought he was going to continue the line of questioning, but he didn't. With her heart pounding, she turned to Simon Owens and asked how long he'd been in the colonies.

"Oh, not very long. My parents wanted to keep me from the insurrection, but I overcame their objections at last and purchased my commission." He beamed proudly. "And do you enjoy country living?"

"Oh, most assuredly. There's so much to do here, and

the scenery is so lovely," Lilly answered honestly. She wanted to keep him talking so Colonel Wilkins wouldn't have a chance to question her further about Octavia's habits. "Don't you agree?"

"Well, to be truthful, no. It's too warm most of the time, and I understand that in a few months the weather will be bitterly cold." Simon placed his fork on his plate and studied Lilly for a moment. "Wouldn't you rather live in London? It's ever so much more civilized."

Lilly almost snapped that she'd prefer to live with the alligators and snakes than with him anywhere, but she smiled and looked at him innocently. "Well, I'm sure the colonies have some disadvantages, but I do have lots of friends and would hate to leave them."

"Well, Colonel Wilkins, I've ordered the good Madeira to be poured," Jonathan interrupted. "Tell us of the news you received today."

Colonel Wilkins glared at Jonathan. "I don't wish to discuss the dreary matters of war at table."

"Come now, we've waited all afternoon for the news," Jonathan urged. "Ever since you received the letter, I've watched you, and you seem to be calculating or plotting for a renewed attack. Share your news with us."

"Miss Arledge certainly isn't interested in the—"

"Of course she is. She's a true Tory, as we all are," Jonathan interrupted, not to be diverted from his path.

"Very well, if you insist. I hadn't wanted to disturb the tranquility of the evening with bad news, but I shall." Colonel Wilkins carefully folded his napkin, laid it beside his plate, and traced the creases with his thumb. "I feel that I can delay the news no longer. Cornwallis surrendered in Yorktown."

For several seconds the silence was so great that Lilly felt she could hear her radishes growing in the garden.

She looked from one to the other of the men seated near her, and each face was marked with disbelief. Her father's mouth gaped open in astonishment. Clearly he'd thought the letter contained word of some great victory.

"I am devastated by this news," Colonel Wilkins continued and hung his head. "All day I've been trying to ascertain the effects this defeat will have on our cause and I find the repercussions far reaching and incomprehensible."

Lilly touched his hand in a gesture of comfort. "Sir, do you think it is possible that the letter . . . well, that perhaps the letter is misleading? That the defeat may not be so overwhelming? Or maybe completely untrue? You know that the Patriot spies have intercepted missives before and . . ."

Her words faded away as she recognized Colonel Wilkins's face of defeat. Without speaking further, she withdrew her hand. Her father was watching her. In fact, almost every man at the table was looking at her. For the remainder of the meal, she simply answered questions and volunteered nothing. She felt as though she were on trial for a crime she didn't realize she had committed.

After supper, when the men were having their cigars and brandy, Lilly thought she would step out for a breath of fresh air. Simon Owens asked if he could accompany her. Under her father's watchful eye she assented, though not as graciously as she might have if she'd truly wanted company.

For the first time she seriously considered the possibility that the British might lose the war. What would happen to her? She glanced back at the house. Already she loved Carolina Moon even though she still felt guilty about the circumstances under which she lived there.

Without a doubt, if the British lost the war, she and her father would have to leave Carolina Moon.

The sky was lovely. Stars twinkled to life around a spectacular moon that rode high above the trees. Lilly loved the sense of space and freedom that accompanied living on such a vast plantation. Birds called from their nesting places in the trees, crickets chirruped from their hiding places, and the bullfrogs sang in their reverberating bass from the swamps. She would find leaving hard and could easily understand Ethan's passion for his home.

Simon made inane remarks about the beauty of the sky, but Lilly simply wanted to look at it, to drink in every nuance of the place. They walked the dim path through the garden and, when Simon suggested that she might want to rest, Lilly sat on the bench she'd occupied with Ethan.

Folding her hands across her lap, she wondered where Ethan was tonight. Did he know of Cornwallis's defeat? Was Ethan still in danger? Could he be injured somewhere? Was he looking at the same stars and thinking of her?

Ethan lay on the ground near Vince's Fort. He'd been directed here after he'd left Carolina Moon. Marion wasn't here, but the militia in this area needed help until replacements could arrive. Ethan had gathered about thirty men and would remain here for a few more days before heading north to join Marion.

On October twenty-eighth, a detachment of Tories under Colonel Hezekiah Williams had raided the fort. Having been warned of the impending raid by spies, the eighty or so men who populated the fort were safely away by the time Williams's superior force arrived. The Tories had burned the fort and returned to Orangeburg empty-handed except for a few stragglers they captured.

Looking up at the moon, Ethan thought of Lilly. When he'd left Carolina Moon, he hadn't known how he felt about her living in his home, but now he was glad she was there. He couldn't—and wouldn't—be happy about his mother living in the small guest cottage while Jonathan enjoyed all of the amenities the Kendalls had worked for. But Ethan had wanted Lilly to see Carolina Moon the moment he'd met her.

He wondered if she'd enjoy the formal English garden and its intricate design, the pathways that led to secluded nooks set among bowers of flowering plants. He'd loved to play there as a boy. The cluster of live oaks came to mind, and he smiled. The next time he was at Carolina Moon, he'd show her *his* special tree. Maybe they could climb together.

Cornwallis's loss had lightened the spirits of the Carolina Militia. Even though the small band evacuated Vince's Fort to avoid being beaten by the superior number of British troops, they weren't disheartened. Nobody had considered that Cornwallis could have been defeated so resoundingly. In fact, only two or three days before the battle Cornwallis had tried to evacuate all the British troops from Yorktown.

When the American victory had been announced, the celebrating among the militia lasted well into the night. Even now the men would raise their cups in salute to Washington as they ate their evening meals.

Ethan thought back to the last time he'd seen Lilly. He regretted his anger more than anything he'd done in a long time. He seldom lost his temper, but that night when everything he'd worked so hard to build seemed to be tumbling around him, he'd lashed out at Lilly.

Thinking more rationally now, he realized she couldn't have reported him—she knew nothing to report. He'd have to apologize the next time he saw her.

Kissing her beneath the Carolina moon seemed to be a compelling occupation that filled his thoughts, and Ethan could hardly wait until he could return to Lilly. He wondered if she'd ever forgive him.

Several days later Lilly smiled inanely at Simon's attempt to be amusing. How could he prattle on about such nonsense when the British and Loyalists were facing defeat? she wondered. He'd been following her for days, trying to please her and make her like him. His chatter drove her to hide from him on occasion, but he sometimes found her, as he had tonight. Did he think her head was filled with nothing but fripperies and that she wouldn't be concerned about Lord Cornwallis's defeat? Simon Owens never seemed to think a serious thought.

After a few moments Simon slid his arm around her, and Lilly leapt to her feet. "How dare you presume to . . . Who do you think you are?"

"God's blood, Miss Arledge, I meant no disrespect," Simon babbled. "I . . . I like you a great deal. Your father will have my request for your hand tonight. I never meant to . . . I'll go at once and speak to him."

"Simon, no!" she called after him, but he'd already disappeared among the tall boxwoods. If he succeeded in asking for her hand, she'd simply refuse him as she had countless others. Lilly had no intention of marrying a man with no more gumption than Simon Owens displayed.

She looked at the silhouette of the house and decided that she didn't want to go back inside yet. Her father would find her far too quickly if he agreed to allow Simon to press his suit.

After supper this evening she'd gone to her room and changed into something warmer to wear while walking about the grounds. The night air was cool, and she pulled her shawl closer about her shoulders. Her long-sleeved gown covered almost every part of her except her bodice. The shawl helped but wasn't completely effective.

Lilly strode out of the garden thinking of Simon. She couldn't really blame him for his actions. He'd been here for several days and had seen her in nothing but risqué attire. She was sure he couldn't know that her father selected her gowns for her.

Ever since the evening when Colonel Wilkins had announced Lord Cornwallis's defeat and surrender at Yorktown, a pall had fallen on Carolina Moon. The soldiers, who were in and out constantly because the plantation was located near their outpost at Dorchester, seemed to feel that the defeat signaled the end of the war—and a tragic loss for the British.

Taking little notice of her direction, Lilly hurried toward a copse of live oaks. During the past few days she'd discovered them and delighted in climbing upon a low-hanging limb and thinking of Ethan and her home in Charleston. These trees were old, perhaps even hundreds of years, and their lower branches nearly touched the ground. She could step onto one of them more easily than she could have stepped into a carriage in Charleston.

Ethan must have loved these woods when he was a boy. As she settled herself on one of the limbs, she pictured him, slim and scrappy, climbing among the branches as easily as Tartuffe. Several times recently she'd seen the old cat perched high up in a tree and surveying the land. He'd adapted to Carolina Moon as well as Lilly had.

Ethan couldn't believe what he saw. Lilly was rushing across the lawn toward his grove of trees. How could she have known where to find him? He'd waited until dark to climb the tree, hoping to spot the soldiers who were probably around. He'd talked to a man earlier who'd told him that Carolina Moon had become a favorite spot of the young British officers.

He'd seen Lilly come out of the house with a man in uniform. Ethan couldn't deny the jealousy that colored his thoughts. Never before possessive of the women he'd courted, Ethan found the emotion strange and unsettling. He had no claim on Lilly. He supposed that he might return one day and find her engaged or married. That thought disturbed him even more than his jealousy. How did he really feel about her?

Ethan couldn't answer that question. It was one he'd wrangled with for the last few days. At first he'd liked the idea of having her tucked away here at Carolina Moon and out of the tenuous calm in Charleston. Now he wasn't sure.

These soldiers had been at the outpost for some time, and Ethan didn't want them around Lilly. With a father like Jonathan she could be forced to marry any one of the wealthier men. The British officers were all wealthy and represented established and respected families, which was tempting to a man like Jonathan Arledge.

Now here he lay across a limb a few feet above her, and she hadn't noticed him. How could he climb down to her level and make his presence known without frightening her into a screech that would bring all her father's guests into the yard?

Suddenly he felt a heavy weight on the middle of his back and the telltale claws that had been his misfortune to experience twice before. "Damn you, Tartuffe!" Ethan hissed as he teetered back and forth and then fell to the ground with a thump.

He heard the leaves rustle and then saw the hem of a lady's gown approaching. Ethan looked up and grinned, feeling very foolish.

Lilly knelt beside him and giggled. "Ethan, are you injured?" She was amused to note she'd asked him the same question in her own bower, and now that scene was being repeated here!

Dusting himself as he went, Ethan rose and chuckled. "No, but before I climb another tree, I'm going to look for that devil's spawn of a cat, no matter where I am."

"A good habit, I'm sure," Lilly agreed. She felt light-hearted and giddy. Ethan was home—he was safe.

They stood looking at each other in the dim light. What should she do, she wondered. She wanted to throw herself into his arms, but she was too much of a lady. Remembering his cruel words the last time she'd seen him, she thought he might not be interested in her any longer.

"Lilly," he whispered and lifted her into his arms. He swung her around and hugged her, kissing her soundly as he stopped whirling. "Lilly, I'm happy to see you."

Before she could stop herself, her arms snaked around his neck, and she kissed him again and again. She felt so good in his arms, as if the weight of the world rested on someone else's shoulders for a little while. For a few moments Lilly acted like a schoolgirl again, but the reality of her age and her relationship with Ethan soon intruded, and she became more subdued.

"Put me down before I'm completely senseless!" she

cried and laid her head on his shoulder. "What if someone should hear or see us?"

"Then I fear we would both be in trouble. I'm a rebel, and you're consorting with one." Ethan let her slide through his arms until her feet touched the ground, but he didn't let go of her.

"Are you truly unhurt?" Lilly asked, feeling a little embarrassed for acting so foolishly. She looked up into his eyes, the jade color barely visible in the moonlight filtering through the sparse leaves on the live oak.

"Only my pride, Miss Arledge," he quipped and kissed her again. "Were you waiting for me in my tree?"

"Is this your tree?" she asked and glanced up into the branches. The trunk was as thick as a wagon wheel was round, and the limbs were wider than her hips. "One could easily hide here, lying atop a fat branch, and never be seen."

"True enough. How have you been?" Ethan gazed down into her eyes. In the dim light they were like onyx, black and glimmering. He brushed a wisp of hair off her forehead and inhaled the scent of jasmine that always seemed to cling to her.

"I have been well." Lilly smiled and rested her cheek against his chest. "Do you think perhaps we should find a more secluded spot to chat? I fear a certain Major Owens will be seeking my company this evening."

Ethan led her into the deep shadows of the thatch of live oaks until the house could hardly be seen through the abundance of branches. He laid his cloak on the ground, and they sat down, Lilly with her feet curled beneath her.

A barricade seemingly rose between them as they sat silently for a few moments, and Lilly wondered how to broach the subject she instinctively felt caused the silence. Cornwallis. To her, his defeat was a stunning loss; to Ethan, the defeat was a stellar victory. Would they ever move beyond their idealistic differences and truly care for each other without having to avoid certain subjects?

Since the loss occurred on the British side, Lilly decided that she must bring up the subject. "Ethan, I presume you've heard of Lord Cornwallis's defeat and surrender."

Ethan had been thinking of the same topic but didn't want to embarrass her by mentioning Britain's most resounding defeat. "I have. Word of Washington's victory spread quickly."

"I . . . We don't need to discuss the details, but I want to ask how you think this will affect the war. Is it over? Can we be friends again? I mean, the Patriots and the Loyalists." Lilly felt she wasn't expressing herself well.

"I'm afraid it's too soon to tell. But the war is still going on." Ethan stretched out and leaned back on his elbow. "I wish I could say it's over. You don't know how badly I want that to be true."

"No more than I." Lilly looked at him, relaxed beneath his trees. He belongs here, not me, she thought. What will happen when victory is proclaimed by one side or the other? "Ethan, I want to make a request of you."

"What is that, Lilly?" he asked softly.

"I . . . whenever the end comes, let it not affect our friendship." Lilly looked down at her hands. The live oak leaves shifted gently in the breeze, and the dappled moonlight moved like a luminous fluid over her and Ethan. "I do want us to remain close friends."

He drew her down beside him and looked into her eyes. Cradling her in his arms, he whispered, "Lilly, when this is all over, I pray that our friendship will be deepened and will know new dimensions."

CHAPTER 10

TINGLING WARMTH SPREAD THROUGH LILLY'S BODY as Ethan wrapped his arms around her. As his lips closed over hers, she thought that it was highly inappropriate for her to be lying on the ground beneath a tree with a man—especially after the dressing down she'd given Simon Owens earlier.

She didn't care. All she cared about at the moment was that Ethan's arms were around her, that his lips were pressed to hers, that her body nearly sang with joy at his touch. Filled with happiness, she shifted slightly so that her body and his were even closer. The most wonderful feeling came from being cuddled more intimately than ever before. Her breasts were thrust against his chest, and for the first time in her life Lilly wished the fabric weren't there to block the sensation of lying against Ethan.

"Oh, Miss Arledge!" She heard a masculine voice call across the lawn. "Miss Arledge, where are you?"

Ethan stiffened, turned slightly, and peered across the lawn. "Who is that?" he whispered.

"Undoubtedly, Simon Owens," Lilly murmured. "Where is he? Can you see him?"

"No. I can't . . . yes, there he is. Just coming out of the garden. He's going toward the dock and boathouse." Ethan thought for a moment. "Let's go to my mother's to see if he's been there yet. If not, you can say you were there and never heard him."

"How will we get there without being seen?" Lilly clung to Ethan, reluctant to allow anything to interrupt their stolen moments together.

Ethan looked down at her. He didn't want to move, except to get closer to her. "If you don't appear, he'll have every man in the house out looking for you."

"Let me go. I'll tell him I was walking . . . I'll tell him something. If he finds you, he'll . . ." Lilly couldn't say what she thought would happen if the soldiers in the house found Ethan. She simply knew it would be terrible. With the weight of Cornwallis's loss so recently thrust upon them, a single rebel would likely turn them into a lynching mob.

"Don't worry, love. I won't let him find me." Ethan kissed her quickly. "Come, we mustn't tarry."

Hesitantly Lilly allowed him to pull her to her feet. He gathered his cloak and shook the leaves and debris off before they started edging along beneath the protective branches of the live oaks toward the guest cottage.

"Just pray he hasn't checked the guest cottage yet." Ethan held her arm, and they walked as quickly as possible.

The protruding roots and low-hanging limbs impeded their progress, but they reached the cottage without being seen. Ethan waited to see if anyone could be seen approaching the front. "Here, let's go in the back way."

"Shouldn't you remain hidden?" Lilly pleaded, hoping to prevent Ethan from being captured. "I'll go alone."

"No. I'll take you in." Ethan took her hand, and they ran across the twenty feet of open ground before reaching the back of the guest cottage.

He knocked twice, once, then twice again. After a few

moments that seemed like hours, the door swung open and Octavia stood in the doorway.

"Come in, come in." Octavia backed out of the way and gestured for them to enter. "Hurry, Lilly. Prudence has been watching from upstairs, and she said that a soldier is headed this way."

Lilly slipped in front of Ethan and hurried into the parlor. Octavia followed her and pulled her back.

"One moment. There are leaves on your gown." Octavia brushed them off as quickly as possible and then led Lilly into the parlor. "So you see, Lilly, my dear, we've a nice setup. Cook complains about the small amount of space, but we're getting along well," Octavia said loudly so that anyone standing outside the front door would hear.

A loud rapping on the door made Lilly jump despite being prepared for Simon's arrival. She glanced behind her to make sure that Ethan couldn't be seen and dropped into a chair so Simon wouldn't notice how much she was shaking.

"Who's there?" Octavia called through the closed door.

"Simon Owens," came the reply.

Octavia opened the door a little and peered through the crack. "And who is Simon Owens? I don't believe I know you. Are you related to the Owens family of St. Thomas Parrish?"

Simon ignored the reference to relatives and jumped right in to explain. "I'm looking for Miss Arledge. I left her some short while ago taking the evening air in the garden. I had a quick errand to run and when I returned, she'd disappeared. I've called and called with no response. I'm concerned that she may have been walking and hurt herself."

"Miss Arledge is visiting with me, Mr. Owens." Octavia opened the door more fully. "As you can see, she's sitting here quite safe." Octavia turned to Lilly and smiled. "Miss Arledge, this young man is inquiring after your health."

"Please tell him I'm fine and thank him for being worried." Lilly tried not to laugh. She could see Simon's anguished expression, and it delighted her that he felt so badly about her disappearance.

He poked his head in the door and received a withering glare from Octavia, but he ignored it. "Miss Arledge, the hour is growing late. May I escort you back to the house?"

Lilly didn't want to go, but she knew that if she didn't, Simon would probably ask if he could stay and visit. She couldn't chance letting Simon discover Ethan in the house. "How kind of you."

She rose, walked over to Octavia, and hugged her gently. "Thank you for the tea and lovely company. It's nice to have you here to talk with."

"You are a delightful girl, Lilly. Come back soon." Octavia's green eyes glittered. She loved the idea of fooling the British in any way possible.

Lilly gazed at Octavia meaningfully. "Good night. Sleep well."

Lilly stepped outside and drew her shawl close around her shoulders and covered her bosom. "My goodness, but it's gotten much cooler since I went inside. Aren't you cold, Mr. Owens?"

"Call me Simon, please." Simon beamed down at her as they walked across the moonlit lawn. "Miss Arledge, it cannot have escaped your attention that I—"

"Gracious!" She screamed and clutched Simon's arm.

"Did you see that? Something moved! Do you think it's an alligator?"

Simon glanced to and fro. "Where? Close by?"

Lilly clung to him as if she were scared witless. "There, near the— It moved again! It must be an alligator. Can you see red eyes? They glow like coals."

Simon leaned forward and peered into the dark shadows where she was pointing. "Miss Arledge, are you sure? I can't see a thing except shadows."

Not caring whether he saw anything or not, she half-dragged him toward the house. She'd diverted his attention from the proposal he was about to make. Though he was scheduled to stay for another day, she didn't want to cause any questioning of loyalties by refusing his proposal any sooner than she had to. Her father had obviously given Simon approval to ask for Lilly's hand and would not take her rebuff lightly.

If she could avoid answering the question, she would. "Oh, my, run! I see its tail swinging back and forth. That alligator must be fifteen feet long."

Lilly ran as fast as she could. Simon, who still hadn't seen the alligator that existed only in Lilly's mind, hurried along beside her, all the while peering over his shoulder. When she reached the house, she never paused to allow him to open the door. She flung it open herself and sprinted through the main hallway and up the stairs. "Zip! Zip, where are you?"

She left a baffled-looking Simon Owens standing at the bottom of the staircase gazing after her. Lilly scurried into her room and closed the door behind her.

Zip was hanging a dress in the wardrobe and stared blankly at Lilly. "What's the matter? Who after my baby? If it's that no 'count Pappy of yours, I'll take a flat iron to him."

Lilly giggled at the image of her father being chased by Zip brandishing an iron. "No, not Father. It was Simon Owens."

"Harrumph. That goody-goody? He ain't got gumption 'nuff to chase no woman." Zip smoothed the satin and turned to face Lilly again. "He ain't done nothin' wrong, has he? He ain't acted improper to my baby, has he? I'll show that scoundrel right quick—"

"No, Zip, nothing like that." Lilly held her arms up while Zip pulled the dress off. "He wants to marry me. I think he asked Father for his blessing."

"You reckon that boy got enough money to make yo pappy satisfied?" Zip placed her hands on her hips and shook her head gently. "That man's a wonder to me. Makin' a loose woman of his own daughter. Sellin' her to the richest man. Too bad ole King George already married. I believe yo pappy'd have you settin' on the throne if he could'a finagled it."

"Zip," Lilly whispered and bent over the shorter woman so she wouldn't have to speak so loudly. "I've got to find a way to avoid Simon tomorrow. Do you have any suggestions?"

Zip grinned, as always ready to trick Lilly's father. "Honey chile, I believe you got a fever." She placed her hand on Lilly's forehead. "You's sweatin'. How come?"

"I ran all the way from the garden. I told Simon I saw an alligator on the lawn." Lilly giggled behind her hand. Zip caught the idea and nearly laughed out loud. Lilly pointed to the door, indicating that she'd heard a sound outside.

"I don't care who you wants to see. You ain't gettin' out'a that bed till Zip say so," Zip boomed loudly enough for everyone in the area to hear. "Now, you just rest yo'self. I'm gonna git a potion and set right here with you all night. The idea of you bein' out in the garden when the cool night air set in! You act like you ain't got no more sense than a field hand."

Grinning, Lilly slipped into her nightgown and slid between the covers. She could always depend on Zip to do and say the right thing. Tomorrow Lilly would have to answer questions, but for tonight, heaven and hell would have to be moved before anyone came through that door.

Zip opened the door and stepped briskly into the hall. From her bed Lilly could hear the scolding Zip gave to whoever was waiting in the hallway. Suspecting that it was her father, she closed her eyes and moaned slightly.

"Zipporah, I demand to see her. She's my daughter and—"

"She may be yo' daughter, but she my baby. She sick. Probably on account 'a you." Zipporah was whipping herself into a froth of anger. "You go disturbin' her, and Miss Thera's ghost gonna haunt you the rest of yo' days botherin' her baby like that. If Miss Thera'd lived, she'd have you hung for treatin' her baby like that. If Miss Lilly dies, it'll be on yo' head, not mine. Her white as a ghost and broke out in a cold sweat! Lawsy, don't take my l'il kitten away."

Lilly almost laughed out loud. Zip could put on an act to convince anyone of anything. In the hallway Jonathan stammered and stuttered about not realizing the seriousness of the situation. He commended Zip on her diligence and returned to the parlor.

Jonathan Arledge was frightened of almost nothing. But Lilly and Zip both knew he truly feared that his deceased wife would one day haunt him for the way he acted toward their daughter. Regardless of how warped he was, Jonathan loved his wife and always had. When she'd died in childbirth, he'd been mad with grief and never really recovered. Pressed for a name for the infant who survived the birthing, he called her Lilly after the baskets of lilies that stood at Thera Arledge's bier.

From early childhood Lilly knew her father saw her as the cause of his wife's death. Guilt-ridden as a girl, Lilly had grown up with the knowledge that he couldn't love her openly, but because she was his wife's daughter, neither could he turn his back on her completely.

Lilly always thanked God she didn't look like her mother. That would have made her father hate her even more. With hair the color of flames, Thera Arledge had been a stunning woman filled with grace and poise. Zip had made sure that Lilly knew everything about the kind, gentle person who had given birth to her.

With a figure like her mother's—full breasts, narrow waist, and slim hips—Lilly was frightened of marrying and bearing children. She was afraid that she, like her mother, would die in childbirth, though she never admitted her fears to anyone.

Zip returned quickly with a cool pitcher of water. She made a fuss loud enough for everyone to think she was trying to break Lilly's fever. After several minutes Lilly became frustrated with all the unwanted attention. She wanted to be left alone to think about her meeting with Ethan.

"Zip, I'll be fine. I just want to go to sleep," Lilly protested. "Please don't impair your own health looking after mine."

"I'll sleep in the kitchen. You pull that bell ringer and I'll come a'runnin' if you need me." Zip left and went down the stairs.

Lilly knew that Zip would report to Jonathan that Lilly had drifted into a fitful sleep and would be checked on periodically during the night to see if her condition worsened. A single candle burned on the mantel, and Zip had closed the inside shutters.

After a few minutes Lilly did fall into a light sleep. She dreamed that Ethan had come to her. She awoke and felt a hand cover her mouth.

"Shhh!" Ethan whispered. "It's me."

"Ethan?" Lilly murmured against his hand and breathed a little easier when he released her.

"What happened? I heard you scream." Ethan stretched out beside her on top of the covers. He hadn't anticipated finding her in bed when he'd sneaked across the lawn to discover what happened.

Lilly smiled and covered her own mouth. She felt like laughing. "Simon was going to ask for my hand. I couldn't think of any way to prevent it, so I screamed. When he asked what was wrong, I recalled his fear of snakes and alligators. I told him I'd seen an alligator coming toward us."

"He believed you?" Ethan asked incredulously. "What a dolt. Mother almost had to tie me down to keep me from running out of the cottage to see what was wrong."

"Oh, heavens, Ethan," she rasped, realizing for the first time what danger he was in. "Why didn't you stay there? You're in grave danger here. My father is pacified for the moment, but he could come in any time. Zip told him I was ill. Thank goodness she has a quick mind."

"Don't worry about me. I'm used to sneaking in and out of places—especially this one. I used to do it regularly as a boy." Ethan glanced around and was glad to see that she hadn't changed the room much.

"But you were eluding your parents. Now you must elude soldiers." Lilly thought a moment. "And my father and Zip."

"Don't you worry. I'll take care of myself." Ethan snuggled closer. "How did you end up in this room?"

"I . . . I don't really know. I just saw it and liked it, I guess." Lilly couldn't tell him the truth—that she'd picked the room because she thought it was his. She never dreamed that he'd come sneaking in here at night. "I'll move tomorrow if you don't want me here. I've tried to keep it as unchanged as possible."

Ethan chuckled. "I rather like the idea of you sleeping here."

Lilly was thankful that the dim light hid her blush. "I believe you're teasing me."

"Not really." Ethan propped up on one elbow and looked down at her. Her chestnut hair was flared out around her head like a soft halo, and the candlelight reflected in her dark eyes.

He hadn't planned on kissing her; he'd only intended to find out if she was injured and leave immediately. Now he didn't want to leave at all. He wanted to spend the night with her in his arms.

The danger for him was great, he realized. To prevent—or lessen—the possibility of discovery, he got up, walked to the mantel, and blew out the candle. If anyone entered the room, he'd simply slide off the side of the bed away from the door and hide beneath it.

Measuring his steps carefully so he wouldn't knock over the stand with the pitcher and bowl, he finally reached the bed again. "Mind if I join you for a few minutes? I wanted—"

"Here? Ethan, I do like you and—"

"Shhh! Someone will hear you." Ethan climbed over her and lay on the side of the bed nearest the wall. "I won't hurt you. I just wanted to talk. You will recall that we were interrupted."

"This is highly irregular," Lilly maintained and pulled the covers up to her chin primly.

"Lilly, I wanted to apologize for my anger during my last visit. I should have trusted you." Ethan allowed the words to tumble out. He wanted the apology behind him as quickly as possible. "Please forgive me."

"You already apologized," Lilly reminded him. "Your mother made you."

"I did that to appease her," he answered honestly. "Now I'm asking your forgiveness in earnest."

For a few seconds Lilly didn't know what to say. Her throat constricted, and her answer froze before it reached her lips. "I accept your apology wholeheartedly."

Ethan kissed her. Their bodies came together as if drawn by magnets. Ethan still lay on top of the covers and Lilly beneath. To Ethan, his memories were like shadows compared to the real Lilly. Holding her in his arms, he whispered her name over and over again.

Lilly found that she wasn't breathing. Her lungs burned, and her chest ached as she inhaled deeply. She felt his hand wriggling down between the covers and her back, but she didn't care. She wanted him to touch all of her. Guilt assailed her, but she ignored it. She could worry about that tomorrow. For now she wanted to know what love was, what being loved meant. For the first time in her life someone cared for her in spite of who she was, and she could have sung with happiness.

Ethan looked down at her and was filled with desire. He wanted to believe she was innocent, yet some part of him wondered if he hadn't misjudged her. Had she fooled him with a sweet charade? He hoped not. Fighting to maintain control of his passions, he held her close and breathed deeply. Would she welcome his advances or spurn them?

Unwilling to chance being rebuffed, Ethan smoothed her hair out of her face and kissed her again and again. He wanted to store enough kisses in his mind to keep him warm through the cold months to come.

Lilly thought she would lose consciousness if Ethan continued to ply her with such intoxicating kisses. Wriggling closer, she moaned as he plunged his tongue into her mouth and began to plunder its soft recesses. Wanting him to derive as much pleasure from the same gentle exploration, Lilly touched his tongue with her own. When he stopped, she tentatively slid her tongue past his teeth and tried to emulate his actions.

His breathing came in rasps, and he pushed her back against the pillows. Kissing her more fiercely than ever before, he drew his hand along the perimeter of her breast and brushed against her nipple, which swelled and hardened in his hand. Mentally cursing the fabric that kept him from enjoying the silky texture of her breast, he pushed her gown aside and slid his hand inside the opening to capture the taut nipple between his thumb and forefinger.

A noise coming from the hallway stopped him cold. The footsteps were coming toward his door. Ethan slipped away from Lilly and slid off the bed. He hoped she'd understand what was happening.

The door opened slightly. Lilly didn't move, nor did Ethan. From his position under the bed, he could see nothing, and he dared not risk the noise of moving to discover who'd opened the door. He suspected it was Lilly's maid, Zip, but it could easily be Jonathan.

After a few seconds the door closed. Ethan couldn't tell whether the person had entered the room or not, so he remained motionless and intended to do so until Lilly confirmed that they were alone. She hadn't moved a muscle since Ethan withdrew.

Lilly peered through a veil of lashes. Her father had opened the door, watched her for a few seconds, and then entered the room, closing the door behind him. She suspected that he wanted to see for himself that she was ill.

She instinctively knew her face was the color of ripe apples. If her father had looked from the doorway, he would have seen the color of her cheeks and assumed that the scarlet color arose from her fever. She hoped he wouldn't place his hand on her forehead to verify her condition.

After an interminable length of time, Jonathan opened the door and left. When the door shut behind him, Lilly lay stock still for a moment to make sure her father walked away. When she knew he wasn't listening at the door, she rolled over, touched Ethan on the arm, and whispered, "He's gone."

Ethan moved back to the top of the bed. "I suppose that I should leave. If I don't go now, I'll never leave."

"Good night, Ethan," Lilly whispered dreamily.

He kissed her one more time and answered, "Good night, Lilly."

When the sun rose, Lilly almost sprang out of bed. Where was Ethan? She'd forgotten to ask if he was staying more than one night. Since they were on opposite sides of the war, he probably couldn't answer that question for her. As she rummaged through her dresses for something to wear, she remembered that she was supposed to be ill in order to keep Simon Owens from proposing to her.

How could she find out if Ethan had left or not without seeing Simon? Lilly climbed back into bed and allowed the soft feather mattress to caress her on three sides. She would have no choice but to stay in bed until Simon left the plantation.

She heard Zip singing as she came down the hallway, but Lilly couldn't ask her for information. The servant had a temper and would more than likely forget that Ethan's whereabouts were a secret.

"My baby's awake." Zip placed a silver tray on the edge of the bed. "I got some hominy grits and ham to make you feel better."

Lilly didn't really want to eat. She wanted to go out to Octavia's and find out where Ethan was. Knowing she couldn't go, Lilly forced herself to eat. The day would pass so slowly while she wondered about him. Maybe she could slip out after dark and ask Octavia.

The morning dragged by. Lilly became irritable. She dozed off and on, but she didn't get up. Her father came in around noon to check on her, and she pretended to feel nauseated. He had a weak stomach and never could stand to be around anyone who might throw up.

While Dulcie was serving luncheon, Octavia came to visit. She knew that Ethan had come to see Lilly during the night. After Dulcie left, Octavia whispered, "My dear, you should have seen him. He was in such a state."

Lilly smiled and blushed without answering. She couldn't relate the details of Ethan's visit to anyone—least of all his mother.

"I thought I would have to tie him down to prevent him from barging into the group of soldiers sitting in the parlor." Octavia shook her head merrily and winked at Lilly. "Nothing would keep him from checking to make sure you were safe. I was able to slow him down long enough to keep him from acting rashly. I assume he climbed the post on the back of the piazza to get in as he always did as a child."

Lilly giggled at the picture. Little did Octavia know that climbing up and down trellises and support posts had gotten to be a habit with both of them. One of these days Lilly might tell her new friend, but not now. The experience was too fresh and exciting, but she couldn't resist asking if he had left the plantation. "Is he . . . still nearby?"

"I think you'll see him before he leaves." Octavia walked over and kissed Lilly on the forehead. "Don't lock your shutters tonight. I believe he plans to stop and say goodbye."

Nothing was as it should be, Lilly thought. Who could imagine that a man's mother would connive with him to see the woman he couldn't keep from his mind? Lilly was embarrassed enough about her own behavior, and now Octavia was actually telling her she approved of her alliance with Ethan!

CHAPTER 11

LILLY THOUGHT THE DAY WOULD NEVER END. DURing the afternoon, she received a note from Simon saying that he was dreadfully sorry she was ill. He had to return to duty but would be back soon to ascertain her condition. He also stated that he had a very important question to ask her.

Lilly crumpled the note. She knew he was waiting downstairs for an answer, and she couldn't think of anything to say that didn't smack of sarcasm. "Zip, tell him I'm far too weak to respond, but thank him for his concern," she instructed.

Confident that Zip would handle the situation, Lilly thought of Ethan. How long would she have to wait for his visit? How long would he remain with her? Would he kiss her again? Her questions made her restless—she tossed and turned and flopped about until she almost convinced herself she was ill.

She knew that her anxiety was due to the danger in which Ethan would place himself if he came to her bedroom again; but if she went out, her father would know her illness was a ruse. She had to remain in her room for at least one more day.

When Zip retired for the night, Lilly flung back the covers and rose. She paced back and forth until her feet were freezing. She didn't realize Ethan had entered her bedroom until she noticed the candle flickering and felt the cool air from the open window. She spun on her heels and almost fell into his arms.

After kissing her once, he blew out the candle and carried her to the bed. "Lilly, I can't stay more than a few minutes. I couldn't leave without seeing you once more."

"I'm glad. Lying here all day, I kept hoping you'd come back." Lilly knew she shouldn't have said such a thing to a man, but she felt they didn't have time for all the niceties and game-playing that most couples had. Ethan risked his life every day. To have forced their relationship into a preordained mold simply to satisfy convention would have jeopardized it forever.

No matter how hard she scolded herself for acting so boldly with Ethan, she couldn't get past the fact that she might never see him again. What would she do if that happened? Their ideological differences prevented her from seeing him in public, and by all realistic measures she shouldn't have been attracted to him. He stood for everything she did not—except that they both wanted peace. Was this the way a woman felt when she fell in love the first time? Did being in love mean something as simple as both parties liking the same foods or books? Could it simply be that they didn't argue? Could they be really different and be in love?

Since she had no prior experience in matters of love, Lilly didn't know the answers to her questions. In fact, the longer she knew Ethan, the more questions she discovered she couldn't answer.

"I can't ask when you're leaving. I don't want to know," Lilly said and peered up into his eyes. "Ours is a very extraordinary . . . friendship, wouldn't you say?"

"To say the least. I don't really know how to categorize it, and I don't think I really would want to try . . . yet," he added with a slight emphasis. He'd given a great deal of consideration to their relationship. When he held her in his arms as he was doing now, he never wanted to leave. When he lay on the cold, damp ground trying to sleep, her image swam before his eyes and spoiled his attempts to rest. "I want to know that you enjoy . . . being with me. That's all I ask for now."

It was more than enough for Lilly. She wanted to be with him every moment of the day, to explore this new-found wonder that he brought about. Nothing else seemed to matter when Ethan was near.

They lay together in silence for a long time before Ethan whispered, "I have to leave. I don't know when I shall return."

Lilly felt her heart pounding and wondered if Ethan noticed it as well. She didn't want him to leave, to risk his life; she wanted him here with her, safe and sound. "Ethan, promise me you'll be careful."

"I promise, Lilly." Ethan kissed her lightly and wondered if he'd ever be able to leave. Now he understood how the militia lost so many men when the battles and marches took them close to their homes. The men would sneak off to spend a few minutes with their wives or girlfriends and never return. If Ethan didn't have such a commitment to winning this war, he would have been content to remain with Lilly.

He knew he couldn't live with himself, however, if he abandoned the effort now. He felt that the war was drawing to a close. If the militia lost all its men, then the British would win easily with no opposition. On nights like this one he wished he had no convictions.

"If I don't leave now, I'll never leave," he murmured, nuzzling against her hair, which smelled of jasmine. It was a fragrance that would haunt him for many long nights ahead.

Lilly didn't trust her voice to answer, so she simply nodded. Their last kiss was poignant, sweet, searching, and she knew that he was trying to build memories as she was.

"Be safe, Lilly. Think often of me." Ethan kissed her forehead and rose. It took all his willpower to walk away from her.

Ethan watched the house for a long time before heading across the lawn and into the woods. He didn't want to expose Lilly to any more problems with her father. Nor did Ethan want anyone to know he'd been in the house.

When he reached the woods, he followed a narrow tributary to the north until he found the area where he'd left his horse. Mounting, he rode silently through the deep woods and tried to concentrate on his task.

So many of the militia thought that since Cornwallis had surrendered, the war was over. Gates, Marion, and Washington all disagreed. Those three generals knew that the outcome of a war depended not on one soldier alone, but upon the entire enterprise. Clinton still held New York. Wilmington, Savannah, and Charleston were still occupied. There was much yet to be done.

Many men had deserted, if indeed a man could desert an informal militia. South Carolina's militia comprised men who were volunteers. Nobody could really blame them for heading home to tend their farms and families when the most celebrated British general had surrendered.

The real test of strength was yet to come. Finding a way to expel the British from America's cities wouldn't be easy, nor could it be accomplished without manpower. Ethan was heading toward upcountry South Carolina, searching for men who'd be willing to remain with the militia for a while longer.

Drake Hastings, a British captain who'd turned Patriot spy, had sent word that men were to be had around the Tyger River area and Gowan's Fort. Ethan rode as quickly as he could over the rough terrain well off the more traveled roads to reach his destination.

Ethan knew that Drake Hastings was related to Lilly in some way by marriage. Lilly's cousin, Noelle Arledge, had married Captain Hastings of the British Army shortly after he'd disclosed that he was in truth a spy for the Patriots, according to Bowie Gallagher. Since going with the Patriots on a full-time basis, he'd been promoted to colonel. His bravery was legendary.

Ethan wondered about the end of the war. Would the three cousins—Lilly, Noelle, and Erin—come together with their families and make peace? Lilly and her father were the only Tories in the family. How would the others respond to them after the war?

Since he knew Erin, Ethan thought she'd forgive her cousin easily. Jonathan was another matter. Lilly had intimated that he had always been the scoundrel in the family and wasn't likely to change. Bowie had given Ethan a letter to take to Noelle Arledge Hastings instructing her to provide whatever comfort she could to him. Ethan hoped he'd reach Tyger Rest without encountering trouble.

Lilly awoke with a terrible headache. Long after Ethan left, she had lain awake staring at the window. She didn't want to get out of bed but knew she couldn't remain in bed all day. Sooner or later she'd have to go downstairs.

Zip brought Lilly a cup of tea and some hominy, which she played with for a few minutes, but she ate little. Lilly decided she wanted to see Octavia, so she rose and dressed quickly. She pulled on her homespun to work in the garden—whether it needed tending or not.

The fresh air was cold and invigorating. She hugged her cloak close about her and took a small spade into the garden. She found Octavia already there.

Octavia glanced up to see who was coming toward her. "I see you had the same idea as I had."

Lilly didn't really know how to answer, so she nodded. Octavia was sweet, and Lilly already loved her as a friend. Her reserve came when she looked upon Octavia as Ethan's mother. Since Lilly didn't know exactly how she felt about Ethan, she didn't always feel completely at ease with his mother.

He hadn't said where he was going, and Lilly hadn't asked. She didn't want to know anything that she could inadvertently pass on that could be used against him, even though he fought on the opposite side of the war. Where Ethan was concerned, Lilly wanted to remain neutral.

As she dug the weeds from around the seedlings, Lilly pictured Ethan in her mind. She could feel his touch and shivers of pleasure darted down her spine. She knew little of the act of love, and what she knew was subject to an interpretation given by her friend Mari, who knew no more than Lilly. The two girls had spoken of kissing and of "that other thing," as Mari called it, but neither had any concrete information. Lilly didn't get the idea that Mari had experienced the same quivers of excitement and desire, or if she had, she'd never mentioned it. Lilly could almost feel Ethan's hand on her breast and blushed with the memory of how she'd felt.

Had Mari ever allowed a man to touch her breast? She was more forward than Lilly. Until Ethan had done it, Lilly never thought she would enjoy it and was embarrassed that she did. If he'd ever had any doubt about her character and morals, he most certainly didn't now—thanks to her own lack of discipline.

But he'd come back. And he hadn't touched her so intimately again. Did that mean he didn't enjoy touching her? She'd always supposed that men really liked that sort of thing, but now she wondered. "A man's pleasure and a woman's curse," Zip had called it. Lilly didn't know what to believe now.

"Lilly, my dear!" Octavia called for the third time.

"Oh, I'm sorry, Mrs. Kendall. I . . . I suppose I was daydreaming."

Octavia laughed and shook her head gently. "I'm not scolding, dear. I just wondered if you felt well."

"Oh, I'm fine. Why do you ask?" Lilly felt foolish now.

"You look so flushed." Octavia removed her gloves and touched Lilly's forehead. "No fever. Well, I suppose it could be because of the cool air."

"Must be," Lilly mumbled and began to dig again. She didn't want to look silly in Mrs. Kendall's eyes, so she resolved to work harder and pay close attention to what she was doing.

"Lilly, dear, you're forgetting. You promised to call me Octavia. I feel so old when you call me Mrs. Kendall." Octavia placed her spade on the ground and reached over to pat Lilly's hand.

Lilly's smile made Octavia feel wonderful. The young woman was so intense, so understanding, and so caring that Octavia would have been proud to claim Lilly as a friend anytime, but especially now. They were on opposite sides of the war, but Lilly's sight went beyond today and took into consideration the fact that sometime in the future everybody would have to forget the war, whether they were victors or losers.

After a moment Lilly said, "I try to call you Octavia, but old habits are hard to break."

"I know." Octavia sat back on her heels and surveyed the vegetable garden.

"Octavia, may I ask you a rather personal question?" Lilly said, wondering if she could really voice her fears.

Octavia leveled her gaze at Lilly. Something was troubling the girl, and Octavia hated to see the pain across Lilly's face. "Of course you may. Ask me anything you wish. I'll answer as honestly as I can."

Now that she'd been given permission to ask a personal question, Lilly didn't know how to phrase it. She simply blurted it out. "You're so, I mean, giving birth is difficult, and you're tiny. Did . . . did you have any trouble?"

Octavia closed her eyes for a moment. She'd never considered that Lilly might be frightened of having children. During the course of their friendship, Lilly had confided that her mother died in childbirth. "My dear Lilly. Nobody can say whether you'll have difficulty bearing children or not. I won't gloss over the facts. It's a painful and humbling experience, but also the most beautiful. Many small-boned women give birth with no complications."

"I . . . I'm sorry to ask something so personal, but I don't really know anyone else to ask." Lilly returned to her gardening. She was embarrassed to have asked the question but glad to know its answer. "I love babies. I'm just scared of the unknown, I guess."

"We all are, Lilly. You're not alone." She allowed her gaze to take in the expanse of lawn and the formal ornamental garden. She loved every inch of Carolina Moon. "What do you suppose will happen to us when the war is over?"

"Nobody can say, Octavia. I pray that we can all be sensible and go back to being friends and neighbors. Someone has to win and someone has to lose. I hope that one side can be as gracious in victory as the other will be gracious in defeat."

"Fine sentiments. I pray you're right." Octavia sighed and half smiled. I guess we'll always have a few who never want to let the war be over."

"I'm sure that's true. I hope there aren't too many of them, though," Lilly answered and stuck her spade in the earth. "What of Ethan, Octavia? What will he do?"

Octavia gazed at Lilly. She could see the spark of interest in those large brown eyes that almost seemed to speak. "I always expected him to come back here and take up where he left off. We were never really politically minded people. We were country people who loved our home and land. Ethan felt compelled to fight for . . . but you know that. You probably know how deeply he feels about self-government."

Lilly shook her head. "Not really. We . . . we sort of avoid talking about either side."

"Smart policy. Well, he feels quite strongly that we should have a voice in our government." Octavia looked up at the cornflower-blue sky punctuated by a glaring sun that mocked them as the cold wind blew and cut through their cloaks. "I hope that people will feel that way after the war."

The days passed quickly. Octavia and Lilly spent a short time in the garden each day as November grew cooler. Octavia supervised the cleaning staff, and Lilly watched and learned. She'd never been trained in the finer arts of housekeeping, although she'd managed to muddle through.

As time passed, Lilly and Octavia became fond of each other. They spoke little of Ethan, as if by agreement, but Lilly always wondered whether Ethan had returned home or not. She found that she couldn't ask. Spending time with Octavia became the focal point of Lilly's day. It was as if by substituting his mother for Ethan, Lilly somehow felt closer to him—and she always walked to the small copse of live oaks each night before retiring.

The nights passed slowly. Lilly often lay awake, wondering if Ethan would slip through the window again. Even if he came to see Octavia, Lilly didn't know whether he would come to see her.

Lilly always seemed to be in trouble with her father when he was home. He stayed home more and more, always with a few troops to insure that they wouldn't be attacked.

Ethan rode down a lane past rattling bushes and shrubs. Bowie had mentioned this when he'd given Ethan the directions to Noelle's house. In the moonlight he could see a large patch on the roof and wondered what had happened. Then he recalled something about Indians setting the house on fire.

The terrain was far different here from the low country. Ethan had ridden up and down hills, through dense forests, and across cold, rushing streams. He found the landscape beautiful and intimidating. He—and his horse—grew tired much more quickly, but he never tired of looking at the mountain peaks that appeared to be getting much closer.

Ethan had made several stops at farms along the way

and enlisted the help of several men. At the moment they were camped south of Noelle's plantation, Tyger Rest, on the banks of the Tyger River. He'd spend the night here, if Noelle could spare the room, and head toward Gowan's Fort in the morning.

He tied his horse to a tree, stepped onto the broad porch, and rapped loudly on the door. He heard the sound of footsteps stop.

"Noelle!" he called, hoping to allay her fears. "I'm Ethan Kendall, friend of Bowie Gallagher. He sent me here to recruit men for the—"

The door swung open, and a petite woman peered out at him. "You know Bowie? Do you know my husband as well?"

"No, ma'am. I've heard of Colonel Hastings but never met him," Ethan admitted and reached inside his cloak for the letter of introduction Bowie had given him. "Here. This letter is from Bowie Gallagher."

"Come in." Noelle stepped back into the keeping room and closed the door behind him. "Please, make yourself at home. I'll send Mandy for some coffee."

Noelle stepped to the back door and called across the short distance to the kitchen. Within a few seconds she returned to the keeping room and sat on the end of the sofa closest to the fire. "You must be freezing. Warm yourself here by the fire until Mandy comes."

Ethan stood in front of the fire and held out his hands to warm them. While the circulation began to come back, he studied Noelle. She looked almost nothing like her cousins. All of them had vastly different coloring, but like the other two girls, Noelle was beautiful.

Noelle read the words of the letter and smiled. She glanced up at Ethan and nodded. "Ah, Bowie says you and my cousin Lilly are good friends."

"As close as we can be, ma'am. You see, she's a Tory. That makes being friends difficult during this war." Ethan loved the twinkle in Noelle's eyes. She seemed to be filled with joy for some reason. Then he noticed. Below her full breasts, her waist was thick and rounded. Noelle was pregnant.

She gazed at him, and he quickly looked back at the fire. Embarrassed to be caught staring at a pregnant woman, he babbled on, "Of course, Lilly and I try not to talk about the war. Being on different sides makes . . . friendship tough."

Noelle wondered if he'd almost said love. She could see that Ethan cared a great deal for Lilly, and Noelle was delighted. Lilly had seemed so alone. Her last letter spoke of Jonathan as if she hated him. She mentioned the horrible fashions she was forced to wear and how her father wanted her to be "kind" to the soldiers he brought home.

"Mr. Kendall, would—"

"Call me Ethan. I'm much more comfortable with that." Ethan grinned and removed his cloak now that he was getting warmer. "Is Colonel Hastings here?"

"No, I'm sorry to report that he isn't. He is with Greene's forces. He fought with Daniel Morgan at the Cowpens, but now his regiment is with Greene." Noelle read the last few lines of Bowie's letter. "A little girl! How wonderful."

Ethan grinned. "That man is mad about his little girl. I'll bet she's going to be the most spoiled child in all of Charleston when this war is over."

Noelle sighed and folded the letter. "When the war is over. . . . I hope it's soon." She placed her hand across the bulge in her stomach. "Mr. Kendall . . . Ethan, I'm going to have a baby soon."

"My congratulations to you and Colonel Hastings, ma'am." Ethan strode to a wing chair and sat down. "Lilly will be happy to hear the news—that is, if you don't mind my telling her about it."

"Oh, no. Please do," Noelle hastened to assure him. "Ethan, will you take a letter to her for me?"

"I will. She's at my plantation, Carolina Moon." Ethan smiled and scratched at a spot on his breeches. He wondered what she was doing.

"Your plantation? What's she doing there?" Noelle asked and rose as Mandy entered the room. "Ah, here's the coffee. Gracious, Ethan, Mandy put a platter of ham and hominy and two baked apples on the tray for us. Are you hungry?"

Ethan grinned broadly. "You bet I am. I haven't eaten a decent meal in days."

"There are biscuits, too." Noelle signaled to Mandy, who went back into the next room. "Come, Ethan, let's eat at the dining table. We can continue to talk there."

Once they were settled at the table and their plates piled with food, Noelle repeated her question. "What's Lilly doing at your plantation? Has something happened to Uncle Jonathan?"

Ethan's jaw tightened, and his fork clattered to the plate. "Pardon me, ma'am, but that man's a low-down, stinking—"

"Yes, that's my uncle. My father used to say, 'My brother is lower than a snake's belly,' and I heartily agree." Noelle patted the corners of her mouth with her napkin. "But what about Lilly?"

"Both of them are at Carolina Moon." Ethan's fingers flexed into a fist, and he pounded the table. "I'm sorry, ma'am, but I get furious when I think about him. He's working for John Cruden, the Commissioner of Sequestrated Estates. Jonathan came out and looked over my place and decided to make it his own. Now he and Lilly are settled there, and my mother is living in the guest cottage."

Noelle reached over and patted Ethan's hand consolingly. "I'm so sorry. I heard that was being done all over the low country. Some people weren't even allowed to take their clothing with them."

"If it wasn't for Lilly, I don't know where my mother would be. Lilly stood up to her father and insisted that he allow Mother to remain at the guest cottage instead of sending her off without a place to live." Ethan breathed slowly, trying to keep from losing his temper completely. "He actually struck Lilly across the face."

Noelle cupped her chin in her hands. Erin, her other cousin, had indicated that Uncle Jonathan might abuse Lilly, but Noelle had tried not to believe it. "I'm so sorry. Do you think she would come and stay with me?"

"I don't think so, but you can ask her in your letter." Ethan considered the idea for a minute. He'd see her less if she came all the way up here, but she'd be out of her father's abusive reach. "If she wants to come, I'll escort her, Mrs. Hastings."

"I would appreciate that. You're a kind man, Ethan. And please, call me Noelle." Noelle ate in silence for a few minutes and then looked at Ethan. "I believe Lilly has a good friend in you, Ethan."

The next morning, Ethan rode away from Tyger Rest with a full stomach and full saddlebags. Gowan's Fort was about twenty-five miles north of Tyger Rest, and Ethan covered the distance fairly quickly. As he came into view of the fort, he sensed that something was wrong. His horse shied, prancing from side to side on the narrow road. Ethan listened, but heard no calls to indicate that the sentries had seen him coming.

Ethan spotted a woman walking toward him. As she got closer, he wanted to dismount and retch. The woman had been scalped and was wandering aimlessly. He jumped down and ran to the woman. "Ma'am, what happened? Who did this to you?"

"All dead. They're all dead. Them Cherokees and Tories just killed everybody." She reached up and touched her still-bleeding head. "Will hair grow back? I'm gonna die, too. When I get to heaven, I won't have any hair."

Ethan closed his eyes and tried to breathe deeply. He could smell death. "Stay here, ma'am. I'll go and have a look."

He led her to a fallen tree and helped her to sit down. "Don't move. I'll get help for you."

Before the woman could answer, Ethan ran for his horse and urged him into a full gallop. She couldn't be right. The woman must be wrong. There were no Tories up here that he knew of. Where had they come from? Where had they gone?

Ethan rode, unhindered, into the fort. Its gates hung open, exposing the full stench of death to him. Bloated bodies lay scattered everywhere. Men, women, children. Almost falling from his horse, Ethan tried to dismount. He collapsed on the ground and heaved until nothing else could come up. The devastation was beyond anything he'd ever seen.

He'd find no help in this area. When he could stand again, Ethan made a cursory search to make sure there was no one left alive. Satisfied that he could do nothing for anyone at the fort, he rode slowly back to the woman who sat as still as a statue on the log where he'd left her.

Without knowing what he could do with her, he lifted

the woman into his saddle and climbed up behind her. "Where can I take you, ma'am? Do you have kin around here?"

Her chin touched her chest, and she wanly shook her head. "All a' my kin's back there dead. I ain't got nobody left."

Ethan decided that he'd take her to Noelle's. He had no other choice. The woman smelled of blood and death, and Ethan almost retched again, but he held on to her. She needed a loving hand to help her recover.

Toward the middle of November Lilly made her nightly trek to the copse of live oaks. She often climbed onto one of the low-hanging limbs and hoped that if someone looked for her, she would be hard to find. At other times she wore an old cloak and sat in the browning grass.

This particular evening she removed her cloak and spread it out on the ground under the densest foliage. She didn't want to be discovered, but she wanted to lie on her back and gaze at the sky. Though she was chilly, she loved to stare at the stars as they flickered into view, taking their places among myriad others that looked down on her. The moon rose like a golden ball over the skeletal limbs of the cypress trees reaching toward the heavens. She ignored the wisps of clouds that stretched like silken streams over the stars and moon, only to drift away again.

The moon seemed brighter, more alive with its golden color than usual. As it rose higher, the color gradually changed and bathed Carolina Moon in a web of silvery light. Lilly lay there, wondering where Ethan could be, when she heard a sound. A twig snapped. A leaf crunched. Someone was walking toward her.

She glanced toward the house and wondered if one of her father's cronies had followed her. Lilly wasn't afraid of them. She could—and had—put them in their place. If whoever was coming toward her was a guest at Carolina Moon, she didn't care. She'd send him on his way. But if the person was a stranger, there was no telling what desperate act a drifter might commit.

Then she decided that whoever was creeping toward her might not have seen her. Or it might be an animal. Lilly looked longingly at the limbs above her. If only she'd climbed up instead of lying down.

Listening carefully, she lay as still as a mouse. It seemed that the noise was human because there wasn't enough of a disturbance for it to be an animal. She didn't know whether to be relieved or dismayed.

Her heart pounded, and she felt that it could be heard all the way back to Charleston. She closed her eyes and forced herself to breathe slowly for a minute, hoping to maintain her composure. If she lay still enough, whoever was walking toward her would never be able to see her in the darkness.

"Lilly," Ethan called, hoping that she was still alone. He knew about where she was, having seen her spread her cloak and lie down before darkness fell in earnest.

He'd watched for a few minutes to see if anyone joined her. During that time, he didn't like the way he felt. He didn't like the way he'd felt for several days. The rational part of him knew that Lilly didn't have any part in the massacre at Gowan's Fort, but she was a Tory, and when he'd seen the devastation, he'd hated all Tories. He tried to tell himself that some of the Patriots weren't as fair and honest as others, too, but he simply couldn't imagine anyone low enough to do what those Indians and Tories had done, and he got sick every time he thought of it.

All the way home from the upcountry, he'd tried to decide whether to tell her about the massacre or not. He'd have to wait to make that decision. For now he wanted to forget it and be happy for a few minutes—shutting out the war completely.

"Lilly," he called softly. This time he caught her attention.

"Ethan? Over here." She moved so he could see where she was. "I'm here."

Ethan tumbled down onto her cloak and drew her into his embrace. He needed comfort and love, open and honest and undemanding. He knew of no place else to get that kind of reception. "Lilly, I'm so happy to see you."

Before she could answer, he ground his lips on hers in a kiss far more passionate than any they'd shared. They fell back on the cloak and spent the next few minutes making up for the time they'd lost. Ethan couldn't get enough of her sweet kisses this time.

When he drew back to look at her, he knew she didn't understand what had happened to him. He realized, at the same time, that he couldn't tell her right now. He didn't want the ugly realities of the war to intrude on their mutual joy.

Holding her so tightly he thought her fragile bones would break, he nuzzled against her soft, free-flowing hair. "My God, but I missed you, love."

CHAPTER 12

LILLY'S HEART SEEMED TO TAKE FLIGHT. *LOVE.* HE'D called her love. Taking advantage of his pause, she kissed him, darting her tongue into his mouth. She set off another barrage of kisses.

Ethan was almost wild with desire. He needed her desperately, but he couldn't take advantage of his condition or hers. He rolled away from her and sat up. "Lilly. We can't go on doing this. We're going to end up . . . what I mean to say is, if we . . . well, you're young and innocent and don't know where all this could—"

"Ethan, shhh." Lilly sat up and put her arm around him. "Just lie here beside me and let me comfort you. I . . . I'm not sure what's happened, but you're distraught."

He glanced at her. The glade was far too dark for him to see her face now that the moon had deserted them for the security of hiding behind an ominous-looking cloud. He wanted to make love to her. It was as simple as that. For the last few miles he'd thought of nothing but her soft, silky skin and the taut nipple he'd captured between his thumb and fingers that one night. He wanted to forget war and destruction and death. For a day or so he wanted to pretend that it didn't exist. He wanted to pretend that he and Lilly were fighting for the same cause.

Drawing his fingers down her cheeks, he lay back with her. Her arms encircled him and pulled him close, and he allowed her to comfort him for a few minutes. He felt like a storm-tossed ship reaching safe harbor.

His desire for Lilly almost consumed him. He couldn't remember when he'd felt this way about a woman and finally concluded that he'd never felt this way before. The relationship that had begun only a little more than a month ago in Charleston had blossomed into—into what? Love.

Ethan couldn't afford to be in love. He was a soldier. He refused to place a woman—Lilly—in a situation where she would wonder about his safety day and night. Maybe after the war was over, he might consider marriage. Marriage? He sat bolt upright and stared back at Lilly.

He'd never thought seriously about marriage in his life, and here he was not only thinking about it, but trying to decide when would be the best time to consider it.

"What's wrong?" Ethan acted like she'd bitten him.

"Wrong? Eh, nothing," he lied, trying to think of a way to convince her that the problem was not something she'd done, but something he'd thought of. "I'm sorry. I just . . . never mind. I'll tell you about it some day."

Lilly studied him carefully. He seemed to be nervous all of a sudden, as if he'd remembered something really important, something he should have done or didn't want to do. She felt embarrassed now and sat up beside him. "Tell me what's wrong. You've been . . . upset ever since you arrived, and now you act as though you'd just discovered I have bubonic plague or something worse."

"I apologize. I just had a thought that startled me. I'm sorry if I upset you." Ethan slid his arm around her and pulled her close. "Don't mind me. I'm fidgety because I've been on the trail too long alone."

"If it will help you to talk to someone, go ahead. You know I won't . . . Your words go no farther than from your mouth to my ears. I would never say anything to jeopardize your life." Lilly brushed a hank of hair out of his face and caressed his cheek. "I like you a lot, Ethan."

He stared at her. She liked him a lot. Was he too late? Had she fallen in love with him already? Ethan cursed himself for not ending this relationship sooner, when he still had the willpower. "Lilly, I like you a lot, too. We're facing a terrible situation. The war is still going on. I'm in danger every day. I don't want you to worry about me."

"You can't control my mind, Ethan. I already worry about you, and you can't say anything to make me feel any different than I feel now." Lilly spoke slowly, thoughtfully. "We will eventually have to face the most horrible part of the war—the reconciliation. I think we can be mature enough to understand each other's role in this abominable war."

Lilly was right. He admired her for being able to say the words he wanted to say himself but couldn't. She was telling him that she loved him, that she would wait! He couldn't bring himself to answer with words.

Ethan eased Lilly back on the cloak and kissed her again. For now they needed no words between them. He needed her to hold him, to kiss him, and to ask no questions. In time he would volunteer the answers, but not now.

Lilly responded as passionately as she knew how. She kissed him in return for his kisses and ran her fingers through his thick blond curls. He smothered her with kisses over her eyelids, across her cheeks, down her neck, across her cleavage, until she almost cried out for him to do more.

Rain began to fall. At first it pattered on the leaves and grass and then fell in a deluge. Ethan sprang to his feet and pulled Lilly up with him. "Come on, love, we can reach the cottage before we get drenched."

They didn't. By the time they arrived at the cottage, both of them were soaked. Ethan rapped lightly on the back door as he had before, and Octavia opened it without lighting a candle or saying a word.

When she saw that Lilly was with Ethan, she drew them into the parlor. "Ethan, toss a log on the fire." Octavia walked to the staircase and called, "Prudence!"

She returned to the parlor and helped Lilly remove her cloak. "For heaven's sake, where were you two?"

"We were—"

"Ah! Prudence," Octavia interrupted. "Find my umbrella and go up to the main house. Lilly needs dry clothing. Tell Zip to explain to Mr. Arledge that Lilly will remain with me until this torrential downpour subsides. I won't have her falling ill again."

"Yas'm," Prudence said and ambled out of the cottage.

"Ethan, go into the pantry and remove your clothing. I'll find a way to make sure it dries." Octavia took Lilly's arm and guided her up the staircase. "I'll find a dressing gown for you to wear until your dry clothing arrives."

Lilly allowed herself to be led away from Ethan. Though she would rather have stayed with him, she followed Octavia up the staircase without resisting. Lilly knew better. When Octavia made up her mind, there was no changing it.

She saw Ethan shrug and hurry into the kitchen, presumably to hide in the pantry until his clothing dried out. When they reached Octavia's room, Lilly smiled wanly. "I'm so sorry to trouble you. Your house is much closer than the big house."

"Nonsense. You're no trouble at all." Octavia threw a log on the grate and helped Lilly to undress. "My dear girl, your skin is like ice. How long have you been out . . . walking?"

Lilly sneezed. "Not too long. I try to get away alone. All those men Father brings home are disgusting. I ran into Ethan."

"Well, he should be ashamed for not paying attention to the weather. Anyone with a grain of sense would have noticed that the moon had hidden behind those clouds." Octavia scuttled about, searching for a dressing gown that would fit Lilly. "This will have to do."

"Thank you." Lilly slipped on the robe and found her legs bare from the knee down. She considered what Octavia had been saying about the moon and clouds. Ethan's mother had been watching for him. Lilly sat down and gazed at Octavia. "How did you know to expect Ethan tonight?"

Surprised at how quickly Lilly picked up on her blunder, Octavia stopped puttering for a moment and faced Lilly. How much could the young woman be trusted? Would she falter and let information slip as Octavia herself had? She doubted it. Lilly rarely talked to anyone else. Octavia decided to be honest. "I have a place where I get messages from Ethan."

Tears warmed Lilly's eyes. Octavia had knowingly placed her son's life in Lilly's hands. "I won't ask where. And don't tell me."

"Whatever you think is best, my dear." Octavia felt relieved.

"Be assured that no one will ever hear anything from me that could jeopardize Ethan's life." Lilly hugged Octavia.

Both women sat there for a few minutes, holding and comforting each other. Lilly knew that Octavia must worry about Ethan tremendously. Every battle she heard about must send her into hysterics until she knew her son was safe.

During the past few weeks, Lilly had come to feel the same way. I love him, she told herself. Could she tell him?

Prudence returned quickly with Lilly's dry clothing. After she'd donned her dress and cloak, Lilly took Octavia's umbrella and ran across the lawn after saying a quick goodbye to Ethan. If someone had become suspicious and was watching Octavia's house, Lilly didn't want to be the one to give away Ethan's whereabouts.

By the time she reached the back door, she was sneezing in earnest. She folded the umbrella, shook it, and leaned it against the inside door facing.

Zip stood there, arms akimbo, waiting for Lilly. "Ain't got sense to git out of a shower 'a rain. I raised you better than that. Lawsy mercy, I cain't believe you a full-grown woman and don't have no more sense than to go walkin' in the rain."

Lilly would have answered, but she started sneezing again. Still scolding, Zip toddled along behind Lilly and stopped only long enough to ask Applejack to bring water for a bath.

When Lilly reached her room, all she wanted to do was have a cup of tea and go to bed. She was shivering so badly that she could hardly talk.

Zip lit a fire, and the room was soon warm and cozy. "Miss Thera, if you up there a-lookin' down here, don't be blamin' ole Zip if Lilly catches her death a' cold." Zip raised her hands in supplication and, still muttering, moved about the room looking for something to do.

Applejack and one of the house servants arrived with buckets of steaming water. Zip supervised while they made several trips to fill the tub for Lilly's bath. By the time Lilly lowered herself into the hot water, she was beginning to get warm.

The bath soothed her, and she climbed out reluctantly. Zip helped her to dry off and put on a nightgown. Within minutes Lilly snuggled down into the warmth of her—Ethan's—feather mattress and fell asleep.

When Lilly opened her eyes again, sunlight was streaming through the windows. She glanced around and saw that she was alone. Before Zip brought breakfast, Lilly raced to the window and peered out at the cottage. The trees were whipping back and forth in the stiff wind, but there was nobody in sight. She couldn't spot anything exciting going on, nor did she think she would, but she wanted to see Ethan again. Had he gone yet?

Raindrops glistened on the grass and piazza, and the storm clouds were clearing. By noon the grass should be dry enough for Lilly to visit Octavia.

Zip opened the door and brought in a tray. "I hopes you ain't got a cold. Now eat all this and don't leave a drop. Feed a cold and starve a fever."

"Mari says starve a cold and feed a fever," Lilly said almost automatically as she tore into her breakfast, having discovered that she was starving.

"Harrumph. I know you ain't foolish enough to believe that silly girl." Zip pulled a morning gown from the wardrobe and laid it across the bed. "What you gonna do with all them men's clothes I stuck in the dressin' room?"

Lilly stared wide-eyed at Zip. Had she noticed something? Had she seen Ethan? Lilly gulped down a mouthful of food. "Why do you ask?"

"Well, I knows it ain't right to take folks clothes and all, but Applejack sure needs a new shirt." Zip placed a pair of slippers and pattens by the bed.

"I'll ask Olivia about them. I think she'll be happy to give him one of them, but I don't believe we should ask for more." Lilly returned to her eating with gusto. She'd go right after breakfast to see Octavia—and Ethan.

Lilly dressed carefully. She wore the same dress she usually wore for working, but took extra time with her hair and pinned a pretty kerchief around her shoulders and over her bosom. By the time she reached Octavia's door, Lilly was glad Zip had laid out the iron pattens. The mud was thick in places, and the extra height kept her gown and slippers clean.

She sat down and listened to Octavia prattle on about so much needing to be done. Lilly wrote while Octavia called out chores that needed to be done.

"I said washing," Octavia repeated and placed her hands on her hips to watch Lilly for a moment. "I think your mind is occupied elsewhere."

"What? Oh, I'm sorry. I guess I was daydreaming." Lilly carefully listed washing on the next line. "Now I'm all caught up. What's next?"

"You wore your pattens?" Octavia asked and waited for Lilly's nod. "Good. Go down by the creek and gather some mushrooms."

"Mushrooms?" Lilly repeated.

"Yes. I fancy a bowl of mushroom soup on a cold day like this." Octavia disappeared into the kitchen and returned with a basket. "Follow the river to the first creek and then follow it a ways. You'll come to some rocks, a peculiar formation that looks like a fat sea turtle. There are mushrooms around there that are fine for cooking. Run along. Don't dawdle."

Lilly did as she was told. Her cape whipped around her in the wind, but she pulled it close and followed the river. At the first creek she branched off and walked for a long time before coming to some rocks. She studied them for a moment and decided that they might possibly resemble a turtle.

Walking along the bank, she spied the mushrooms and began to pick. She had to hold on to her cloak with one hand and pick with the other. The basket tumbled along in the wind, but she caught it before it spilled all her mushrooms and placed a small stone in the bottom to keep the basket from blowing away. The ground was strewn with rocks, but up ahead the boulders jutted out of the ground and rose into a bluff that soared above the little stream. As Lilly walked along selecting the nicest of the mushrooms, she heard a noise and stopped. It sounded like a low whistle, but she heard it only once. She glanced around and saw nothing, so she continued to pick her mushrooms, wondering how many Octavia would need.

A little higher on the bluff she could see better. She could see the entire plantation. Lilly sat down on a stone and enjoyed the beautiful view for a few moments. Then, humming softly, she returned to her chore. She decided that the wind would bother her less if she picked in the shelter of the large boulders.

As she rounded a particularly large one, she ran into Ethan face to face. She dropped her basket, fell into his arms, and welcomed his kisses. He lifted her easily and carried her into a small cave formed by the seams in the rocks.

"I used to play here as a child." Ethan put her down when they entered a tiny room. "My humble playhouse, Miss Arledge."

Lilly looked around. There were jars of water and food, blankets, books, candles, and clothes. "You have a lovely home."

"Yes, I do." He wrapped his arms around Lilly. "I wanted to come up to your room last night, but Mother refused. She said I'd track mud across the piazza and all over the lovely carpet, and you'd be in danger."

"She's probably right," Lilly admitted, although she would have gladly stayed up all night scrubbing the carpet and eradicating any trace of Ethan's visit if he'd come. "Your mother is a very wise woman."

Ethan nodded and hitched his thumb in his breeches. "She likes you a lot."

"I like her, too." Lilly sat down on a blanket and pulled her knees up to her chin. "I never had a mother. Zip tried, but it wasn't the same. If I'd had a choice of mothers, I would have wanted her to be like Octavia."

"That's a kind thing to say." Ethan joined Lilly on the blanket. "I wondered how she'd get you up here."

"You mean she knows you're here?" Lilly asked and stared at Ethan.

"Yes. And now you do." Ethan fell silent for a few moments and studied Lilly's lovely face. "You are the only two people in the world who know where I hide out."

"I would never tell anyone," Lilly whispered, staggered by the knowledge that she held such power. Ethan—and Octavia—must both trust her a great deal to give her this information. "Why did you bring me here?"

"I wanted to see you. I'm leaving tonight just after

dark, and I may not have a chance to see you before I go." Ethan wanted to dispense with all this conversation and kiss her, but he felt they needed the time to get to know each other better.

Lilly closed her eyes briefly. "Ethan, don't go. There's no real fighting around here right now. Stay here with . . . with us."

Ethan looked away. He hadn't told her about the massacre. He didn't want her to be aware of all the ugliness in this war, but she had a right to know. If the Tories and Cherokees persisted in raiding and killing, they might find Carolina Moon. As quickly as possible, leaving out the goriest of the details, Ethan told her about Gowan's Fort.

"Oh, Ethan, how horrible for you. How horrible for all of us." Lilly rested her forehead on her hands. "We're killing our friends, neighbors, even relatives." Lilly sighed and leaned back against his shoulder. She wanted to forget the war existed for a little while. She lived with it day and night, constantly worried about Ethan and the dangers he faced. "Ethan, I'm so sorry you were exposed to all that cruelty. Will we ever be free of the nightmares associated with war and death?"

"I pray so." Ethan didn't want her to cry, so he changed the subject. "I stayed with Noelle."

"Noelle? You saw her? How is she?" Lilly perked up and looked at him with renewed interest. "How did you find her?"

Ethan chuckled. "She's a lot like you. Sort of spunky and stubborn."

"I am not stubborn," Lilly retorted, knowing that she was. Zip complained of it all the time. "Well, not much anyway."

"I have a letter from her to you." He pulled the folded paper from his saddlebag and handed it to her.

"Will you excuse me while I read it?" Lilly didn't wait for his permission.

Dearest Lilly,

Your young man is handsome and courageous. Congratulations for choosing well. I believe that all of us have done well. Ethan tells me that Erin has a beautiful little girl. I will have our first child soon. Will try to send word after the birth occurs. Please don't endanger Ethan's life by telling Uncle Jonathan about this letter. He really cares nothing for me anyway.

I love you and look forward to the day when we can be together. Immediately after the war I'm going to make Drake take me to Charleston for a long visit. Won't that be wonderful? Erin and Bowie, you and Ethan, and me and Drake—and all our babies.

Until then, keep safe.

With love,
Noelle Arledge Hastings

Lilly reread the letter quickly and folded it up. She tucked it in her pocket and gazed at Ethan. Had he read the letter? She couldn't ask him. "My cousin Noelle is quite taken with you."

"She's a lovely lady." Ethan pictured Noelle as she folded the injured woman into her arms. "She's a true . . . lady." He'd almost said Patriot, but he didn't want to embarrass Lilly by pointing out that her cousin was on the opposite side of the war. He hoped that within a few months it wouldn't matter.

"She's going to have a baby." Lilly's eyes glistened

with tears of joy for her cousin. "Noelle is so sweet. She deserves to be happy."

"So do you, Lilly. So do we all." Ethan hadn't planned to keep Lilly away from the plantation so long. He thought that Jonathan might become concerned and send a party of soldiers looking for her. "I think you should go."

"Oh, Ethan, I don't want to go. I want to stay here with you." Lilly wrapped her arms around him and kissed him. How could she even think of going back to those dullards who sat around the parlor and smoked and drank until they were senseless?

Ethan's will was weakening fast. He couldn't push her away even though he knew he should have. Before he knew what was happening, they were reclining on his makeshift bed of blankets and pinestraw. Her kisses thrilled him, sent shivers of passion flying through his body until he trembled like a leaf in a hurricane. "Lilly, we mustn't. You must leave—now."

"Don't you like me?" Lilly asked, wondering if she'd misunderstood his previous advances.

"Of course I like you," Ethan admitted and held her close. "That's the problem. I like you too much."

He walked her back to the stream and helped her pick enough mushrooms to look plausible for an excuse. Their last kiss was lingering and filled with desire. "I'll try to see you before I leave tonight."

For the rest of the day Lilly's heart sang. She was in love. He'd said he liked her too much. That was the same as love, wasn't it? She sped through her chores, sipped the delicious mushroom soup almost without tasting it, and hurried off to her room. She wanted to be alone, to think about Ethan, to recall his words, the exact timbre of his voice, the intonations, the pressure of his kisses.

* * *

Jonathan Arledge had a houseful of guests. Lilly sat through supper, answering questions, smiling absently, and making a halfhearted attempt to be charming. The roast duckling tasted like shoe leather to her, even though the men at the table kept remarking about how delicious it was. The crab soup seemed more like dishwater.

Simon Owens turned to Colonel Wilkins and asked, "The evacuation of Wilmington went well, I presume?"

"Son, withdrawing from a conflict seldom goes well. Even if there were no casualties, supplies were lost, and morale . . ." His voice trailed off for a few seconds. "Morale is lower than ever, this coming on the heels of Lord Cornwallis's defeat."

"Well, sir," Simon continued and glanced at Lilly as if to see whether she noticed how well informed he was, "I'm sure that our army can be better used elsewhere."

Lilly heard no more. The British had evacuated Wilmington on November eighteenth. That left Charleston and Savannah in the hands of the British in the South, with a few small outposts. With each passing day Lilly wished for the end of the war.

Ethan's life was more important to her now than ideals, though she could never agree with him about his choice of loyalties. The end of the war could signify the beginning of a wonderful new relationship with him.

After supper she walked to the garden to be alone. The men were all smoking cigars and drinking brandy that belonged to Ethan. Lilly knew that he wouldn't come near the house with so many soldiers around, but she wanted to see him badly. She couldn't safely find her way to the cave in the dark and wouldn't even try for fear of being followed. Her only choice was to wait until he came to her.

Deciding that the cold air was too uncomfortable, she returned to the house. The laughter coming from the library told her that her father and his friends were well on their way to passing out. That made her happy. If they were already this far into their cups, she'd have no problems with them tonight.

When she reached her room, she removed her gown and shoes and dressed for bed. Zip had a cold, so Lilly hung up her clothes and put her shoes away. She rang for a maid and asked for warm milk to be sent to Zip and ordered a cup of tea for herself. While she waited, she warmed herself by the fireplace.

The tea arrived and, as she sipped it, Lilly thought about how lucky Noelle and Erin were. Both were married to fine, handsome men and both had—or were about to have, if Noelle hadn't delivered yet—babies.

Lilly could imagine the tiny wriggling form, a product of the love between her and Ethan, but the idea of giving birth still frightened her—even after she'd talked with Octavia about it. Lilly drained the pot of tea into her cup and sipped thoughtfully. If she married Ethan, would it make Octavia happy or sad? Since they were friends, Lilly wanted to believe that happiness would be the outcome, but maybe Octavia would turn out to be strangely protective of her son.

The sounds of reveling ceased downstairs, so Lilly assumed that her father and his friends were either passed out or asleep. She didn't really care which. She simply didn't want them to bother her.

Lilly wondered where Ethan was. He'd said he would try to come to her tonight. Had he heard of the British withdrawal from North Carolina? Should she tell him?

The hour grew late, and Lilly gave up. She blew out her candle, banked her fire, and crawled into bed exhausted. No matter how hard she tried, she couldn't fall asleep. Somehow she knew that Ethan wanted to talk to her, and she refused to miss the opportunity. She rose, walked to the window, threw back the shutters, and unlocked it. He wouldn't have any trouble getting in if he came. She watched the rectangular patch of moonlight that lay across her bed and finally nodded off to sleep.

Later Ethan gazed down at her, knowing he should leave her asleep, but he couldn't. He needed to say good-bye, to tell her how he really felt. Lying down beside her, he slipped his arms around her and covered her mouth in case he startled a scream from her. "Shhh, Lilly," he cooed when he saw her eyes open wide. "It's me."

Nodding that she understood, Lilly felt an overwhelming sense of relief that he'd stopped to see her. She couldn't let him go into battle again without telling him she loved him. "Ethan, I—"

"No, Lilly. Let me say what I have to say. I'm already late." Ethan made himself more comfortable. "I think I love you, Lilly. No, I know I love you. But this war is still too awful for me to ask you to make a commitment. I don't want you staying up nights, worrying about me. I'll be back as soon as I can."

"Ethan—" she began.

"No, don't say anything. I want you to think about what I said." Ethan rose and stepped through the window onto the piazza.

"Ethan Kendall, I love you, too." Lilly leapt from the bed and chased after him. She kissed him gently and then gazed at him, memorizing the way the moonlight shadowed his face. "Don't you worry about me, either. We're going to come through this fine."

CHAPTER 13

LILLY STROLLED AMONG THE CAMELLIA BUSHES, CUTting prime blossoms with which to decorate her room. She hummed merrily as she clipped an especially lovely crimson bud that was just opening. With her arms full of fragrant blooms, she sat on one of the benches in the garden to trim some of the excess leaves from the stems.

Simon Owens walked into the little nook and sat beside her for a few minutes, watching her as she worked. He slid to one knee and grabbed her hand. "Miss Arledge, it cannot have escaped your attention that—"

Almost panicking, Lilly interrupted, "Did you hear someone call my name? I'm sure I did. Please excuse me."

She tried to rise, but he held her hand too tightly and continued. "My feelings are of a most tender and wondrous nature where you are concerned. Dare I name it love? I've spoken with your father, and he assures me—"

"You really must—"

"—that you will consent to make me the happiest of men and marry me."

Lilly stared in disbelief. Not only had Simon not realized that she'd been avoiding him for the past few days, but he didn't take the hint that she wasn't receptive to his proposal. That seemed rather odd to her.

Before Lilly could speak, Simon continued. "Don't answer now. Think about it. This war is almost over. I'm from a wealthy family. You'll live in London in luxury."

London? Lilly hadn't thought about the possibility that some people would return to England if the British lost, but she supposed it would be the easiest route for some extreme Loyalists. For now her problem was Simon. How could she turn him down gently? "Simon, I'm honored that—"

"No. Think about it. Don't answer." Simon rose, leaned over, and kissed her forehead. "I'll speak with you again concerning this matter."

Lilly watched him walk away. He and her father were up to something. She imagined that her father would speak with her next about the proposal. Not wanting to have her day spoiled completely, Lilly took her flowers and arranged them in a vase on the dining room table.

"Ah, Lilly, my dear. Here you are." Jonathan Arledge stepped inside the room and closed the double pocket doors behind him. "I understand Simon has asked for your hand in marriage. You have my blessings. He's a fine boy. Rich."

Lilly poked the last camellia into the vase so hard that she snapped the stem. "Father, Simon Owens is not the right man for me."

"You haven't turned him down, have you?" Jonathan demanded and knocked a silver pitcher off the sideboard. "I forbid you. You go right back and tell him you've changed your mind."

Jonathan stared at her with wild eyes. She understood in that moment that he was hedging his bet. Regardless of who won the war, Jonathan would be sitting in the lap of luxury. If the British won, he owned Carolina

Moon. If the Patriots won, he'd go to England with Lilly and Simon.

"Father, I haven't answered yet. Simon asked me to think it over for a few days." Lilly picked up her scraps and moved toward the kitchen.

"Wait, Lilly. You must accept his proposal. He's from a very prominent family." Jonathan sounded desperate. His face was beaded with perspiration in spite of the cool temperature.

Lilly gazed at him and suddenly felt sorry for her father. From the beginning of the war, he'd been a staunch Loyalist, not because of his convictions, but because he believed that England was stronger militarily and would win easily. Now, when it appeared that the Americans might win, he was panicking. All of the people he'd cheated and stolen from would be waiting to exact their revenge if the rebels won.

"I have said I'll think about it." Lilly left the room. Jonathan couldn't force her to marry Simon, at least not legally. She hurried out the back door and headed down to Octavia's house.

Lilly found Octavia pruning shrubs. "Ah, here you are. I was coming down to visit."

"Well, I think you should find your gloves. We'll finish the pruning and then work in the vegetables a bit." Octavia motioned toward the garden. "I think we can have fresh radishes and onions tonight. Maybe a few greens."

"Oh, that sounds wonderful. I'll be right back." Lilly ran to the toolbox where she kept the small gardening tools and removed her gloves. She stopped to get a basket for their vegetables and hurried back to Octavia.

The two women spent an hour pruning the boxwoods and azaleas. Lilly stood back and surveyed their work.

"These should be wonderful in the spring. I asked Applejack to help us."

"Yes. The colors are lovely. They always bloom around Easter." Octavia picked up the basket. "I think we'll be glad of Applejack's help."

"Here he comes." Lilly waited for the black man to join them. "Applejack, will you please take all these trimmings to the compost pile for us? Then come back. We may still need you."

Lilly and Octavia went to the garden and pulled radishes, onions, and greens. Lilly sat back on her heels and looked at the laden basket. "I can almost taste those now."

Time seemed to pass more quickly when she worked outside, except for today. She wanted to ask Octavia if Ethan had mentioned that he'd fallen in love. Octavia didn't speak of Ethan, and neither did Lilly for a long time. Finally Lilly could stand the silence on the subject no more. "Octavia, when do you think Ethan will be back?"

"I don't know, dear. You know, Lilly," Octavia began and sat down on a piece of cloth she always carried when gardening. "I think the war's over for all practical purposes. Why do men have to be such fools and keep dragging this thing out forever? If women ran the wars, things would be done logically, don't you think?"

Lilly giggled at the idea of hundreds of women dressed in silks fighting for freedom or to preserve their heritage. "I'm not sure how that could work, Octavia. I think the best option is to have people get along."

"I'm sure you're right, my dear." Octavia sighed and shook her head. "It seems to me there's a better way to resolve our differences."

"Well, since we have no say in the issue, our ideas are

purely conversation." Lilly stood up and dusted the debris off her dress. "I suppose I'd better go and dress for supper. I hate the idea of eating with all those silly men, but I have no choice."

"I admire you, Lilly. You're such a levelheaded, intelligent young woman. Your life is still ahead of you. I know you're going to make some man a fine wife one day." Octavia smiled and tears welled up in her eyes. She could see that Lilly wanted to ask questions about Ethan but hesitated because of their ideological differences. It was just as well. Octavia loved Lilly and didn't want to put any more pressure on her than was already there. *I hope that young man is my son.*

Ethan sat on a log and sipped hot coffee. His feet were nearly frozen from wading through the Ashepoo River. He'd caught up with Greene at the new camp at Round O and was still trying to warm up several days later. He thought that the proper way to run this war would be to send all the soldiers home for the winter and to reconvene in the spring, but nobody asked him for his opinion.

General Greene sent for Ethan. When he stood in front of the general, Ethan felt slightly rumpled. The general's clothes were immaculate while Ethan's were dirty and wrinkled. But the general still had his horse, and Ethan's had broken a leg and had to be destroyed. "Kendall, I've a mission for you. I want you to go into Charleston and see what's going on. Can you do it?"

"I'll try, sir. I hope you don't mean to send me as Major Kendall again. You know they discovered who I was," Ethan explained. "You say the word, sir, and I'll be on my way."

* * *

Lilly couldn't get rid of Simon Owens. He followed her around the plantation like a suckling puppy after its mother. She was glad Ethan was away, because she didn't think he'd like watching this charade. Lilly continued to put off answering Simon.

When she mentioned draughts one day, he challenged her to a game. "If I win, you must marry me."

Lilly studied him a moment. She didn't know very much about him. For all she knew, he could be a master at the game. Judging from the way he went about everything else, she doubted it. But she didn't want to make him angry. "Mr. Owens, I'm sure your skills would put mine to shame. Thank you for asking, though."

Once she told him that she couldn't marry him—whether the result of a game or a decision—Simon would go directly to her father. Then her father would lash out at her. So Lilly bided her time. She planned to hold out as long as she could without committing herself.

Several days passed, and Lilly could hardly control her anxiety. She hadn't heard from Ethan and was worried that something dreadful had happened. Lilly and Octavia didn't mention him, for fear of being overheard.

Late one afternoon Lilly slipped away from Simon. She sat on a tree limb and watched him search futilely for her. Without being seen, she sneaked down the riverbank, careful not to leave tracks in the mud, and followed the creek to the pile of rocks where she'd met Ethan before. She climbed up to a perch where she could see the plantation and observed the small figure of Simon Owens as he went from building to building looking for her.

When she was satisfied that Simon didn't know where she'd gone, she scrambled the rest of the way up through the boulders to Ethan's little hideaway. Lilly went in and sat down on the blankets. She felt much better, simply sitting among his possessions in his room than she had back at the house. After a few minutes she decided to tidy up. The room was so small, it took no more than five minutes' work to complete.

She lay down on the blankets and fresh pine straw and fell asleep. When she awoke, Ethan was sitting across the room watching her sleep. "How long have you been here?"

Ethan didn't answer her. He crawled the short distance to her and took her in his arms. For fifteen minutes he'd fought the urge to awaken her, but decided that if she was tired enough to sleep on a stone floor, he couldn't be that cruel. "I noticed that you tidied up. You even put fresh pine straw under the blankets. Thank you."

Lilly beamed. She didn't know whether he'd notice or not. "I didn't mean to change anything. I just wanted to make you more comfortable. You've grown a beard!"

"Yes. I've no inclination to shave in the cold rivers." Ethan lay down beside her, cradling her head in the crook of his arm. "I was afraid I couldn't get back here this quickly. I have only tonight."

"You have to leave tonight?" Lilly squeezed her eyes shut to keep the tears from seeping out. She'd hoped he was home for good. She was getting increasingly upset about being with him for just a few stolen moments at a time.

"Yes. I . . . I'm going on an assignment in a few days' time. I asked for a day's leave to see you." Ethan didn't want her to worry. "I'm glad you were here. It means we can spend a little more time together."

"What time will you leave?" Lilly asked and immediately realized that she didn't really want to know. She wanted to enjoy every moment as it came, not watch the clock.

Ethan snuggled closer. "I leave just after midnight."

He kissed her softly, relishing the touch that had haunted him so frequently during the past few days and weeks. Ethan knew that he wanted more than kisses, and that was one reason he'd stayed away so long. There was nothing to do at camp but think of her, and he'd thought of her until his body ached.

Their kisses changed and became more passionate. Ethan could feel her nipples hardening through the fabric of her gown and wanted to rip away the offending cloth. He wondered if she wore no corset. Desire ran rampant through him, and he drew away. "Lilly, we must stop this now while I can maintain control."

"No, Ethan. I wish to . . . I don't wish to stop." Lilly had made up her mind this morning that when Ethan next appeared, she would allow him to make love to her. She loved him and was ready for the next step in their relationship. When he stared at her, his mouth hanging agape, she blushed. Maybe she had mistaken his ardor, and he didn't want the same thing as she did. "Unless you don't—"

"No, Lilly, my darling, that's not it at all." Ethan could hardly breathe. This lovely young woman, the woman he loved, was asking him to make love to her. "Do you know what you're asking?"

Lilly lay her head on his shoulder and stared into his deep green eyes. Yes, she knew. She wanted to be a part of him forever. If something dreadful happened, then she would remain a spinster until her death. She inhaled deeply and answered, "I think I do. I don't believe I want to talk about it, though."

Ethan kissed her again. He wasn't sure what was going on, but it seemed she'd come to some sort of decision about their relationship. And then he didn't care why.

He just knew that they belonged together in every sense of the word. Their kisses became more passionate, more demanding as he worked with the lacings of her gown. Out of desperation he pulled back, quickly undid the garment, and pulled it over her head. Her body was naked from the waist up. She untied the straps of her petticoats, and he almost ripped them off before undressing himself.

Lilly looked away for a moment while Ethan removed his breeches. She'd never seen a man without his clothes, and she felt the scarlet color warming her cheeks. When he lay next to her again, she turned to face him. "Ethan, I'm sorry I'm so naive."

"Shhh. Don't be sorry for anything, love," he whispered and enfolded her in his arms. Her body felt like silk against his, and Ethan's arousal became immediately obvious.

He stroked her breasts gently and then followed with moist kisses that cooled her skin and made the nipples as hard as pebbles. His beard, still short enough to be a little wiry, tickled her skin, and she could hardly stop moving. Lilly writhed beneath his touch and knew she really wanted him to continue. His skin was rougher than hers, especially with the beard, and his chest and legs were tickly with golden hair that sent little shivers all through her.

Lilly was hardly breathing. Her lungs began to burn, and air whooshed out as he traced a cool trail from one nipple to the other. Lilly felt as though she were living in a fantasy world of sensation. Every touch seemed to have a rippling effect on her, growing into ever widening circles of responses that she hadn't known existed. "Ethan," she whispered. "Will this hurt?"

Ethan hesitated. He should stop now before something

happened they couldn't take back, but he couldn't. He wanted her, needed her more than he'd ever wanted another woman in his life. Did love make the difference? Could it be the ingredient that enhanced his desires until he could no longer control them? "My darling, relax. You may feel momentary pain, but it will be over before you know it."

Lilly heard his words echoing in her as though they were in a great cavern. Her body arched at his touch as he moved his fingers from one place to another, constantly stroking and tracing little circles around her nipples and down her stomach. When his fingers touched the downy thatch of hair that grew between her legs, she gasped. She could feel the gentle movements that brought his fingers closer and closer to the most private part of her body, a place no man had ever seen or touched.

She was on fire. Scalding through her veins, her blood searched each cell until every part of her body cried out for him. Lilly grasped his golden curls and held on, hoping to maintain her contact with a reality that was changing so rapidly she couldn't even speak.

And then he was over her, poised between her legs. She didn't know how he'd gotten there, but he was. He lay over her body and cradled her head and shoulders in his hands, all the while kissing and cooing words of love to her.

No longer in control of her own body, Lilly arched against him again, rubbing that small center of sensation against him, seeking something she couldn't define. Her heart pounded, and blood rushed through her, carrying alarm signals that went unanswered by mind and muscles. Lilly didn't know how much more she could stand without exploding. Every part of her sang with desire.

Ethan said a quick prayer, hoping he was doing the right thing, but knowing he was beyond the point at which he could withdraw. Despite the cool November air, both of their bodies were damp with wanting. He held himself above her and looked down at the intensity of her expression. Lilly wanted him as much as he wanted her. Their union would be the most splendid event of his life.

Lilly held on to his neck and wriggled against his lower body. She never felt so alive, so uninhibited, so free. He showered her with kisses all over her face and neck, settling finally on her mouth again. Cuddling a breast in his hand, he plunged his tongue into her mouth and explored as he thrust himself into the warm cradle of her passion.

When Lilly cried out in pain, his mouth muffled the sound, but it echoed in his heart. He lay as still as possible, waiting for her to adjust to him and to catch her breath. Within a few seconds he felt her wriggle a little beneath him, and he began to rock slowly back and forth to bring her back to her previous level of desire.

She writhed again, feeling the frenzy begin to build inside where the heat had cooled slightly when he made her his. Lilly began to feel light, weightless, as if her body no longer had any substance, but was more like the glimmer of foxfire. Desire whipped through her with the speed of lightning, and the messages sent from her mind changed, urging her to give in to that indefinable something that seemed to be controlling her.

Ethan quickened his pace. He knew he could hold back no longer and hoped that Lilly would find the same gratification as he. When he felt her fingernails in his back and the demanding motion of her hips signaling her pleasure, his entire being seemed to explode; raging tides shot through him until he lay in a quivering heap beside her.

They lay silently for a long time before Ethan spoke. "Lilly, I didn't want our first time to be like this . . . in a cave. I wanted our passion to be met in comfort. I apologize for not waiting."

Her eyes damp with tears of the joy of becoming a woman and sorrow for leaving her girlhood, Lilly kissed him. "Don't apologize, my love. It was I who demanded today's revelry. If you are unhappy about it, then I should be the one to apologize."

"Meoooow!"

Ethan and Lilly sat up in unison. Tartuffe pounced onto Ethan's lap and bared his teeth. "Meooow!"

"Tartuffe!" Lilly exclaimed and lifted the fat tom off Ethan's stomach. "Bad boy."

"I'll say," Ethan agreed as blood began to seep out of a nasty scratch. "I don't have to worry about you with that hellcat around."

Lilly smiled and scratched Tartuffe's ears. "I told you he was very protective of me."

"You'd think I would have learned by now. Isn't there some way to communicate with him that we're friends?" Ethan asked and reached out to rub the cat's fur.

"He'll get used to you." Lilly sighed. "Tartuffe, I think the time has come for you to make friends with Ethan. Now go along and catch mice."

The cat looked from Lilly to Ethan, curled up his tail, and strolled out the door.

"I think I've been snubbed." Ethan chuckled. "An attack cat."

They lay back down, and Ethan stroked her back as he kissed her gently. "Lilly, we've just shared a wonderful experience. I feel that I took advantage of you and—"

"No, Ethan," she interrupted and touched his lips with her fingers. "We did what we both wanted. Don't destroy the beauty of it by rationalizing it. It was right. The time had come."

Tomorrow would be time enough to consider the consequences of her actions. For today she simply wanted to love and be loved.

Lilly moved gracefully about the parlor from guest to guest. She felt that every man could look at her and see the difference in her appearance. She was truly a woman now. And she belonged, body and soul, to Ethan Kendall.

She could even put up with Simon much more easily now that she knew she would never have to marry him. The moment she'd lain with Ethan changed everything in her life. Simon may want her now, but he wouldn't if he knew about Ethan. If her father kept insisting, she'd tell him what had happened. Then she and Ethan could go away together.

The men were all looking at her. Her gown, as usual, was quite revealing. Her skin was tender from Ethan's touch and slightly pink from his more passionate caresses. She hoped no one would notice.

When her duties for the evening were finally over, Lilly retired to her room to think of Ethan. Since she'd spent most of the afternoon with him, she didn't know whether he could stop by before he left or not. She hoped so.

His timing was tight, so she tried not to build up her hopes too much. Besides, with so many British officers in the house, she didn't really want Ethan to run the risk of being caught. He might have eluded them once, but she didn't want him to try again.

The house was quiet. She didn't even hear the usual creaking sound of the house settling tonight. The eerie silence bothered Lilly, and she couldn't sleep. She kept thinking of Ethan and of the magical episode that now bound them together.

Lilly had been flushed with pleasure ever since. Her smile had never been brighter than today. She was in love and was loved in return. Nothing in her life had ever prepared her for the splendor of that feeling, and no matter what happened now, nothing could take that sensation away from her.

Then she heard the small sound. Her window slid open a little farther, and Ethan was with her. Their kisses were born of hunger and memory and desire, of desperation for the time they would be separated.

Ethan nuzzled her ear and whispered, "I couldn't leave without kissing you goodbye. Be a good girl until I get back."

"I will. I always am," Lilly told him.

"Ah, but you weren't this afternoon," he reminded her.

"Ethan Kendall, how dare you say such a thing?" Lilly scowled at him.

"Because I love you." Ethan kissed her long and hard, reluctant to leave. "And now I must go. Think of me often, my love."

Before Lilly could answer, Ethan was gone. Knowing that she could do nothing now and that there was no reason to stay awake, Lilly fell asleep soon after he left. When she awoke the next morning, it was to a cold rain that beat against her windows and forced her to stay inside.

Day after dreary day of dark gray skies and ominous thunder, Lilly watched for Ethan's return. In the light of day her loss of innocence caused her to be plagued by guilt. She'd been brought up to know that intimacy of any sort—even kissing—was wrong before marriage. There was no way she could undo what she'd done. More than anything else, insecurity remained with her night and day. Now that she'd made love to Ethan, would he lose interest in her?

When she could stand the tension no longer, she pulled on her pattens, found an umbrella, and walked down to Octavia's for comfort. Her father and his friends had left the morning after Ethan had, so Lilly was virtually alone in the big house.

Octavia's bright smile cheered Lilly a little. She tried to put forth a happy demeanor, but she knew Octavia could see through the ruse. "Octavia, I'm concerned about Ethan. Have you heard from him?"

"No, I haven't," Octavia conceded and rose to look out the windows. "I'm worried, too. He should have been back by now."

CHAPTER 14

ETHAN ARRIVED AT THE FIRST SENTRY OUTPOST. HE hid among the low branches of the trees and watched for a while to learn how often they changed the guards and how frequently they checked this point. Not only did he need this information now, but it would be invaluable when he tried to leave Charleston, particularly if he were running from a lynch mob.

While lying flat across a limb, he noticed the branches were close enough for him to climb from one tree into the next. Ethan pulled out some Spanish moss and hung it on his clothes so he would blend well with the tree limbs. He hoped he could crawl across the expanse of branches without being seen.

Ethan was more than halfway across when a soldier came and stood directly beneath him. Ethan had no choice but to wait until the man left or chance being discovered. Ethan glanced at the limbs above him. He'd come to expect that damned Tartuffe to appear when the moment was most inopportune. Thank heaven the cat was at Carolina Moon! When the soldier finally returned to his tent, Ethan was stiff from the cold.

Since he hadn't shaved after he last saw Lilly, Ethan could almost depend on not being recognized. He'd grown thinner in the past few weeks, and the tattered clothing he wore was very different from his red woolen coat and white doeskin breeches. His job was to sit in or around taverns and listen for information. He planned to sneak into the headquarters to see if he could find any letters or plans that would give the Patriots the advantage.

He nearly fell when he moved from one tree to the next. The limbs were not quite as sturdy as he'd imagined they would be. Nevertheless, he made the journey successfully. Once across that British checkpoint, he didn't have to worry too much. The British trusted their sentries to keep the people in Charleston in and all the others out, but Ethan had found a way to slip into and out of the city without anyone's knowledge.

Ethan made his way into town. In his dark clothing he blended in with the shadows as he shuffled along close to the buildings and trees.

He walked past the wharf where women called out to a group of soldiers, but no one confronted him. The soldiers were so busy exchanging quips with the women that they didn't see him. Ethan wasn't scared, but he was cautious. Until he could find a way to blend in with the lower-class elements of Charleston, he'd keep out of the way of the British officers.

The streets were crowded, much more so than when he'd left. So the reports were true. The British were bringing all their troops in from the area. That should make feeding and housing them much more difficult. If the British officials were concerned with those kinds of issues, then Greene's task would be much easier.

Ethan came as close to the headquarters as possible without making his presence obvious. Pulling a tattered cloak around him, he leaned against a fence and watched through eyes that appeared to be closed in sleep or stupor. He overheard two officers talking about the British installation at John's Island. Ethan could feel his heart pounding as the officer mentioned that the camp was impregnable except over an expanse of water where the boats could easily be seen.

The South Carolina Legislature was meeting at Jacksonboro. The city was vulnerable to an attack from John's Island. By now Ethan knew that Greene would have moved his forces from Round O about six miles back across the river between Jacksonboro and the British troops. He intended to make the legislature invulnerable to attack. Ethan's part would be to find out what he could in Charleston, get back out, and lead an expedition across New Cut where the canal was shallow enough to ford without boats. The entrance was guarded by two galleys, but men on foot could easily pass unnoticed.

Ethan shuffled along, his head down. He bumped into a red coat, and he looked up into Greg's eyes.

"Ethan!" Greg pulled Ethan to one side. "My God, man, what's happened to you?"

"Not so loud, Greg." Ethan didn't know whether to hug his friend or knock him senseless. He hoped Greg would be kind enough to remain quiet about his identity.

"I understood you were a spy. How could you do that, Ethan? You almost got me arrested for—"

"Quiet, Greg." Ethan sighed and shook his head. "I'm sorry if I damaged your reputation. I never intended to hurt anyone."

Greg shrugged. "It's about over now, anyway. There's nothing going on."

"After this is over, we'll talk about it over a bottle of rum. For now I'm in a hurry." Ethan started to walk away but stopped. "You're a good friend, Greg. Oh, yes, I'm going to marry Lilly Arledge."

"You're what?" Greg caught up with Ethan and matched his stride. "Come to my place for a drink. We need to discuss this."

"Sorry, I'm headed out of town. I'm not exactly the city's most popular citizen with the British." Ethan stopped again and placed his hands on his friend's shoulders. "I love Lilly. I'm going to marry her as soon as this war's over."

"Well, I always thought that I'd marry her, but I suppose if she loves you . . . She does love you, doesn't she? Does she know you're a spy? I mean a rebel?" Greg asked, with a lilt of hope in his voice.

"She knows. She doesn't like it, but she knows," Ethan admitted. "You know her father confiscated our plantation, and they're living there."

"I won't ask if you ever get to see her." Greg's tone was bitter.

"And I won't answer." Ethan winced at his friend's tone. Greg loved Lilly and had said often enough that he wanted to marry her, but her father always refused him. Both Greg and Ethan were committed to their sides in the war, but they were unwilling to destroy their friendship. Ethan wondered if Lilly might come between them. "Goodbye old friend."

"Tell Lilly I send my best wishes on her wedding day." Greg studied Ethan for a moment and then walked away.

Lilly was nearly desperate to see Ethan. For several days she'd imagined him lying dead somewhere or injured in some filthy British prison ship. She'd heard of the horrors perpetrated in jails. Several times when she knew she was alone, she hurried up to the cave to see if Ethan had come back. Each time she came back even more depressed.

"Octavia, I'm scared," she admitted one morning while they were embroidering napkins. "What can we do to find out if he's . . . injured?"

"Nothing. We must wait for him to return. Anything we do . . . any inquiries we make may endanger him even more." Octavia made a wrong stitch and had to pull out her work.

Lilly looked on in astonishment. Octavia's work was always perfect. This error simply demonstrated how upset she was over Ethan's disappearance.

Until today Lilly had been plagued by the knowledge that she might be pregnant. She felt relieved but also a little let down when she found out she wasn't. During the past few days, she'd been thinking a great deal about having children. She wanted several children because she'd grown up so lonely as an only child.

Lilly walked through the gardens alone. She'd come to love the stillness at twilight as the sun sank behind the cypress trees. Its glow reddened as it reached the horizon, and heavy clouds of deep purple accented the evening sky. There would be rain tomorrow, she thought. Cold rain.

"Ah, Miss Arledge, here you are." Simon Owens appeared at the edge of her little nook. "May I join you?"

He had become a nuisance. He kept after her day and night to answer him about his proposal. Lilly almost told him to leave her alone but knew that she'd regret her quick words. "Please do, Mr. Owens."

He shook his head and wagged his finger at her. "I've asked you to call me Simon. We're going to . . . I mean, we've become close enough to use a more intimate form of address, don't you think?"

"I'm sorry. I keep forgetting." She spotted a movement in the bushes and started to warn Simon, but her alarm came too late. Tartuffe leapt at Simon and landed on his shoulders, digging his claws in. "Tartuffe!"

Lilly jumped up and pulled the cat off Simon's back. She couldn't help giggling a little. "I'm so sorry, Simon. Tartuffe's very protective of me."

"Devil cat," Simon growled and flexed his shoulders.

As the silence between them lengthened, Lilly watched the first star twinkle to life. Little star, heed my wish, she thought. Keep Ethan safe and bring him home to me soon.

"Lilly!" Simon shouted and shook her.

"What? Oh, I'm sorry. I was . . . I was wishing on a star," Lilly answered in her confusion and resolved to let him wonder what she wished for.

"Say yes tonight, my dear. Make me the happiest of men," Simon begged, taking her hand in his. "I'll be the most loving and kindest of all husbands. I'll never give you cause to regret marrying me."

Lilly closed her eyes, and an image of Ethan appeared. She loved him. Whether she married Ethan or not, she would never be satisfied with another man. "Mr. Owens . . . Simon, I'm fond of you, but I'm not prepared to marry at this time."

"I can wait a few more days for your answer, my dear." Simon patted her hand. "I don't want to rush you. My father, the Earl of Dunsmore, always insisted that a lady's mind was a delicate organ and needed more time than a man's to . . . well, to make decisions."

Ah, so that was why her father was so eager for her to marry Simon. His father was an earl. She should tell poor Simon that she loved someone else, but if she did he was sure to tell her father. Lilly wasn't prepared to risk Ethan's life to spare Simon's feelings.

* * *

She'd heard that the troops at Dorchester were skittish about being so far from Charleston with Greene camped nearby. Lilly suspected that at any moment the troops at Dorchester would abandon the fort and head for Charleston. Maybe when they left, Ethan could come home and marry her. By then her father would have fewer objections.

One afternoon her father sent for her. When she arrived in the library, he asked, "Why haven't you given an answer to young Simon?"

"I don't love him, Father. I've tried to tell him, but he refuses to listen." Lilly knew her father wouldn't understand, but she had to try.

"Love? What has love to do with it? Bah. You'll marry him and you'll do it soon. On Christmas Day I expect to see the two of you wed." Jonathan glared at her and pounded his fist on the desk. "You think it over and you'll see that I'm right about this. Don't make me angry."

"But, Father," she began, feeling hemmed in like a fenced animal, "I've never had a normal courtship. All the men who've called on me were friends of yours. People you wanted to impress."

"And you should be glad. That pup Greg Weston has asked me a dozen times to allow him to approach you. I could have said yes to him, and where would you be?" Jonathan scowled at her. "You could be living in near poverty."

"At least I'd be with someone who cares for me." Lilly didn't know how to tell her father that she didn't want any of them. "But I'm not interested in Greg. I'm much—"

"The matter is not open to further discussion." Jonathan dismissed her with a gesture. "You will obey my wishes in this matter, or I'll take a cane to your buttocks."

Lilly ran all the way to Octavia's house. By the time she reached the door, she was frantic. What if Ethan didn't come home before Christmas? Would her father truly force her to marry Simon? Christmas was little more than two weeks away.

When Octavia opened the door, Lilly fell into her friend's arms. "Oh, Octavia, the most horrible thing has happened."

"Not Ethan? He hasn't—"

"No, no, that's not it at all." Lilly gasped for breath and sat down when Octavia gestured.

"Then what can be so horrible, my child?" Octavia asked and seated herself beside Lilly on the brocade sofa.

"Father says I have to marry Simon at Christmas."

Ethan slid across the limbs more easily this time. He'd learned which ones would support his weight better than others. If he hurried back to camp, maybe the next day he could visit Lilly. General Greene was an understanding man. He wouldn't try to prevent a man from seeing his love if he came back right away.

But Ethan was wrong. General Greene refused to let any man leave camp until after the next action. This was too important a conflict to lose because of a shortage of men.

Though Ethan understood, he didn't like it by half. He lay back on his blanket and peered up at the stars. He knew it was too cold for Lilly to be outside tonight, but Ethan thought of her anyway. She loved stargazing, and he loved her because the simplest things made her happy.

Ethan regretted making love to her. It had been the most wonderful experience of his life, but he didn't know how it would affect her emotionally. Some women were less stable than men. Ethan felt that if he could have been there to make sure she understood that he loved her, everything would be all right.

He couldn't stand it. Ethan rose, rolled up his blanket, and walked the hundred yards to Greene's cabin. Ethan rapped sharply on the door. "Ethan Kendall, sir," he called.

General Greene had already undressed for the evening. Ethan stepped inside and blurted, "Sir, I must go. My love is in possible danger. If I haven't your permission, I'll have to desert."

Greene looked intently at Ethan for a moment. "You have twenty-four hours, son."

Lilly sat beside her window and stared out at the moon. The cold, crisp December air fluttered her gown, but she didn't pay any attention. Her life had become too miserable to care about anything. She had no idea where Ethan was, and her father was about to marry her off to a young man for his money.

She wouldn't do it. She'd run away and find Ethan. Lilly resolved that she would pack a few clothes and leave tomorrow night immediately after dark. She'd tell Octavia her plans in case she missed Ethan somewhere along the way.

Now that she'd made up her mind, Lilly returned to her bed. She could stay in the cave until Ethan came or until her father relented.

Ethan stood outside his cave and stared at the plantation. The only light was one burning in the kitchen. He knew that everyone would be in bed now and probably asleep, but he waited a little longer to be sure. He didn't want to encounter one of those soldiers that Jonathan kept around all the time.

He had seen Lilly's light go out a few moments ago and assumed she was probably still awake. Thinking of her made Ethan want to abandon his watch and run to her without regard for safety—either hers or his.

When he was satisfied that everyone had settled down for the night, he began his approach to the house. Instead of following the creek and river as he was sure Lilly did, he angled off through the woods so he could remain unseen longer if anyone was watching. His hideout was difficult to see even if someone were standing nearby, but he didn't want to have soldiers watching this place the next time he returned.

At the edge of the woods he waited for a few minutes. He heard a noise and stood stock still. Judging from the sounds, he decided it must be an animal. Out of the corner of his eye he could see something moving. Very slowly he turned to see what was coming toward him.

It was Tartuffe.

"Sneaking up on me again, eh, pal?" Ethan whispered.

The cat simply rubbed himself against Ethan's legs and purred.

Ethan looked down, astonished that the cat seemed to like him. "Does this mean you're not going to attack me again? Can we be friends?"

She heard a noise. Ethan. It must be. She listened carefully and looked toward her window. A dark figure was crawling in.

Tears flowed freely. It was Ethan, and he was uninjured. Their joyous kisses prevented all thought of conversation for several minutes.

Finally Ethan pulled away. "My God, what has come over you?"

"I was so scared you were dead. Octavia and I have been in agony these past days, fearing that you were dead or in a filthy prison ship." Lilly cuddled in his arms, relishing the feeling of safety and comfort. "Are you back for good?"

Ethan kissed the top of her head. "No. Not for a while yet. Stop worrying. I can take adequate care of myself."

"I know you can. It's just that when you were gone so long, we . . ." Lilly's voice trailed off. She didn't want him to think she was a goose with no more sense than to prattle on about nothing while important issues went undiscussed. "Forgive me. Can I get you something to eat?"

"Nothing." Ethan liked knowing that someone cared enough about him to worry, although he didn't like burdening her. His logic made no sense to him, but he felt like he'd come home when he stepped into her arms. "I saw Greg."

Lilly thought about that for a minute. "You've been in Charleston. Did you see Mari?"

"No. As you can see, my beard has grown thicker, and my clothes are filthy." Ethan hesitated for a few seconds.

"Oh, you have clean clothes there in the dressing room. I asked Zip to leave them there." Lilly indicated the door to the adjoining room. "Except for one shirt and one pair of breeches, which I gave to Applejack."

"I see. I'd like a change of clothes actually." Ethan slipped out of his dirty breeches and shirt.

He walked over to the pitcher and poured a little water into the bowl while Lilly found clean clothes for him. He really wanted to shave off his itchy beard but knew he would need the disguise for a short time longer. When he was satisfied that he'd washed off all the dirt and muck of the trail, he took the shirt and breeches and laid them aside.

Lilly was studying him raptly, and he smiled at her intent gaze. He would have loved to watch her perform even the simple task of bathing, too. "I must be back by midnight tomorrow. I have little time since I am forced to travel at night."

Lilly swallowed hard. She'd hoped he could stay for a few days. "How long can you remain here?"

"No more than an hour." He grinned, lifted Lilly into his arms, and carried her to the bed. "And I don't intend to spend it talking about my wardrobe."

For a fleeting moment Lilly again considered the frightening possibility of having children, but when Ethan began to kiss her, she forgot everything but him.

His lips captured her nipple, and he nibbled softly, coaxing it into a tight bud. He held her close and with splayed fingers massaged her bare back. Soft moonlight fell across her face, and she looked up at him, eyes smoldering with passion. She nuzzled his ear and whispered, "I love you, Ethan."

Her words were like fat on a fire to him. Her lilting voice sent him into a near frenzy as he delighted in the feel of her flesh. The soft swell of her bosom tantalized him, and Ethan could restrain himself no longer. After making sure she was ready to accept him, he plunged inside her.

Lilly no longer controlled her body. She moaned as Ethan lifted her to new heights of sensuality. Without moving she seemed to be floating, lighter than air, like a feather drifting with the currents. Ethan was her only anchor in reality.

He brought her to the brink of ecstasy several times, but slowed his pace until she thought he was torturing her intentionally. She nibbled on his ear and whispered, "Now, Ethan, love me now."

Ethan's thrusts became almost savage with need of her. Lilly's hips rose to meet his, and their passion exploded into a flash of light much like a falling star, blazing gloriously for a few moments and gradually fading.

A movement startled both of them, and they looked up. Tartuffe crawled up on Ethan's chest and licked him several times on the chin.

"Lord have mercy!" Lilly exclaimed. "I never thought I'd see that cat do something like that with a stranger."

"I'm not a stranger. He's pushed me out of trees twice and nearly ripped my stomach out." Ethan scratched the cat between the ears. "Besides, you told him to be nice to me."

Tartuffe jumped off Ethan and climbed out the window. Lilly rested her head on Ethan's shoulder and played with the golden curling hair on his chest until she started getting drowsy.

For a short time Ethan lay with her in his arms. He waited until her breathing was even and he knew she had fallen asleep. Slipping his arm from beneath her head, he gazed at her one last time. He dressed quickly and quietly. Trying to memorize the silken feel of her skin, he reached down and caressed her cheek longingly. When he left, he knew that this experience might have to last for several weeks. Greene had said Ethan might not get away again until after Christmas.

Ethan slipped out the window, made his way across the piazza, and never looked back. His chest felt constricted, as if a rope had been tied there and was getting tighter and tighter. The end of the war had come for Ethan; he wanted to finish his assignments and return to Carolina Moon and Lilly.

Lilly awoke feeling refreshed and happy. Ethan had come home. He was safe. She sat up quickly and glanced around. She'd been asleep when he left, and there was no trace of him. It was almost as if she'd dreamed of his visit, but Lilly hugged herself. Last night was no dream.

She hurried through her morning toilet because she wanted to go down to see Octavia. Ethan hadn't said whether he was going to see his mother or not, but Lilly knew he must have. She'd know the moment she saw Octavia.

The two women met outside but neither mentioned Ethan's visit. When Lilly threw her arms around Octavia, the older woman squeezed her tightly, and their talk centered on everything but the subject that was foremost in their minds. As they picked the last of the radishes, Lilly marked the look of contentment on Octavia's face. Ethan was a thoughtful son, Lilly decided.

Octavia couldn't mistake the happiness that seemed to envelop Lilly. Her smile was wide, her eyes sparkling with excitement. Ethan had told Octavia that he intended to marry Lilly when the war was over. She didn't know that yet, Octavia surmised, but Lilly knew that Ethan loved her.

Had the two become lovers? Octavia gazed more intently at Lilly. It could be possible. Though Octavia would never broach such a sensitive subject, she decided that they had. She wasn't a judgmental person, but she wanted to warn Lilly to be careful. Society wasn't as openminded as Octavia Kendall.

* * *

Lilly avoided her father whenever possible. She knew that he would pressure her about her decision concerning Simon's marriage proposal. She spent long hours at Octavia's or walking in the woods, but Lilly always took care to walk in the direction opposite to the way she would go to Ethan's cave.

One day she found herself at the cave and didn't know how she'd gotten there. She'd started out through the woods, following a barely perceptible path. Stepping inside to avoid the cold wind that blew on the bluff, she immediately became immersed in memories.

She sat on the blanket and then lay down. She could smell Ethan's spicy scent almost as well as if he were with her. Tears came to her eyes, but she refused to allow herself to cry. Sentimentality had no place in her life at the moment. She could easily allow herself to wallow in self-pity but always scolded herself for such indulgence.

She lay back and looked up at the dome of rock over her. This was a perfect place for Ethan to hide. It was high enough to command a view of the area and hidden well enough to be safe. Now it was special for another reason. It was the place where Lilly had become a woman.

After a few moments of musing, she decided that she'd better go. If anyone had seen her walking through the woods, they might have followed her, and she didn't want to lead anyone to this place. She took the same trail down as she'd taken to arrive there. Now that she noticed it, the trail was rather well marked here, so she picked up a broken limb and began to sweep leaves over the path to hide it better.

She stopped and looked back. Satisfied with her work, she continued until she came to a point where the trail divided. She took extra care to disguise the way she'd come.

From then on she was more careful about where she went.

The afterglow of Ethan's visit soon wore off for Lilly. Her days became routine again, her life mundane. When she was alone, she indulged in secret fantasies of his visits. Her dreams were haunted by his face. Sometimes she awoke during the night and could almost believe he'd been home again.

CHAPTER 15

ETHAN WAITED FOR A SIGNAL FROM THE SENTRY AND then entered the camp. He went straight to Greene to thank him for allowing the leave against his better judgment.

Greene was giving orders to the men who would take part in the expedition. "Ah, Kendall, I need you. Come in."

Ethan obeyed and waited for the general to continue. "Now, we'll separate into two groups. The galleys are far enough apart for us to slip between without them ever knowing we're there. We'll have to go through at low tide."

Ethan had seen the armed galley placements and concurred. Timing would be an essential factor, however. Once the tide started coming back in, the galleys were free to move about Wadmalaw Sound and might catch the Patriots in the middle of their mission.

On December Thirteenth two units moved separately toward John's Island. The first, led by Ethan Kendall, reached New Cut and crossed without incident. They waited on John's Island for the other unit.

Ethan went to Greene, who had come along as an observer. "Sir, if we wait much longer, our men will be unable to ford the river again. I've sent messengers, but they report that they cannot locate our remaining troops."

"This is a terrible situation. We can't signal the other unit, or we'll give away our position. We can't go on and complete the mission with half our strength." Greene stared across the cut as if he were thinking of something else. "Send me the messengers."

Ethan called for the messengers and listened as Greene issued orders. "Go back to camp and bring artillery." To the other he said, "Find a boat and be quick about it."

Waiting with Greene, Ethan had to admire him. The general had taken a bad situation and was trying to turn it around. Ethan considered the problems they faced. They'd never be able to risk this same mission again because the British would be alerted to their plans. "Sir, if I have your permission, I'm going to take my men and try to reach the objective."

Greene gazed at Ethan in the dim light for a moment. "Good luck, son. We'll be waiting when you return."

Ethan rousted his men, and they began to search for the British camp. When they reached the campsite, they found it abandoned. The British had discovered the expedition's purpose and driven all their cattle into the woods. They then moved their campsite to James Island.

When he'd assured himself that no British troops remained on John's Island, Ethan and his men returned to the New Cut. The water was now too high for them to ford. Faced with waiting for low tide again, Ethan was glad when he saw the cannon mounted in a small boat fire on the first galley.

The galleys kept their distance, allowing the smaller boat to ferry the Patriots across to safety. Ethan hurried to find General Greene. "Sir, there were no British soldiers left on John's Island. They were apparently warned of our arrival and drove all their cattle into the woods. They withdrew to James Island."

Greene smiled and nodded. "For a mission that went so awry, we have succeeded."

"What do you mean, sir?" Ethan asked.

"You've effectively eliminated the danger to Jacksonboro. The British cannot attack directly from James Island, and if they move in this direction, we'll have plenty of time to evacuate our legislators."

"I'm happy to have taken part, sir." Ethan grinned. He liked the idea of the British on the run. If they were that skittish, then he felt sure that all the outposts would be abandoned soon.

Lilly spent the days before Christmas juggling her time. The house was to be full of guests, and she ordered the cleaning of silver and the preparation of food. Green boughs were placed on the mantels in every room to make the house seem more festive.

But in the back of her mind was the deadline her father had set. Christmas was fast approaching, and she would have to marry Simon or leave. Her father would never accept the fact that she couldn't marry a man she didn't love—especially if the man was rich.

That night Ethan slipped into her bedroom. She was delighted to see him and smothered him with kisses. "I've missed you so. How long can you stay?"

"I must leave before daybreak in two days." Ethan held her close. He'd missed her as much as she'd missed him—maybe more.

Lilly hesitated to speak with Ethan about her problems because he had so many himself, but she wanted to be honest. "Ethan, Simon Owens has asked me to marry him."

"Turn him down," Ethan answered simply.

Closing her eyes briefly while she gathered her thoughts, Lilly caught a whiff of Ethan's spicy scent and was reminded of the day in the cave. She'd have to remember to tell him, but now she wanted to talk about her problem. "It isn't as simple as that."

Ethan heard a touch of apprehension in her voice. "Tell me what's wrong."

"My father is insisting that I marry Simon." Lilly inhaled deeply and continued. "He's given me until Christmas. Simon and I will be married Christmas Day whether I agree to it or not."

Staring blankly at her, Ethan began to understand why she was so upset. Jonathan Arledge was in effect selling his daughter to the highest bidder. "Tell him you've accepted my proposal."

He slid off the bed and knelt beside her, taking her hand and pressing it to his lips ardently. "Miss Arledge, during the past weeks I have fallen so helplessly in love with you that I'm sure it can't have escaped your notice. My adoration for you is surpassed only by your beauty, which blinds me as I look at you and taunts me in my dreams. I can no longer live without making you my own. Say you'll accept my humble proposal, and I shall be the happiest of men."

"I accept most joyously." Lilly kissed his forehead. "It cannot have escaped your attention that I love you and cannot live without you. I'm glad you've finally noticed."

Ethan climbed back into the bed. "What will you do?"

"I'll tell my father we're betrothed," Lilly said and peered out the window over Ethan's shoulder. "Oh, dear, it's getting light."

He jumped out of bed and blew her a kiss as he disappeared through the window. She heard no footsteps, so she felt sure nobody else did, either. But the servants might be up. Would they tell anyone? Lilly felt sure that the Carolina Moon servants wouldn't, but what of her own people? Dulcie or Applejack could be awake.

Ethan reached the woods without incident; however, there his luck ran out. Before he could flee, a tremendous black man tackled Ethan and pinned him down. The man's huge fist was drawn and ready to strike when Ethan recognized the shirt that barely reached across the wide expanse of chest.

"Applejack?" he asked, eyeing the fist to make sure it didn't crush his face.

"Who're you? Howcum you know who Applejack is?" the black man asked hesitantly.

"You're Lilly's friend. She told me she gave you my shirt." Ethan searched his memory for anything Lilly had mentioned about Applejack. "Er, she said she played draughts with you."

Applejack grinned and slid off Ethan's stomach. "That's me. Tell me who you is."

"I'm Ethan Kendall." Ethan half expected Applejack to hit him anyway, but he didn't.

"Miz Octavia's boy?" Applejack asked and studied Ethan warily. "I guess you is at that. Them green eyes'd give you away in a minute."

"Yes. She's my mother," Ethan agreed readily.

"She a fine woman, that Miz Octavia." Applejack continued to study him. "But you ain't comin' from Miz Octavia's. You's comin' from the big house."

Ethan didn't know exactly how to answer. Anything he said might send the black man into a frenzy. There was a wild look in the dark eyes. "I've been to see Lilly."

"What you be doin' wif Miss Lilly in the middle of

the night?" Applejack's eyes widened as he began to understand. "Lawsy mercy. I's gonna kill you fo' sure."

"Wait! Wait a minute. Lilly and I are going to be married. We're . . . I love her. I would never do anything to harm her." Ethan's life was nothing in this man's hands. The strength of Applejack's fist would crush Ethan's face before he knew what had hit him. "I love her."

Applejack hesitated. "I knows Miss Lilly's in love, but how I know it's wif you?"

Ethan was amazed. "You do? How do you know?"

Grinning a toothless grin, Applejack chuckled a little. "I can see it in them big brown eyes of hers. She mopes around here for days on end lookin' like she about to keel over. Then all of a sudden, for two or three days, she look like an angel. She almost sparkle."

"Sparkles, eh?" Ethan grinned, too. He could imagine. He'd seen her when she was happy. Applejack was certainly observant. "Well, Applejack, are you going to kill me or let me live to marry Lilly? If you kill me, Jonathan will force her to marry Simon Owens. He's already set the date."

"That simpleton ain't got no need to be marryin' Miss Lilly. He ain't man enough to handle that little spitfire." Applejack studied Ethan again. "I believe you might be. I'se gonna let you go, but if'n you don't marry Miss Lilly, I'll find you and tear yo flesh off yo bones wif my teeth."

Lilly's heart pounded when she opened the door to Jonathan's study. She knew the day of reckoning had come. All along she'd intended to tell him about Ethan if her father forced her to accept Simon's proposal, but now she couldn't. He'd know that she'd been seeing Ethan and send out a search party. With Ethan probably up at the cave, Lilly couldn't run the risk. She'd simply have to refuse without giving her father a reason.

"Well, daughter, have you come to a decision?" Jonathan asked with a wide grin.

She knew he thought he'd won the game already. "Yes, Father. I'm going to refuse Simon's proposal. I'll tell him—"

Jonathan exploded out of his chair, rounded the desk, and grabbed her arm. "You'll do no such thing. You'll accept his proposal and marry him on Christmas Day."

"No, Father. I won't. It's not fair to—"

"I don't care about fair. I'm damned if you're going to continue ruining my life." Jonathan's anger consumed him. He struck her across the face twice. "You killed my wife, and you've been useless to me ever since. But now you'll marry him and repay me for all you've cost me."

Lilly's face went blank. She stared at her father as if she could see through him.

"By the gods, you won't do that this time." Jonathan hit her with his fist, harder than he'd ever hit her before.

Lilly's teeth bit into her lip, and she tasted blood just before everything turned black.

When Lilly awoke, her head felt like it had been hit with an anvil. She clasped both sides and tried to keep it from splitting. "Oh, dear, what happened?"

"That good for nuthin' pappy of yours hit you, that's what. I'm gonna kill that man one of these days." Zip paced back and forth at the foot of the bed. "Him sayin' you fainted. Harrumph."

Lilly touched her face. She could feel the swelling of her lip from the inside. She found a bruised spot beneath her left eye. "Do I look awful?"

"You looks like somebody done took a hammer and pounded yo face," Zip answered honestly.

Sliding out of bed, Lilly felt woozy, but she steadied herself and walked to her mirror. The swollen face that looked back at her was alien to her. "Oh, heaven above, I look horrible."

"It worse than you think. Yo pappy say for you to dress fo' supper. He gonna announce yo' engagement to that weasel Simon." Zip almost spat the name.

"Oh, Zip. I can't marry him. I love Eth . . . someone else." She'd almost said Ethan's name, but Lilly couldn't trust herself to talk about him, not while he was still wanted for treason by the British.

"I knows who you loves," Zip announced and crossed her arms. "You ain't a-foolin' ole Zip."

"How do you know who I love?" Lilly asked skeptically. She'd never really talked about Ethan to Zip, so there was no logical explanation.

"That scoundrel Applejack done jumped Mistah Kendall this mornin' after he come out'a this room. Now, I—"

Lilly spun around and almost fell. "He didn't hurt Ethan . . . Mr. Kendall, did he?"

"No'm. Mr. Kendall noticed his shirt. I guess you told him you gave a shirt to ole Applejack." Zip grinned and patted Lilly on the back. "Anyhow, Mr. Kendall said some stuff that kept Applejack from killin' him."

"That's good." Lilly's body went limp with relief, and she fell onto the bed with her eyes closed. "What did Mr. Kendall say?"

Zip beamed and crossed her arms. "Applejack say Mr. Kendall say he gonna marry you. Now, I don't like it you a marryin' a reb, but I like it a sight better than that Simon worm."

Lilly sighed with happiness. She'd wondered what Zip would think of her "l'il kitten" marrying a Patriot. A few months ago Lilly would have been the first to deny that such a possibility existed. "Tell my father that I can't come to table. I refuse to go anywhere with my face in such a mess."

"I'll tell 'em, but he already said you have to come down anyhow. Say you bein' punished for sassin' him." Still muttering, Zip left the room.

Lilly closed her eyes briefly. What was going to happen to her? She knew that Ethan would be furious if he saw the way she looked. How could she send a message to him? Applejack. She'd send Applejack.

When Zip returned, she repeated Jonathan's words. "He say if you don't dress and come down, he gonna come up here and drag you down in yo' dressin' gown."

Lilly could have guessed that her father would insist on her coming downstairs, though she couldn't understand what pleasure he would derive from seeing her in such a state. "What am I going to do, Zip?"

"I reckon you gonna put on one of them hussy dresses and take yo'self off down there." Zip pulled out the most provocative of Lilly's new gowns. "Wear this'n. Won't nobody look at yo' face when yo' bosoms is hangin' out."

Lilly didn't care anymore about the dresses. She slipped this one on, and Zip arranged her hair. "Thank you, Zip. I don't know what I'd do without you."

When Lilly went down for supper, she lifted her chin and gazed at each man in the room as if to dare them to mention her disfigurement. Her father rushed to her side and put his arm around her solicitously.

"You see what I mean? Oh, my poor angel," he cooed lovingly. "You must be more careful on the stairs."

Lilly gazed at him as though she could see through him. His words flowed over her but didn't really sink in.

Simon came to her and knelt. "My dear, how dreadful. If only it could have happened to me instead."

The random thought passed through Lilly's mind that she would have much preferred the event never happened at all. "You're very kind."

She could hardly eat. Lilly sipped her soup but found the roast pork too difficult to chew. When the meal was over, she started to rise, but her father stopped her.

"Just one moment, my dear." Jonathan rose and lifted his glass. "My daughter has told me that she and our good friend Simon Owens are to be wed on Christmas Day. She was searching for me to tell me of her happy news when she fell."

Lilly couldn't speak. Simon beamed at her, reached over, and patted her hand. The rest of the men raised their glasses in a toast. Lilly rose slowly, glared at her father, and returned to her room.

Ethan saw Applejack climbing up the rocks. Something awful must have happened, or Lilly wouldn't have sent him looking for Ethan. He stepped farther out so the slave could see where to climb in the growing darkness. "Here, Applejack."

Applejack hurried up to the ledge and started jabbering breathlessly.

"Slow down. Catch your breath first." Ethan led the big black man into the interior of the cave. "Sit down. Now, tell me what's wrong."

"Miss Lilly say don't come tonight." Applejack delivered the message exactly as Zip had repeated it to him.

Ethan gazed at the man for a moment and dropped to the blanket beside him. "Why not?"

"Miss Lilly say to tell you she sick." This time Applejack looked away.

Ethan noticed the muscles in the slave's jaw working angrily. "I understand, Applejack. Now tell me what's really wrong."

Applejack looked at the rebel. Zip had said that Lilly loved this man. The rebel had said he loved Lilly. Applejack fought with himself for a moment before deciding that the rebel could decide what was best for Miss Lilly. "That devil of a pappy of hers beat her."

Ethan leapt to his feet and grabbed his gun. "I'll kill the bastard."

He started out the door, but Applejack jumped up and caught him. "No, sir. Don't do nothin' that gonna hurt Miss Lilly. You got to stop and think. You cain't go runnin' off like a dawg after a fox unless you got a plan. I believe you better talk to Miss Lilly first."

Hesitating, Ethan looked back at the man. "You're right. I'll wait until after I speak to her."

Ethan sat back down and, filled with hatred, fingered the smooth wood of his musket. He forced himself to calm down and breathe regularly. If Applejack hadn't stopped him, he would have killed Jonathan Arledge in a fit of rage and been no better than the man he eliminated. "Thank you, Applejack. Sometimes two men are needed to make the right decision."

Applejack beamed. "Yessuh, sometimes is right. Miss Lilly would'a been mighty upset you come bustin' down there and git yo'self shot by one of them Redcoats."

"Oh, should you be staying here?" Ethan asked, concerned that Applejack might be missed. "I don't want to get you in trouble with Jonathan."

"He ain't never beat me. I'd break that l'il rat like a nut." Applejack shook his head from side to side. "I'm gonna git him one of these days for hittin' Miss Lilly, too."

"No, Applejack. That's not the way. You'd be hanged for murder, even if Lilly begged and pleaded for your life." Ethan patted his new friend on the shoulder. "We'll find a way to get rid of him."

"What you gonna do, Mistah Kendall?" Applejack asked and stared wide-eyed at Ethan.

"The first thing I'm going to do is hire a parson to marry me to Miss Lilly. The second thing I'm going to do is evict Jonathan Kendall from my home." Ethan didn't know exactly how he was going to accomplish either task, but he knew he could try. "Applejack, you go and tell Miss Lilly not to worry about anything. I'll take care of her from now on."

"Yessuh. I'm on my way." Applejack left immediately.

After a few minutes Ethan could hear a deep voice singing a soulful song. He couldn't make out the words, but he knew that Applejack was the singer. The voice rang through the trees and was haunting in quality, but it finally died away.

Ethan waited until dark. He saw the light in Lilly's room and gradually made his way down the hillside to the creek. The route was shorter this way, but he was in greater danger of being seen. He didn't care. He wanted to get to Lilly and assure her that she would be fine and that her father would never harm her again. In a few days' time she and Ethan would marry.

Lilly left the light burning. She stared at herself in the mirror, hating what she saw. This was her fault. If she hadn't challenged her father's authority, he might never have struck her. Even though she knew this was wrong, she couldn't help trying to believe it. She didn't want to think her father hated her, despite the horrible things he'd said.

Before she saw him, she knew Ethan had slipped into her room. She turned and stared at him. She loved him more than she ever thought she could love anyone, but she couldn't expose him to her father's malice.

"Go away." She buried her face in her hands to hide her ugliness. "I asked you not to come."

"You don't think I'd let you suffer through this alone, do you?" Ethan asked and walked toward her.

"Stop. Don't come closer. Leave now and you won't get hurt." She looked up at him and implored him to do her will.

Lilly's eyes were almost glazed with fear, and Ethan felt his heart breaking. She was trying to protect him from her father. "Lilly," he whispered and crossed the room.

He lifted her in his arms and held her as tightly as he could without hurting her. He carried her to the rocking chair in front of the fire and sat down with her in his arms. He began to rock and whisper love words to her. For several hours he sat there holding and comforting her as he would a child. He knew that talking rationally wouldn't help at all. She simply needed to know that he loved her.

Before sunrise he carried her to the bed and covered her up. "Don't worry, my darling. I'll be back, and Jonathan Arledge will never hurt you again."

Several days later Greene called for Ethan again.

"Have you another mission for me, sir?"

"Yes. I have some letters and information to be taken to Captain James Armstrong. He's expecting someone to meet him near Dorchester on December thirtieth." Greene smiled. "I believe your home is in the vicinity, isn't it? Spend Christmas with your family and take the dispatches to Armstrong on the thirtieth." Greene shook Ethan's hand. "Congratulations, son. Remain with your new wife until after the New Year."

Ethan took the leather pouch and mounted his horse. He rode directly to the Episcopalian Church in Dorchester to find the parson. When he found him, he explained the situation as best he could. "So you see, sir, Miss Arledge must be taken from the grasp of that devil . . . beg your pardon . . . her father. I hope you'll do the honor of marrying us."

"Ethan, I married your father and mother. I wouldn't miss this chance to perform your ceremony." The parson gathered his belongings and told his housekeeper to expect him after Christmas. "And I'm delighted to outsmart the British every chance I get."

They rode the short distance to Carolina Moon. Ethan had arranged with his mother to have the ceremony at her cottage, but they decided to have it at midnight on Christmas Eve. He hadn't told Lilly because he didn't know if he could get everything together or not.

Lilly went through the day glumly. Tomorrow she was to be married to Simon Owens. As night fell, she decided that she wouldn't go through with it. She'd hide until Simon had to return to his unit.

When supper was over and everyone started going to bed, she sneaked out. She'd hidden her cloak down at the river and had to walk about a quarter of a mile without it, but every step was worth the trouble. She was free.

Climbing the rocks in the dark was difficult, but she managed. The moon rose, pregnant, above the cypress trees and showered the rocks with a golden glow that helped her considerably. But by the time she reached the little cave, she was exhausted.

She lay on the blanket and thought of Ethan. He'd promised that she wouldn't have to marry Simon, but she thought that it must have been a "piecrust promise"—easily made, easily broken. Without divine intervention she'd be Mrs. Simon Owens by this time tomorrow night.

Ethan and the parson arrived at the guest cottage after dark. He could hardly wait for midnight to arrive when Lilly would become his wife.

Smiling, Ethan remembered how he'd vowed to remain a bachelor, flirting with all the girls but serious about none. Now he couldn't imagine life without Lilly. He couldn't get her out of his mind.

He went searching for Applejack. He found him in the barn, carving a little animal out of wood. "Applejack, will you come over to the cottage around midnight and sing a song?"

"Howcum you want me to sing at midnight?"

"Because that's when I'm marrying Lilly." Ethan clapped Applejack on the back. "And I want you to stand up for me."

Applejack grinned broadly. "You got the right man, Mistah Kendall. I'll be there."

Octavia and Prudence had worked diligently for days with Zip's help to make Lilly a wedding gown. Its soft blue color would be beautiful with her eyes. There were few flowers blooming, but Prudence had gathered a few camellias for Lilly to hold. Everybody had pitched in to help while Lilly recovered from her bruises.

A little before midnight Zip would sneak out of her

quarters and be waiting at Octavia's. Ethan would slip into Lilly's room and spirit her away. At midnight the parson would perform the ceremony. Everything had been planned to the minute.

Octavia bustled about, making everything perfect for her son's marriage. He'd gone after Lilly and should be returning any moment. Applejack and Zip were waiting with Prudence in the kitchen, so if anybody from the main house happened to come, they wouldn't be seen. Everything had to appear normal.

Ethan crawled along the piazza beneath Jonathan's window. For some reason the light was still on. Ethan raised his head and peeked inside. Jonathan was passed out in a chair, and the rum bottle had rolled out of his hand and spilled on the floor.

Continuing on, Ethan came to Lilly's window. It was dark inside, and he slipped in quietly. He walked over to the bed and reached down to kiss her. Ethan kissed a pillow. She wasn't there. He searched the room as best he could and still didn't find her. He thought of lighting a candle but knew that would be dangerous. The only reasonable thing to do would be to send Zip over to look for her.

Almost falling off the piazza, he forced himself to be more careful. Ethan wasted no more time. He ran full speed across the lawn and into his mother's cottage. "She's gone."

CHAPTER 16

FOR A MOMENT NOBODY SPOKE. ETHAN TURNED TO Zip. "Go and make sure she hasn't gone somewhere else in the house. I couldn't very well search for her."

While Zip was gone, Ethan paced back and forth in the little kitchen. Something was wrong. Those pillows had been shoved under the quilts to look like someone was sleeping there. Lilly had left of her own accord, but where had she gone and with whom?

Ethan silently cursed himself for taking so long to return. He'd known of Lilly's desperate situation, and he should have dealt with it sooner. Lilly couldn't be expected to live in a house where she was physically abused at the whim of a man whose mind was so obviously twisted.

He searched his memory. Had Lilly mentioned knowing anyone in the area? He thought of Erin and Noelle, but Lilly probably wouldn't know how to find them even if she had the means to try. She had to be somewhere closeby.

Ethan glanced over at Applejack. "Come on. I know where she is."

Ethan's scent was strong on the blanket. She closed her eyes and imagined his arms around her, his lips on hers. Why hadn't he returned? Why had he deserted her? For the past few days she'd thought of nothing but him. She didn't need him to rescue her—she'd done that herself. But she hated to think that he didn't keep his word. Then she chided herself for being so selfish. There was a war going on, after all.

She rose to her knees and clasped her hands together in supplication. "Dear Lord," she prayed aloud. "I know I don't deserve someone as fine and upstanding as Ethan Kendall, but I do love him, and there isn't anything I can do about that. Don't let him be hurt. I'd rather he didn't keep his promise than be injured."

"Your prayers are almost answered," Ethan said and swept into the cave with Applejack. "I'm not a liar and I'm not injured."

"Ethan! Oh, Ethan!" She flew into his arms. "I was so worried about you. You've been gone longer than I thought you would be." Lilly knew she was jabbering like a three-year-old, but she didn't care. Ethan was here and he was safe. Then she noticed Applejack standing behind Ethan. "Applejack. What are you doing here?"

"Lilly, the question is, what are you doing here?" Ethan lifted her in his arms and kissed her. "Everybody is at Mother's waiting for you."

"Who's waiting for me?" she asked, suddenly puzzled by the whole situation. "What's going on?"

Applejack was grinning happily and was dressed in a clean shirt and breeches. Ethan was wearing a white brocade vest over dark green satin breeches. His cravat was of finest lawn with an emerald pin, and his coat was of green satin trimmed in black velvet.

"Mother, Prudence, Zip, and the parson." Ethan kissed her again. "We're going to be married if you'll consent to come out of hiding long enough."

Tears of joy clouded Lilly's vision for a few seconds, but her heart sang. This single moment of happiness almost made up for the lifetime of misery inflicted upon her by her father.

When Ethan kissed her tenderly, Lilly thought she would explode with pleasure. Never had she imagined that she'd find a man like Ethan, and in a few minutes he would belong to her forever. Lilly felt as though her life was beginning anew.

Without waiting any longer the threesome started back toward Octavia's. Ethan insisted on taking the long way through the woods in case someone was watching. "With Zip searching everywhere for you, there's no way of knowing who may have heard the commotion and become suspicious."

In the darkness they took more than thirty minutes to reach Octavia's house, and when Ethan opened the kitchen door, everyone was relieved to see Lilly safe. Octavia, Zip, and Prudence whisked her away to dress her in her new gown.

"How could you keep this a secret?" she asked finally when Prudence handed her a bouquet of camellias and brightly colored Carolina jasmine. Lilly lifted the flowers to smell them. "This is so lovely. Where did you get the jasmine?"

"I grow it in the kitchen," said Octavia. "I adore the fragrance, so I always keep a pot around. It does better in the yard, but I force it to bloom in the house by exposing it to cold weather for a few weeks and then bringing it inside." Octavia smiled proudly. She took a little sprig of blooms and stuck it in Lilly's hair. "There. That's lovely. Well, my dear, you've been indisposed for the past few days. We all chipped in to make it special."

The gown was one her father had bought from Mrs.

Hawkins, but Octavia had cut a piece from one of the underskirts to make an embroidered inset to be worn over the bosom so that the dress was modest enough for a bride. The inset was lovely, done in pink and white silk roses with dark green leaves. Zip had made sure that Lilly didn't notice that the gown was missing, and Prudence had done the pressing and basting.

"This is the happiest day of my life." Lilly hugged her three friends. She was glad that her bruises had healed and weren't obvious unless she looked closely. "You have all made me feel so ashamed of the way I've acted for the past week."

"Nonsense. You were hurting." Octavia walked around Lilly and studied her critically. She took an emerald brooch from a small case, pinned it to a velvet ribbon, and tied it around Lilly's slender neck. "You look perfectly lovely."

The four women joined the men downstairs. Lilly's eyes met Ethan's, and she was overjoyed to see his look of approval. She glanced at Applejack, who began to sing. Everything seemed perfect.

The minister introduced himself and began the ceremony. Lilly was so happy, she hardly heard the words. Octavia, Zip, and Prudence were all dabbing at their eyes and trying to appear inconspicuous. When the parson said the last words, Ethan slipped a ring on her finger. It was a simple band studded with small emeralds.

"Oh, Ethan, it's lovely." Lilly could hardly see the ring through her tears of joy.

"No lovelier than you, love." Ethan kissed her gently. "It was made for my great-grandmother. The first bride in each generation since has been given this ring."

Octavia stood there a moment watching her son and

his new bride. "Enough is enough. Let's go into the dining room and celebrate."

When they reached the dining room, Lilly noticed an array of sweetmeats and punch. Everyone ate heartily, all together, rebel and Loyalist, black and white. Lilly kept stealing glances at her lovely ring. It was a family heirloom, a treasure she would always hold most dear.

When they were finished, Ethan proposed a toast. He poured everyone a glass of wine.

"Where did you get that?" Lilly asked, knowing that the only keys to the wine cellar were in her father's pocket.

"Me, Miss Lilly. I done it," Applejack confessed. "When Mr. Jonathan was passed out last night, I sneaked the keys and took two bottles."

"Applejack, you're a wonder." Lilly stood on her tiptoes and hugged him. "I'll never be able to repay you."

"To my lovely bride," Ethan began. "May our lives be long, our children many, our quarrels few, and our love neverending."

Everybody touched glasses and sipped their wine. "That was lovely, Ethan," Lilly said.

"I meant every word." Ethan kissed her again and held her tightly for a moment. "Now go with Zip. I'll be along shortly."

I'll be along shortly. The words rang in her ears as she crossed the yard and walked up the steps. When she reached her room, she allowed Zip to help her undress. The nightdress she wore was new. It was made of lawn and lace with blue satin ribbons.

Lilly walked back and forth, waiting for Ethan. Hours seemed to pass before he slipped through the window. Lilly launched herself at him and kissed him fervently. "I'm so sorry. I should have trusted you. Instead I took matters into my own hands and almost missed marrying you."

"Oh, no. You couldn't have gotten out of marrying me that easily. I'd have hunted all over the world for you." Ethan carried her to the bed and blew out the candle on the table.

"How long can you stay?" Lilly asked, steeling herself for his answer.

"Until after the new year." Ethan removed his clothes and climbed into bed with her.

The room was cool, but the embers in the fireplace cast a gentle glow to the room. Lilly snuggled up to Ethan. "Where will you stay? I think it's getting too cold to stay in the cave."

"I'll let you know. At night I plan to sleep with my wife." Ethan kissed her again.

He could hardly believe what he'd said. He'd called her his wife. Filled with joy, he untied the ribbons and lifted her so he could remove the nightgown. "You don't think I'm going to let that wisp of cloth keep me away from you, do you?"

Lilly giggled and slid her hands around his neck. "I hope not."

Ethan pulled her into his embrace. "I love you, Mrs. Kendall."

"And I love you, Mr. Kendall," Lilly admitted, feeling happier than she'd ever been in her life. She belonged to someone, and someone belonged to her.

Kissing her long and hard, Ethan thought he was a lucky man. Suddenly he pulled back and looked around.

"What's wrong? Did you hear something?" she whispered.

"No." He glanced around the room.

"Then what are you looking at?" Lilly tried to follow his gaze but couldn't see anything out of the ordinary.

"Not at—for." Ethan peered over her and then settled back. "I'm looking for Tartuffe. He's not going to spoil my wedding night."

Lilly giggled and then covered her mouth. "Applejack came and got him this afternoon. Said something about needing him in the barn to catch mice."

Ethan nodded happily. "Good for Applejack. Very intelligent man."

Ethan slid his arms around her and pressed her body against his. With splayed fingers he massaged her back as he kissed her gently at first and then with more passion. He couldn't get enough of the taste of her. His lips moved down her neck, teasing and kissing, to her breast where he sampled the sweet nectar of her. He felt her body tense and wriggle with her own need, but Ethan didn't hurry. Tonight he wanted to make their loving special for her.

With one hand he traced small circles around her other breast and then trailed down her ribs to her flat stomach and into the soft nest of curls. His index finger found the tight little bud of her sexuality and caressed it slowly and gently until he could hardly keep her still.

Lilly was wild for Ethan. She wanted him inside her, filling her in that glorious fashion that made her think of him every minute of the day. She craved that exquisite feeling of love and being loved she'd shared with nobody else. But he seemed to be in no hurry.

"Two can play this tantalizing game, darling," she murmured and slid her hands down his chest to his stomach. Lilly didn't know exactly what to do. She found his maleness stiff and throbbing and closed her hand around it.

Ethan groaned. For a moment he lay there, allowing her to learn about him, to explore as he'd explored her body. Then he could stand no more. He raised himself above her and guided himself inside the moist warmth of her body.

Lilly gasped. The feeling of being suddenly filled and caressed and loved was still very new to her. As they moved and rocked, Lilly felt the power building inside her. From somewhere deep in the pit of her stomach, it began growing and stretching, igniting every cell with fiery rapture until she quivered with satisfaction.

Ethan kissed her more deeply, plunged his tongue in her mouth, ravished her. He could no longer control himself. This woman who was his wife charged him with a desire he'd never known. He felt her around him, contracting spasmodically, and erupted into her, releasing a million tiny explosions to each part of his body.

They lay there, spent and happy until Zip tapped lightly on the door. Ethan pulled on his breeches and ran to let her in. "I'm gone. Take care of my darling wife."

He kissed Zip on the cheek, stopped to kiss Lilly, and slid his feet into his boots. With his shirt flying behind him like a flag, he slipped out the window and was gone.

Zip tucked the covers around Lilly and patted them. "You sleep late. I'll tell Mistah Jonathan you real sick."

The two women talked for a few minutes about what disease Lilly might have and then Zip left the room. Lilly fell asleep again and dreamed of Ethan.

When Lilly awoke, she stretched lazily like Tartuffe after one of his catnaps. She glanced around and saw that she was alone. She looked at the ring on her finger and knew she couldn't wear it in public yet. Her father couldn't know that Ethan was anywhere around or he'd send every British soldier in the area hunting for the rebel.

Jonathan burst through the door. "What's this I hear about your being ill?"

Lilly pulled the covers up to her chin and stared at her father for a moment. "I'm sure I have some kind of influenza. Zip has a touch of it herself."

"Influenza? Bah." Jonathan paced back and forth. "You're not going to put me off with this act."

"Zip said the servants told her that an entire family near here died of the influenza." Lilly didn't want to say too much for fear of contradicting something Zip might have already said.

"Lilly, are you all right?" came a call from the door, followed by a light tapping. "It's Simon."

Jonathan opened the door and pulled Simon into the room. "She's fine. Doesn't she look fine to you?"

Simon shook his head. "This influenza is nothing to take lightly. Several people have died of it. Even some of our soldiers."

"Can't you see that this is a ruse?" Jonathan asked, staring from Lilly to Simon.

"I see that my intended is ill and that you are treating her discourteously." Simon glanced at Lilly and then confronted Jonathan. "If you don't leave her alone until she's well again, I'm going to have you flogged."

Lilly almost laughed. She coughed several times to cover up her faux pas and lay back as if the effort exhausted her.

"Jonathan, her health is to be considered here. Women are much more delicate than men." Simon pushed Jonathan toward the door and turned for a last word to Lilly. "Rest now, my darling. We shall be married on the first day of the new year."

The door closed, and the two men disappeared. Later Zip came up with the news that Simon and the rest of the soldiers had been called away. Thankful for her reprieve, Lilly spent the remainder of the day in her room. She knew that Jonathan would be furious if he discovered her ruse.

Lilly wanted to go to Ethan. She didn't know exactly where he was or what he was doing, but she wanted to be with him. She'd never been so happy in her life. Toward evening she dressed and went downstairs.

"Dulcie, send someone to gather the servants. I want to hand out Christmas presents." Lilly ensconced herself in a chair in the parlor and tried to look wan and pale in case her father came in.

Octavia brought in some packages and kissed Lilly. "Where's your father?"

Lilly shook her head and shrugged. "I haven't seen him since this morning. He was in a rage because I was sick and couldn't marry Simon."

Octavia laughed. "Think how he'll be when he learns you married a rebel."

"I don't look forward to that. He's bound to be furious." Lilly looked around. The room was filling with people. "Maybe he won't bother us."

"He'd better not try."

"Ethan!" Lilly exclaimed and jumped up to hug him. "What are you doing here? You must leave before you're discovered. I can't bear to think of living without you."

He lifted her in his arms and kissed her to resounding cheers from the staff. "Why, I'm celebrating Christmas with my wife, of course. Where else would I be? And don't worry. We've nothing to fear."

Lilly glanced at the servants. None of them would talk. "But what about Father? What if he comes in?"

"I don't think he'll be able to come down for a while." Ethan grinned and winked at Applejack. "Somebody drugged his wine."

When all the servants had arrived, Octavia, Ethan, and Lilly handed them mittens and fruit. For Dulcie, Zip, Prudence, and Applejack there were extra gifts. Lilly had made a little lace collar for Octavia and gave it to her happily. "I hope you like it."

Octavia handed Lilly a small package. When she opened it, tears came to her eyes. The housekeeping keys were tucked away in a little silver dish. Lilly knew how closely Octavia supervised the staff at Carolina Moon and how much she prided herself on how well she did it. "This is . . . a most precious gift."

Lilly lifted the keys and put them in her pocket. Then she saw the emerald brooch she'd worn for her wedding. "Octavia, I . . . this is too much. I can't accept—"

"Nonsense. Of course you can and will." Octavia hugged her daughter-in-law. "The brooch was my grandmother's. It's passed down to the first bride."

Ethan's package was next. Lilly had knitted him a scarf of thick wool and a pair of stockings to match. She smiled shyly. "The stockings aren't very stylish, but they'll be warm."

Ethan handed her a little box. "This is from me."

As Lilly tried to open the box, her hands were shaking so hard that Ethan had to help her. "I'm sorry. I just didn't expect anything so—"

The box fell open and exposed a strand of glittering emeralds to match her wedding ring. "Oh, Ethan, these are lovely. I . . . oh, I could dance for joy. I've never been this happy in my life."

"You may do that, too." Ethan took her hand and led her to the ballroom. "Here's your orchestra."

Lilly looked at the array of black faces. They certainly weren't the musicians she was accustomed to in Charleston, but as they struck the first chords, she decided they were perfect. Lilly and Ethan danced for hours. When she declared she couldn't take another step, Ethan lifted her in his arms and carried her up the stairs.

"One day soon we'll be able to do this without sneaking around," Ethan declared as he closed the door behind them.

He painstakingly removed Lilly's gown and then his own clothes, and they climbed into bed together. As they lay in each other's arms, Lilly looked up at him. "Ethan, do you like babies?"

Ethan drew back and gazed at her intently. "Are you going to have one? I mean, could you tell this soon? Are you ill?"

Lilly laughed and kissed his cheek. "No, no. Don't worry. I just wanted to know."

"Didn't you listen to my toast? I said many children." Ethan hugged her close and chuckled. "We can start now if you like."

Ethan woke Lilly before dawn. "I can't stay during the day. Don't tell your father that we're married unless you have to. I'm planning a little surprise for him."

"Are you leaving? I thought you were going to be here until after the new year." Lilly felt tears sting her eyes. For the last few hours she'd felt truly married. They'd presided over Christmas for the servants, danced until the wee hours, and then gone up to bed together. She didn't want to lose that wonderful feeling of belonging so soon.

"I'll be back. Don't worry." Ethan kissed her and held

her for a long moment. "I love you, Lilly, more than I ever thought I could love anyone."

When he was gone, Lilly buried her head in her pillow and sobbed. She loved Ethan so much that her heart actually ached when he left her. Christmas had been so splendid with him, Octavia, and the servants—a Christmas like she'd never known before.

He hadn't said where he was going, so she could only surmise that he was in danger. She tried hard to fall asleep again, but had little success. When Zip came in, Lilly was already dressed.

Lilly was pleased to see that Zip was wearing the new kerchief she had given her. Lilly touched her ring, and a surge of happiness burst through her. She knew she should remove the ring before her father saw it, but she didn't want to take it off yet. "You're up early this morning, Zip."

"You is, too." Zip hummed as she moved about the room, tidying everything, straightening pictures, making the bed.

Lilly watched her carefully for a few minutes, unable to figure out what had happened to make her so sprightly. "What's going on, Zip? What's happened to make you so cheerful this morning?"

"Does a body have to have a reason to be cheerful? Does a squirrel have to have a reason to run up a tree?" Zip never stopped working. She opened the shutters and peered out. "It's a mighty bright and cheery day."

"I've lived with you for seventeen years, and you've never been this cheerful. What's going on?" Lilly demanded and crossed her arms over her breasts. "We're not leaving until you confess."

Zip stopped and looked at Lilly. "Ain't I taught you better manners than that? You a busybody worser'n them women in Charleston, always messin' in ever'body else's business."

Lilly stood her ground firmly. "You're not going to change the subject on me. Now, tell me why you're so . . . so cocky this morning."

Zip grimaced as if she realized she'd never be able to continue her chores until she placated Lilly. "Well, if you must know, Miss Nosy, me and that scoundrel Applejack gonna finally git married."

"Zip!" Lilly exclaimed and rushed over to hug the woman who had been a mother to her for the past seventeen years. "I'm thrilled. Best wishes to you. We'll have a wedding feast for you."

"Now, there you go. I ain't as young as you, and I don't need nothin' fancy. Me'n that ole buzzard just gonna—"

"You'll do no such thing." Lilly hugged Zip again. "This is wonderful. I'm so excited. I can't wait to tell Octavia."

Lilly ran out the door and down the stairs. She stopped in the kitchen to tell Dulcie about the meals for the day and then hurried out the back door. By the time she reached the cottage, Lilly was out of breath.

"Octavia!" Lilly called as she let herself in. "I have the most wonderful news."

Octavia came from the kitchen and stared at Lilly. Could she mean that Jonathan was leaving Carolina Moon? "What is it, my dear?"

"This is splendid news." Lilly could hardly contain her glee. "Zip and Applejack are going to be married."

Trying not to appear let down, Octavia hugged Lilly and smiled. "I thought there was something going on between those two."

Lilly began to pace. "We need to plan a small reception. Where are they going to live? Oh, my, that's a problem."

Octavia shook her head at Lilly's enthusiasm. "No, it's not a problem. They can live in the guest cottage out past the barn. I always intended it for my mother-in-law, but since I don't have one any longer, they can have it. It's perfect for them. Just a bedroom, parlor, and kitchen, not nearly as big as this house, but comfortable."

Lilly clapped her hands together joyfully. "Oh, that would be perfect. When can we look at it?"

"We'll look at it today. When are they to be married?" Octavia asked, taking the pragmatic approach.

"I don't know. I didn't think to ask."

Lilly hurried back to the house. She wanted to make the arrangements as soon as possible. Applejack had been courting Zip for years, and Lilly wanted to have everything done quickly before her friend could back out again.

When Lilly walked into the house, she ran into her father. "Good morning, Father," she said and walked past him.

He reached out and caught her hand, gripping it so tightly that she couldn't escape. "Not so fast. Are you feeling better?"

"Yes, sir," Lilly answered and felt her new ring bite into her fingers. She prayed that her father wouldn't see it.

"The wedding is set for the first day of the new year. Sick or well, you'll stand before the parson." Jonathan grasped his head. "Head full of horseshoes this morning. Bloody awful headache."

As she slipped her hand in her pocket to hide her ring, Lilly couldn't suppress her smile. Her father always said that when he'd had too much to drink. She couldn't help wondering if the drug made the headache worse. "I'm sorry, Father, maybe you're coming down with the influenza, too."

"Now, see here, young lady, you're a bit too flippant to your father. Simon Owens is a fine young man with lots of money and connections. We'll be sitting pretty in England. Let all these low-country rebels stew in their humidity and swat mosquitoes while we're consorting with the bluebloods." Jonathan chuckled and then winced. "I'd hate to have to discipline you to convince you of your duty. You know how much this means to me. And to you and Simon, of course."

Lilly bit her tongue. "Yes, Father. Whatever you say."

"I can see us now. We'll be invited to court, of course. King George will know how loyal I've been." Jonathan's eyes glistened with excitement. "I'll be getting the recognition I've been due all these years."

"Yes, Father." Lilly tried to understand her father but couldn't. He seemed more interested in money and power than in the people around him.

When he'd finished boasting, she continued her search for Zip and found her in the attic. "What are you doing up here?"

Zip, sitting on a low stool, turned to Lilly. "I'se lookin' for a dress Miss Octavia say up here."

"What kind of dress?" Lilly asked and looked around the attic. Like the rest of Carolina Moon, the attic was as neat as could be. Several trunks were placed against the walls, and assorted furniture was situated so that even though the room was filled, it didn't look overly cluttered. Lilly gasped when she noticed the mahogany cradle in one corner. She walked over and ran her fingers along the highly polished wood.

Zip glanced at her. "I ain't gonna be needin' that!"

Giggling like a schoolgirl, Lilly blushed. "No, but maybe I shall."

"As I was saying. I'se lookin' for some kinda fancy dress Miss Octavia say I can wear to marry that ole cuss in." Zip sat back and stared at Lilly. "I don't know how-cum I let him talk me into doin' this. I better go tell him I changed my mind."

"No." Lilly put her hands on Zip's shoulders and kept her from standing. "Now, listen to me. I'm grown. I'm married. You need to think about yourself for a change. Applejack loves you. He's always loved you. And you're going to marry him if I have to truss you up like a Thanksgiving turkey and shake your head for you when the parson asks if you'll take Applejack to wed."

Zip's eyes widened. Lilly kept her face stern and her eyes narrowed and menacing. She realized that she was wagging her finger at Zip as if she were a little girl who needed to be told what to do. Unable to maintain her austere expression any longer, she burst into laughter and hugged her friend. "Oh, Zip. I want you to be as happy as I am. You deserve it."

CHAPTER 17

EVERYONE AT CAROLINA MOON, WITH THE POSSIBLE exception of Jonathan, who knew nothing about the two weddings, was excited and happy.

Zip and Applejack's wedding day was clear and cold. Lilly thought wistfully of Ethan, wondering where he was and knowing he'd want to be here. For some reason he and Applejack had gotten close. She'd even heard that they were challenging each other at draughts.

Lilly dressed in her own wedding gown, that being the most decent dress she owned, and walked down to the little cottage. Nobody had mentioned the wedding to Jonathan for fear he would do something to stop it. Lilly suspected, though she didn't know for sure, that her father's wine had been drugged again. Had the house been filled with soldiers as it was before Christmas, the wedding would have been less open.

As it was, every servant deserted the main house to see the two lovers joined in wedlock. Lilly agreed to stand up for Zip. Nobody mentioned who would do so for Applejack, but she knew that Ethan would have wanted to. When she reached the small house, she entered and found everyone else already gathered. To her surprise, Ethan had returned and stood up for Applejack.

The ceremony was even simpler than Lilly's, but just

as beautiful, and she blinked back tears as she remembered her own recent vows.

Octavia and Lilly had worked hard to make the spare cottage into a tiny love nest for the two servants. They'd made curtains for privacy, replaced the worn furnishings, and stocked the larder. There were big bowls with fresh stems of cedar and pretty camellia blossoms in the center of every table. The house took on a pleasing fresh scent.

Octavia, who loved to entertain, had planned an excellent supper of catfish, fresh greens, potato dumplings, and corn sticks. There were pitchers of milk and a bottle of wine. Everyone ate until they could no longer stuff in another bite.

Long after Octavia, Ethan, and Lilly left, the celebrating continued. Ethan and Lilly walked hand in hand back to the main house. Lilly loved the feeling of belonging, of being mistress of her own plantation, of being free to walk openly with the man she loved. She suspected that they wouldn't be able to do so again for a long time to come.

As they lay in bed together, Lilly snuggled into the curve of Ethan's arm. "Ethan, I've been thinking about this war. We're in a pretty touchy predicament here."

"What do you mean, love?" Ethan didn't really want to spoil their evening with a philosophical discussion, but he didn't want to say anything to discourage her. Lilly had a bright, inquiring mind and needed the freedom to express herself.

"We're married, husband and wife. You're a rebel. I'm a Tory. What are we going to do when the war is over? Will our friends hate us for marrying each other?"

Ethan laughed and squeezed her tight. "I don't really care what people think. And, Lilly, I never faulted you for remaining loyal to the king. As long as I feel a person has deep feelings about the side he chose, I still think highly of him. I'm quite fond of Greg. Oh, dear, I forgot to tell you something he said."

"What? I'm sure it was something silly. He can't be serious for a minute." Lilly laughed. She could hardly wait to see her friends and tell them of her marriage.

"I told him we were to be married." Ethan recalled the look of jealousy that had passed over Greg's face. "He was quite jealous of me, but he relented and asked me to pass on his good wishes."

Lilly smiled, imagining how jealous Greg would be. Even though she'd always discouraged him from falling in love with her, he had. "If you should see him again, would you—"

Interrupting, Ethan kissed her nose. "If I should see him again, I'll duck because I feel sure he'll shoot me on sight."

"He wouldn't do that." Lilly defended her friend. "At least, I don't think he would."

"Well, maybe not. But he looked pretty angry that I got you and he didn't." Ethan held her close. "I'm a happy man, Lilly. You've made me the happiest man alive."

"I'm happy, too, Ethan." She hesitated a few seconds and then continued. "I never thought I could be this happy."

"I have to leave again. I came back for the wedding, but I have to meet someone." Ethan felt Lilly tense in his arms. He knew she was afraid for him. "I'll be back soon. Don't worry about anything."

* * *

"Octavia, he said for me not to worry, but I can't help it," Lilly confided and put down her needlework. "How can I not worry?"

Octavia placed her sewing in her little sweetgrass basket. "Lilly, I don't know. During the warm months, we can work outdoors and occupy our hands and our minds. When the weather's as cold as it is now, all we can do is think."

"Isn't there anything at all we can do?" Lilly asked, hoping Octavia would think of some task that would keep them busy for a few days.

"Well, maybe there is." Octavia stood and crossed her arms. "Lilly, go put on your work clothes. Something you don't mind spoiling."

Lilly, glad to have something to do, hurried to change clothes. She dug in the back of the wardrobe for an old homespun gown that had been dyed using indigo. Excited to feel useful again, she was back at Octavia's in a few minutes. "What are we going to do?"

"You'll see." Octavia led Lilly to the barn, where they asked for some milk. From there she went to the spinning house were all her dyes and yarns were kept. "Take this pot of indigo."

When they returned to the main house, Octavia went to an unoccupied room that opened off Lilly's room upstairs. Lilly looked puzzled. "What are we going to do with milk and indigo?"

"Make paint." Octavia poured a few drops of the indigo into the bucket with the milk. "How's that?"

Lilly studied the "paint" for a moment. "What are you going to paint?"

"A nursery. We'll be having babies around here soon, *I hope,*" Octavia said, emphasizing the last two words. "How about a nice light blue for a boy?"

Lilly blushed and smiled. "Do we have a choice?"

"About the baby? I doubt it. We do have a choice about the paint." Octavia added a few more drops until the color was almost sky blue. "How about now?"

"I think it's perfect." Lilly took a clean turkey feather and began to paint the wainscotting. "I saw the cradle up in the attic. It's lovely."

"No need to bring it down yet. I think it's a little early for that. You can use this as a guest room if you have to. We won't make it too babylike."

Lilly laughed. "I can't imagine those soldiers liking . . . what color is this?"

"Heavenly blue." Octavia stroked the paint on as smoothly as she could. "My mother told me how to make it."

As Lilly painted, she began to think of her baby in this room. She would love to have a little boy with golden curls and green eyes like Ethan. She wanted a little girl, too, but she wanted the boy first. Ethan would probably want a boy.

"What are you thinking about, Lilly?"

Lilly didn't really want to give voice to her thoughts, so she stopped painting, looked at the freshly painted wall, and then at Octavia. "How long will this last?"

"Forever." Octavia finished up a panel and glanced at their handiwork. "My mother had walls this color. I remember them from childhood, and the last time I saw that house, the walls were still this color."

"Octavia, don't you think Ethan should have been back by now?" Lilly dipped her feather in the bucket and brushed the mixture on the wall. "I mean, didn't he say he'd be back today?"

"I think you're right." Octavia stopped painting, laid

her feather on the lip of the bucket, and gazed at Lilly. "Do you think something's happened?"

"I don't know. I'm going out to the cave to see." Lilly glanced back at the wall. "Can you finish this last panel?"

"Yes. You go. I think . . . I don't know what I think." Octavia picked up her feather and made several meticulous strokes. "Go now."

Lilly hesitated no longer. She ran to her room, found her heaviest cloak, and hurried out the back door. She made no pretense of going through the woods. She and Octavia both felt that something was wrong.

At the point where the creek branched off the river, she waited a few seconds to see if she was being followed. When she saw no one, she dashed down the narrow pathway until she arrived at the rock formation. From there she scrambled up the boulders until she reached the hidden mouth to the cave.

She hesitated for a moment, afraid of what she might find when she went inside, but her fear for Ethan was so great that she overcame her own fears. When she stepped into the small room, she was alone. Ethan wasn't there, nor did it look like he'd been there recently.

Almost overcome with relief, she sat down on the blanket. How foolish she was to be so scared for nothing. When Ethan returned, she would tell him how silly she was, and they would laugh together about it. But Octavia had sensed something, too. Their intuition had seemed to be honing in on the problem at the same time. Ethan would laugh and call them both silly.

Lilly stood, took one last look around, and left the cave. She decided to walk back through the woods instead of taking the more open route along the riverbank. As she strolled down the hill, she heard a sound and stopped.

She peered around, saw nothing, and continued on her way until she heard the sound again. Lilly began to feel ill. Something inside her told her that something was terribly wrong. She turned around twice very slowly and looked at every possible hiding place for an animal or human.

Taking a few more steps forward, she heard it again. This time it sounded like her name. She wondered if she really heard the sound, or if it was all in her head. Could she be imagining this? Lilly turned again. This time a small cluster of bushes caught her attention. Without waiting for more evidence, she started toward them. She ran faster and faster. When she was no more than ten feet away, she tripped on a honeysuckle vine and fell hard. She didn't even hesitate but bounced back up and ran again.

When she reached the bushes, she slowed down and peered over them. Ethan lay there, blood matted and clotted on his head. Now she could hear the barely perceptible call. "Lilly . . . Lilly. Help. Mother."

"Oh, God help us! Ethan, I'm here." Lilly climbed over the bushes and sat down beside him. His temple was an ugly open wound. "Here I am, darling. I'll go get help."

"No. Stay." Ethan reached for her. "Stay."

"All right." Lilly cradled his head against her breast and wondered how long it would take for Octavia to send someone looking for her. Who would she send?

Octavia was an intelligent woman; she'd send Applejack. Lilly prayed that Octavia would send him. For now, all she could do was sit and hold her husband's head as he bled on her.

"Ethan, can you walk?" Lilly asked, hoping he could. "If I help you, can you walk as far as the cave?"

"Don't think so." Ethan tried to sit up. He slumped back against her. "Maybe if you help."

Lilly stood and tried to pull him up with her. She succeeded in getting him to a standing position, but didn't know how she could ever get him to walk. Tears streaming from her eyes, she moved behind him and tried to slide her feet under his. "Lift your feet, one at a time."

It seemed to take forever for Ethan to place his feet on hers. "Ethan, my darling, do you remember how you used to dance when you were a boy? With your feet on your mother's?"

"Seems silly. Don't know if I did." Ethan's head rolled to one side.

"Ethan, don't faint on me now. I'll lift my foot and move forward. All you have to do is lift yours." Lilly knew that the possibility of going up the hill with Ethan standing on her feet was remote, but she had no choice. She couldn't leave him there alone and she couldn't sit by and do nothing while he died. "Come on. We have to try. Right foot first."

Her legs were hardly strong enough to force Ethan's feet forward, but she managed to take several steps before they had to rest. "Go again. Right . . . left . . . right . . . left."

After more than thirty minutes had passed, they were still a good distance from the cave. Lilly kept trying, but she was almost ready to give up. Ethan muttered and mumbled, could hardly lift his feet, but she urged him on. By the time an hour had passed, they were nearing the cave. "Just a little farther."

Lilly heard a noise, the unmistakable sound of feet shuffling through the leaves. There was no place to hide, except for a live oak. "We've done this before, Ethan."

She almost dragged him to the lowest limb and sat him

down. With every ounce of strength she laid him across the limb and stretched him out. She climbed up with him. From where she sat, she could see the path.

After a moment she spotted Applejack. "Over here," she called lightly.

Applejack perked up and looked her way. For a few seconds she didn't think he'd find her, but she waved vigorously. "Here!"

He ran to the tree. "Miss Lilly, what . . . Lawsy have mercy. What happened to Mistah Ethan?"

"I don't know. Help me get him into the cave." Lilly jumped down while Applejack lifted Ethan off the limb.

"You go on to the cave. Don't worry." Applejack hurried along behind her.

Dear God, don't let him die, she prayed as she reached the cave. She waited for Applejack to lay Ethan across the blanket and then she covered him with another one. "Applejack, go and tell Miss Octavia. We need a doctor. Find out where—"

"You knows I can take care of him, Miss Lilly. I'se the best horse doctor in the colonies," Applejack reminded her.

"Yes, I know but this is . . . You're right. Go for more blankets and whatever you need. Tell Miss Octavia. Don't let my father know." Lilly stopped to think for a minute, to see if she could think of anything else. "Food. He'll need something to eat."

Applejack didn't waste any time. He lit out of the cave as if he were being chased by a pack of wild dogs. Lilly cradled Ethan's head on her lap and tried to pray again. Why had this happened? *What* had happened?

Ethan was shivering. Lilly removed her cloak and placed it over him, but it didn't seem to help. Finally she slid under the covers with him and wrapped herself around him as much as possible.

What was taking so long? Had Applejack run into trouble? Lilly wanted to scream. Everything seemed to be moving so slowly that time stood still. What would she do if her father came up here? Or Colonel Wilkins? She had to protect Ethan at all cost.

Finally Applejack arrived. He ran into the cave and dropped a pile of blankets. Wrapped inside one of them was hot soup in an earthen jar and a pot of salve.

Lilly watched while Applejack cleaned the wound and looked at it. To her, it appeared to be a deep gash, but Applejack seemed relieved. When the wound was dressed with thick smelly salve and a clean bandage, he moved aside to let her feed Ethan.

"Jus' a l'il at the time, Miss Lilly," Applejack cautioned.

"Oh, Applejack, what would we do without you?" Lilly ladled the thick broth into Ethan's mouth and waited for him to swallow. "I'm sure glad you're one of us."

"Me, too, Miss Lilly." Applejack grinned and placed more blankets over Ethan. "Miss Lilly, you better put yo' cloak back on or you'll be catchin' yo' death a cold."

"I'd rather Ethan have it. He's freezing." Lilly smiled at her old friend.

"No'm, he ain't. He's plenty warm. You put on that cloak, else I'll send you back to the big house," Applejack threatened good-naturedly. "I cain't nurse both of you."

"All right." Lilly slipped on her cloak and was glad for the warmth. She hadn't realized how very cold she was. "What about Miss Octavia?"

"She'll come when she can. She's keepin' yo' pappy busy."

"What's she doing?" Lilly looked at Applejack curiously.

"She's a playin' the harpsichord and singin' some songs while they drink they wine." Applejack grinned. "She cain't sing no better'n a barn owl, but them men won't say nothing. They jus' keep on smilin' while she screechin' the words."

"What men?" Lilly felt sick. She knew what men. Colonel Wilkins and Simon were back.

"Them redcoats that been here ever since we moved in."

Lilly had to return to the house. They would tire of Octavia's entertainment before long and begin looking for her. "Applejack, I'll send Octavia and Zip to help. I'll manage those men. Keep an eye open for Octavia and Zip."

She paused a minute to kiss Ethan goodbye while he slept and hurried out the door. Lilly ran along the trail by the river. As she neared the house, she slowed down enough to catch her breath. She looked at her clothes and saw bloodstains on her bodice. Almost stricken dumb with panic, she stopped and tried to decide what to do. She couldn't reach her room without going past the parlor and being seen.

Ethan could climb up and down the posts on the piazza, but she couldn't. She would have given anything for a trellis at that moment. There was but one thing to do. Lilly turned around, walked to the edge of the river, and walked in at the shallowest point. Once there, she squatted down and drenched herself. When she came out of the water, she picked up a handful of mud and smeared it all over herself. Nobody would be able to tell the difference between the blood and the red mud from the riverbank.

Shivering furiously, she hurried up to the house and entered by the front door. Everyone would see her. She closed the door quite loudly and stepped into the foyer just outside the parlor.

"Lilly!" Octavia spotted her and sprang up from the harpsichord so quickly that her chair overturned. "What happened to you?"

"Oh, I'm so embarrassed. I'm the clumsiest person I know." Lilly hung her head so nobody could see her eyes. "I was walking along beside the river and fell in."

The men in the room stared in amazement. Simon hurried to her side and called for a servant. "Here, take Miss Arledge upstairs and—"

"I'll do it," Octavia interrupted. She glanced at the maid and instructed her to put plenty of water on to boil and to bring it up to Miss Lilly's room.

Octavia took Lilly's arm and helped her toward the stairs. "Come, my dear, I'll take care of you."

As they reached the landing, Lilly heard a voice filter up from the parlor. It said, ". . . thought that woman would never quit."

Another said, "If she's going to do that every evening, I'll stay in camp."

Lilly giggled and quickly coughed to cover it up. She and Octavia were in stitches by the time they reached Lilly's room.

Octavia closed the door and listened to make sure they weren't followed. "Oh, Lilly, what really happened?"

"Ethan's been shot. Applejack's taking care of him."

"I know that much . . . how is he?"

"I don't exactly know. He looks terrible and he's unconscious or sleeping. I can't tell." Lilly peeled off her dress and laid it across a chair in front of the fire.

Octavia nodded. Applejack had given her much the same report. She'd go see for herself as soon as Lilly was comfortable. "What about you? What happened?"

Lilly stopped and moved as close to the fire as possible. She was shivering in earnest now. "I got blood on my dress. I knew someone would see me come in. The only way I could get past without anyone noticing the blood was to be drenched and have mud all over my clothes."

"You mean you jumped in the river voluntarily when the temperature outside is near freezing?" Octavia stared in disbelief.

Lilly nodded and stripped the remainder of her clothing off. She slipped into a dressing gown to wear until her bathwater arrived. "I couldn't think of anything else to do."

Octavia hugged her. "You are a foolish girl, but I love you. Why didn't you just wait until they were asleep?"

"I thought of that, but I think they would have missed me. Especially since Simon is back. Father wouldn't have let me miss supper," Lilly explained and held her hands up to get warm.

"You're probably right. They've both been asking where you were. I told them you were—"

Lilly clapped her hands over Octavia's mouth. The sound of footsteps coming down the hallway alerted Lilly to the presence of someone outside the door. "And I simply slid into the river. I thought I would wash away, but the current isn't very strong. I swam once in the Ashley and—"

A knock interrupted her. Octavia opened the door. Simon peered through the doorway, but Octavia stopped him. "Sir, this is a lady's bedchamber. You are not welcome here."

"Mrs. Kendall, I'm—"

Octavia glared at him and folded her arms across her chest. "I don't care if you're the king of England. No decent man presents himself at an unmarried lady's door and expects to be . . . This is unheard of. What a cad you are. Miss Arledge is not receiving visitors."

She slammed the door in Simon's face and pushed the latch. As she stepped away, she muttered, quite loudly, "Of all the forward notions. Can you imagine? That man is no gentleman, Lilly."

"Well, Octavia, he means well, I'm sure." Lilly defended him so loudly that he could have heard her downstairs. She shoveled some coals from the fireplace into the bed warmer and rubbed it between the covers for a few minutes.

"He has no breeding, Lilly. Avoid men like that." Octavia winked at Lilly and sat in the rocking chair.

For the second time they heard footsteps and then a knock. Octavia rose and walked to the door. Before Octavia opened it this time, she called, "Who's there?"

"Dulcie, the cook, Miss Octavia."

Octavia unlocked the door. Dulcie marched in followed by three maids, all bearing buckets of steaming water. They poured it in the bathing tub and left.

Lilly poured in some fragrance grains, removed her dressing gown, and stepped into the water. "Oooh, this is wonderful. I was freezing."

"I hope you don't take a cold, my dear." Octavia pulled her chair close to Lilly. "Tell me more about Ethan."

"You're to take Zip and go up to the cave." Lilly explained that the three of them, along with Applejack, could take turns nursing Ethan.

Octavia thought for a moment, noticed that Lilly was almost done, and repeated Lilly's motions with the bed-warming pan. "Don't forget Prudence. I'll send her up there, too. She's the most dispensable of all of us. Your father will want you around while Simon's here. I need to be in and out, or he'll suspect something. Zip must be around, too. What a dilemma."

Lilly drizzled the warm water over her body once more and stood up. She dried quickly, slipped on her nightgown, and slid into bed. "Oh, this feels wonderful, Octavia. Thanks for warming the sheets again. Now go and get Zip. Show her the way to the cave. We've got to establish a schedule."

The clock downstairs struck midnight before Lilly finally stopped shivering and fell asleep. She couldn't risk going out now, not after dunking herself in the river and having a bath. She'd go first thing in the morning.

Lilly awoke early. She slipped on a warm dress and cloak and hurried downstairs. The house was quiet, so she slipped out the back door and ran down the path to Octavia's. Once at Octavia's Lilly let herself in, greeted Prudence, and exited out the back. The short distance to the woods would be her biggest danger. Someone on the piazza would be able to see her as she darted across the open space.

When she reached the woods, she waited for a full ten minutes to see if anyone had followed her, then she scurried along the path until it divided. She took care to brush leaves back over the path to hide her route, and halfway to the cave she hid behind a tree to see if she could hear or see anyone else. She was being overly cautious, since the sun hadn't fully risen, but she couldn't risk Ethan's life by being foolish.

After what seemed like an eternity, she arrived at the cave. She found Octavia there with Zip. Lilly nodded to them and sat down beside Ethan. His head was burning up with fever. "Has he regained consciousness?"

"No," Octavia answered and sighed. "He's been like this ever since I came in."

Lilly nodded. "Zip, you go back to the house for a while. I'll stay for about an hour. I don't think I'll be missed. Octavia, why don't you go back, too? Send Prudence up to relieve me."

The two ladies left Lilly alone with Ethan. She snuggled under the covers with him to try to help keep him warm. Applejack would be back pretty soon, after he did his morning chores, and Lilly would feel better.

Ethan seemed to be trying to talk. She moved her head so she could hear more clearly.

"Armstrong."

"Who is Armstrong? Did he do this to you?" Lilly asked. She wished she could do something but felt helpless.

"Find Armstrong," Ethan muttered through the veil of his fever.

"Ethan, darling, shhh. Don't talk now." Lilly fought tears, knowing she'd be no help to Ethan if she cried every time trouble came along.

"Lilly . . . find . . . Armstrong . . . Find . . ." Ethan moved erratically in his sleep. "Important. Armstrong."

For two days Ethan seemed to drift into and out of consciousness. He kept calling for Lilly and the Armstrong man, whom none of them knew.

Again through his delirium, Ethan kept calling for

Lilly. She did her best to assure him of her continued presence but had no way of knowing if he understood. Then he called for the man Armstrong and mentioned a pouch.

For a few minutes Lilly wondered what he could be talking about. Then she retraced her steps along the trail and out to the clump of bushes where she'd found Ethan. After brushing aside the leaves, she found a small leather pouch. With shaking hands, she opened it and read a page of instructions.

Ethan was to take the pouch to Captain James Armstrong near Dorchester. The pouch was to be delivered on December thirtieth—today. Lilly hurried back to the cave. There she found Applejack and talked to him about what they should do. "Do you think we could get to the rendezvous point and back before we're missed?"

"Miss Lilly, you ain't thinkin' a changin' into a rebel, is you?" Applejack asked, and deep furrows formed above his eyes as he scowled at her.

Lilly chewed on her lip. She'd avoided thinking about the consequences if she were caught. "No, Applejack, but . . . but Ethan was supposed to deliver this today. What can we do?"

"Miss Lilly, we gonna do whatever you thinks best." Applejack scratched his head. "I reckon we could be back in a hour if we hurry."

"Let's go." Lilly found Prudence and sent her up to sit with Ethan. After explaining to Octavia what she intended to do, Lilly had to rush. She took a book from the library and tucked it into her cloak. "Octavia, if Father asks for me, tell him you saw me walking across the cotton field with a book in my hand. They can search the back fields and woods all afternoon and never see me when I come back. If they're watching the river, I'm caught."

Applejack had taken two horses and ridden downstream about a mile. Lilly took a small rowboat and rowed herself into the middle of the river. It took all her power to keep from crashing into the rocks near the creek where Ethan was being hidden. She finally reached the trees where she knew Applejack would be and coasted to a stop.

He pulled the boat up the bank into some bushes and then helped Lilly to mount. Their horses cantered along until they reached the road to Dorchester. There Lilly urged her horse into a gallop.

When they reached the point marked on the map, they dismounted and walked the horses into the thick brush beside the road and waited. Armstrong was late. Lilly watched the sun, trying to gauge the time.

She glanced over at Applejack's intense expression. "Applejack, what should we do? He's well beyond the appointed time."

"Miss Lilly, I believe—"

They heard the sound of horses. The horses were at full gallop. Lilly gazed at Applejack and shrugged. She leaned over and whispered, "Do you think that's him?"

"I dunno. You ain't goin' out till you see if he's reb or Tory, is you?"

"No. I'm going to wait right here until I—"

A horse galloped into view. The rider was unmistakably a rebel, but he showed no signs of stopping. Before Lilly could make up her mind what to do, she heard the sound of muskets being fired.

"Uh-oh, Miss Lilly," Applejack whispered. "Looks like we done rode right into the war."

CHAPTER 18

LILLY AND APPLEJACK LAY AS STILL AS POSSIBLE. Scared beyond speech, Lilly simply watched the fray taking place before her eyes. A dozen redcoats were after a single Patriot. She knew that, without doubt, the man was Captain James Armstrong, even though she'd never seen him before.

She didn't know what to do. Since she and Applejack had no weapons, they were obviously no match for the soldiers. Then she noticed a large detachment of British soldiers coming from the other direction.

She and Applejack exchanged stares of disbelief. They'd come that same way not long before. They could have been caught with the papers and hung as spies. She had the hem of her chemise pulled through her legs and tucked into the waist band so she could ride easier. While Applejack watched for any sign that they'd been spotted, she slipped the small pouch through the slits in her skirts and petticoats where pockets were attached and tucked it into the waist of her chemise.

Praying that the British wouldn't discover them, Lilly and Applejack watched in horror as Captain Armstrong was captured and led away. Lilly hung her head. There was nothing she could do at all, but at least the papers hadn't gotten into the hands of the British. She opened her mouth to speak, but nothing came out.

She was a loyal British subject. She'd seen a rebel captured and had papers in her possession that would undoubtedly be valuable to the British. Rationalizing that she was acting as Ethan's agent, and not of her own volition, she waited for a few more minutes to see if either of the British units returned.

When she thought she and Applejack were safe, she leaned close and whispered, "Do you think it's safe for us to go?"

"I dunno, but I cain't stand much more of this." Applejack rose and rubbed his hips. "I'se gettin' too old to be laying on the froze ground."

Lilly was stiff, too. They mounted their horses and rode a short distance through the woods. When it appeared that they wouldn't be caught, they found the road again and rode hard until they reached the boat.

"I can't row this boat back to the boathouse. We'll have to pretend that it got loose from its moorings and drifted this way." Lilly dismounted. "Pull it back to the edge of the water."

Applejack did as he was told and then took the horses. "I'll see you later, Miss Lilly. You go straight to the big house 'cause yo' pappy might have missed you."

"Thanks, Applejack. You're a wonder." Lilly reached up and kissed him on the cheek. "Take care of Ethan."

Lilly sped along until she was pretty near the house. When she rounded the next bend, she would be able to see it. Taking no chances with her story, she removed the little book of poetry from her pocket and began to read as she walked.

When she neared the house, one of the soldiers came

running out to her and called, "Miss Arledge, your father is looking for you."

Lilly looked around as if she were puzzled. "Gracious, I must have lost track of the time."

She hurried into the house to see her father. Lilly found him in the library. "You were looking for me?"

"Yes. Where in the name of the hounds of hell have you been all afternoon?" Jonathan demanded and jumped up to glare across the desk at her.

Lilly put her book back on the shelf, removed her cloak, and sat down in front of the massive desk. "I went for a walk. I've been stuck in this musty old house for weeks," Lilly complained. She pushed back a lock of hair.

Jonathan studied her for a few seconds. "We searched the back fields for you. Where were you."

Lilly lied as calmly as possible. She knew her father was angry enough to become abusive. "I'm sorry, Father, but I decided I wanted to go for a ride in one of the little boats. I took one from the boathouse."

"Boats? What boats?" he asked and sat down.

"One of the little ones." Lilly felt the tension in the room dissolving a little. "Only I didn't know how to guide it very well. I'm afraid it's down the river a ways. I couldn't row against the current."

"Don't you know you could have drowned?" Jonathan pounded on the desk. "You are the most goose-witted girl I ever knew."

Lilly did her best to appear contrite. "I'm sorry, Father. I didn't know that rowing was that hard. I just flowed along with the river until I could grab a tree branch and pull the little boat onto the shore."

"Jonathan, I can't find her—" Simon burst into the room, not noticing Lilly for a moment. "Lilly!" he exclaimed, so upset that he used her given name although he never had before. "Oh, my dear, we've been worried to death about you."

"Lilly, apologize to Simon for making him worry and then excuse yourself." Jonathan removed a cigar from the box on the desk. "Have one, Simon?"

"No, Jonathan, thank you. I'll escort Miss Arledge to her room." Simon waited for Lilly to rise. "I'll be back shortly."

Lilly walked to the door and paused. "Mr. Owens, I'm so sorry to have troubled you. I never imagined that you would be searching for me."

Simon patted her arm solicitously. "We were concerned because we've had reports of rebel activity in the area. We simply wanted to protect you."

"Gracious, I'll have to stay closer to the house, I suppose." Lilly walked past him and started up the stairs.

"Miss Arledge," he called and ran along after her. He fanned himself as if he were overly warm. "I also wanted to make sure . . . well, the parson will arrive on the first day of January. I want to make sure our plans are . . . that nothing's happened to . . . he'll be here on the first."

Lilly felt a sense of desperation rise in her throat and constrict it, almost as though someone were choking her. She could barely croak the words she said to Simon. "Thank you for informing me, Mr. Owens. I'm very tired now."

"Of course, after your busy afternoon you'll need to rest." Simon lifted her hand to his lips and kissed it.

She hurried into her room and closed the door behind her. That had been a close call. If she and Applejack had been gone a few minutes more, then her alibi would have been unnecessary. The British soldiers would have caught her before she could hide the papers.

What could she do with them? If they ever suspected her, then they would search while she was out. Lilly began to look for a place where the papers would be safe until she could return them to Ethan.

She pulled out drawers and looked under every piece of furniture. No place in her room seemed to be safe enough. Lilly was sure Simon would have her watched. He seemed awfully smug and knowing. Could he possibly know about Ethan?

As time for supper came closer, Lilly still hadn't resolved the issue of where to hide the dispatches she'd attempted to take to Captain Armstrong. After dressing carefully, she decided to conceal them in her father's room. She waited until she heard his door close and then peeked out to see if the hallway was clear.

She saw no one. Lilly slipped the pouch into her pocket and took a candle with her across the hall. She tilted the candle so that the wax dripped on the leather pouch until there was a large puddle. Then she opened the bottom drawer of her father's dresser and pressed the pouch to the bottom of the next drawer up.

When she was sure it was stuck, she hurried back across the hall. Lilly couldn't predict how long the wax would hold the pouch, but since it wasn't too heavy, she decided it would remain in place for a few days at least.

After supper she made herself heard around the house. She walked back and forth to the kitchen. When the men were in the library smoking their cigars, she went in and took a book. "I'm going to read for a short time."

"Stay with us, Miss Arledge," Simon pleaded, rushing to her side.

"Oh, you men don't want me around. I'm sure you have more interesting things to do than to entertain a goose of a girl like me." Lilly smiled at him, hoping he wouldn't pursue the issue. Colonel Wilkins studied her carefully as she smiled and talked for a few moments. Then all she wanted to do was get away. "If you need me, Father, I'll be in my room."

Lilly hurried up the stairs. She couldn't leave the house until after dark—if then. Simon's demeanor told her that she was suspected of something, although she didn't know exactly what. He could simply be interested in spending some time with her, but she doubted it.

The night seemed endless. All through the hours she heard people in the hallway and out on the piazza. She was cut off from Ethan and didn't know how to escape. Applejack would take care of Ethan, but Lilly wanted to see him, to assure herself that he was all right.

The last day of December was somber. Gray clouds blotted out the sun, and during the afternoon a dull rain began to fall. Lilly stood in her room, peering out the window toward the cave. She wanted desperately to go to Ethan but dared not risk it.

Zip came in for a few minutes. She reported that Ethan was better. He was conscious now and asking for Lilly.

Lilly told Zip to tell him and the others the reason she hadn't come to the cave—she was being watched.

Lilly went about her housekeeping chores as if she hadn't a care in the world. She had one objective—to keep the soldiers away from Ethan. They didn't know where he was, Lilly assumed, since he was still safely hidden.

Ethan's safety was of primary importance. If the soldiers caught him now, he would surely die. With an injury like his, life on one of those filthy prison ships would kill him—if he lived that long. Lilly realized that the British would probably hang him as a traitor if they found him.

Lilly brought a rocking chair down from the attic and put it in the nursery. Even though there was no reason to call it a nursery yet, she decided to make it as much of a baby's room as possible. She was filling time, time she wanted to spend with Ethan. The baby's room was as close as she could come.

Since Lilly went down to Octavia's house every day, today could be no exception. She put on her pattens and took her umbrella and walked across the yard as if nothing out of the ordinary was going on—except that today she carried a change of warm clothing and some food with her.

Octavia wasn't home. She was up in the cave with Ethan. Lilly had known that her visit would be with Prudence, but nobody else would know. "Prudence, I wish I could go up there, but I just can't risk it."

"Miss Lilly," Prudence began, sitting down on the sofa, "that man got all of us lookin' after him. Don't you go up there. If them Tories . . . 'scuse me, Miss Lilly, them soldiers are watchin' you, you'll lead them right to him."

Lilly paced back and forth in front of the fire. "Why are they watching me? Have I done something unusual? I can't remember having said or done anything to make them suspicious. Do you think they're watching Octavia, too?"

Prudence shook her head. "I don't know, but she ain't comin' back durin' the daylight. They sure ain't watchin' Applejack and Zip. Them two can come and go as they please."

Lilly stopped pacing and smiled at Prudence. "I guess I'll go back to the house and see what I can find out. Maybe I'll overhear something as I do my chores. My wedding to Simon is scheduled for tomorrow. Prudence,

I'm not going to be there. I've got to escape somehow. Hide this bag. Send it up to the cave if you can."

The soldiers were in the parlor when Lilly arrived at the main house. She found a cloth and went in, pretending to dust, to see if she could hear anything. The men were discussing the most recent rebel action—they were talking about Captain Armstrong.

Lilly shielded her emotions as she lifted each porcelain figurine and dusted it lovingly. After a moment she noticed the men weren't talking, but she continued her task as if she hadn't heard them stop.

"Lilly, my dear," Jonathan said and walked over to her. "Isn't there someone here who can do this? You're my daughter. You don't have to dust."

Sighing wistfully—she hoped—Lilly placed the piece of porcelain back on the mantel. "Father, I've nothing to do. I've read until my eyes are aching. With all this dreary rain I can't go walking. What's there to do?"

Jonathan rolled his eyes. "Well, you're disrupting our conversation. Can't you go somewhere else?"

"I suppose, if I'm intruding." Lilly started to leave the room but stopped at the door to say, "Supper will be in a few minutes."

Ethan tried to sit up. His head felt as large as a washtub, but he couldn't afford the luxury of being indisposed. Applejack insisted on rebandaging the wounds. "I'm fine, Applejack. Don't fret over me."

"If somethin' happens to you, Miss Lilly gonna string me up by my toes. She sets a great store by you, Mistah Ethan." Applejack peeled the dirty bandage off, looked at the wound, and added more salve.

Ethan wrinkled his nose in disgust. "What's that stinking salve you keep pasting on my head?"

"Horse liniment." Applejack wound a fresh bandage around Ethan's head. "And don't say nothin' bad about it. You ain't dead, is you?"

"I suppose you're right." Ethan tried to ignore the smell by thinking of Lilly's wonderful fragrance of jasmine. "Is Lilly all right?"

"She fine. You know she cain't come up here. Them redcoats watchin' her like she was a pot of gold." Applejack finished the bandage and leaned forward to examine his work. "You'll do."

Ethan felt his head and found the wound still tender. He winced. "What's going on down there?"

"I don't know. I hears that soldier planning to marry her tomorrow, and she tryin' to find a way not to marry him."

Leaning back, Ethan began to think of ways to prevent the wedding from taking place. He could think of only one way. Lilly had to be out of the house until it was too late. He knew that the British were pulling back to Charleston very soon. If Ethan could find a way to kidnap Lilly until the soldiers were gone, she would be fine.

Lilly went upstairs and changed clothes for supper. When she came downstairs, Simon took her arm and escorted her into the dining room. "Thank you . . . Simon." Lilly deliberately called him by his first name, hoping to put him off-guard.

He blushed profusely. He glowed like a coal in a hot fire. "Allow me, Lilly," he said and pulled out a chair for her.

While they were eating, he reached under the table and rested his hand on her knee. Lilly gasped aloud. Seeing that everyone had heard, she pretended to be choking. After a few moments of coughing, she smiled sweetly.

"Thank you for your concern. I'm just so . . . excited about . . . well, I'm excited."

Simon grinned foolishly. Lilly had succeeded in convincing him, without ever saying anything positive, that she was looking forward to the wedding scheduled for the next day.

Even Jonathan's face beamed with pleasure. Lilly thought wryly that men were exceedingly easy to fool, especially when they thought a woman was acceding to their wishes. The remainder of supper took on a festive air. Dulcie's wonderful dishes tasted like sawdust to Lilly, but she ate ravenously. She didn't know when she would eat a good meal again.

". . . caught that Armstrong chap not far from here," said one soldier down near her father.

Lilly pretended not to notice the conversation because she knew several of the men at the table were watching her for a sign of recognition of the name or perhaps fear. She smiled at Simon. "Simon . . ." she said and blushed shyly. "I wish the weather would clear up . . . for tomorrow. I hate this dreary rain, don't you?"

"Oh, yes. Yes, I do." Simon gazed at her for a moment. "Maybe it will. Who knows?"

". . . saw a woman and a big slave riding that way," the voice down the table continued.

"I would so like some fresh flowers. It's far too early for the bulbs to be blooming, don't you think?" Lilly hated to speak when there was information she needed to know being discussed at the other end of the table, but she wanted to appear disinterested.

"Flowers?" Simon asked, looking puzzled.

"Yes, you know, for my hair or for a little bouquet." Lilly lowered her eyes coquettishly. "I wish I had time to commission a new gown."

"They think maybe the woman is a spy. She disappeared before the unit coming from the other direction ever saw her," the soldier said.

"I painted the little room off my bedchamber. I plan to use it for a nursery. There's no telling how long this war will last and . . ." Lilly wanted desperately to keep Simon's attention. He obviously wanted to hear the conversation at the other end of the table.

Colonel Wilkins shook his head sadly. "We're pulling back. It's too dangerous for so few of us out here. Greene's men are camped outside Jacksonboro, cutting us off from our main force."

"You do like babies, don't you, Simon?" Lilly touched her hand to Simon's knee.

Simon seemed to forget all about the important conversation going on among the men. "Why, yes, of course."

He took Lilly's hand and held it tightly. Lilly smiled and fluttered her eyelids at him, trying to make him feel special. She hated this charade but felt that if she could convince him of her innocence without ever mentioning that she thought she was being watched, then he might call off the sentries.

When supper was over, Lilly walked to the door of the dining room. "Simon, it's so stuffy in here. Would you mind foregoing your cigar and brandy for a short time? I would love some fresh air."

"Certainly, Miss . . . Lilly. Gentlemen, if you'll excuse us, I'm taking my . . . lovely fiancée for fresh air." Simon took her arm, and they walked out onto the piazza.

The cold air nearly froze Lilly in her thin gown, but she pretended not to notice. "Oh, dear. This is so sad."

"What is? Why are you sad?" Simon stopped and gazed down at her.

Lilly dabbed at the corners of her eyes with her handkerchief. "A girl dreams of a pretty wedding with lots of her friends around. Oh, I'm so sorry, Simon. I didn't mean to imply that . . . oh, dear, how thoughtless of me. It's just the cold, damp air. I'd so hoped to be married in the spring."

"I'm afraid that's impossible, Lilly." Simon slipped his arms around her and held her close. "My unit is being withdrawn soon."

"What do you mean? You won't be here with me? I'm to remain here all alone?" she asked, as if the idea horrified her. "Oh, Simon, say you won't leave me here in the country with nothing to do but swat flies and bake in the humidity."

"Well, Lilly, there's not much I can do. Charleston is already packed with people. Why, I hear that General Leslie has had to destroy many of our horses for lack of forage. We can hardly feed the people."

"Oh, how awful. When are you leaving? Can you stay for a little while . . . after the wedding?" Lilly felt herself blushing. She'd never consciously baited anyone in her life. Here she was picking this man for information and using her sexuality to keep him from being aware of what was happening to him. She leaned against his chest.

"Well, I don't think . . . I'll try to get a leave or something . . . I mean . . . it's not easy, with the war still going on and . . . I want to be here, of course, but . . ." Simon babbled like a baby.

Lilly could feel the evidence of his attraction to her. She broke free of his embrace and turned away from him. Simon immediately dropped into one of the chairs and crossed his legs.

"Oh, Simon, how simply awful. We'll be married but separated. With nobody here to protect us if those rebels . . . if they go on a murderous rampage." She clung to the post as if prostrate with fear of living out in the country alone without protection.

Simon, who apparently couldn't get up without embarrassing himself, cleared his throat. "Well, it won't be as bad as all that. We'll win this war shortly and . . . well, everything will be all right."

Lilly straightened her shoulders. The rain was falling as heavily as it had been all day. From her vantage point she could see no soldiers posted as sentries. "Simon, those rebels could dance right in here and burn us in our beds."

Rising, Simon straightened his kid breeches and walked over to Lilly. "Don't you worry. We've sentries posted on the river and on the road to protect us. Nobody can get in or out without us knowing about it."

Lilly smiled and batted her eyes at him. "I should have known you'd take measures to protect us. How foolish of me not to trust you. I hope you'll forgive me." Lilly reached up and kissed him lightly on the cheek. "We've an exciting day tomorrow. I must get some sleep."

Without looking back, Lilly ran into the house and up the stairs to her room. She'd found out where the sentries were posted outside the house. Now all she had to do was make sure she could escape the sentries inside the house.

She gave Simon enough time to regain his composure and return to the other men. She knew he would be as cocky as any man who'd made a conquest, but she wasn't through with him yet. Lilly had to be sure she could evade the sentries completely.

After a few minutes she went to the library, where the men were gathered, and peeked inside. "Simon," she called. "Could I see you for a moment?"

"Certainly, my dear." Simon excused himself and stepped into the hallway. "What's wrong?"

"Simon," she said in a voice hardly above a whisper. "I . . . I've been thinking. We're not certain . . . Oh, I need to sit down."

Simon escorted her to the parlor, and she sat on the sofa near the fire. "Thank you. You're such a dear man."

"And you are a treasure." Simon seated himself beside her. "Perhaps I should close the door."

Lilly glanced about, as if in a panic. "Oh, no, someone would . . . I mean, they might think we . . . my reputation would be ruined."

"I hardly think that's the case." Simon slid his arm around her. "We're to be married tomorrow."

"That's what I want to talk to you about." Lilly smiled like a shy, virginal bride to be. "You're leaving immediately after the wedding takes place. Am I correct?"

Simon nodded. He seemed to regret having to confirm her suspicions. "I'm sorry, Lilly. But I am, after all, still a soldier."

"But on your wedding day. Oh, those brutes." Lilly scowled and shrugged helplessly. "They're so mean. Don't they understand that . . . well, that we need some time?"

Smiling happily, Simon hugged her close. "Lilly, my darling. This war is bound to be over soon. We'll be together the rest of our lives."

Lilly forced a dewy tear from her eye and promptly blotted it with her handkerchief. She didn't want Simon to realize that there were no real tears. "But I'm afraid something awful will happen. What if . . . what if you're injured . . . or worse?"

She turned her head toward his shoulder and pretended to sob. When she thought of the possibility of

Ethan's death or injury, the tears came forward, and she cried until she'd dampened Simon's shirt. "Oh, how careless of me. I'm so sorry. But, Simon, I'll have nothing to remember you by. No sweet caresses. No . . . baby. My life will be ruined."

"Oh, Lilly, my dear. I had no idea all these things were worrying you. Don't even think such awful thoughts. I'll be back sooner than you think." Simon patted her consolingly. "Don't worry."

"Simon," she said, blotting the corners of her eyes once again for effect, "I'm going to be perfectly honest with you." She slipped her hands into her pockets and crossed her fingers for the lie she told. "I want to have a baby. May I come . . . oh, I feel like such a . . . such a bad woman. May I come to your room later?"

Simon stared at her in disbelief. "Lilly, are you saying what I think—"

Lilly leapt up, went to the window, and peered out into the night. "You hate me now, don't you? Oh, this is the worst mess I've ever been in."

Simon sprang to his feet and put his arms around her. "Lilly, my dear sweet innocent, I think nothing of the sort. I adore you."

Closing her eyes to hide her true feelings, Lilly hung her head for the horrible tricks she was playing on poor Simon. She silently asked the Lord for forgiveness and hoped he'd understand. She glanced up at Simon. Her tears had wet her lashes, and they were stuck together in little spikes when she fluttered her eyelids. "Oh, Simon, you are too kind."

"Lilly, my dear, maybe it would be better if I came to your room," he suggested.

"Oh, no." Lilly gazed at him wide-eyed with fear—real fear. He couldn't come to her room. "No, my father would hear you. He's a light sleeper. And Zip often checks on me before she retires and as soon as she rises. You would have no way . . . and, Simon," she whispered, as if to impart a secret, "I've been hearing people in the hallways at night."

Simon flushed. "Lilly, I think you must be imagining the footsteps."

His embarrassment confirmed to her that he was having her watched at night. "I'll come to you. If I run into anyone in the hallway, I can pretend I'm going downstairs for a glass of water. It would be most embarrassing if anyone thought you were coming . . . Oh, please, Simon, promise me you won't humiliate me by coming to my room. I'll try to come to your room by one—our wedding day."

"Of course, darling." Simon hugged her reassuringly. "I'll wait for you."

Lilly's smile was broad and sweet. "Oh, Simon, you're so wonderful."

CHAPTER 19

LILLY RETURNED TO HER ROOM AND OPENED HER window to see if she could hear anything coming from downstairs. Her patience and plotting were soon rewarded.

Not long afterward she heard Simon talking to one of the other soldiers about sentry duty. "I think that since we are so few men and the perimeters of this plantation must be guarded, we can forego the sentry post inside the house. Tomorrow will be a busy day, what with us moving our headquarters, and I believe the men need a rest."

"Yes, sir," came the reply.

Hugging herself gleefully, Lilly put on her thickest, darkest dress without the panniers. She pulled her hair into a long braid and secured it with a dark ribbon. The night would be dark, but she couldn't carry a candle or lantern, so she waited until the house was absolutely quiet and opened the door just a little. She peered into the hallway and saw no one.

Lilly walked down the hallway in her stockinged feet to avoid being heard. The rain pattering on the roof and blowing against the windows would be enough noise to cover any slight sound she might make. Simon's room was at the back of the house. She was running the risk of being seen if he was still awake, but he wasn't expecting her for another hour.

Her cloak flew around her face, and the umbrella whipped back and forth when she stepped out into the wind, but she managed to control both. Lilly moved stealthily away from the house until she could see Simon's windows. The yellow glow from his window told her he was expecting her—and that he probably couldn't see out into the darkness very well.

Offering a prayer for her safe escape, Lilly darted across the lawn, through the gardens, and past Octavia's house. When she reached the woods, she hid beneath the low-hanging branches of a live oak and waited. She crouched there for fifteen minutes or more to make sure she wasn't followed.

She would have to hide until late in the afternoon, but she didn't care. She tasted her first real freedom and loved it.

Taking a wide-ranging route, she came to the hill upon which stood the cave where Ethan would be. She paused again to watch for signs that she was being followed.

Ethan would have to be moved before dawn. Her course of action might cause him to be discovered if Simon searched for her.

Without waiting any longer than necessary, she peered across the plantation. She spotted several fires that were probably the sentry outposts. Then she went inside to find Ethan.

"Ethan!" she cried when she saw him sitting on the blanket. "Oh, Ethan, I'm happy to see you awake. Why are you alone? Except for Tartuffe, of course."

"I don't need to be nursed. I sent Applejack back to his bride." He grinned crookedly and scratched between the cat's ears. "I'm happy to see you, too. What are you doing here? Tartuffe and I are good friends now."

"The most awful thing has happened." Lilly sat beside him and hugged him. "The British—Simon and Colonel Wilkins in particular—think I've turned rebel."

"Why would they think a thing like that?" Ethan asked and slipped his arm around her. God, but he'd missed her.

"Well, let me start at the beginning." Lilly snuggled into the crook of his arm. "When you were unconscious, you were calling for someone named Armstrong. I finally figured out what you were talking about and went searching for the pouch."

Ethan stared at her in astonishment. "Did you find it?"

"Yes. I'm sorry, but I read the instructions to you and decided that you were incapable of carrying out your duty, and I didn't want you to be accused of shirking it, so I took the pouch to Captain Armstrong."

"You did? Lilly, that was too dangerous. That mission could have . . . What happened?" Ethan closed his eyes. If the British had caught her with those papers, she would be dead now in all probability.

She explained all about the boat and Applejack's part in the adventure. Lilly told the tale without much emotion because she didn't want to upset Ethan any more than was absolutely necessary. "We just hid out until we saw them. The British trapped him, Ethan. I don't know where they took him. They came at him from two directions, which leads to the bothersome part of this story for me."

Ethan gazed at her, wondering how she'd ever found enough courage to do what she'd done. "What's that, my love?"

"The British soldiers saw a woman and a slave riding along that road. I suppose they were lying in wait for Captain Armstrong," Lilly explained and removed her damp cloak. "Simon and Captain Wilkins suspect that the woman was me."

"Have they questioned you about it?" Ethan asked. He rose and paced the floor. Lilly was in graver danger than she thought. "What did they say? Did they see you coming back from there?"

"No. They haven't asked anything. They're talking around the subject in my presence. I assume they think I'll act suspiciously." Lilly folded the umbrella and laid it to one side. "I've got to go back. I've played a trick on Simon. We're supposed to be getting married tomorrow, and I'll have to tell him. I thought I could simply hide out, but I can't. That isn't fair to him."

Ethan stared at her for a few seconds. "You don't have to be fair to him. He's the enemy."

"He's not my enemy. He's been very kind to me, Ethan." Lilly felt so ashamed of herself. She should have stood up to her father, no matter what. Now she'd embarrassed a nice man for the sake of her own comfort. "You've got to leave. When I tell them I'm married to you, I'm afraid they'll come looking for you."

"I won't go without taking you with me." Ethan pulled on his cloak. "Come on. We'll get two horses and—"

"No. I can't go, Ethan. Not until I've told the truth." Lilly stood up. "I love you, but I must be honest with Simon."

Ethan nodded. He understood her need to be truthful, but he didn't want to leave her unprotected. "Lilly, I'll walk you back to the house. I'm going to get a horse and go for help. Wait as long as you can to give me a chance to get far enough away to avoid being caught. I can't ride too fast with this head injury, but I'll be back as soon as I can."

"Take Applejack with you." Lilly put her arms around Ethan. "He's a good thinker and will help to protect you."

"Good idea." Ethan calculated the distances. "I may be gone as much as a day, depending on how much cooperation I can get from General Marion."

Lilly lay her head on his shoulder and relished the warmth that seemed to emanate from him. She felt his forehead. "You're still running a fever. What are you going to do?"

"Don't worry. Let's go." Ethan pulled her cape around her and gazed down into her eyes. He'd dreamed of seeing them again ever since he was injured. He ached to take her in his arms and make love to her again, but he knew the time wasn't right. Too much could happen and too much could go wrong.

Their kiss was tender and then passionate. Ethan hungered for her. He wanted to forget the war and live out the rest of his days with Lilly in peace. But like Lilly he felt duty-bound to do what he could for his country.

They walked slowly down the path through the woods. Lilly hated every step because the closer she got to the house, the more danger Ethan was in and the sooner he'd have to leave her. She tensed as she heard a sound in the bushes.

"Tartuffe," Ethan whispered and kissed the top of her head.

Soon they were directly behind Octavia's house. Ethan and Lilly watched the main house for a few minutes to see if they could spot any sentries or unusual movement. The light still shone from Simon's window. "That's

Simon's room, there with the candles burning. He's still waiting for me."

"He can wait forever." Ethan kissed her and held her tightly. He didn't want to let her go. "Please be careful. I'll be back as soon as I can."

Lilly nodded and started to walk away. "Oh, Ethan. You be careful. I heard the soldiers talking about withdrawing to Charleston. I don't want you to run into them on your way back."

Ethan watched her until she reached the door. She didn't look back, and he knew that she would have if she didn't fear for his safety. He waited for a few minutes longer to make sure that nothing unusual happened. He heard no shouting, no alarm given. He went to awaken Applejack.

Applejack wasn't asleep. Ethan explained briefly what he wanted, and the slave dressed quickly without complaining. They went to the barn, saddled two horses, and led them out.

"We've got to avoid the roads and river. Lilly says there are sentries posted there." Ethan swung into the saddle and headed southeast through the thick brush. "We may have to walk through the worst of this, but I think we can ride safely for a while."

Lilly slowly made her way up the stairs. She wanted to change clothes before she went to see Simon because she didn't want him to know she'd been outside. She did everything in her power to protect Ethan from being caught.

Somewhere deep inside, she knew that she was doing the right thing by being honest with Simon. She pulled on a simple homespun dress and lifted her chin. Lilly walked quietly to Simon's door and paused. Could she do this? Should she do this at this hour?

No, Ethan wasn't far enough away yet. She'd have to give him at least an hour's start. She still had to deal with Simon for now. She could tell him the complete truth in the morning when Ethan was well away.

Summoning her courage, she tapped on the door. Lilly heard footsteps as Simon crossed the room. When he opened the door, she stepped inside quickly.

"My dear, I thought you would never come." Simon put his arm around her and led her to a chair. "Can I offer you a glass of wine?"

Lilly burst into tears. Great sobs of agony shook her shoulders, and she wrung her hands. Anyone who saw her could tell that she was in a state of emotional turmoil that couldn't be easily resolved. "Oh, Simon. I can't. I'm sorry. I led you on, but I can't. Can you . . . hic . . . ever forgive me?"

Simon stared at her in disbelief. "What are you saying? What can't you do?"

"Oh, I know you'll hate me for telling you." Lilly stared at him through wet eyes that were opened wide. "I . . . I can't be . . . intimate . . . with you now."

"Don't worry about anything, my dear. Everything will be all right." Simon knelt before her and smiled. "I promise not to hurt you."

"It's wrong. I can't do it." Lilly began to sob again. She wanted to tell him the complete truth, to get all the weight off her shoulders, but she couldn't yet. Not yet.

"Lilly, this is a perfectly natural act. We're not being bad. We're going to be married in a few hours and—"

The sobs came harder. Lilly knew that if she continued, she'd awaken everybody in the house. Simon must have thought so, too.

"All right. Come with me. I'll walk you back to your room." Simon patted her on the shoulder and helped her to stand. "We'll talk about this in the morning."

"Th . . . th . . . thank you for being so understanding." Lilly sniffed and touched her handkerchief to her eyes. "You're so kind."

"You're simply having some strong emotional feelings about getting married. There's nothing for you to fear." Simon stopped outside her door. "Good night, my dear. Sleep well and don't worry."

Lilly felt awful. She looked awful. Her eyes were puffy and red, and her face was all splotched with color. She removed her clothes, pulled on a nightgown, and climbed into bed. This night had turned out to be simply terrible. What a miserable beginning for the new year.

When Ethan and Applejack came close to the British encampment at Dorchester, they saw little activity. The few soldiers who remained were packing crates and casks onto wagons to be transported back to Charleston.

The two men rode on in silence. They were heading toward Jacksonboro, just outside Charleston. General Marion was there, sitting on the newly formed legislature. Ethan wanted to ask for Marion's help.

Dawn came and went almost unmarked. Gray clouds still cluttered the sky, but Ethan thought the weather might improve later in the day. The ride to Jacksonboro would take until nearly noon.

Ethan wondered what Lilly was doing. Had she been able to convince Simon that she couldn't marry him? She seemed to believe that Simon would understand, but Ethan didn't think so. No man liked to be fooled.

What about Jonathan? Ethan thought Jonathan would probably be angrier than Simon. Her father had a lot to lose if she didn't marry the Englishman. "Say, Applejack, what do you think Jonathan will do when Lilly refuses to marry Simon?"

"Well, sir, Mistah Ethan, that man's liable to do anything. I think he's dangerous." Applejack wiped the drizzle off his face and looked at Ethan. "He's like to hurt Lilly if we don't git back to stop him."

The wedding was scheduled for six o'clock in the evening. Lilly had set the time that late because she claimed to have too much to do.

She prayed that Ethan had gotten away safely. Every minute she waited to tell Simon and her father that she couldn't go through with the marriage would help Ethan. But she wanted to spare Simon all the embarrassment she possibly could.

Taking the umbrella, she headed toward Octavia's. Lilly wanted to be free to discuss Ethan. She also wanted to consult with Octavia about how to break the news to Simon. She found her sitting in the parlor staring at the fire.

"Sit down, my dear." Octavia gestured to Lilly's favorite rocking chair. "Join me and get warm."

Lilly gazed at her friend for a moment. Octavia sounded glum and wasn't doing anything. Lilly had never seen Octavia without something in her hands. She was either working in the gardens, knitting or embroidering, darning or mending, or writing in her journal.

Almost afraid to ask questions, Lilly dropped into the chair and stared at Octavia. "Is something wrong?"

"Wrong? Nothing really." Octavia sighed and continued to stare into the flames.

"Something must be," Lilly protested and slipped out

of the chair to sit at Octavia's knee. "You can tell me. Is it Ethan? Has he been hurt again?"

"Oh, Lilly, it's a combination of things." Octavia attempted to smile and touched Lilly's face. "You're so young and your life is before you. This morning I feel so old."

"But you're not old. You've plenty to live for." Lilly hadn't expected to be the one consoling Octavia. She'd expected to seek advice from her mother-in-law. "Tell me what's troubling you."

"I'm going to be honest with you, dear. I love you and I think you know it." Octavia glanced at Lilly and then back at the flames. "When you first came here, the day your father came with all the troops and removed me from my house, I prayed that all of you would perish."

Lilly hugged Octavia sympathetically. The woman couldn't be blamed for not wanting a bunch of usurpers in her house. "I understand. You don't have to fret about that at all."

"No, Lilly. You were so sweet, so understanding, so loving. I still wanted to hate you." Octavia's eyes were glazed with sorrow. "I knew you weren't to blame, but you were the person I saw the most. I hated your father and still do. I've regretted my feelings for you ever since. God didn't mean for us to hate, no matter what happens to us."

Lilly felt tears sting her eyes. Octavia was in pain, great emotional pain. Lilly hugged her close and pressed Octavia's head to her bosom and rocked her as she would a child. "Octavia, don't worry about it. It's over."

Octavia lifted her head and looked at Lilly. "I knew you would understand. You're the kindest person I ever knew. It's not over, Lilly. I love you as I would my own daughter. If anyone has to live in my house other than me, I would choose you, but I still hate your father."

"There are a lot of people who hate him, Octavia. You aren't alone. Sometimes I think I do," Lilly admitted. "But he's in pain, too. He adored my mother and when she died, he blamed me. I can understand his . . . moods."

"Dear child, you've been through so much. I hope life is kind to you from this day forward." Octavia sat back in her chair and looked down at Lilly. "My greatest prayer was that your father would be out of my home by the new year. The answer to my prayer was no."

"Don't give up yet, Octavia. Ethan's gone for help." Lilly tried to encourage Octavia with good news. "He'll be back soon."

"You mean he's not in the . . . hiding place?"

"No. He's been gone since about two this morning."

Octavia's lips curved upward slightly. "Alone?"

"No, Applejack is with him." Lilly moved back to her rocking chair. "I pray they'll be back today. I . . . I need him to be back today."

Lilly couldn't burden Octavia any further. Jonathan Arledge had caused enough problems at Carolina Moon, and Lilly didn't want to add to them. She would have to face Simon alone. She would have to decide the best way to handle him.

Later she found him in the parlor with several other men. "Simon, may I speak with you?"

"Of course, my dear," Simon answered and excused himself.

He followed her into the hallway. For lack of a better place, Lilly took him to the ladies' parlor. Nobody but her used the room anymore, and they could be alone for this very private conversation. She closed the doors to assure privacy.

"What is it, Lilly?" he asked.

"Please sit down, Simon." Lilly wanted to make him comfortable if she could. She moved to the sofa, and he sat beside her. "I've been very dishonest with you, and I want to apologize for my behavior."

"Lilly, don't worry—"

"No, Simon," she interrupted and placed a hand on his chest. "Let me speak. Then you may say what you wish without interruption."

He nodded for her to go on.

"I have always tried to be truthful with people. I pride myself on my honesty." Lilly stared at her hands for a moment. She wrung them until they were red. She looked into Simon's eyes so he would know she was being completely honest now. "I cannot marry you."

CHAPTER 20

SIMON GAPED AT HER AS IF HE DIDN'T UNDERSTAND the words she'd spoken. "Cannot marry me?"

"No. I cannot." Lilly inhaled deeply. She knew that her confession would hurt Simon, and it pained her to be the cause of it, but she had no alternative. "I am already married."

A lopsided grin broke across Simon's face. "You're teasing me, aren't you?"

"No." She said it as simply as she could. "I tried to prevent your proposal, Simon, I really did. But you went on, ignoring my signals. Then you spoke to my father. He's rather dictatorial, as you've observed."

"He struck you, didn't he?" The dawning of knowledge was apparent on Simon's face. "He threatened you to make you accept my proposal."

Simon rose and walked to the window. He stared out across the fields and then turned back to Lilly. "Why didn't you tell me? I would have . . . I could have—"

"No, Simon. It wouldn't have changed anything." Lilly walked over to him and touched his arm. "He uses people, Simon. He's used me for years, and I've been too weak to stop him, but now I'm not going to let him use me anymore."

"What are you going to do?" Simon looked down into her eyes. "I'm afraid he'll beat you again."

"I'm sorry to have involved you in this sordid mess at all, Simon. You're a kind, decent man." Lilly returned to her seat. "I hope I haven't embarrassed you too much. If you wish, you may say that you discovered some horrible secret about me and retracted your proposal. My father wanted your money. That's why he wanted this marriage. I shall uphold your story, no matter what you choose to say."

"Lilly . . . Miss Arledge—"

"You can call me Lilly. We've been through a great mess together." Lilly tried to smile at him. He seemed to be taking the whole matter rather well.

Simon smiled. "Oh, Lilly, what a mess we have indeed. I've deceived you as well. I believed I was marrying an heiress to a large fortune."

"You believed that . . .?" Lilly giggled. "Yes, we do have a mess. What shall our story be?"

"Well, as I see it, we've both been the deceiver and the deceivee, if there is such a word." Apparently lost in thought, Simon peered out the window. "Perhaps we should have a rousing fight. That way neither of us will appear to be completely to blame, nor completely blameless."

Lilly smiled, feeling better about the whole situation since she hadn't hurt him as badly as she thought. "That seems like a wonderful plan. What shall we argue about?"

"Well, supposing we argue about money. That's always a good one. My parents have had some jolly good fights over money."

"But what shall I say?" Lilly asked, wondering if she

could make this disagreement seem real enough to call off the wedding.

"You ask for money to refurbish this place. I'll refuse. You ask for money for gowns. I'll refuse." Simon cocked his head to one side. "I never knew a woman who couldn't think of a reason to ask for money."

"Well, I'll try." Lilly leaned forward to whisper in Simon's ear. "Where shall we stage this fight?"

"Why not in the hallway where everyone can hear?" Simon took her arm, and they walked to the door. "Lilly, I do care for you. I think you are a fine person."

Lilly kissed him on the cheek. "And I like you, Simon. I hope that after our horrible argument we can part friends."

"We'll be friends forever. Nobody can have lived through our riotous engagement and not come out friends." Simon gazed at her. "One or two more points to clarify."

Knowing that he was about to ask her to be more specific about her marriage, Lilly nodded. "I am married to Major Ethan Kendall."

"I see. Does that mean you're no longer . . . you've turned rebel?" Simon asked, staring blankly at her.

The way Simon looked at her, Lilly felt as if she'd grown green hair. "No. It means I'm in love with a man who happens to be a rebel. Does this change our arrangement?"

Simon sat down again. "Lilly, you're married to a rebel?"

Lilly could see that this would take a better explanation, so she seated herself again. "Simon, I met Ethan in Charleston. I, like everyone else, thought he was a Tory. I fell in love with him. When I found out he wasn't a Tory, I still loved him. Can you understand?"

"I don't know." Simon shook his head slowly as if all the new information she'd given him was a foreign language.

"Think of it this way," Lilly began. She hoped she could make Simon see her point of view. It would be nice if they could part as friends. "Before the war we were all the same. After the war we'll all be the same again, no matter who wins. We've got to find common ground, a basis for renewing our civilization."

"I can understand that. I've often wondered what was going to happen after the war was over. Neighbor against neighbor; brother against brother—"

"Wife against husband. The list goes on and on, but someday we're going to have to heal those old wounds and . . ." Lilly thought about how she could explain her feelings. "Just be people again."

Simon leaned back and gazed at her with new understanding. "I see what you mean. When this is all over, regardless of who wins, everyone will still be here and will someday have to forgive and forget."

Lilly felt triumphant. "Exactly. Each relationship that forms now between the two sides makes that healing process easier."

As Simon looked at her, she had the impression that he'd changed his opinion of her. "You know, Lilly, you're an intelligent woman. I thought I would never admit that, but I have." Simon chuckled and shook his head. "Maybe I'm glad you're married to the rebel instead of me. I don't know how I could handle a woman with good sense."

"Shall we fight?"

"One more thing. Why did you virtually invite yourself to my bed last night and then uninvite yourself?"

Lilly had hoped he wouldn't ask that question. She'd

tried to answer all his queries honestly thus far. This one might prove the most difficult. She didn't really know if she could risk telling the truth. After gazing into Simon's eyes for a moment, she concluded that she would be honest. "Simon, I knew about the sentries posted in the house. Ethan was hurt. I needed to see him. In fact, I was going to run away instead of facing you today. I found that I couldn't."

"You saw him? Here? Last night?" Simon jumped up and faced her.

Answering honestly became easier for Lilly. "Not here. I went to where he was."

"Where? How could he have been here without us knowing?"

"I won't answer, Simon." Lilly stood and stared directly into his eyes. "If it were the other way around and I were married to you, I wouldn't tell him, either."

"That makes a kind of sense, I suppose." Simon walked back and forth for a few seconds. "I wonder what Jonathan will say to this news."

Lilly shrugged. "I guess I'll find out soon enough."

Simon took her arm, and they walked to the door once again. "You're an extraordinary woman, Lilly Arledge. I'm glad I came in second. Shall we fight, my dear?"

Lilly nodded as he opened the door. They walked a few steps into the hallway and stopped. Simon motioned for her to begin.

"Simon, I need money for a new dress. All these clothes are dreary, and everybody's seen them."

"I've known you for several weeks, and I've yet to see you wear the same outfit. I can't afford a closet full of new clothes every time the season changes."

"But, Simon—"

"No, Lilly. I'm a soldier. I don't make much money."

"How about the money for new draperies and furnishings? This place hasn't been redecorated in years. I need—"

"I already told you I don't have any money."

Lilly heard footsteps in the parlor, but the door didn't open. "But—"

"No, Lilly. No."

"And our wedding trip. Where are we going? I'd like to go to Paris."

"You're mad! Lilly, there's no money for clothes, furniture, and certainly none for a trip to Paris." Simon smiled slightly as he moved closer. "Not a chance."

Lilly noticed the door to the parlor open slightly. "You're the meanest man I ever met. I can't live with anyone who won't allow me a little fun."

"Mean, am I? Hah. I never saw such a money-grubbing witch as you." Simon slammed his hand down on the banister.

Lilly stepped backward as if she were afraid of him or seeing him for the first time. "I refuse to walk into a prison and lock myself in, and this marriage sounds more like a prison than anything I can think of."

"Shall we agree to call this mess off?"

"My pleasure," Lilly agreed and turned to walk up the stairs.

"Lilly! Stop!" Jonathan threw the doors open and ran into the hallway. "Children, this is just a case of nerves. You'll work these problems out."

Spinning on her heel at the landing, she shouted, "Never!"

Simon glared at Jonathan and stared up the stairs. "Never in a million years. Thank you for your hospitality, but I'm leaving."

When they reached the top of the stairs, out of view

of the crowd gathering in the hallway, Simon lifted her and spun her around. He whispered, "Should you ever really need money, perhaps you could take up stage acting. Goodbye, Lilly."

"Goodbye, Simon." Lilly's feet touched the floor as he gently set her down, and she smiled as he turned and strode jauntily down the hall.

She hurried into her room. Jonathan Arledge wasn't likely to accept the defeat of his plans easily. She sat in her rocking chair and waited for him.

Within seconds he burst through her door. "What is the meaning of this?"

"I'm not marrying Simon, Father," Lilly answered calmly. "The argument you witnessed wasn't for your benefit, but for Simon's."

"What? What are you talking about." Jonathan slammed the door behind him and walked toward her.

"I told Simon I couldn't marry him. We agreed to stage the fight to protect his reputation." Lilly remained calm and spoke evenly though she could see the anger in her father's eyes.

"That's preposterous," Jonathan blustered and knocked a porcelain vase off the mantel. "You go down there right this minute. I don't care what you have to do, but you tell him you've changed your mind and—"

"No, Father. I am not marrying Simon." Lilly tried to keep from allowing her protective veil to drop over her eyes. This time she was determined to face her father and stand up to him, no matter what. "I'm already married."

"Nonsense. That's the most—"

Lilly waved his protest aside. "I'm married to Major Ethan Kendall."

"Kendall? That traitor? What a fool you must think me if you . . . I'm not foolish enough to believe—"

"It's true. I was married here on Christmas Day." Lilly rose and looked her father in the eye. "There's nothing you can do about it."

"Yes, there is," Jonathan sputtered and glowered at her. "He's a rebel. I'll make sure he's hanged. I can do that, you know. Then you can marry anyone. Nobody will ever know you were married to a rebel."

"You'll do no such thing. I'm married to him, and I'm going to remain married to him." Lilly stared with all the power she could muster. "I love him. You're going to do nothing to him, except get out of his home."

"Hah! This is my home. He has nothing." Jonathan glanced around the room. "All this is mine. You live here at my pleasure."

"No. Carolina Moon belongs to Ethan and Octavia and, by right of marriage, now me." Lilly watched her father as he grew angrier. She never doubted that this conversation would end in him beating her, but she refused to cower anymore. "Leave my home immediately. You have until six o'clock to pack your things and leave."

Jonathan threw his head back in laughter. "My stupid little Lilly. You've never listened to me. You should have married Simon, and all this would have never happened."

He lunged at her. Lilly jumped behind her chair, and Jonathan crashed to the floor. "I'm not going to stand here and allow you to injure me again."

"I'm your father. I have the right to discipline you." Jonathan's face was screwed into a grimace that bared his teeth and made him look like a mad dog.

"Yes, but discipline is far different from what you do.

You beat me because you enjoy it. You won't ever derive that pleasure again!" Lilly stood her ground and looked down at him.

Jonathan scrambled to his feet. "You'll pay for your attitude."

When he threw himself at her, Lilly couldn't step away in time. He hit her chin and then her stomach. She gasped for breath but couldn't get any air. She could taste the blood in her mouth but didn't take her eyes off her father. Lilly was backed up against the mantel.

He grinned, and a strange gleam appeared in his eyes. "Now you see that you must obey me."

He walked toward her. Lilly fought to keep from crumbling beneath his vicious gaze. Her hand closed around a silver candelabra. "Don't come any closer."

"You won't hit me. You're too stupid and scared of me." Jonathan stepped menacingly closer.

Somewhere in the house Lilly heard a door slam, but she couldn't take her eyes off her father for one second. "Stop where you are, Father. I'm warning you."

"Hah! So the kitten envisions herself a tigress, eh?" Without further warning, he launched himself at her, pinning her against the mantel.

Lilly screamed and struck him with the candelabra. Jonathan groaned and fell at her feet. Stunned by her bravery, Lilly stood there looking down at him.

The door flew open, and Simon entered carrying his musket. "I see you've handled this yourself."

He propped the musket against the wall and crossed the room. "Are you all right?"

"I'm fine. I think," she added.

Simon knelt beside Jonathan and felt his pulse. "He isn't dead."

"Thank goodness." Lilly stared at her father's prostrate form on the floor as Simon stood and put his arms around her.

"It's over, Lilly. He won't do this to you again." Simon lifted her and started toward the bed.

"If you hurt her, you—"

"Ethan!" Lilly shouted joyfully.

Simon stopped and turned to face the door. He allowed Lilly to stand and watched her run across the floor to Ethan's arms. "Mr. Kendall, I presume?"

Ethan kissed Lilly and held her close. "You must be Simon Owens."

"I am," Simon replied and stood stiffly erect.

Ethan glanced at Jonathan and then back at Simon. "Did you kill him?"

Simon chuckled. "No, but Lilly almost did. He's still breathing."

Applejack appeared in the doorway behind Ethan and spotted Jonathan on the floor. He hurried over to see if he could help him, but Jonathan seemed to be coming to.

Simon watched for a moment and then turned back to Ethan. "Sir, I understand I'm to congratulate you for your marriage to Lilly."

"Thank you, Simon," Ethan said simply, knowing that Simon had been planning to marry Lilly.

"I feel that I must warn you, however." Simon smiled and walked toward Ethan. "This woman is a spitfire if ever I saw one and quite intelligent. I don't know how you're going to manage to live happily with a woman you're constantly having to work hard to outthink."

Ethan grinned and kissed Lilly. "Well, I know it won't be easy, but I love her. I suppose we'll just fight it out."

Simon chuckled. "I can vouch for that."

"Ethan what are you doing here? What happened?"

Lilly asked as she watched Applejack carry her father out the door and down the hallway. "Tell me everything."

"I have a detachment of Marion's men. We're here to escort Jonathan Arledge off my, eh, our property." Ethan squeezed her and kissed the top of her head. Then his lips met hers, and they were melded together in a passionate embrace.

For a moment Simon watched the two and then cleared his throat. "I see that my presence is no longer needed. Mr. Kendall, since you have a detachment of men and I have but three, what are your plans for us?"

Ethan gazed at Simon for a moment and then looked down at Lilly. "Sir, I feel that I've taken enough from you already. If you're willing to pack your belongings and leave, you may do so unharmed and without fear."

"You're very kind." Simon started toward the door, but Ethan stopped him.

"The end is coming, Simon. Someone must start the mending process." Ethan put out his hand. "I propose that it begin with us."

"Thank you." Simon shook Ethan's hand and smiled at Lilly. "I wish the two of you a long and happy life together. And, Ethan, I hope we meet again when peace has come to South Carolina."

"You will be welcome here, Simon." He watched as Simon walked down the hallway. "Oh, you forgot this." Ethan held up Simon's musket.

Simon returned and took it. "You are quite a gentleman, Ethan Kendall."

Within the hour Simon and his men were gone. Lilly, Ethan, Octavia, Zip, Applejack, and Prudence were sitting in the parlor enjoying the feeling of freedom when Jonathan came down the stairs.

He stepped into the room and glanced at all the people. "What are you doing in my house? Get out. All of you, get out and never come back. Traitors!"

Ethan stood and gazed at Jonathan. "Sir, you are to leave my house immediately and not return unless you're invited. From the looks of Lilly's face, that invitation may be a long time in coming."

"You have no authority to—"

"I have. All the British troops are in Charleston. If you can find enough of them to come and fight for you, then do so." Ethan crossed his arms and continued to stare at Jonathan. "You may take one horse of Applejack's choosing and your own personal servant. Applejack, Zip, and Dulcie will remain with Lilly. If you hurry, you can catch Simon and his men on their way to Charleston."

"That is the most preposterous—"

Ethan stepped toward Jonathan. "And if you ever touch my wife again, I will chase you to the ends of the earth and gleefully separate your head from your body."

Jonathan glanced at everyone in the room. He was obviously certain that Ethan meant what he said. "I shall return."

He left the room, and Ethan turned to Applejack. "Go and bring a horse for him. For us as well. I want to make sure he leaves my property."

While the two men were gone, the women set to work preparing a feast for their celebration. Lilly put on her most festive gown and the emeralds Ethan had given her. A single tear slid down her cheek as she slipped the ring on. "I'll never take this off again," she vowed.

Everybody at Carolina Moon celebrated this New

Year's Day with hams, greens, and black-eyed peas. Lilly, in her new role as mistress of the plantation, and Zip worked side by side setting the table while Dulcie and Prudence ladled the food into bowls. Octavia, now a guest, watched approvingly from the doorway.

By the time the food was ready, Ethan and Applejack had returned. Lilly hurried over to Ethan. "Will he be all right?"

"I think so." Ethan held her close, inhaling the scent of jasmine that he loved so well. "He won't bother us again."

They sat down. Tonight Zip, Applejack, Dulcie, and Prudence ate at the dining room table with Ethan, Lilly, and Octavia.

Applejack finally put down his fork and looked around. "This is good food. But it don't taste no different on these purty plates. I'd jus' as soon eat outa my ole tin plate and not have to worry."

Dulcie started cleaning off the table, and everyone jumped up to help. She looked at Lilly and smiled. "Miss Lilly, you and Mistah Ethan go on. We'll take care of this."

"Would you like to go for a walk?" Ethan asked. "It's not raining, though it's cold."

"I'd love to." Lilly found her warmest cloak and followed him out to the piazza.

They walked down the graceful steps and across the lawn. Without speaking, they strolled hand in hand through the formal garden but didn't stop. Neither of them wanted to remain within the restrictions of the boxwoods, roses, and camellias. Before either of them really noticed where they were going, they ended up in the little grove of live oaks.

Ethan shrugged and looked at Lilly. "Would you like to sit in a tree with me, love?"

Lilly grinned and moved toward the lowest hanging limb. "I'd like nothing better."

Lifting her as easily as a feather, Ethan kissed her and then deposited her on the limb. He climbed up beside her. "You know, Lilly, I never thought I would marry at all. But this is beyond my wildest imagining. I married a woman who likes trees as much as I do."

"Well, I have to be honest, since this seems to be the day for it. I never thought I'd marry a man and sit in a tree for pleasure," Lilly admitted. "That morning of the party, when you first spotted me in the tree—"

"Ah, yes, wearing a lovely yellow silk dress, as I recall." Ethan slipped his arm around her and snuggled close.

Lilly laid her head on his shoulder. "That was the first time I'd climbed that tree in ages. Since I was a little girl."

"I suspected as much. Although it didn't turn out badly, I have to admit." Ethan swung his feet back and forth for a minute. He glanced around. "Except for—"

Ethan fell to the ground and lay there looking up at Lilly. "Except for that damned cat. Tartuffe, I thought we were friends."

Lilly laughed and slid off the limb. She knelt down beside him. "Are you hurt?"

Ethan stood up and dusted himself off. "Only my pride."

Lilly took his hand, and they began to walk with Tartuffe following aimlessly along as if he had nothing better to do. They walked past Zip and Applejack's cottage and then Octavia's.

After a moment Ethan stopped and looked at Lilly. "I think we'd better ask Mother to move back into—"

"Nonsense." Octavia stuck her head out her door. "This is my home, now. If you'll invite me up for meals occasionally, we'll get on splendidly. Now go on and stop this sappy talk outside my door."

Lilly and Ethan kissed Octavia and then went on walking. They strolled down by the river and stopped for a moment on the dock. The moon had risen, like a great orange pomegranite, and moonlight poured over them and their plantation.

For a moment Lilly didn't say anything, and then she looked up at Ethan. "Didn't you once say to me that I was being rather shortsighted, or something like that, when I referred to this as the Carolina moon?"

"I seem to recall addressing the issue." Ethan pulled her into his arms, and they watched the moon drift higher in the sky.

"Since you named your plantation Carolina Moon, I think you owe me an apology." Lilly lifted her face to his and was rewarded with a kiss.

Ethan looked down at his bride and felt himself filled with love. They'd been through a lot together, but the war wasn't over. They'd won today, but tomorrow might be different. The British were bottled up in Charleston, with no more than a couple of miles of land outside from which to obtain their food and forage for their horses.

Ships were coming in with food and staples, but the crowds were overwhelming. He knew that within the year America would be free of the British, unless some drastic change occurred.

The South Carolina Legislature would continue to meet, almost within sight of Charleston, simply to flout the British authority. Marion's men, led by Colonel

Maham, would continue to keep pressure on the British when they left Charleston for any reason. More blood would be shed, but the taste of victory was strong in Ethan.

He gazed down at Lilly, feeling love well up within him for his strong, intelligent wife. Simon had been right about one thing. Ethan had married a spitfire.

She'd be a Tory until the end, and he wouldn't try to change her. But they'd formed a truce at Carolina Moon. "Lilly, we've still a fight to win, but I think we can walk this property and know it's ours. You're right about the Carolina Moon. It belongs to us."

EPILOGUE

May 1782
Charleston, South Carolina

LILLY FELT A SURGE OF EMOTION AS SHE RODE DOWN Meeting Street with Ethan. She gazed at the people milling along and then at the wispy clouds that hovered over the harbor. "I can't wait to see Erin and Noelle. And Erin's baby, of course."

Ethan smiled indulgently at his wife. He recognized the hint of desire in her voice. "We'll have our own baby soon."

Lilly smoothed her skirt over the growing evidence of her condition and grinned shyly. "Do you want a boy or a girl?"

"I'd like a girl who looks like you. Black hair, incredible brown eyes, beautiful . . ." His voice trailed off as he leaned down to kiss her nose.

Feeling a blush creep into her cheeks, Lilly averted her eyes. Though they'd been married only a short while, less than a year, their love had produced a child to be born in the fall. Her thoughts turned to her father, and her smile changed to a grimace. What would he say when she saw him? "Do you think Father . . ."

"I don't want to think of him at all." Ethan waited

until the carriage came to a complete stop and then leapt to the ground. "Here, let me help you. I don't want to risk anything happening to you or that little bulge in your tummy that's begun to kick me when I try to sleep."

"Do you think we're doing the right thing?" Lilly let him lift her to the ground and then took his arm. As they walked up the steps, she hesitated and glanced around. "Staying here, I mean? Instead of going to my father's?"

"I think your father and I will both be more comfortable if we don't have to stay in the same house." Ethan rapped on the door. "Times might be tense for a while, but everything will work out."

The door swung open, and 'Lasses stepped outside. "Lawd, if it ain't Miss Lilly! Come on in the house. Miss Erin and Mr. Bowie in the parlor with Miss Noelle and Mr. Drake. Lawsy, what a happy day."

Lilly hugged 'Lasses and followed the servant into the parlor. Before 'Lasses could announce them, Erin and Noelle jumped up and bounded across the parlor to greet her.

"Oh, Lilly, how wonderful to see you!" Erin threw her arms around her cousin.

Noelle waited until Lilly could extricate herself from Erin and then drew her youngest cousin into her arms. "Lilly, you look wonderful. Such a pretty glow in your cheeks."

By now Bowie and Drake had reached the door and were shaking hands with Ethan. Lilly blushed as the two men brushed kisses on her cheek. "We're happy to be here."

"Come in. We were about to have a cup of coffee." Erin escorted Lilly to a chair and then sat down near her. "Tell me everything."

"Well, we've been isolated for the past few months

while planting was done. You tell me what's going on."
Lilly glanced from one cousin to the other. "And where is your darling little Star? I can't wait to see her."

"Oh, come with me. We'll leave the men to talk while we go and peek at the baby." Erin beamed with pride. "She's the most beautiful baby you've ever seen."

"Well, my two boys are the most handsome. Can you imagine twins?" Noelle asked, glowing with pride.

Erin glanced at her cousin and touched her thickening waist. "My, but we're productive."

Lilly nodded. "Quite a houseful when they all get older, I'll bet. I hope they'll be as close as we were."

They stopped to look at the round pink faces of Noelle's twins. After a moment Lilly looked at Noelle and grinned. "They must be a handful."

"You're right, but they're fun most of the time," Noelle admitted.

Lilly and her two cousins went next door to the nursery. Erin glanced inside and then motioned for Lilly and Noelle to follow. "Star's almost a year old. Isn't she wonderful?"

Peering down at the sleeping baby, Lilly had to agree. The child looked angelic. She felt a twinge of jealousy but knew she could wait a few more months for the birth of her own child. She followed Erin and Noelle into the little sitting room that served as Erin's morning room. "Oh, Erin, you're so lucky."

"I know. It's like a dream." Erin pulled on the cord hanging beside the door.

In a few minutes 'Lasses came in. "Yas'm?"

" 'Lasses, bring our coffee here, please," Erin said and then sat on the brocade sofa with her cousins. "Now, tell us everything."

"I don't exactly know what to say. Ethan and I married. We've been living at Carolina Moon with his wonderful mother." Lilly felt the warm color stain her cheeks. "I'm going to have a baby."

"I can see that." Noelle reached over and hugged her cousin. "I know you're happy."

"Erin," Lilly began and gazed at her older cousin. "Do you mind if we stay here? I can't . . . I mean, I don't want to go home. You know how Father is. And with Ethan—"

"You mean you don't know?" both Erin and Noelle chorused.

Lilly looked from one to the other. "Know what?"

With her arm still draped around Lilly's shoulder, Noelle sighed. "Uncle Jonathan left with the British. Lots of Loyalists did."

"You mean he . . . he left without even telling me?" Lilly gazed steadily at Noelle. "What about our house?"

Erin patted Lilly's hand. "Your house is damaged, but it can be lived in. Uncle Jonathan was a . . . well, to be honest, Lilly, the man was worse than a wharf rat."

"That's right," Noelle chimed in. "And he knew he couldn't live here after the British left, so he went with them."

Lilly felt as if a burden had been lifted from her shoulders. "Thank God. I hated the thought of having to face him again."

For a few minutes the girls talked about the people who'd been streaming back to town, about the repairs, about the new government, and about their changed lives. The conversation began to lag, and Erin rose and strode to the window. "Look here, Lilly. You can see where the ships were sunk in the harbor. There are crews working now to clear the lanes."

Lilly and Noelle joined Erin at the window. They

watched the ships move slowly through the water in the entrance to the harbor.

"Do you remember the last time we were all together before the war?" Lilly asked and then glanced at her cousins. "It seems as if hundreds of years have passed since then. I've grown into a woman."

"Many things have changed," Noelle agreed.

"Foolish little girl dreams," Erin added and grinned wickedly. "But dreams do come true."

Erin opened the window, and the girls walked onto the piazza. "Look. Construction and repairs are going on every way you look. The face of Charleston is changing."

Somewhere in the house a clock chimed the hour. Lilly closed her eyes and let the familiar sound flow over her for a few seconds and then jerked to attention. "Why didn't the bell toll in the steeple of St. Michael's?"

With a quick glance at Noelle Erin shook her head sadly. "The British took it, along with many of our treasures."

"What do you mean? They stole the bells of St. Michael's?" Lilly asked incredulously. "Those huge bells?"

"That's right." Noelle slipped her arm around her cousin's waist. "The scoundrels."

Lilly looked at Noelle and then at Erin. She felt a wave of homesickness, for the gayer times before the war, but it didn't last long. She was too content with the present to dwell for long on the past. "I think I want to go home . . . I mean to Father's house."

"Whatever for?" Erin asked.

Before Lilly could answer, Ethan bolted onto the piazza and grabbed her around the waist. "Did they tell you? Your father's gone for good."

"Take me home, Ethan." Lilly looked up at her husband, her eyes aglitter with unshed tears. "I don't mean home," she amended, "I mean to his house."

"Why, my darling?" he asked, gazing at her with concern.

"Because I want to start changing everything there this very minute. By the time this baby comes, that house will have not one single reminder of that tyrant." Lilly's fists clenched in anger.

"But you don't have to start now, darling," Ethan reminded her. "We've got plenty of time, and you've had a long journey. You need rest."

"Yes, little Lilly," Erin agreed. "You have plenty of time—and we'll help. Take some time to rest before you begin. Relax, daydream. Be lazy for a few days."

"You can change everything in the house by the time your baby comes. Don't do anything foolish." Noelle stared at her young cousin with concern. "We'll make sure everything's changed in time."

"America is changing, Charleston is changing, and I'm changing. But most of all," she said thoughtfully, "I'm glad we're free to change." She rubbed the swell of her stomach gently, remembering the daydreams of her youth. She recalled her wish as clearly as if she'd said it aloud yesterday. Each of the girls had wanted a husband and babies, and to avoid war.

The war hadn't been avoided. Many of her friends were dead or injured. The cost had been great, but from the strife of war she'd met her own dear husband. She glanced up at Ethan and smiled. "Yes, some dreams do come true."